HILARY MANTEL is the author of fourteen books, including *A Place of Greater Safety, Beyond Black,* and the memoir *Giving Up the Ghost.* Her two most recent novels, *Wolf Hall* and *Bring Up the Bodies,* have both been awarded the Man Booker prize. *Bring up the Bodies* also won the Costa Book of the Year.

From the reviews of *A Change of Climate*:

'There are very few novels that not only bristle with ideas but leave you asking questions about those ideas, again and again, your world turned upside down. That Mantel has managed to do this, combining it with black comedy that is larky, snappy and as light as Norfolk's summer skies, is a formidable achievement'
Sunday Times

'A beautifully crafted novel' *Guardian*

'Taut, poignant and beautifully observed' *Sunday Telegraph*

'Strong and intelligent, and there is nothing merely clever, and nothing counterfeit about [*A Change of Climate*]. It is the real thing, and confirms Hilary Mantel as one of the best novelists of her generation' *Scotsman*

'A work of exquisite craftsmanship that asks enormous questions' *Independent*

'A complex and highly intelligent portrayal of injustice, bereavement and the loss of faith, Mantel's wry style – evident from her earliest work – here delivers acute dialogue and some arresting loco-descriptive sequences ... Hilary Mantel has created that rare thing, a page-turner with a moral dimension'
Daily Telegraph

'The force and intelligence of this novel derives not merely from the quality of writing (Mantel's prose is as precise and imaginative as ever) but from the subtlety of this "secret's" unravelling ... A mature, wise and enriching novel' *Harpers & Queen*

'The best book she's written . . . a risk-taking book about safety, about how having any sense of security is false . . . She writes about punishing subjects so freshly it is as if they had never been written about before'   *Observer*

'The aftershock of this excellent novel is considerable, as considerable as the unresolved moral questions which Hilary Mantel is surely unusual among contemporary novelists in addressing'   *Spectator*

'Hilary Mantel's sixth novel has the tension of a first-rate thriller and the breadth of a family saga . . . its compassion and its intellectual energy mark her as the novelist of her generation who will achieve a lasting greatness'   *Literary Review*

'Mantel writes imperturbable prose studded with surprising images and interspersed with snatches of acutely – and often hilariously – caught dialogue . . . working at the peak of her powers, she clenches all these concerns together into a novel that simultaneously horrifies and heartens'   *TLS*

By the same author

Wolf Hall
Bring Up the Bodies
The Assassination of Margaret Thatcher
Beyond Black
Every Day is Mother's Day
Vacant Possession
Eight Months on Ghazzah Street
Fludd
A Place of Greater Safety
An Experiment in Love
The Giant, O'Brien
Learning to Talk

NON-FICTION
Giving Up the Ghost

HILARY MANTEL

A Change of Climate

4th ESTATE · London

4th Estate
An imprint of HarperCollins*Publishers*
1 London Bridge Street,
London SE1 9GF
www.4thEstate.co.uk

HarperCollins*Publishers*
1st Floor, Watermarque Building, Ringsend Road
Dublin 4, Ireland

This edition published by 4th Estate 2010

18

First published by Viking 1994
Republished in Penguin Books 1995
Published in paperback by Harper Perennial 2005,
reprinted 2 times

A catalogue record for this book is available from the British Library

This novel is entirely a work of fiction. The names, characters and incidents portrayed in it are the work of the author's imagination. Any resemblance to actual persons, living or dead, events or localities is entirely coincidental.

ISBN 978-0-00-717290-0

Printed and bound by CPI Group (UK) Ltd, Croydon CR0 4YY

MIX
Paper from responsible sources
FSC
www.fsc.org
FSC™ C007454

This book is produced from independently certified FSC™ paper to ensure responsible forest management.

For more information visit: www.harpercollins.co.uk/green

To Jenny Naipaul

NOTE

All the characters in this book are fictitious, except that of the Archbishop of Cape Town, which is based on his real-life counterpart, Geoffrey Clayton. I have used some of his words, taken from writings and sermons.

The settlement of Mosadinyana is fictional. The township of Elim is invented too, but I am indebted to the memoirs of Hannah Stanton, who served in the township of Lady Selborne.

Cases similar to that of the Eldreds may be found in the Law Reports of Botswana.

Charles Darwin, *The Descent of Man*, 1871:
'We are not here concerned with hopes and fears, only with the truth as far as our reason allows us to discover it. I have given the evidence to the best of my ability . . .'

Job 4:7:
'Consider, what innocent ever perished, or where have the righteous been destroyed?'

1970

SAD CASES, GOOD SOULS

One day when Kit was ten years old, a visitor cut her wrists in the kitchen. She was just beginning on this cold, difficult form of death when Kit came in to get a glass of milk.

The woman Joan was sixty years old, and wore a polyester dress from a charity shop. A housewifely type, she had chosen to drip her blood into the kitchen sink. When Kit touched her on the elbow, she threw down the knife on to the draining board and attempted with her good hand to cover Kit's eyes.

By this stage in her life Kit was not much surprised by anything. As she ducked under the woman's arm she thought, that's our bread-knife, *if* you don't mind; but she said, 'You shouldn't be doing that, Joan, why don't you come away from the sink, why don't you sit down on this chair and I'll get the first-aid kit?'

The woman allowed herself to be led to a chair at the kitchen table. Kit pulled a clean tea-towel out of a drawer and wrapped it around Joan's wrist. The towel was a checked one, red and white; Joan's reluctant blood seeped black against the cloth. Her cuts were light, early, indecisive: the practice cuts. 'Just wiggle your fingers,' Kit said, 'make sure you haven't done any damage.' The woman looked down at her hand in dry-eyed dread, while the child scrambled on a stool and brought down a box from a cupboard.

'Lucky it's half-term,' Kit said, unpacking the bandages and the round-ended scissors. 'Otherwise I wouldn't have been here. I was upstairs. I was reading a book. It's called *Children of the*

New Forest. Have you read it? It's about a family like ours, two boys and two girls, but they live a long time ago, in the olden days.'

I'm all fingers and thumbs, she thought. She heard her voice, running on. She was learning first aid at school. They told you, 'Reassure the patient.' 'They live in the forest by themselves.' Joan nodded: again her dumb dazed nod. 'They're Royalists. They have to hide from their enemies.'

Kit was afraid that Joan might faint, dropping as a dead weight to the flagstoned floor. 'I'll get you a glass of water,' she said. 'Or I dare say you could have hot sweet tea.'

She thought, poor Joan. Perhaps dead is what she wants to be. It's just as Dad always says: you can never find a sharp knife when you need one.

As she stood filling the kettle, she heard her mother's car. She knew the crunch and scrape and wheeze of it, as it lurched up the drive. Relief washed through her body, turned her legs to water. She put the kettle on the hob, and was wiping out the sink with disinfectant when her mother came in.

Anna put her bags down on the table. She saw, more in sorrow than in surprise, Joan's figure slumped across it. 'Tea for me as well, Kit,' she said.

That night Kit caught the tail-end of a whispered conversation: 'You didn't *say* she was a suicide risk, Ralph.'

'I didn't say because I didn't *know*.' She closed her bedroom door; she didn't want to listen to her parents' private thoughts.

Three days later, she came into the kitchen and found her mother on her hands and knees by the sink, working on the flags with a scrubbing brush. 'The blood's gone,' Kit said, puzzled. 'I wiped it up.'

Anna didn't answer her, but rose from the floor, lifted the bucket and threw the soapy water into the sink.

By this time Joan had left, taking everything she owned in the two carrier bags with which she had arrived. Sudden exits were not infrequent among their visitors; they were not like the visitors that other households get. Ralph made inquiries of the police, the Salvation Army, and the Department of Health and Social Security, but he drew a blank. When Anna came to check the first-aid kit – restocking it was one of her responsibilities – she noticed that Joan had taken an extra bandage with her. They saw this as a hopeful sign.

In those years, when the children were growing up, the house was full of people like Joan. Ralph brought some of them from the hostel in London, which was maintained by the charitable trust for which he worked. Others he took in when Social Services didn't know what to do with them, or when there were no beds at the local psychiatric hospital. Sometimes they turned up of their own accord, crouching out of the wind in one of the outhouses until he came home. 'So-and-so's a sad case,' he would say; and over the years, this was what the family came to call them: the Sad Cases. Other people he called Good Souls. 'Your Aunt Emma is giving so-and-so a lift to her drugs clinic in Norwich – she's a good soul.'

And this was how the world was divided, when Kit was growing up – into Good Souls and Sad Cases. There was no wickedness in it.

ONE

On the day of Felix Palmer's funeral, his wife, Ginny, met his mistress, Emma. They had met before, of course. The county of Norfolk is not so populous that they could have avoided each other. Their conduct at these meetings had been shaped by Ginny's lofty and wilful ignorance of the situation: by Emma's sang-froid: by Felix's natural desire to maintain an arrangement that suited him.

Over the years they had coincided in draughty parish halls, in charity committee rooms and at the caucuses of local groups concerned with the protection of what, in the decade just beginning, would be known as 'the environment'. They had bumped into each other in Norwich, shopping in Jarrold's department store; they had exchanged small-talk at exhibitions of craftwork, and occupied neighbouring seats at the theatre.

Once, travelling to London, they had found themselves sole occupants of a first-class carriage. For half an hour they had found enough that was anodyne to pass the time. Then Ginny, excusing herself with a smile, delved into her bag and pulled out a fat paperback book. She retired behind it. Emma examined its cover. A svelte woman, with a small crown perched upon her wimple, stood before a manor house with anachronistic chimney-stacks. The title was in florid gold script: *Wyfe to Crookback*. Emma looked out of the window. The landscape was a sad East England green; crows wheeled over the fields. As they moved from the edge of England to its heart, Emma herself took out a book.

They parted at sooty Liverpool Street with a nod and a smile. London forced no collusion on them, but Norfolk did. A handful of farming and professional families played host to both. At a round of weddings and christenings they had made polite, even warm conversation. At a dozen New Year's Eve parties they had wished each other luck and happiness: and sometimes almost meant it.

Now, on this February morning, Ginny stood surrounded by a knot of mourners. Friends and business associates had turned out for the occasion; Felix had been well-liked in the district. The church occupied high ground, and a ripping wind billowed coats and snapped at woollen head-scarves and brought a flush to aching faces. The mourners could sense the presence of the sea, hidden from them by a belt of pines.

Some of them lingered in the church porch, reading the notices about flower rotas, dusting and brass-cleaning; others stood among the gravestones, looking depressed. They had double-parked in the open area beyond the church gate, and would have to wait their turn to get away. Ginny, leaning on the arm of her son, moved from group to group, offering a few tactful words to soothe their feelings; she understood that death is embarrassing.

Her own family – her son Daniel, who was an architect, her daughter Claire, who was a buyer at Harrods – had been as gentle and as careful of her feelings as anyone could wish. But – even as she deferred the moment – Ginny felt that it was Emma to whom she wished to speak, to whom naturally she should be speaking. Patting her son's arm, smiling up and dismissing him, she made her way across the grass with a short, precisely regulated stride, her high heels spiking holes in the ground like some primitive seed drill.

Ginny Palmer was a sharp, neat, Wallis Simpson sort of woman, to whom black lent an added definition. As she advanced on Emma, she took from her pocket a crisp lace-edged handkerchief, folded it very small and polished the tip of her nose: a gesture quite unnecessary, but somehow drawn out of her by the occasion. You see me, the widow: fastidious but distraught.

Emma Eldred kept her hands in her pockets; she had forgotten her gloves. She wore the coat that she had worn for years, to go out on her doctor's rounds, to go shopping, to go out walking and to meet Felix. She saw no need for any other coat, in her ordinary life or on a day like this; it was dark, it was decent, and – she felt obscurely – it was something Felix would have recognized.

Emma Eldred was not a large woman, but gave the appearance of it: forty-eight years old, her face innocent of cosmetics, her broad feet safely encased in scuffed shoes decorated by leather tassels which somehow failed to cut a dash. Emma had known Ginny's husband since childhood. She might have married him; but Felix was not what Emma considered a serious man. Their relationship had, she felt, borne all the weight it could. As Ginny approached, Emma shrunk into herself, inwardly but not outwardly. A stranger, only partly apprised of the situation, would have taken Ginny for the smart little mistress, and Emma for the tatty old wife.

The women stood together for a moment, not speaking; then as the wind cut her to the bird-bones, Ginny took a half-step closer, and stood holding her mink collar up to her throat. 'Well, Ginny,' Emma said, after a moment. 'I'm not here to act as a wind-break.' She drew her right hand from her pocket, and gave Ginny a pat on the shoulder. It was a brusque gesture, less of consolation than of encouragement; what you might give a weary nag, as it faces the next set of hurdles.

Ginny averted her face. Tears sprang into her eyes. She took out her tiny handkerchief again. 'Why, Emma?' she said. She sounded fretful, but as if her fretfulness might turn to rage. 'Tell me why. You're a doctor.'

'But not his doctor.'

'He wasn't ill. He never had a day's illness.'

Emma fixed her gaze on the tassels of her shoes. She imagined herself looking right through her dead lover; through his customary tweed jacket, his lambswool pullover, his striped shirt, through the skin, through the flesh, into the arteries where Felix's blood moved slowly, a dark underground stream with silted banks. 'No one could have known,' she said. 'No one could have spared you this shock, Ginny. Will you be all right, my dear?'

'There's plenty of insurance,' Ginny said. 'And the house. I'll move of course. But not just yet.'

'Don't do anything in a hurry,' Emma said. She had meant her question in a broad sense, not as an inquiry into Ginny's financial standing. She raised her head, and saw that they were being watched. The eyes of the other mourners were drawn to them, however hard those mourners tried to look away. What do they all think, Emma wondered: that there will be some sort of embarrassing scene? Hardly likely. Not at this time. Not in this place. Not amongst people like ourselves, who have been reared in the service of the great god Self-Control. 'Ginny,' she said, 'you mustn't stand about here. Let Daniel drive you home.'

'A few people are coming back,' Ginny said. She looked at Emma in faint surprise, as if it were natural that she would know the arrangements. 'You should come back too. Let me give you some whisky. A freezing day like this . . . Still, better than rain. Claire's staying on over the weekend.' Ginny raised her hand, and twitched at her collar again. 'Emma, I'd like to see you. Like you to come to the house . . . Mrs Gleave is making vol-au-vents . . .' Her voice tailed off entirely.

8

Emma's brother, Ralph Eldred, loomed purposefully behind them: a solid figure, hands scrunched into the pockets of his dark wool overcoat. Ginny looked up. The sight of Ralph seemed to restore her. 'Ralph, thank you for coming,' she said. 'Come back with us and have some whisky.'

'I should take myself off,' Ralph said. 'I have to go to Norwich this afternoon to a meeting. But naturally if you want me to, Ginny . . . if I can be of any help . . .' He was weighing considerations, as he always did; his presence was wanted on every hand, and it was simply a question of where he was needed most.

'Why, no,' Ginny said. 'It was a courtesy, Ralph. Do run along.'

She managed a smile. It was her husband's under-occupation that had freed him for his long years of infidelity; but Ralph's days were full, and everybody knew it. There were advantages, she saw, in being married to a man who thought only of work, God and family; even though the Eldred children did look so down at heel, and had been so strangely brought up, and even though Ralph's wife was worn to a shadow slaving for his concerns.

Ralph's wife Anna wore a neat black pillbox hat. It looked very smart, though it was not remotely in fashion. Lingering in the background, she gave Ginny a nod of acknowledgement and sympathy. It was an Anna Eldred nod, full of I-do-not-intrude. Ginny returned it; then Ralph took his wife's arm, and squired her away at a good clip towards their parked car.

Ginny looked after them. 'You wonder about marriage,' she said suddenly. 'Are marriages all different, or all alike?'

Emma shrugged, shoulders stiff inside her old coat. 'No use asking me, Ginny.'

Inside the car, Ralph said, 'It's not right, you know. It's not, is

9

it? For Emma to find out like that. More or less by chance. And only when it was all over.'

'It was all over very quickly,' Anna said. 'From what I gather.'

'Yes, but to have no priority in being told –'

'I expect you think Ginny should have rung her from the hospital, do you? Just given her a tinkle from the intensive-care unit?'

'– to have no right to know. That's what galls me. It's inhuman. And now Ginny gets all the sympathy, all the attention. I'm not saying she doesn't need and deserve it. But Emma gets nothing, not a word. Only this public embarrassment.'

'I see – you think that as Emma was the *maîtresse en titre*, she should be allowed to put on a show of her own?' Anna sighed. 'I'm sure Felix has left her some fine diamonds, and a château for her old age.'

A contractor's van drew up in front of the Eldreds' car, adding to the traffic jam; restoration work was going on at the church. Two workmen got out, and began to untie a ladder from the roof-rack. A lesser man with Ralph's schedule would have fretted at the delay. But Ralph showed his impatience only by a little tapping of his forefinger against the steering wheel. There was a school nearby, and the voices of children drifted from the playground, carried on the wind like gulls' cries.

The couple who blocked them drove off, nodding, raising hands in a stiff-fingered wave. The contractor moved his van. Ralph pulled out on to the road. Anna saw the children dashing and bumping and careening behind a fence: bullets trussed in duffle coats, their faces hidden under hoods.

The route home lay inland, through narrow lanes between farms: flat airy fields, where tractors lay at rest. Ralph pulled up to let a duck dawdle across the road, on its way from a barnyard to nowhere. 'I'll tell you,' he said. 'I'll tell you what's the worst of it. Emma's got nothing. Nothing. She's given twenty years to Felix and now she's on her own.'

'Emma's given something,' Anna said. 'I think to say that she's given twenty years is being melodramatic.'

'Why is it,' Ralph said, 'that women manage to be so cool in these situations? What's all this keeping up a good front? Why do they think they have to do it? I heard Ginny talking about *insurance policies*, for God's sake.'

'I only mean, that Emma's life has suited her. She had what she wanted – a part-time man. Felix didn't use her. The reverse, I think. She could have married. If she'd chosen to. She didn't have to wait on Felix.'

'Married? Could she?' Ralph turned his head.

'Look out,' Anna said, with a languor born of experience. Ralph put his foot on the brake; a farm truck slowly extruded its back end from a muddy and half-concealed driveway.

'Sorry,' Ralph said. 'Could she? Who could she have married then?'

'Oh Ralph, I don't mean any one person, not this particular man or that particular man . . . I only mean that if she had wanted to marry, if that had been what she preferred, she could have done it. But marriage entails things, like learning to boil eggs. Things that are beyond Emma.'

'I can't see men beating a path to her door.' Ralph edged the car painfully down the lane, squeezing it past the truck, which had got stuck. 'Not Emma. No beauty.'

'Felix liked her.'

'Felix was a creature of habit.'

'Most men are.'

Ralph fell silent. He was very fond of his sister; no one should think otherwise. Emma was kind, clever, wise . . . and lonely, he'd supposed: a little figure glimpsed on a river bank, while the pleasure craft sped by. This notion of her as a manipulator, of Felix as a little fish that she played at the end of her stick and hook . . . Seems unlikely to me, he thought. But then, what do I know?

The journey took them a half-hour, through back roads and lanes, through straggling hamlets of red brick or flint cottages, whose only amenity was a post-box; between agri-business fields, wide open to a vast grey sky. Ralph pulled up with a jolt at the gate of their house. Anna shot forward, one hand on the dashboard and one on her hat. 'Can I leave you here? I'm late.'

As she unravelled her seat-belt, Ralph turned to look at her. 'Those people at the funeral, all those friends of Felix's, how many of them do you think knew about him and Emma?'

Anna took her house keys from her bag. 'Every one of them.'

'How did Ginny bear it?'

'Easily. Or so everyone says.' Anna swung her door open and her legs out, setting her high heels daintily into the mud. 'What time will you be back?'

'Seven o'clock. Maybe eight.'

Nine, then, Anna thought. 'Everybody knew except you,' she said. 'I suppose you still feel a fool.'

'I suppose I do.' Ralph reached over to close the passenger door. 'But then, I still don't see why I should have known. Not as if their affair was the flamboyant sort. Not as if it was . . .' he searched for the word, '. . . torrid.'

Torrid, Anna thought. She watched him drive away. Interesting how our vocabulary responds, providing us with words we have never needed before, words stacked away for us, neatly folded into our brain and there for our use: like a bride's lifetime supply of linen, or a ducal trove of monogrammed china. Death will overtake us before a fraction of those words are used.

TWO

Anna, as Ralph vanished from view, plucked the afternoon post from the wooden mail-box by the gate; then picked her way over rutted ground to the front door. The drive was more of a farm track than anything else; often it looked as if a herd of beasts had been trampling it. The mail-box was something new. Julian, her eldest boy, had made it. Now the postman's legs were spared, if not the family's.

The Red House was a farmhouse that had lost its farm; it retained a half-acre of ground upon which grew sundry bicycle sheds, a dog kennel and a wire dog-run with the wire broken, a number of leaning wooden huts filled with the detritus of family life, and an unaccountable horse-trough, very ancient and covered with lichen. Recently, since Julian had been at home, the hedges had been cut back and some ground cleared, and the rudiments of a vegetable garden were appearing. The house and its ramshackle surroundings formed a not-displeasing organic whole; Julian's attempt at agriculture seemed an imposition on the natural state of things, as if it were the bicycle sheds that were the work of nature, and the potatoes the work of man.

The house itself was built of red brick, and stood side-on to the road. It had a tiled roof, steeply pitched; in season, the crop-spraying plane buzzed its chimney-stacks and complicated arrangements of television aerials. There were a number of small windows under the eaves, and these gave the house a restless look: as if it would just as soon wander across the lane and put down its foundations in a different field.

Two years before, when it seemed that the older children would shortly be off their hands, Anna had suggested they should look for a smaller place. It would be cheaper to run, she had said, knowing what line of reasoning would appeal to Ralph. With his permission she had rung up Felix Palmer's firm, to talk about putting the house on the market. 'You can't mean it,' Felix had said. 'Leave, Anna? After all these years? I hope and trust you wouldn't be going far?'

'Felix,' Anna had said, 'do you recall that you're an estate agent? Aren't you supposed to encourage people to sell their houses?'

'Yes, but not my friends. I should be a poor specimen if I tried to uproot my friends.'

'Shall I try someone else, then?'

'Oh, no need for that . . . If you're sure . . .'

'I'm far from sure,' Anna said. 'But you might send someone to look around. Put a value on it.'

Felix came himself, of course. He brought a measuring tape, and took notes as he went in a little leather-bound book. On the second storey, he grew bored. 'Anna, dear girl, let's just say . . . a wealth of versatile extra accommodation . . . attics, so forth . . . an abundance of storage space. Leave it at that, shall we? Buyers don't want, you know, to have to exercise their brains.' He sighed, at the foot of the attic stairs. 'I remember the day I brought you here, you and Ralph, to talk you into it . . .' His eyes crept over her, assessing time's work. 'You were fresh from Africa then.'

I was tired and cold that day, she thought, tired and cold and pregnant, rubbing my chilblains in that draughty wreck of a drawing room; the Red House smelled of mice and moulds, and there were doors banging overhead, and cracked window glass, and spiders. To pre-empt his next comment, she put her hand on his arm: 'Yes, Felix. It was, it was a long time ago.'

Felix nodded. 'I remember saying to you – it's the sort of place you come to grips with in your own good time.'

'And we never have.' She smiled.

'You filled it with children. That's the main thing.'

'Yes. And for all their presence improved it, we might as well have stabled horses. Well, Felix – what's the verdict?'

'There'd be interest,' he said cautiously. 'London people perhaps.'

'Oh – fancy prices,' Anna said.

'But consider, Anna – do you really want to do this rather drastic thing?'

Felix closed his notebook and slipped it back into his pocket. They went downstairs, and had a glass of sherry. Felix stared gloomily over the garden. Slowly the conventions of his calling seemed to occur to him. 'Useful range of outbuildings,' he muttered, and jotted this phrase in his book.

That evening Felix telephoned Ralph. 'Why don't you hang on?' he said. 'Prices are going up all over East Anglia. A year from now you might make a killing. Tell Anna I advise staying put.'

'I will.' Ralph was relieved. 'I take her point, of course – Kit and Julian away, Robin will be off in a year or so, and then there'll be just the two of us and Becky, we'll be rattling around. But of course, it's not often that we're just the family. We get a lot of visitors.'

'You do, rather,' Felix said.

'And we have to have somewhere to put them.'

Two days later, while Ralph and Anna were still debating the matter, their boy Julian turned up with his suitcase. He wasn't going back to university, he said. He was finished with all that. He dumped his case in his old room in the attics, next door to Robin; they had put the boys up there years ago, so that they could make a noise. Julian offered no explanation of himself, except that he did not like being away, had worried about his family and constantly wondered how they were. He made himself pleasant and useful about the house and neighbourhood, and showed no inclination to move out, to move on, to go anywhere else at all.

Then Kit wrote from London; she phoned her parents every week, but sometimes things are easier in a letter.

I'm not sure yet what I should do after my finals. There's still more than a term to go and I have various ideas, but I keep changing my mind. It isn't that I want to sit about wasting time, but I would like to come home for a few weeks, just to think things through. Dad, I know you mentioned to me that I could work for the Trust for a year, but the truth is I've had enough of London – for the moment, anyway. I wondered if there was something I could do in Norwich . . .

'Well,' Ralph said, re-reading the letter. 'This is unexpected. But of course she must come home, if she wants to.'

'Of course,' Anna said.

Her perspective altered. She felt that she must settle to it, give way to the house's demands, perhaps until she was an old woman.

When on the afternoon of the funeral Anna let herself into the wide square hall, she peeled off her gloves slowly, and placed them on the hall-stand, a vast and unnecessary article of furniture that Ralph had picked up in an antique shop in Great Yarmouth. 'No other family in the county,' she had said at the time, 'feels they need an object like this.' She looked with a fresh sense of wonder and dislike at its barley-sugar legs and its many little drawers and its many little dust-trapping ledges and its brass hooks for gentlemen's hats, and she saw her face in the dim spotted oval of mirror, and smoothed her hair back from her forehead, then took off her coat and threw it over the banisters.

The Norfolk climate gave Anna a bloodless look, tinged her thin hands with violet. Every winter she would think of Africa; days when, leaving her warm bed in a hot early dawn, she had felt her limbs grow fluid, and the pores of her face open like petals, and her ribs, free from their accustomed tense gauge, move to allow her a full, voluptuary's breath. In England she never felt this confidence, not even in a blazing July. The thermometer might register the heat, but her body was sceptical. English heat is fitful; clouds pass before the sun.

Anna went into the kitchen. Julian had heard her come in, and was setting out cups for tea.

'How did it go?'

'It went well, I suppose,' Anna said. 'We buried him. The main object was achieved. How do funerals ever go?'

'How was Mrs Palmer?'

'Ginny was very much herself. A party of them were going back to the house, for vol-au-vents provided by Mrs Gleave.' Anna made a face. 'And whisky. She seemed very insistent on the whisky. If you'd have asked for gin – well, I don't know what!'

Julian reached for the teapot. 'Nobody would have gin, would they, at a funeral?'

'No, it would be unseemly,' Anna said. Mother's ruin, she thought. The abortionist's drink. A mistress's tipple. Flushed complexions and unbuttoned afternoons.

'And how was Emma?'

'Emma was staunch. She was an absolute brick. She turned up in that old coat, by the way.'

'You wouldn't have expected her to get a new one.'

'Oh, I don't know. A lesser woman might have hired sables for the day. And implied that Felix had given them to her.'

Anna smiled, her hands cradling her tea-cup. 'Your old dad and I were talking on the way home. About how he went on for so long, without knowing about Felix and Emma.'

'Twit,' Julian said.

Some three years earlier, the year before Kit went to university, Ralph Eldred had been in Holt for the afternoon. It was a Wednesday, late in the year; at Gresham's School, blue-kneed boys were playing hockey. The small town's streets were empty of tourists; the sky was the colour of pewter.

Ralph decided – and it was an unaccustomed indulgence on his part – to have some tea. The girl behind the counter directed him upstairs; wrapped in bakery smells, he climbed a steep staircase with a rickety handrail, and found himself in a room where the ceiling was a scant seven foot high, and a half-dozen tables were set with pink cloths and white china. At the top of the stairs, Ralph, who was a man of six foot, bent his head to pass under a beam; as he straightened up and turned his head, he looked directly into the eye of Felix Palmer, who was in the act of pouring his sister Emma a second cup of Darjeeling.

The twenty minutes which followed were most peculiar. Not that anything Emma did was strange; for she simply looked up and greeted him, and said, 'Why don't you get that chair there and put it over here, and would you like a toasted tea-cake or would you like a bun or would you like both?' As for Felix, he just lowered his Harris tweed elbow, replaced the teapot on its mat and said, 'Ralph, you old bugger, skiving off again?'

Ralph sat down; he looked ashen; when the waitress brought him a cup, his hand trembled. The innocent sight that had met his eyes when he came up the staircase had suddenly and shockingly revealed its true meaning, and what overset Ralph was not that his sister was having an affair, but his instant realization that the affair was part of the world-order, one of the givens, one of the assumptions of the parish, and that only he, Ralph – stupid, blind and emotionally inept – had failed to recognize the fact: he and his wife Anna, whom he must go home and tell.

Ask him how he knew, that moment he swivelled his head under the beam and met the bland blue eye of Felix: ask him how he knew, and he couldn't tell you. The knowledge simply penetrated his bone-marrow. When they brought the toasted tea-cake, he took a bite, and replaced the piece on the plate, and found that what he had bitten turned into a pebble in his mouth, and he couldn't swallow it. Felix took a brown paper bag out of his pocket, and said, 'Look, Emma, I've got that wool that Ginny's been wanting for her blasted tapestry, the shop's had it on order for three months, I just popped in on the off-chance, and they said it came in this morning.' He laid the skein out on the white cloth; it was a dead bracken colour. 'Hope to heaven it's the right shade,' he said. 'Ginny goes on about dye batches.'

Emma made some trite reply; Felix began to tell about a church conversion over in Fakenham that had come on to the firm's books earlier that week. Then they had talked about the salary of the organist at the Palmers' parish church; then about the price of petrol. Ralph could not make conversation at all. The loop of brown wool remained on the table. He stared at it as if it were a serpent.

Ralph arrived home alone that evening – which surprised Anna. No cronies, no hangers-on, no fat file of papers in his hand: no rushing to the telephone either, no flinging of a greeting over his shoulder, no distracted inquiries about where this and where that and who rang and what messages. He sat down in the kitchen; and when Anna came in, to see why he was so subdued, he was rocking on the back legs of his chair and staring at the wall. 'You know, Anna,' he said, 'I think I'd like a drink. I've had a shock.'

Alcohol, for Ralph, was a medicinal substance only. Brandy might be taken for colic, when other remedies had failed. Hot whisky and lemon might be taken for colds, for Ralph recognized that people with colds need cheering up, and he was all for cheerfulness. But drink as social unction was something that had never been part of his life. His parents did not drink, and he had never freed himself from his parents. He had nothing against drinking in others, of course; the house was well-stocked, he was a hospitable man. When the tongue-tied or the chilled called on him, Ralph was ready with glasses and ice-buckets. His eye was inexpert and his nature generous, so the drinks he poured were four times larger than ordinary measures. A local councillor, upon leaving the Red House, had been breathalyzed by the police in East Dereham, and found to be three times over the legal limit. On another occasion, a female social worker from Norwich had been sick on the stairs. When these things happened, Ralph would say, 'My uncle, Holy James, he was right, I think. Total abstinence is best. Things run out of control so quickly, don't they?'

So now, when Anna poured him a normal-sized measure of whisky, he judged it to be mean and small. He looked at it in bewilderment, but said nothing. After a while, still rocking back on the chair, he said, 'Emma is having an affair with Felix Palmer. I saw them today.'

'What, *in flagrante*?' Anna said.

'No. Having a cup of tea in Holt.'

Anna said nothing for a time: then, 'Ralph, may I explain something to you?' She sat down at the table and clasped her hands on the scrubbed white wood. It was as if she were going to pray aloud, but did not know what to pray for. 'You must remember how Emma and Felix used to go around together, when they were young. Now, you know that, don't you?'

'Yes,' Ralph said. He stopped rocking. The front legs of his chair came down with a clunk. 'But that's going right back – that's going back to the fifties, before she was qualified, when she was in London and she'd come up for the odd weekend. That was before we went abroad. And then he married Ginny. Oh God,' he said. 'You mean it's been going on for years.'

'I do. Years and years and years.'

'Would it be . . . for instance . . . when we came back from Africa?'

Anna nodded. 'Oh, yes. It's so many years, you see, that people no longer bother to talk about it.'

'And you knew. Why didn't I know?'

'It's hard to imagine. Perhaps because you don't notice people.'

'But people are all my life,' Ralph said. 'God help me. Everything I do concerns people. What else do I ever think about?'

'Perhaps you don't think about them in quite the right way. Perhaps there's a – gap – in the way that you think about them.'

'Something missing,' Ralph said. 'Well, there must be, mustn't there? If that's the case I'll have to sit down and talk to myself and try to examine it, whatever it is, this lack, won't I? Otherwise it's obvious I'm not fit to be at large.' He shook his head. 'I'll tell you what puzzles me, though. There's Emma living in her cottage right on the main street in Foulsham, and there's Felix over at Blakeney, and since we know innumerable people in between –'

'Yes, we know people. But it's as I say, they don't talk about it any more.'

'But why didn't somebody tell me?'

'Why should they? How would they have broached the topic?'

'Why didn't *you* tell me?'

21

'What would you have done with the information?'

Ralph was still shaking his head. He couldn't take this in – that his discovery, so exciting to him, was stale and soporific to everyone else. 'What I can't understand is how in a place like this they could conduct what must be so blatantly obvious – I mean, the comings and goings, she can't go to Blakeney I suppose so he must come to Foulsham, his car must be parked there, all hours of the night –'

Anna smiled.

'No,' Ralph said. 'I don't suppose it's like that, is it? I suppose they go to teashops quite a lot. I suppose it's a – mental companionship, is it?'

'I think it might be, largely. But people like Felix and Emma can get away with a lot, you know. They have everything well under control.'

'It's never damaged their standing,' Ralph said. 'I mean, their standing in the community. Do the children know?'

'Kit knows. The boys know, I suppose, but they never mention it. It wouldn't interest them, would it?'

'What does Kit think?'

'You know she always admires her aunt.'

'I hope her life won't be like that,' Ralph said. 'My God, I hope it won't. I don't want Kit to turn into some plain woman driving about the countryside in a tweed coat to share a pot of tea with some old bore. I hope somebody flashy and rich comes and carries her off and gives her diamonds. I don't mind if she isn't steady. I want Kit to have a good time.'

'How old-fashioned you are!' Anna laughed. 'You talk about her as if she were a chorus girl. Kit will buy her own diamonds, if it crosses her mind to want any.' Anna looked down at the minute solitaire that had winked for twenty-five years above her wedding ring. 'And Ralph, there is no need to insult Felix. You like him, you always have, we all like him.'

'Yes. I know. But things look different now.'

He put his empty glass down on the table. This is more than a failure of knowledge, he thought, it is a failure of self-knowledge. Anna poured him another whisky. He ignored it, so she drank it herself.

Sitting at the kitchen table, Julian said, 'I thought Kit would have come home for the funeral.'

'It was mainly our generation,' Anna said. 'There were a lot of people there. I think three Eldreds were enough.'

'An elegant sufficiency,' Julian said.

His mother laughed. 'Where did you get that expression?'

'I heard Kit say it. But didn't you think she'd have wanted to be there? As she's so friendly with Daniel Palmer these days.'

Felix's son, the architect, had a flat above his office in Holt. He was interested in Kit; he had taken her to the theatre, and out to dinner, and invited her to go out in the boat he kept at Blakeney. Anna said, 'I think Kit regards Daniel as a provider of treats. A funeral is not a treat.'

'When will she be coming home, then?

'Not till Easter. She's got her exams in a matter of weeks, you know.'

'Yes, I do know. You don't have to keep mentioning things like that. Terms. Exams.'

'We have to talk about you, Julian. But perhaps not this afternoon.' She looked over the rim of her cup. 'What have you done today?'

'I started putting in those poles for the back fence.'

'And have you seen your girlfriend?'

The slight vulgarity and childishness of the expression struck Julian. It was as if his mother had spilled her tea on the table, or put her fingers in the sugar bowl.

'I'm going over tomorrow. I just wanted to get a start on

that fence, as the rain was keeping off. I wish Kit would come home soon. I want her to meet Sandra's mother. I want to know what she'll think of her.'

So Sandra will be with us for another summer, Anna thought. With Julian you had to glean things, here and there.

A few days after the funeral, Emma went to the shrine at Walsingham. She was not sure why; her faith, if it still existed, was not something she displayed in public. But when you cannot cope with grief, she reasoned, you can do worse than observe the forms that have helped other people cope with it. At Felix's funeral the minister had said that, even in the depth of misery, the familiar forms of prayer can lift the heart towards Christian joy. Very well, Emma thought grimly, let's try it. Something is needed. For Ginny, there were undertakers. There was the question of probate. There was the business of organizing Mrs Gleave and the vol-au-vents. But for me there is nothing. An empty space. A lack of occupation. It is as if I have been told of a death that has taken place in a distant country. It is as if I have no claim on sympathy, because I have heard of the death of a person my friends do not know. There is no body. There is no corpse. Just this absence, this feeling of something unfinished.

Skirting Fakenham, taking the back roads towards the shrine and the sea, she found her car alone on the road. Across the flat fields towers spiked the snow-charged sky, the clouds pregnant and bowed with cold; Norfolk is a land of churches, some open to the sky, their chancels colonized by nettles, their naves by blackthorn and brambles. In those not yet redundant, congregations dwindle; the Samaritans' notices, flapping in the porches, attest to the quality and frequency of rural despair.

In Walsingham, the car park was empty. The streets were devoid of tourists and pilgrims, and the old buildings – half-timber and brick and stone, steep roof and Dutch gable – seemed to have moved closer together, as if the town were closing itself down for the winter. By the Anglican shrine, plaster saints looked out from shop windows: and woven saints, with tapestry eyes. Touches of gilt glinted here and there on a cardboard halo; postcards were for sale, and prayers printed in mock black-letter on mock scrolls. You could buy candles, which you might put to secular use; other windows displayed recordings of plainchant, and pots of honey in stoneware jars, and boxes of Norfolk Lavender soap. Walsingham tea-towels were on offer, jars of chutney, tins of shortbread, Earl Grey tea-bags in cod Victorian packaging; and there were herb pillows, Olde Englishe Peppermint Lumps, pot-pourri and fluffy toys, wall-plaques, paperweights and scented drawer-liners – all the appurtenances, in fact, that you would expect to find at an ancient pilgrim site. Trade was poor. The only visible inhabitant was a woman with a shopping basket over her arm and a pug dog on a lead. She nodded to Emma and walked on, huddling into the shadow of the Abbey's wall.

Emma went up the path to the church. It was a building put up in the 1930s, and its exterior, disappointingly plain, hid its dim papistical contents: devotional candles blinking, sad-eyed virgins pouting in gold frames. She asked herself, what would my father have said, what would my father have said to a bauble-shop like this? Matthew Eldred seemed very far away, very old and dead and gone. Not so Felix. Alone in her cottage in Foulsham, she still listened for the sound of his key in the lock.

Emma lurked about towards the back of the church, away from the altar. Finally she sat down on a chair at the end of a row. She gave herself permission for tears, but she was not able to cry. Like her sister-in-law Anna, she had trained herself out of it. The thought of Felix lay like a stone inside her chest.

Outside, some sort of building work seemed to be going on; she could hear the monotonous thump of hammers and the whirring of drills. In my family, she thought, we practise restraint and the keeping of secrets, and the thoughts we respect are unvoiced thoughts; even Felix, an open secret, was a secret of a kind. But our secrets do not keep us. They worry at us; they wear us away, from the inside out.

On the back wall were wooden plaques, names and dates: thanks given, intentions stated. *Thanks for preservation in a motor accident, 1932. For reunion of husband and wife, after prayer at the shrine, 1934. Success in an examination, Thanks, 1935.* What minute considerations we expect God to entertain, Emma thought. *Thanks for a happy death, prayed for at the Holy House.* Who put that here, and how did they know it was happy? Some plaques gave nothing away. Upon these the visitor might exercise imagination: *Prayers Answered.*

Near these plaques, the water from the Holy Well was made available in buckets. Pilgrims might help themselves, by dipping with assorted vessels; a table, stacked up with prayer books, held also the abandoned top of a Thermos flask, some paper cups of the kind tea machines dispense, and some beakers of moulded plastic, each one frilly at the rim, as if it had been gnawed. Emma thought the arrangements unsanitary. She went out, her gloves in her hand.

In the porch was a vast book, well-thumbed, its pages ruled into columns. A notice promised ALL WHOSE NAMES ARE INSCRIBED IN THIS BOOK WILL BE PRAYED FOR AT THE SHRINE.

Emma took her pen out of her pocket, turned to a clean page and wrote down the date. She did not put Felix's name in the book. because she believed that energy should be directed towards the living, not the dead. She did not put her own name, because she believed she would manage well enough. But she wrote the names of her brother and his wife:

RALPH ELDRED

ANNA ELDRED

Beneath she wrote:

KATHERINE ELDRED

then hesitated, and skipped one line, before

JULIAN ELDRED

ROBERT ELDRED

REBECCA ELDRED

It was half dark when Emma left the porch. Between the church and the road there was no pavement; she crept uphill by the high wall, protected only by heaven's benevolence from the cars behind her. Eddies of sleet swirled in a huddle of stone and flint, slapping at window glass and melting underfoot. Sitting in an almost empty café, her hands around a mug of hot chocolate, she thought of that other frozen afternoon, when Ralph's curly head emerged up the staircase of the Holt tea-room, and dipped under the beam, and swivelled, gaze focusing ... If Ralph had not come upon them that particular day, his sensibilities skinned by the cold, he would have continued in his obstinate and peculiar ignorance; when Felix died, they would have stood at his graveside as two old family friends, and Ralph would have given her not a word of sympathy except that due between decent people when a contemporary has quit the scene. And that, she thought, would have suited me.

Lines of poetry ran through Emma's head. Auden, she thought. She was pleased at being able to identify it, because she was not a literary woman. They were insistent lines, stuffed with a crude menace.

> The glacier knocks in the cupboard,
> The desert sighs in the bed,

> And the crack in the tea-cup opens
> A lane to the land of the dead.

Emma shared the café with one be-skirted cleric, who was reading the *Daily Telegraph*. An oil stove popped and hissed at her back. She thought again of crying, but she was afraid the man might put his newspaper down and try to console her. Instead she buttoned her coat, and braced herself for the twilight and cold, the drive home to Foulsham. I hardly know what I am any more she thought: a Good Soul, or a Sad Case.

> O look, look in the mirror,
> O look in your distress;
> Life remains a blessing
> Although you cannot bless.

THREE

Kit sleeps, blanketed in heat. She rolls on to her back. Her lips move. What is she saying? Mama, mama: milk, milk, milk. Her wrist pushes her hair back from her forehead. She turns over again. The sheet creases beneath her, damp from her body. An institutional counterpane slides to the floor.

Kit's hand clenches and unclenches – fat baby fist. The air is too hot to breathe. Soon Felicia will come, in her blue scarf, and lift her out of the mist of mosquito nets.

Her eyes open to an expanse of white wall. She turns her eyes, and sees the polished floor and the fallen bedcover, and her own bare arm dangling from the sheets, like someone else's limb. It is 7.30, a dirty London morning, traffic building up. There is a hint of spring in the air.

In her dream, she has been to Africa.

She sits up slowly, pulling the top sheet across her breasts, as if someone had come into the room. She is in her term-time lodging, a women's hall of residence. Her little gold watch ticks away on top of a pile of textbooks. Her jeans and warm plaid shirt are folded on a chair. Outside in the corridor her fellow residents are going in and out of bathrooms in their towelling robes, their hair in various arrangements of turbans and pins. They stop to exchange words, to say that the central heating is ridiculous, it is like being in the tropics, a complaint will definitely have to be made. Lavatories flush. From the basement drifts the aroma of breakfasts seething on a range, pallid scraps of bacon, mushrooms stewed black. Toast hardens in its racks.

In Norfolk, at the Red House, her mother Anna dreams of a cell. She feels against her bare legs the rasp of a prison blanket, and under her hand the metal of a prison bedstead. A woman's voice tells her, 'The colonel has refused your request for a mirror.' Anna wakes.

The room is cold. Ralph has pulled the blankets over his head. She sits up, massages her temples with her fingertips. With little circular motions, as if it were vanishing cream, she rubs the dream away. She forgets it. Forgetting is an art like other arts. It needs dedication and practice.

As for Kit — she washes and dresses and goes down the big carved staircase, down the corridors smelling of parsnips and polish. On her way from breakfast she plucks a letter out of the pigeonhole marked 'E'.

The letter is from her father. Ralph is a good correspondent — whereas in other families, as she knows, fathers never put pen to paper. She slides the letter into the pocket of her jeans, to read at lunchtime over her salad roll and yoghurt; jogs out across the dappled dampness of Russell Square, towards the Tube and the Thames and an airless lecture room.

Her dream trails after her, contaminating her day.

Julian, with no reason to wake, sleeps till half-past eight. Bright letters float from a summer sky, and form themselves into nonsense words. It is his usual dream; deprived of the terror it once held, it still carries its component of frustration.

Emma does not dream. She has taken to insomnia, walking the rooms of her cottage in the small hours, the hours of deep rural silence. She does not draw the curtains; outside her cottage a street light burns, and shines on her medical books in their orderly shelves, and the washing-up she has left in the sink.

★

Ralph dreams of his father.

This is the town, the date, the place, to which his dreams return him: Ralph walks on cobblestones, his wrist manacled in his grandfather's hand, his eyes turning upwards to scan the column of his grandfather's body. Wind soughs around the streets and the high stony houses and their chimney-pots. Ralph is three years old. His grandfather lifts him into his arms, and wraps him in his coat to keep out the cold.

'In my day, Ralphie,' he says, 'we used to have donkey races round the market-place. And in my grandfather's day, they used to have pig-hunts, and chimney sweeps dipping for pennies in a basin of flour. And then they used to have fireworks after, and burning of Boney.'

His Uncle James says, 'Poor Ralphie! He does not know who Boney is.'

Ralph turns his head, against Grandpa's woollen shoulder. He lifts his chin and wriggles his body, trying to turn in Grandpa's arms. There is his father, Matthew Eldred, one step behind them. But the shoulder blocks his view; or perhaps it is Uncle James who stands between himself and Matthew. His father is there, he knows; but Ralph cannot see his face.

This is Ralph's first memory: the cobbles, the deep moaning of the wind, the thick cloth of his grandfather's overcoat sawing against his cheek.

The Eldred family belonged to the country which is called the Brecklands; it is a country bounded by chalk and peat, but covered by a mantle of shifting sand. Its open fields are strewn with flint or choked with bracken; they are edged by fir trees twisted into fantastic forms. It is a country of flint-knappers and warreners: latterly of archaeologists and military personnel. There are barrows and mounds, tumuli and ancient tracks; there are oaks and elms. The Romans have left their coins, their skeletons and their fragments of terracotta; the military have set down their huts and wire fences among the ruins of monasteries and castles. Everywhere one senses the presence of standing water, of wading birds, of alders and willow, and of swans rising against the sky.

This is meeting-house country, chapel country; the churches are decayed or badly restored, and the sense of the past is strong, seeping and sinister. Halls and churches have perished, fire eaten thatch, air eaten stone; buildings rejoin the landscape, their walls reduced to flint and rubble strewn across the fields. Some artefact you drop tonight may be lost by morning, but the plough turns up treasure trove. In this country, man's work seems ephemeral, his influence transitory. Summer scorches the heath. Winter brings a pale damp light. The sky is dove-coloured; the sun breaks through it in broad glittering rays, like the rays which, in papist prints, signify the presence of the Holy Spirit.

Matthew Eldred, Ralph's father, was born near the market town of Swaffham in the year 1890. His family were printers, lay preachers. His grandfather had printed pamphlets and tracts. His father had printed handbills and auction catalogues and stock lists, and the privately financed memoirs of clergymen and schoolmasters. Their homes, and the homes of their friends, were temples of right-thinking, of inky scholarship, sabbatarian dullness; their religion was active, proselytizing, strenuous and commonsensical. They saw no need to inquire into God's nature; they approached Him through early rising, Bible study and earnest, futile attempts at humility. The Eldreds were as clever in charity as they were in business – casting their bread on the waters, and rubbing their hands in anticipation of the plump milky loaves that would come back to stack upon the shelves of their family and friends.

Matthew Eldred's brother James, who was four years his junior, was ordained in the Church of England just after the end of the Great War. He left almost at once for the African missions, and so he missed Matthew's wedding; Matthew married a grey-eyed girl called Dorcas Carey, whose father was a local wood merchant, and whose connections outside the county – her elder sister had married a Yorkshireman – had been examined and then forgiven.

James reappeared a decade later – thinner, cheerful, somewhat jaundiced – for the baptism of his brother's first child, Ralph. Dorcas wore a look of bewilderment; after a decade, she had got something right. Another baby, a daughter, followed two years later. James was still, as he termed it, on furlough, but he was not idle; he was working in the East End of London in a home for derelicts and drunks. When Ralph was four years old, Africa opened and swallowed Uncle James again. Only letters came, on tissue-thin sheets of paper, and photographs of naked native children and round thatched huts: of unnamed clergymen and lady assistants with large teeth and white sun-hats: of catechumens in white gloves and white frocks.

Ralph has these photographs still. He keeps them in brown envelopes, their subjects named on the back (when Uncle James' memory has obliged) in Ralph's own large, energetic handwriting. And dated? Sometimes. Uncle James peers at some fading spinster, weathered by the African sun; at some wriggling black child clothed only in a string of beads. 'How would I know? 1930?' Ralph makes the record on the back of each one; makes it in soft pencil, in case Uncle James should reconsider. He has respect for dates; he cares for the past. He files the envelopes in his bureau drawers. One day, he thinks, he might write the history of his family. But then his mind shies away, thinking of what would have to be omitted.

His father and mother stand in pewter frames on his bureau,

watching him as he works. Matthew Eldred has grown stout; his watch chain stretches across his belly. Self-conscious before the photographer, he fingers his lapel. In middle age, Dorcas has the face of a Voortrekker or an American plainswoman: a transparent face, that waits for God to do his worst.

When Ralph was eight years old and his sister Emma was six, Matthew moved his family and his business from Swaffham to Norwich. He began by printing ration books, and ended by growing rich.

The war came. 'Do you wish,' Emma asked Ralph, 'that you were big enough to fight?' Emma doubled up her fist and pounded at the drawing-room sofa, till her fist bounced back at her and dust flew up, and her mother came from the kitchen and slapped her.

A year or so later, they heard talk behind closed doors. 'Yarmouth Grammar School moved to the Midlands ... Lowestoft evacuated yesterday ...' They had visited the seaside – a pointless excursion, the children thought, because the beaches were mined – and seen the first wave of London evacuees, decanted from pleasure steamers, fetching up in coastal villages with their gas masks. They stood by the road and stared, these children, stubble-headed and remote. Now the children were moving on again, deeper into England.

Emma turned her eyes on Ralph. 'What is it like, evacuated?' she hissed.

He shook his head. 'It won't happen to us, I don't think. It's the ones from the coast that are going.'

'I mean,' Emma said, 'how do you fix it?'

He put his finger to his lips. He did not think, then or later, that his parents were cruel: only staid, elderly, without imagination.

When the war ended, there was more whispered discussion.

His parents debated taking in an orphan – perhaps the child of some local girl who had given way to an airman. Or an older child, a companion for Ralph ... They had heard through some church connection of a most unfortunate Lowestoft case, a boy of Ralph's age exactly: whose father, a gas-company worker, had been killed when the bomb fell on Lorne Park Road, and whose mother had died when Waller's Restaurant received a direct hit. 'What was she doing in a restaurant, that's what I'd like to know?' Mrs Eldred said. There was some suggestion that the child might have lived a giddy life before his bereavement. The project was dropped; Ralph's companion faded away, into the realms of might-have-been.

For when you surveyed – his father said – when you surveyed the want in this world, when you peered into the bottomless pit of human improvidence and foolishness, it occurred to you that if there was to be charity it must be systematic.

Much later rationing ended. In the Eldred household it continued. 'There's nothing wrong with economy,' his mother said. If you wanted anything nice to eat, you had to eat it outside the house.

When Ralph was fifteen years old, he went to stay with his aunt in Yorkshire. The Synod of Whitby, his Uncle James called the Yorkshire set; they were too dour, cramped and narrow for James' High Church tastes. The trip north had been intended as a holiday, Ralph supposed; by now he was beginning to be critical of his family, and it seemed congruent with everything else in his life that a holiday and a penance should be so very alike.

The Synod occupied a dark house, and inside it were brown shadows. It contained an unreasonable number of upright chairs, with seats of slippery polished brown leather; it was as if preparations were constantly in hand for a public meeting, a chapel get-together. In the dining room the chairs were high-backed and unyielding, of a particularly officious type. Small meals were sanctified by a lengthy grace. The bookcases had glass fronts, and they were locked; upon the sideboard stood vases of dark glass, like cups of blood.

His cousins crept on slippered feet; clocks ticked. His uncle sat at his desk, making up accounts; his aunt slid her knitting down the cushion of her chair. She sat and stared at him, a bloodless woman the image of his mother; her pale lips moved. 'You should get out, Ralph. Go on the bus. Go up the coast a bit. A boy needs fresh air.'

Ralph left the house. He took the first bus he saw out of the town. It was a normal, hostile east coast day; no one else was on a pleasure jaunt. There were points where the road hugged the coast; a few isolated houses tumbled away towards a sea less glimpsed than felt, towards an impression of sliding subsiding rocks, of coal boats and fishing boats, of salt and chill.

He got off the bus. The place was nowhere he knew. The weather now was overcast but blustery; chinks of blue sky showed here and there, like cracks in a thick white basin. He fastened his coat, as his aunt, if she had seen him, would have enjoined him; and he wrapped his despised muffler around his throat. He descended a hill, one-in-four, and saw before him the cold sweep of a bay.

The tide was going out. A solitary walker picked his way along the cliffs. In the middle distance were other figures, with rucksacks and boots; their heads were down, their eyes searching the sands. Ralph, too, lowered his eyes to his shoes, and threaded his way among the seaweed and rock pools.

Ralph had gone twenty yards towards the ocean. Its sound was subdued, congruous, a rustle not a roar. He bent down and plucked from the sand at his feet what he took to be some muddy stone. A sharp pang of delight took hold of him, a feeling that was for a moment indistinguishable from fear. He had picked up a fossil: a ridged, grey-green curl, glassy and damp like a descending wave. It lay in his palm: two inches across, an inch and a half at its crest.

He stood still, examining it and turning it over. Inside it was a gentle hollow; he saw that it was a kind of shell, smoothness concealed beneath grit and silt. He looked up across the beach. The melancholy and windblown figures wheeled towards him, and came within hailing distance. They closed in on him, with their ribbed stockings and their cold-weather complexions.

There was a woman among them, her sharp nose scarlet above a swaddling of scarves. She stared at the fossil in his hand; she pulled off her gloves, hauled them off with her teeth. He dropped the fossil into her hand. She turned it over and back again, ran her forefinger down its mottled curve, feeling the ridges. She laid it against her face; she tasted it with her tongue. 'Gryphaea,' she said. 'Don't you know?'

He shook his head; stood before her, like the dumb unconverted heathen. 'It's a bivalve – like an oyster, you know?'

'Oh, yes.' He was disappointed; something so ordinary after all.

She said, 'It's a hundred and fifty million years old.' He stared at her. 'You know how an oyster lives in its shell? This is the ancestor of oysters.' He nodded. 'It lived here when the sea was warm – if you can imagine that. Here was its soft body, inside this shell, with its heart and blood vessels and gills. When it died all those soft parts rotted, and the sand filled up the cavity. And then the sand compacted and turned into rock.'

There was a circle of people around them, their breath streaming on the air, eyes fixed on her hand; they were coveting what he had found, as if it were a jewel. 'The sea moved,' a

37

man said. His face was a raw ham beneath a bobble hat. 'I mean to say, what had been sea became land. But now the sea's eating away the land again – all this east coast,' he waved his arm, gesturing towards the Wash – 'you can see it going in your lifetime.'

A man in a balaclava – green, ex-army – said, 'I served with a bloke from Suffolk whose grandfather had a smallholding, and it's in the sea now. Whole churchyards have gone down the cliff. Whole graveyards, and the bones washed out.'

The woman said, 'You've stopped this little creature, my dear. On its way back to the sea where it came from.'

'When it was alive –'

'Yes?'

'What did it eat?'

'It cemented itself on the sea-bed, and sucked in water. It got its nourishment from that, from the larvae in the water, you see. It had a stomach, kidneys, intestines, everything you have.'

'Could it think?'

'Well, can an oyster think these days? What would an oyster have to think about?'

He blushed. Stupid question. What he had meant to say was, are you sure it was alive? Can you truly swear to me that it was? 'Are these rare?' he asked.

'Not if you want a smashed-up one. Not if you're content with fragments.'

The woman held his find for a moment, clenched and concealed in her fist; then put it into his outstretched palm, and worked her fingers back painfully into her gloves. She wanted the fossil so much that he almost gave it to her; but then, he wanted it himself. Bobble-hat said, 'I've been coming here man and boy, and never got anything as good as that. Two-a-penny brachiopods, that's what I get. Sometimes I think we're looking so hard we can't see.'

'Beginner's luck,' the balaclava said. He stabbed a woolly finger at the object he craved. 'Do you know what they call them? Devil's toenails.' He chuckled. 'I reckon you can see why.'

Ralph looked down at the fossil and almost dropped it. Saw the thick, ridged, ogreish curve, that greenish, sinister sheen . . . All the way home in the bus he forced himself to hold the object in his hand, his feelings seesawing between attraction and repulsion; wondering how he could have found it, when he was not looking at all.

When he arrived at the house he was very cold and slightly nauseated. He smiled at the cousin who let him in and said he had better go upstairs right away and wash his hands. 'Did you enjoy yourself, love?' his aunt asked; he gave a monosyllabic reply, a polite mutter which translated to nothing. The ticking of the parlour clock was oppressive, insistent; he could imagine it buried in the earth, ticking away for a hundred and fifty million years. He took his place on one of the leather chairs, and wondered about the animal whose back the leather had adorned: what skin, what hair, what blood through living veins? His aunt quibbled about how the table had been laid, twitching the fish knives about with her forefinger. Smoked haddock came, with its thin-cut bread and butter, a pale juice oozing across the plate. He ate a flake or two, then put down his fork. His aunt said, 'No appetite?' He thought of the bones spilled down the cliff, into the salty whispering of the tides; *Gryphaea* sucking in its nourishment, the aeons rolling by, the devil walking abroad.

His mother made Satan into the likeness of some strict schoolmaster: 'The devil finds work for idle hands to do.'

The toenail was upstairs, locked in his suitcase.

When Ralph came home from Yorkshire, he and Emma played their Bible games. They always played them when they had some decision to make. Now Emma said, 'I want to decide whether when I grow up I'm going to be a doctor or a lawyer, or just a broody hen who stays at home like my mama.'

You were supposed to pick a verse at random, and it would give you guidance; but you needed a keen imagination to make anything of the verses they turned up. 'Try this one,' Emma said. '"And thou shalt anoint the laver and his foot, and sanctify it." Exodus 40:11. Very helpful, I'm sure.' She began to sing a hymn of her own composition: '*How daft the name of Jesus sounds . . .*'

Ralph took out the fossil from his coat pocket, where he was keeping it for the while. 'Look at this,' he said. 'It's the devil's toenail.'

Emma gave a startled wail. 'It's horrible. Whatever is it?'

He told her. Her face brightened. 'Give it me.' He dropped it into her cupped hand. 'Can I take it to school to frighten girls with?'

'No, you certainly can't. It's valuable. It's mine.'

'I'm an atheist,' Emma said.

'Not an atheist a minute ago, were you?'

These were the books on their shelves, old, crumbling: *The Christian's Secret of a Happy Life*. And dusty, brown: *Christ is All*, H. C. G. Moule, London, 1892. Slime-trailed, musty: F. R. Havergal, 1880: *Kept for the Master's Use*. Earwiggy, fading: *Hymns of Faith and Hope*. And *A Basket of Fragments*, R. M. McCheyne, published Aberdeen, no date, pages uncut.

A year later Ralph went back to Yorkshire. His request surprised his family, and gave some pale gratification to the Synod, who had found him a quiet boy who offered no offence, and were glad that someone in the family seemed to like them. He spent his days on the beaches and in the town museum. He did not speak of his discoveries at home, but he found a schoolmaster to encourage him – a man whom, he realized later, he should have enlisted on his side when the quarrel came. He studied alone after school, sent for books with his pocket-money and puzzled over geological maps; he walked fields, hills, coastal paths, examined ditches and road-cuttings. When he was tired and discouraged and there were things he could not understand he thought of the woman on the Yorkshire beach, putting out the purple tip of her tongue to taste the fossil, its silt and grit, its coldness and its age.

There was a trick he had to perfect: to look at a landscape and strip away the effect of man. England transforms itself under the geologist's eye; the scavenger sheep are herded away into the future, and a forest grows in a peat bog, each tree seeded by imagination. Where others saw the lie of the land, Ralph saw the path of the glacier; he saw the desert beneath copse and stream, and the glories of Europe stewing beneath a warm, clear, shallow sea.

Today his fossil collection is in cardboard boxes, in one of the attics of his house. Rebecca, his youngest child, had nightmares about them when she was five or six. He blamed himself, for not giving a proper explanation; it was Kit who had told her they were stone animals, stone lives, primitive creatures that once had swum and crawled. The baby saw them swimming and crawling again, mud-sucking and breathing at her bedroom door.

But in those days, when he was a boy, Ralph kept his finds in his bedroom, arranged on top of his bookcase and on the painted mantelpiece over the empty grate. Norfolk did not yield much for his collection. He combed the Weymouth and Cromer beaches for ammonites and echinoids, but his luck was out; he had to wait for the summer, for his exile to the slippery chairs. He endured all: his uncle's homilies, the piano practice of his female cousins. His mother dusted the fossils twice a week, but didn't understand what they were. 'It's Ralph's interest,' she told people. 'Old bits of stone, and pottery, things of that nature, little bits and pieces that he brings back from his holidays.' Geology and archaeology were thoroughly confused in her mind. 'Ralph is a collector,' she would say. 'He likes anything that's old. Emma – now, Emma – she's much more your modern miss.'

Emma said to her brother, 'Ralph, how can you talk so casually about 500 million years? Most of us have trouble with . . . well, Christmas for example. Every December it puts people into a panic, as if it had come up on them without warning. It's only very exceptional people who can imagine Christmas in July.'

Ralph said, 'What you must do is to think of yourself walking through time. To go back, right back, to the very beginning of geological time, you'd have to go round the world forty-six times. Suppose you want to go back to the last Ice Age. That's very recent, as we think of it. It would be like a cross-channel trip. London to Paris.'

'I wouldn't mind a trip to Paris,' Emma said. 'Do you think it's any good me asking?'

'Then, to reach the time of the dinosaurs, you'd have to go right around the world.

'I feel confined, myself,' Emma said. 'To the here and now.' She sat twisting at one of her plaits, pulling at it, finally undoing it and combing her fingers through her heavy brown hair. She glanced at herself covertly in mirrors these days. 'Geese turn into swans', her mother said; she meant well, but it was hardly science.

A frieze of evolution marched through Ralph's head. Each form of life has its time and place: sea-snail and sea-lily, water-scorpion and lungfish, fern tree and coral. Shark and flesh-eating reptile; sea-urchin and brontosaurus; pterodactyl and magnolia tree; cuttle fish and oyster. Then the giant flightless bird, opossum in his tree, elephant in his swamp; it was as clear in his mind as it might be in a child's picture book, or a poster on a nursery wall. The sabre-toothed cat, the little horse three feet tall; the Irish elk, the woolly mammoth; then man, stooped, hairy, furrow-browed. It is a success story.

At seventeen Ralph could be taken for a man, but not of this primitive textbook kind. He was tall, strong, with a clear skin and clear eyes, like a hero in a slushy book. Sometimes women looked at him with interest on the street: with a speculative pity, as if they feared other women might exploit him.

Ralph would go back to the Brecklands, in those years after the war, threading his bicycle along the narrow roads, between concrete emplacements and through lanes churned up by heavy vehicles. What he saw was victory: fences broken, orchards cut down, avenues of trees mutilated. Gates hung from a hinge, posters flapped on walls. Everywhere was a proliferation of little huts made of corrugated iron – rusting now, and without their doors. Farm workers ran about in scrapped jeeps they had salvaged. Heaps of rubbish festered amid the pines. The wind was the same, its low hum through the stiff branches. The thread-like trunks of birch trees were the same, viewed across tussocky fields; herons flapped from the meres.

The Ministry of Defence did not mean to relinquish its hold on the district. Its fences and KEEP OUT notices divided the fields. Ralph would pull his bicycle on to the grass verge, while a convoy rumbled past. Once, holding his handlebars and standing up to his knees in damp grass, he reached down for what caught his eye; it was a flint arrow-head. He turned it over in his palm, then put it in his pocket. He remembered the moment when he had found the fossil; here was another secret, buried life. He need not take it to a museum; these things are common enough. He took it home and put it on his mantelpiece, meaning to save it for his Uncle James to see when he was next in England. 'Ah, an elfshot,' his mother said, and smiled.

'You like that old country, Ralph,' his father said; the thought did not displease him. Matthew himself had kept friends in the area, church people, other businessmen of a charitable, socially responsible bent. These were the days of meeting-room hysteria and sudden conversion, of dipping people in rivers and calling it baptism. American preachers had come to the bases to service the raw spirituality of their compatriots, and found a ready audience in the poor, cold towns. 'A plain font is requisite,' said Matthew. 'Nothing else.' He hated display: Roman Catholic display, evangelists' display, emotional display. A plain mind is requisite: nothing else.

Emma said she wanted to be a doctor. His father said, 'Yes, if you wish to, Emma.'

Everything was permitted to her, it seemed to Ralph. She was a decisive girl, bossy, full of strong opinions strongly expressed. When Emma's opinions cut across those of her parents, they saw contrariness; they saw a defect of character. They tried, therefore, to correct her character; it did not seem important to them to correct her opinions, for Emma was a female, and what influence could the opinion of a female have in the real world? Her opinions might damage her, and she would then revise them – but they would not damage the social order.

At least, that was how Ralph supposed they thought. For when it came to his opinions, his desires, it was a very different story.

'So you don't want to go into the business, Ralphie.'

This was how his father joined battle: obliquely, from the flank. He made it seem that there were only simple issues at

44

stake, a change in family expectations. But soon enough, his weighty battalions were deployed. The issues went beyond the family. They became larger than Ralph had bargained for. They became universal.

First his father said: 'Ralph, you've never given me any trouble. I thought you believed in the religion that you were brought up in.'

'I do,' Ralph said.

'But now you are setting yourself up against it.'

'No.'

'But you must be, Ralph. We believe that God created the world, as is set down in the Bible. I believe it. Your mother believes it.'

'Uncle James doesn't believe it.'

'James is not here,' his father said flatly. It was incontrovertible; James was in the Diocese of Zanzibar.

'I believe it as a metaphor,' Ralph said. 'But I believe in evolution too.'

'Then you are a very muddle-headed young man,' his father said. 'How can you entertain two contradictory beliefs at the same time?'

'But they aren't contradictory. Father, most people got all this over with by the turn of the century. Nobody thinks what you think any more. Nobody thinks there's God on one side and Darwin on the other.'

'When I was a young man,' Matthew said, 'I attended a lecture. It was given by a professor, he was a distinguished scholar, he was no fool or half-baked schoolboy. He said to us, "What is Darwinism? I will tell you. Darwinism is atheism," he said. I have always remembered those words. I have seen nothing in my life since to convince me that he was wrong.'

'But if you thought about it now,' Ralph said, 'if you thought about it all over again, you might be able to see that he

45

was wrong.' Something bubbled inside him: intellectual panic? 'What's the point of just repeating what you were told when you were a boy? You can be an evolutionist, Darwinian or some other kind, and still believe that everything that exists is intended by God. It's an old debate, it's stale, it was never necessary in the first place.'

'My own beliefs,' his father said, 'have never been subject to the vagaries of fashion.'

Days of war followed. Silences. Ralph couldn't eat. Food stuck in his dry mouth; it was like trying to swallow rocks, he thought. He hated quarrels, hated silences too: those silences that thickened the air in rooms and made it electric.

Matthew closed in on him, and so did his mother: a pincer movement. 'Are you going to take evidence, what you call evidence, from a few bones and shells, and use them to oppose the word of God?'

'I told you,' Ralph said, 'that there is no opposition.'

'There is opposition from me,' his father said: shifting the ground.

'It is impossible to have a discussion with you.'

'No doubt,' Matthew said. 'I am not a scientist, am I? I am so backward in my outlook that I wonder you condescend to talk to me at all. I wonder you condescend to stay under my roof. Good God, boy – look around you. Look at the design of the world. Do you think some blind stupid mechanism controls it? Do you think we got here out of chance?'

'Please be calm,' Ralph said. He tried to take a deep breath, but it seemed to stick half-way. 'It's no good waving your arms at me and saying, look at God's creation. You don't have to force it down my throat, the miracles of nature, the design of the universe – I know about those, more, I'd say, than you.' (More than you, he thought, who have lived your life with your eyes on your well-blacked boots.) 'If I believe in God I

46

believe from choice. Not because of evidence. From choice. Not because I'm compelled.'

'You believe from *choice*?' Matthew was revolted. 'From choice? Where did you get this stupid notion from?'

'I thought of it myself.'

'Can you believe in anything you like, then? Can you believe the moon is made of green cheese? Is there no truth you recognize?'

'I don't know,' Ralph said quietly. 'We used to go to sermons that said the truth was what God revealed, that you don't find the truth by looking for it. At least, that's what I think they were saying. Well – not to put too fine a point on it – I can't wait around all my life. If I've been given the faculty of reasoning, I may as well use it to dig out what truth I can.'

'You'll kill me, Ralph,' his father said. 'Your pride and your self-regard will kill me.'

Ralph was afraid his father might ask, with one old divine, 'What can the geologist tell you about the Rock of Ages?' He spared him that, but not episodes of choking rage, which terrified Ralph and made him regret what he had begun.

His mother took him aside. 'You are making your father very unhappy,' she said. 'I have never seen him more miserable. And he has done everything for you, and would give you anything. If you do this thing, if you insist on it, if you insist on this as your life's work, I'll not be able to hold my head up before our friends. They'll say we have not brought you up properly.'

'Look,' Ralph said, 'what I want is to go to university. I want to read geology. Just that, that's all. I didn't set out to upset anybody. That was the last thing on my mind.'

'I know you have your ambitions,' Dorcas said, with that frayed sigh only mothers can perform. 'But your abilities, Ralph, are not for you to enjoy – they are given to you to use for the Christian community.'

'Yes. All right. I will use them.'

'You've closed your mind,' she said.

Astonishment wrenched him out of his misery. She left him incoherent. 'Me? I've closed my mind?'

'You spoke to your father of reason,' she said. 'You'll find there is a point where reason fails.'

'Stop talking at me,' he said. 'Leave me alone.'

His mother left him alone. Her mouth drew in as though she were eating sour plums. If James were here it would be different, Ralph thought; he wanted to cry like a child for his uncle, of whom he knew so little. James could talk to them, he believed, James could ridicule them out of their caution and their scruples and their superstitions, James could talk them into the twentieth century. James is not like them, he knows it from his letters; James is liberal, educated, sympathetic. Ralph saw himself losing, being driven into the ground. All he believed, all he wished to believe – the march of order, progress – all diminished by his father's hard deriding stare and his mother's puckered mouth.

Why didn't he fetch in the schoolmaster who encouraged him? Why didn't he appeal to his headmaster, who knew him to be a bright, studious, serious boy? Why didn't he get some other, reasonable adult to weigh in on his behalf – at least to referee the argument, make sure his father obeyed the laws of war?

Because he was ashamed of his father's stupidity, ashamed of the terms of the quarrel. Because in families, you never think of appealing for help to the outside world; your quarrels are too particular, too specific, too complex. And because you never think of these reasonable solutions, till it is far too late.

'Ralph,' his father said, 'be guided by me. You are a mere boy. Oh, you don't want to hear that, I know. You think you are very adult and smart. But you will come to thank me, Ralphie, in the days ahead.'

Ralph felt he was trapped in an ancient argument. These are the things sons say to fathers; these are the things fathers say to sons. The knowledge didn't help him; nor did the knowledge that his father was behaving like a caricature of a Victorian patriarch. His family had always been cripplingly old-fashioned; till now he had not realized the deformity's extent. Why should he, when all his family's friends were the same, and he had spent his life hobbling along with them? They were churchgoers; not great readers; not travellers, but people who on principle entertained narrow ideas and stayed at home. He saw them for the first time as the outside world might see them – East Anglian fossils.

'There will be no money for you, Ralphie,' his father said. 'And you will hardly be able to support yourself through your proposed course at university. You may try, of course.'

'James will help me,' Ralph said, without believing it.

'Your Uncle James has not a brass farthing of his own. And you're quite mistaken if you think he would set himself up against his own brother.'

'Of course, I could see it coming,' Emma said. 'After all the fine theories and pieties have been aired, what it comes down to is their hand on the purse-strings. That's their final argument.'

Ralph said, 'It isn't God who's diminished by Darwin's theory, it's man. Man isn't any more lord of the universe. He's just a part of the general scheme of things. But there is a scheme of things, and you can put God at the top of it if you like.'

'But you don't like,' his father said. Another flat statement. It was not evolution that was the issue now, it was obedience. Even if his father had taken that last point, Ralph thought, he had done himself no service by raising it. If Man was diminished, then Matthew Eldred was diminished: a lord of the universe was precisely what he wished to be.

'If you like,' Ralph said, 'and I do like – you can still believe that Man has a unique place in creation. You can still believe that he has a special dignity. Only Man is rational. Only Man is an intellectual animal.'

'Bandying words,' his father said. He seemed satisfied with the phrase, as if he were a doctor and this were his diagnosis.

I except you, Ralph thought. I wouldn't call you rational, not any more.

When the conflict was at its height – when the family were barely speaking to each other, and a Synod-like hush possessed the rooms – Matthew absented himself for a night. He went to King's Lynn, to discuss with some of his business cronies the charitable trust that they were setting up. It was to be an ambitious enterprise, with broad Christian interests: money for the missions, money for the East End doss house with which James kept a connection; money above all for the deserving poor of Norfolk, the aged and indigent farm labourers, those church-going rural folk who had been mangled by agricultural machinery or otherwise suffered some disabling mischance.

It was to be called the St Walstan Trust; Walstan is the patron saint of farmers and farm labourers, and his image is found through the county on screens and fonts. The suggestion came from William Martin, a shopkeeper at Dereham; it was a little High Church for Matthew's taste, but Martin was generally sound, very sound, and the county connection pleased him. Matthew was a local patriot now, a sitter on committees, treasurer of this and chairman of that. Ralph said to Emma, 'I wish that charity would begin at home.'

That evening, the event took place which broke Ralph's resolve. His mother came to his bedroom, upstairs on her noiseless feet. She tapped at the door, and waited till he had asked her to enter; this arch, stiff politeness had come upon the family since the row blew up.

Ralph looked up from his books, adjusting his desk lamp so that it cast a little light into the room. It pooled at his mother's slippered feet as she sat on the bed. She wore her cardigan draped over her shoulders; she took the cuffs of the empty sleeves in her hands, and twisted them as she spoke. Her wedding ring gleamed, big and broad like a brass washer. She had lost weight, perhaps, for it hung loose on her finger, and her knuckle bones seemed huge.

Ralph listened to what she had to say. If he would not capitulate, she said – but she did not use that word – if he would not fall into line, fall in with the plans his father had formulated for him, then she could not say what his father would do about Emma. He might think that as Ralph had gone so badly off course, Emma needed guidance. He might like to have her at home, under his eye. There might, in fact, be no medical school for Emma at all.

His mother sighed as she said all this; her manner was tentative, and her eyes travelled over the peg-rug and the bookcase and the desk, they roamed the wall and flickered over the dark window at which the curtains were not yet drawn. But she was not afraid; and Ralph understood her. She had volunteered, he believed, for this piece of dirty work; she and her husband, his father, had planned it between them, so that there would be no more shouting, no more scenes, only his certain silent defeat.

'Emma might like to be a nurse, perhaps,' his mother said. 'Your father might let her do that, but I only say might. His frame of mind so much depends on you.'

Ralph said, 'You are a wicked woman.'

He didn't know that she was sick then, and that within a few months she would have the first of her many spells in hospital. Despite her sufferings she would have a long life. He was never sure that he forgave her completely. But he tried.

★

After his capitulation, his father began to backtrack at once. 'For a hobby, Ralphie,' he said. 'Keep it for a hobby. But not for what you are seen to do in the eyes of the world. Not for your life's work.'

'I don't want the business,' he told his father. 'I want my own life. I don't want anything to do with all that.'

'Very well,' Matthew said equably. 'I'll sell – when the time is right.' He frowned then, as if he might be misunderstood. 'There'll be money for you, Ralph. And there'll be money for your children. I'll put it in trust, I'll arrange it all. You'll not be poor.'

'This is premature,' Ralph said.

'Oh, you'll be married and have children soon enough, the years go by . . . you could be a teacher, Ralphie. You could go to Africa, like your uncle. They have a great need of people, you know. I would never try to confine you. I would never sentence you to a dull life.' He paused, and added, 'But I hope one day you will come home to Norfolk.'

For months afterwards Ralph never seemed to smile; that was what Emma thought. He kept his shoulders hunched as he walked, as if he wore disappointment like a tight old coat. 'Why did you give in to them?' she asked. 'Why didn't you stick by your principles, why didn't you stick out for the life you had planned?'

He wouldn't talk to her; occasionally, he would just remark that things were not as they seemed, that he saw there were hidden depths to people.

She did not know how he had been defeated. He made sure he did not tell her.

He had his National Service to do; it would fail to broaden his horizons. He would spend it behind a desk, employed in menial clerical work; or in transit in trucks and trains. He began to recognize his character, as it was reflected back to him by other people. He saw a solid, polite, always reasonable young man, who would sort out problems for the dim and timid, who kept his patience and who did not patronize or sneer; who never cultivated his superiors, either, who seemed to have no ambition and no idea how to make life easy for himself. Was he really like that? He didn't know.

He was not excessively miserable. It seemed to him that the boredom, the routine discomforts and humiliations, the exile from home, the futility of his daily round, were all simple enough to endure. What he could not endure were the thoughts of his heart, and the frequent dreams he had, in which he murdered his father. Or rather, dreams in which he plotted the murder; or in which he was arrested and tried, when the murder was already done. The bloody act itself was always offstage.

When he was twenty years old these dreams were so persistent that the memory of them stained and dislocated his waking life. By day he entertained, he thought, little animosity to Matthew. Their quarrel had not affected what he believed, it had only affected the course of his career; and one day Matthew would die, or become senile, or concede the point, and he could resume that career. He must be the winner in the long run, he thought.

So these dreams, these inner revolts, bewildered him. He was forced to concede that large areas of his life were beyond his control.

On one of his leaves, instead of going home to Norwich, he went to London with a friend. They stayed at his friend's sister's house, Ralph sleeping on the sofa. By day, he went sightseeing; he had never been to London before. One night he lost his virginity for cash, in a room near one of the major railway termini. Afterwards he could never remember which station it had been, or the name of the street, so that in later life he couldn't be sure whether he ever walked along it; and although the woman told him her name was Norah he had no reason to believe her. He did not feel guilt afterwards; it was something to be got through. He had not embarrassed himself; there was that much to be said about it.

On his next leave he was introduced to Anna Martin, only child of the very sound shopkeeper from Dereham.

Three years later, Ralph was teaching in London, in the East End. James had come home and was director of what had been the doss house and was now St Walstan's Hostel. Ralph went there most weekends. He slept on a folding bed in the director's office, and was called during the night to new admissions banging on the door, to men taken sick and to residents who had unexpectedly provided themselves with alcohol first, and then with broken bottles, knives, pokers or iron bars. He arbitrated in disputes about the ownership of dog-ends, lumpy mattresses and soiled blankets, and became familiar with the customs and rituals and shibboleths of welfare officers and policemen.

On a Sunday night he collected the week's bedding, and listed it for the laundry, counting the sheets stained with vomit and semen, with excrement and blood. On a Wednesday evening he would drop by for an hour to count the linen in again. The sheets were patched and darned, but stainless. They smelled of the launderer's press; they were stiff and utterly white. How do they do it, he wondered; how do they make them so utterly white?

He became engaged to Anna. They planned to marry when she graduated from her teacher-training college, and go straight out to Dar-es-Salaam, where a dear friend of James was a headmaster and where a pleasant house would be waiting for them, and two jobs as teachers of English to young men

54

training for the ministry. Sometimes, on the London pavements, Ralph tried to imagine himself translated to this alien place, to the heat and colour of this other life. Letters passed to and fro. Arrangements were in hand.

Anna received all this with equanimity. She was planning the wedding, the quiet wedding. A quiet girl altogether; she wore grey, charcoal, dark blue, simple clothes with clear lines. Ralph thought she was setting herself apart, cultivating almost a nun-like air. They did not discuss their religious beliefs; a certain amount was implied, understood. She had taken on the prospect of Africa without demur. 'She hasn't really said much about it,' Ralph told James.

James said, 'Good – I suspect enthusiasm.'

The kind of person not wanted in those climes, he said, was someone who rushed with open arms to embrace the romantic deprivations of the life. Anna's reasoned agreement was a better foundation for their future than constant chatter about what that future might hold.

Later Ralph would think, when we married it was a leap into the dark: we didn't know each other at all. But perhaps when you are so young, you don't even begin to comprehend what there is to know.

As for those nun-like clothes – when he had seen more of the world, and was more accustomed to looking at women, he realized that Anna's style was deliberate, ingenious and contrived by the exercise of a stifled artistic talent. She had made her own dresses in those days; she could not buy what she wanted in Norfolk, and with her tiny means she would not have dared to enter a London shop. She spent what she had on fabric, buttons and trimmings; she cut, pressed and stitched, obsessively careful, tyrannically neat. And so what Anna possessed was unique among the people he knew – it was not sanctity, but chic.

★

55

'Freud said,' Emma told him, 'that religion is a universal obsessional neurosis.' She looked at him over her glasses. 'Tell me now . . . what happened to the dinosaurs, Ralph?'

'Their habitat altered,' he said. 'A change of climate.' She smiled crookedly. He saw that she hadn't expected an answer. 'The trouble with our parents,' she said, 'is that their habitat doesn't change. It hardly varies from one end of the county to the next. Give them a pew, and they're right at home.'

Emma had got her wish. She was at medical school; and home now for Ralph's wedding, her book open on her lap and her feet up on the old sofa that she had thrashed so thoroughly in 1939. Emma had grown heavy; the hospital food, she said, was all dumplings, pastry, suet, and that was what she was turning into, dumplings, pastry, suet. Despite this, she had a suitor, a smart local boy called Felix, not one of their Bible-study set. She dealt with him by ignoring him most of the time, and did not always answer his letters.

She had grumbled with vigour about the business of a new frock for the wedding, even though her father had paid for it; she would pay herself, she said, if Matthew would go and choose the thing, converse with shop assistants and track down a hat to match. Emma resisted the attentions of hairdressers. Anna, the bride-to-be, offered to take her in hand and see that she got a perm. Emma swore when she heard this, so violently that she surprised herself.

'So, Ralph,' Emma said, 'the news from Freud is not all bad. "Devout believers" – that's you and Anna – "are safeguarded in a high degree against the risk of certain neurotic illnesses: their acceptance of the universal neurosis spares them from the task of constructing a personal one." In other words, one sort of madness is enough for anybody.'

'Do you think it is madness?' Ralph asked. 'Madness and nothing else?'

'I don't think it has any reality, Ralph. I think faith is

something people chase after, simply to give life meaning.'

She spoke quite kindly, he thought later. 'And doesn't it have meaning?' he asked.

Emma reserved judgement.

That night his father took him aside. 'I want to talk about the arrangements,' he said.

'It's all in hand. All done. You don't have to concern yourself.'

'I don't mean arrangements for the wedding. Why should I concern myself with the women's business?' His father slid out a drawer of his desk, took out some papers, looked through them as he spoke; this was a family whose members no longer met each other's eyes. 'I mean the arrangements for the future. I have taken advice, and I am going to sell the press. I have a good offer from a publisher of educational books.' Unable to find anything of interest in the papers, he turned them over and stared at their back. 'Education, you know – it's the coming thing.'

'I should hope it is,' Ralph said. He felt at a loss. He ought to be able to give an opinion. 'Well, if your accountant –' he began.

Matthew cut him short. 'Yes, yes, yes. Now then, I propose to invest a certain amount, the interest to be paid to Walstan's Trust.' He had managed to drop the Saint, Ralph noticed. 'I propose to place a smaller amount into a family trust for yourself and Anna and your children. When you come back from the missions, you will sit on the committee of Walstan's Trust, which five years from now will need a full-time paid administrator. If you seem fit for it, you will be able to fill that position.'

'Other people may have claims,' Ralph said. This was all he could do – raise small objections. He could not imagine himself in five years' time. He could not imagine what kind of man he might be, or imagine these notional children of his. I might die in Africa, he thought. There are tropical diseases, and all sorts of strange accidents.

'Well, they may,' said his father. 'But I cannot see very clearly who they would be. Your Uncle James will be wanting a rest by then, and the children of my colleagues on the committee are pursuing their own paths in life.'

'It seems to be looking too far ahead,' Ralph said.

'Oh,' Matthew said, 'I thought the millennia were as naught to you. Really, you know, to plan five years or ten years ahead is nothing. All businessmen do it. We do it when we invest money – though you would know nothing of that.'

'I suppose I wouldn't.'

'My object, my plan – and here I may say the other trustees agree with me – is that the Trust should be forever administered from Norfolk, no matter how wide its interests may become. It is local money that has set it up – and we must keep our feet on the ground. So you will want to base yourself here in Norwich, or elsewhere in the county if you prefer. When you return I will buy you a house, because you will make no money while you are out in Africa. That goes without saying.'

If that is so, Ralph thought, why say it? He said, 'Had you any particular house in mind?' But he could not summon the strength of purpose to put venom into his tone.

'I want the Trust to benefit my own countrymen,' Matthew said, 'not just James' collection of drunks and wastrels. Don't mistake me – I have respect for James' work –'

'Yes, I understand you,' Ralph said. 'You don't have to talk to me as if you were addressing the County Council.'

He thought, from now on I shall take control, I shall order my own life, just as I like. I am going to Africa because I want to go, because Anna wants it. When I return I shall be my own man.

58

He did not feel demeaned when his father wrote out a cheque for a wedding present and put it into his hand. Payment was due, he reckoned, a tribute from the past to the future.

Four days before the wedding James telephoned from London to say that there was a spot of trouble, could Ralph possibly get on the train and come right away? He was due to appear in court as a witness, one of his inmates having assaulted a police constable; his assistant appeared to be having a nervous breakdown, and there was no one but Ralph who could be trusted to oversee the hostel for a day.

Ralph said, 'What will you do when I go out to Dar?'

His uncle said, 'That's another thing – I want to talk to you about that. Don't hang about – take a taxi from Liverpool Street. St Walstan will pay.'

Ralph picked up his coat and hat and strode off to the station. He feared the worst. His uncle was going to tell him that he was needed here, in the East End; that the tropics could wait, and that he and Anna should see about renting some rooms a bus-ride from the hostel. He wondered whether he would say yes and supposed he would. Anna would have to unpack her cotton dresses and put them in mothballs, and begin her married life as an East End housewife visiting street markets with a basket over her arm. He rehearsed some inner rebellions: let James sacrifice himself, James is a clergyman, he has no life of his own. He bought a cup of tea in a café near Liverpool Street. He thought of going back into the station and taking the next train back to Norwich; or alternatively, the next train to somewhere else.

It was half-past five when James came back from court, and the hostel was almost full that night, so before he had any conversation with his nephew he took off his jacket and rolled up his sleeves and began to help with the day's last meal. It was stew – it usually was stew of some sort – but there was all the bread to be cut and margarined. The inmates always wanted bread, three slices per man, whatever the rest of their meal was. They grumbled if they did not get it, as if their rights had been violated.

When the meal was over and the men on the washing-up rota had been identified and corralled and set to their task, James with a twitch of his head beckoned Ralph into his office. They closed the door and with a single purpose, without a word, heaved a filing cabinet at the back of it; they knew from experience that it was the only way they could get a minute without interruption.

'Is it about the posting?' Ralph asked. 'Is there a problem?'

'No, no problem.' James sat down at his desk, and found space for his elbows among the unpaid bills and begging letters and rubber bands. 'Why do I have these rubber bands?' he wondered. 'What are they for? No, Ralphie, there is no problem with Dar-es-Salaam, it is just that something more urgent has come up, and I thought that you should have the chance to consider it.'

Here it comes, Ralph thought: my future on the Mile End Road.

James said, 'Would you like to go to South Africa?'

On the outskirts of Swaffham today there is a goodly selection of dinky bungalows. They have wrought-iron gates and birdbaths, trellises, hanging baskets, shutters and dwarf walls. They have raw brickwork and shining windows, and scarlet floribundas in well-weeded beds. Their carriage lamps are the light of the twentieth century. In the market-place Ralph hears the broad drawling accent in which his grandfather spoke moderated to the foul contemporary tones of middle England.

These bungalow dwellers repopulated the villages of

Breckland, which were empty when Ralph went to Africa. Between settlements, there are still tracts of heather and furze, and black pine plantations: barren, monotonous, funereal, like the contents of an East European nightmare. But the bowed, arthritic pines that line the roads creep to the edges of the small towns, intruding themselves among the DIY merchants and filling stations and furniture warehouses; they gather round the new housing estates, like witches at a christening.

It is only in the land marked off by the military's fences that the old country can be seen. 'Danger areas,' they are called on the map. It is said the army builds models there, of life-sized Belfast streets, and that snipers and marksmen creep behind empty windows and false walls. From the roads you can see Nissen huts, like slugs in formation. Signs read 'No Entry without Permit – Ministry of Defence Property'. Vegetation creeps like serpents around their metal poles. The wind topples them.

To the east, where Ralph and his children now live at the county's heart, the great wheat fields roll on to the horizon, denatured, over-fertile, factory fields. A farm that employed eighty-five men now employs six; the descendants of the other seventy-nine have delivered themselves from rural squalor, from midden and rotting thatch, and live in the bungalows, or in red-brick council houses with long gardens. In spring, primroses struggle in the verges. In June, there are dog-roses in such hedgerows as remain.

Ralph dreams; again, he is three years old. Somewhere behind him, unseen, his father walks, and Uncle James. He curls down inside his grandfather's coat.

They are going to the church. His grandfather will show him the angels in the roof, and the Pedlar of Swaffham carved on a stall end, and the pedlar's dog with its round ears and big chain.

The Pedlar of Swaffham: John Chapman was his name. He dreamt one night that if he went to London, and stood on London Bridge, he would meet a man who would tell him how to make his fortune.

The day after this dream, Chapman put his pack on his back and with his dog set off to London. On London Bridge he stood about, until a shopkeeper asked him what he thought he was doing. 'I'm here because of a dream,' the pedlar said.

'Dream?' said the shopkeeper. 'If I took any notice of dreams, I would be in some country place called Swaffham, in the garden of some yokel called Chapman, digging under his damn-fool pear tree.' With a sneer, the fellow retreated to his merchandise.

John Chapman and his dog returned to Swaffham and dug under the pear tree. There they found a pot of gold. Around the pot ran an inscription. It said, 'Under this pot is another, twice as good.' The pedlar began digging again, and found a second crock: and now his fortune was made.

John Chapman gave candlesticks to the church, and rebuilt the north aisle when it fell down, and gave £120 to the steeple fund. His wife Cateryne and his dog were carved on the stalls, the wife with her rosary and the dog with his chain. John Chapman became a churchwarden, and wore an ermine gown.

But Ralph's dreams? He has shelved them: packed away his specimens and consigned his maps and monographs to a space under the eaves of his father's house in Norwich. He has consented to another kind of life from the life he had planned for himself. It happens to people at Ralph's age, at twenty-five, you realize you are no longer the person you were, and will never become the person you meant to be. But he thinks, after all, there is a living to be made; there is a row to be hoed, and at least I am not a clergyman. He is serving God – a bit – and

Mammon – a bit; his father's friends say he has not *committed* himself, not *wholly*, and he knows he has very little money in the bank. He comforts himself that he understands something of the nature of life, of the nature of hidden things: at least, he has classifications for what lies beneath the surface, he has categories and terms.

From a jelly speck to man the line improves, edging nearer all the time to the summit of God's design. As the species has evolved, the child in the womb grows, grows through its gills and its fur and becomes human. So society creeps forward, from savagery to benevolence: from cold and hunger and murder, to four walls and hearth stones and arts and parliaments and cures for diseases. At twenty-five Ralph believes this; he believes too in the complex perfectibility of the human heart.

FOUR

Lucy Moyo took a bunch of keys out of the pocket of her apron. She was six foot tall, imposing, solid, like a black bolster inside her print frock; the bunch of keys lay in her hand like a toy.

'This is the key for your office,' she said. She held it up. 'These little ones are for your desks and cupboards. This is for the cupboard where we keep the first-aid chest. This one is for the chest itself. Friday nights, Saturdays, you will be wanting that. These keys are for the inside doors of your house. This one is for the pantry and these are for the store cupboards inside the pantry.'

'Are they really necessary?' Anna asked. 'Every one?'

Lucy smiled remotely. 'Mrs Eldred, you will find that they are. This key is for the woodshed where the tools are kept. The baas must be sure that anything to stab and cut, anything with a sharp edge, you understand me, is shown to him or to you or some good person at the end of the day when it has been used and then it is locked up till it is wanted again.'

Lucy pressed the keys into Anna's palm. She folded Anna's fingers over them. 'You must keep all these doors locked. These people are thieves.'

Her own people, Anna thought. And how casually she says it. 'Is Lucy a cynic?' she asked later.

'I don't think we ought to criticize her,' Ralph said. 'She's kept the place ticking over.' His hands moved over his desk, bewildered, flinching. 'She probably knows what she's talking about. It's just the way she puts things, it's a bit bald.'

Lucy said, 'Mr and Mrs Standish, who were here before you, used to sit after their supper most nights and cry. It made me sad to see such old people crying.'

The voyage to Cape Town had taken three weeks. It had allowed Anna a pause for thought, a period of grace. Until the last year of her life, nothing had happened. Then everything had happened together. When she was thirteen or fourteen, she had made up her mind to go to a foreign country: preferably a distant one. Her idea was that she would say goodbye to her parents, and write to them twice a year.

Ralph understood her parents – which was a good thing, because of the time it saved. It would have been a lifetime's work to explain them to someone who had been brought up in a different fashion. In families like yours and mine, Ralph said, it's the girls who have the harder time. He knew, he said, what his sister had gone though. Anna reserved judgement. It seemed to her that Emma was not unduly marked by suffering.

The truth was that Emma frightened her; even her small-talk was inquisitorial, demanding, sarcastic. Without a word but with an impatient toss of her head, she implied that Anna was decorative but useless. At least, Anna took this to be the implication. Nothing could be less true. Her hands had never been idle.

Anyway, she was putting thousands of miles between herself and Emma. If she had stayed in Norfolk people would have expected them to be friends, they would always be saying, Anna and Emma, Emma and Anna. It was not a harmonious combination – not to her ear. As a child, it was true, she had sometimes wished for a sister. Any companions had to run through a parental censorship, an overview of their lives and antecedents. By the time a prospective friend was approved, the attraction had waned on both sides.

Her mother and father were shopkeepers, with the grocer's

habit of measuring out everything: especially their approval. Nothing is free; they stressed that. God has scales in which he weighs your inclinations against your actions, your needs against your desires. Pleasure is paid for in the coin of pain. Pay in the coin of faith, and God may return a measured quantity of mercy. Or then again, he may not.

Anna had been a great reader, as a child. Her parents gave her paper pamphlets, containing tales of black babies and Eskimos and how they came to Jesus. But what she liked were school stories, where the pupils lived away from home in a mansion by the sea, and played lacrosse and learned French from Mam'selle. Her parents said books were a good thing, but when they picked one up to inspect it – to permit or not permit – their faces expressed suspicion and latent hostility.

They eschewed the cinema and the theatre – they did not forbid them, but they knew how to make their views known. No alcohol passed their lips. Women who wore make-up – at least, any more than a smear of tan face-powder – were not their sort. Mr Martin looked at the newspaper, so his wife did not need to bother. She received each day a used opinion from him, just as she received a shirt for laundering, tainted with the smell of smoked bacon and ripe cheese.

Later, when she grew up, Anna realized that her parents were afflicted not simply by godliness, but by social snobbery. It seemed difficult for them to distinguish between the two. They looked up to those customers with big houses, to whom each week they delivered straw-packed boxes containing glacé fruits and tiny jars of chicken breasts in nutritious jelly. They looked down on ordinary customers, who queued in the shop for bags of sugar and quarters of tea. The former paid on account; of the latter, they naturally demanded cash. They were among the first in their district to get the ingenious, time-saving, pre-printed notice, which encapsulated so neatly their philosophy of life:

All through her teens, Anna had been tormented by this notice, and by this thought: what if I fall in love, what if I fall in love with someone *unsuitable*? She knew the chances of this were high; there were so many unsuitable people in the world. But when she came home and said that Ralph Eldred wanted her to get engaged, the Martins looked in vain for a reason to oppose it. It was true that the boy's future was unsettled; but then, his father was a county councillor.

Anna had been a compliant daughter. She had tried to do everything she could to suit her parents, while knowing that it would not be quite enough: *please do not ask for credit* . . . Some unhappy children have fantasies that they are adopted; Anna always knew she was theirs. In adolescence, she fell into reveries, irritating to the people about her, productive of sharp words from her mother. She dreamed of ways of being as unlike her parents as possible. But she didn't know any ways. To despise them was one thing; to free herself from them was quite another.

And she wondered, now, as the ship moved south, whether she was sailing away from them or towards them. After all, they were such charitable people; weren't they, in their own way, missionaries at home? There were no luxuries in their household; money was always needed for good causes. Besides, it was wicked to have luxuries when others had not the necessities: unless you were an account customer, of course.

And if the charity did not proceed from love, but from a sense of duty, did that matter? Were the results not the same?

Anna used to think so. The starving eat, whatever the motive of the bread's donor; perhaps it does not become the starving to be nice about motives.

Ralph saw the issue differently. The Eldreds and the Martins, he said, acted from a desire to make the world conformable. Grocer Martin would like to raise all tramps to the condition of account customers; Betty the grocer's wife would like to see chain-smoking unmarried mothers scrub their faces and take communion monthly. Cold, poverty, hunger must be remedied because they are extreme states, productive of disorder, of psychic convulsions, of demonstrations by the unemployed. They lead to socialism, and make the streets unsafe.

Ralph passed judgement on his father, and on hers. He knew a poem; he would laugh, and say:

> 'God made the wicked Grocer
>   For a mystery and a sign.
> That men might shun the awful shops
>   And go to inns to dine.'

There it was – Ralph hated nothing more than meanness. It seemed to her that he had a spontaneous, uncalculated kindness. She was looking for no more and no less. She slept with him before – just before – the engagement ring was on her finger.

It was she who had made him the offer. When the time came – the one occasion, perhaps in a year, when they had the house at Dereham to themselves – she was seized by fear. Even the touch of his warm hands made her shiver. But he was a young man with little experience – or none, as she supposed – so perhaps the difference between terror and passion was not readily apparent to him.

After the deed was done, she worried a good deal about whether she might be pregnant. She thought of praying not to be, but she did not think she would have God's ear. And besides, in the one way, disgrace would have delivered her. 'I'll look after you,' Ralph had said. 'If that happened, we'd just bring the wedding forward.' When her period came – four days late, late enough to put her into a daze of panic and hope – she leaned against the freezing wall of her parents' bathroom, against the hostile dark-green paint, and cried over the chance lost.

After this she seemed to lose her equilibrium; she had not thought of herself as a complicated person, but now all sorts of wishes and fears were fighting inside her head. Ralph suggested that they should bring the wedding forward anyway; marry as soon as she left her teacher-training college, not wait until the end of the summer. Uncle James came to meet her parents, and talked about this very interesting post that was going in Dar-es-Salaam.

Her mother thought that the climate might be unsuitable, but conceded that Anna had never had a day's illness and had not been brought up to be a shirker. Betty thought, further, that the natives might not be nice. But what surprised Anna was how easily they fell in with James' suggestion, how quickly they agreed that though the engagement had been unusually short the marriage might as well be in June. For the first time it occurred to her that they might be glad to have her off their hands. Think of the expenditure of emotion a daughter entails! With their daughter married, and at the other side of the world, they would have more energy for the affairs of strangers.

Of course there was something improbable, even hilarious, about the idea of being a missionary in Africa. She said, 'I won't have to wear a sola topi, will I? And be boiled in a pot?'

Ralph said, 'I don't think so. Uncle James has never been boiled. Not so far, anyway.'

Then Ralph came to her with the change of plan. If she agreed, they were not to go to East Africa at all. A job was waiting for them elsewhere, in a township called Elim. It was near Johannesburg, north of the city – not far from Pretoria either, he said, as if that would help her place it. He brought a book, newly published, called *Naught for Your Comfort*. If she would read it, he suggested, she would know why people were needed and why perhaps if they valued their own comfort they ought not to go. Then she could weigh up the options, think what was best for them. 'And best for other people, of course,' she said. At that time – the spring of 1956 – she could say such a thing with no ironical intent.

She read the book at once. It painted a picture of a hungry, bloody, barely comprehensible world. She felt ready to enter it. She did not know what use she could be, but Ralph seemed to think their work was cut out for them. And after all, comfort had never been one of her expectations.

She had dreamt about the book too, those last nights before they left England. The dreams seemed to heighten but not betray the text. Policemen strutted in the streets with machine-guns. Acts of Parliament were posted up on every street. The populace was cowed.

When she woke, she shuttled these nightmares out of her head. For one thing, the dream-streets of Elim were too much like the streets of East Dereham. For another thing, they had to jostle for space in her imagination with the images already there: missionaries' tales and childhood geography texts, smudgy photographs of mean proportions; women with their teeth filed sharp, men with cicatrized cheeks. Some other part of Africa, no doubt. Some other time. Still she imagined savannah, long horizons, thatched rondavels standing in kraals: a population simply religious, hymn-singing, tractable. In real life, she had almost never seen a black man.

Ralph had said to Uncle James, 'I hardly think my work at the hostel is going to have prepared me for Africa.'

Uncle James had said cheerfully, 'Don't worry. Nothing could prepare you for Africa.'

Her mother had given her a book called *The Sun-Drenched*

70

Veld. She could read it on the ship, Betty advised. 'One of the *Windows on the World* series, Anna. It cost 9/6.' She picked it up on the day they quit Las Palmas, flicking its pages as they moved through waters where flying fish leapt.

It bore little resemblance to Father Huddleston's text; but no doubt it was true, in its way. 'In descriptions of African wildlife the zebra is often mentioned only in passing. Yet he is a lovely creature; a compact, sturdy little horse with neat mane and flowing tail. And no two of his kind are patterned alike! Having drawn his outline you can paint in the stripes as you please.'

When the sea made her dreamy, unable to concentrate, she gave up on the text, let the book close in her lap and rested her eyes on its cover. It beckoned the reader through arches of the coolest, palest peppermint, into an other-worldly landscape – pink and gold in the foreground, green hills rising in the middle ground and beyond them the lilac haze of mountains. She wondered if the illustrator had confused it with heaven; got his commissions mixed up, perhaps. But then she remembered a book she had seen on Ralph's shelves – a book from his years as a fossil-hunter. The picture on the cover was much the same – strange, impossible colours. She had turned to the inside flap to see what was represented: *On the shores of a Jurassic lagoon*, the caption said. Amid the startling viridescence of the palms, Archaeopteryx flopped and swooped, feathers glowing with the deep autumn tints of a game bird. A little dinosaur, glinting like steel, scurried on spindle legs. The sky was a delicate eggshell. In the background shone a deeper aqueous blue-green – some vast and primitive ocean, with shores that had never been mapped.

But now, how small the sea appeared: a metallic dish, across which they inched. After dark the people who were sailing home stood at the rail, looking for the Southern Cross. And one night it appeared, lying just off-south, exactly where everyone had predicted it would be. Anna saw four dull points of light,

71

pale, hardly distinguishable from the meagre scattering of stars around. She would not have noticed it, she thought, if it had not been pointed out.

They came into Table Bay in the rain, in drizzle and cloud which lifted from moment to moment, then descended again. Through the murk a solid dark mass became visible. 'Table Mountain,' someone told her. A pancake of grey cloud lay over it. The sun broke through, gleamed, was gone – then sent out another searching ray, like an arm reaching into a tent. She could see the contours of the mountain now – its spines of rock, and the ravines and crevices steeped in violet shadow.

What had she expected? Some kind of municipal hill. 'Look there,' a man said. 'That's Devil's Peak.' The cloud was moving now, billowing, parting. The sun was fighting through. The stranger took her arm, and turned her body so that she saw a wisp of cloud, like smoke, rising into the sky.

The Archbishop of Cape Town said, 'You're not like your Uncle James. You're more of a muscular Christian.'

'Oh, James,' Ralph said. 'No, he's never looked strong.'

'But he has endured,' the archbishop said. He seemed to relish the phrase. It gave a heroic quality to James' life. Which, Ralph supposed, it really did possess. From some points of view.

He wished he could have avoided this interview. They did not merit a prelate; only James' letter of introduction had brought them here. They could have gone straight to Johannesburg by rail, and on to Elim. They could have been briefed by an underling from the Pretoria diocese. Or not briefed at all. Frankly, Ralph had expected he would have to muddle through. It was the usual way.

'I wanted James here with me,' the archbishop said. 'Some seven years ago. When I was raised to this – ah – dignity. We had here, at that time, everything one could require. Churches, schools, hospitals, clubs. We had the money and the men. We had the blessed opportunity of leadership. Well, perhaps James saw what would come of it. I cannot claim I did.'

The archbishop limped across the room, setting up little vibrations in the furniture, making the tea-cups tremble. He was a vast, heavy man, seventy years old or perhaps more. He handed himself to a sofa; grunting with effort and pain as he lowered himself, he manoeuvred his stiff leg and propped it on cushions as if it were a false limb, or as if it belonged to someone else. It was a moment before he spoke again. 'We set out with high ideals,' he said. 'The things we wanted have not happened. Well, there was no promise that they would.'

The archbishop seemed shy. Could an archbishop be shy? He spoke gruffly, in short, broken phrases; the phrases were, none the less, well-planned.

'A year before I was enthroned,' he said, 'the electorate threw out Smuts and put the Nationalists in. Then certain laws were enacted, which I presume you know everything about — or if you do not, you will know shortly. You will learn the theory. You will see the practice. You will see that we have come, in effect, to be a police state.' He broke off, waiting for Ralph's reaction. 'Oh, be sure I did not always talk in this fashion. I gave the elected government what leeway I could, for one tries to play the statesman. I understood the machinery of their laws, but I did not know how they would operate it.'

'Apartheid is hard to believe in,' Ralph said. 'I mean, you'd have to see it to believe it.'

The archbishop grunted. '*Separateness*, they used to say. It is the change of language that is significant — it is rather more than the evolution of a term. But I said to myself, when Daniel Malan came in, he is not an oaf. He is a cultured man. He has a doctorate,' the archbishop broke off and gave a short laugh, 'which he got from the University of Utrecht, with a thesis on

Bishop Berkeley. Malan has still some regard for public opinion, I told myself. Then behold, out goes Malan, in comes Strydom, who as you may know was at one time an ostrich farmer. Educated where? Stellenbosch and Pretoria. He is a man from the Transvaal. You will learn what that means. When J. G. Strydom came in I had my moment of despair. That was three years ago now.'

Anna made a tentative movement, in the direction of the tea tray. The archbishop nodded to her, then turned and addressed himself to Ralph.

'You have heard of the Bantu Education Act. They have put you in the picture in London, I hope. You know our pre-eminence in education; the churches have done everything, the government nothing. It is we who have educated the African. We did not know, when we were doing it, that we were going about to embarrass the government. All we have achieved, as they see it, is to create a threat to them. By this Act they mean to remove the threat.'

'I find it difficult to get my mind around it, I suppose,' Ralph said. 'Education is progress, would you not think, it is civilization? I can't imagine that any government in the history of the world, until now, has set out to make time run backwards.'

'Oh, I don't know,' the archbishop said. 'There would be some. It doesn't do to generalize. But you see why they've done it, don't you? Education for the non-Europeans is now put into the hands of Dr Verwoerd, at the Native Affairs Department. Dr Verwoerd's reasoning is, what is the use of teaching mathematics to an African child? A labourer doesn't need mathematics. Give him mathematics, he will begin to think he might try to be a little more than a labourer. Well, Dr Verwoerd would not want him to make that mistake.'

Anna brought the tea. The archbishop tested it. 'Very good, my dear,' he said, 'Such a pleasure, tea, isn't it?' He looked,

Anna thought, as if his pleasures were few. She melted away, back to her tapestry stool.

'The notion is to bring in a new kind of education,' the archbishop said, looking into his cup. 'An education to create coolies and houseboys and fodder for the mines. Two and a half hours a day, taught by little girls who have scraped through their Standard VI. This is not merely the prescription for the children of the illiterate, this is for all – for the children of our brightest mission boys and girls, for the children of university graduates from Fort Hare. The parents have to contain themselves in patience while they see their children stultified.'

'It seems to cut off hope for the future,' Ralph said. 'You can repeal other laws, but how will you undo the effect of this one?'

'Precisely,' the archbishop said. 'In twenty years' time, or in forty years' time, when this idiocy is over, how will you put wisdom into heads that have been deprived of it?'

The archbishop's hand shook a little now. The tea-cup seemed to be too much for him, as a delicate piece of china might be too much for a bear. Anna darted forward, took the cup, returned it to the tray. He did not appear to notice her.

'And so now, how are the churches situated?' The old man turned his head towards Ralph. 'We sit before the government "like the rabbit before the cobra", as Father Huddleston has so memorably expressed it.' His voice was dry. 'Father Huddleston has a gift for the vivid phrase, has he not? Some people say we should close all our schools rather than take part in this fantastic scheme. Others say that any education is better than none. Father Huddleston, if I may quote again, calls that sentiment "the voice of Vichy". Mrs Eldred,' he turned his head again, stiffly and painfully, 'although you are a trained teacher, you will find yourself engaged in amusing children rather than teaching them. We have to try to get them off the streets, where they will get into trouble. This place, you know, Elim –

well, it is not in my cure, but I can tell you something of what to expect. Elim is what they call a freehold township. Africans have been settled there since the turn of the century. They have built houses, they own them. Generations have grown up in Elim. There would be, I don't know, 50,000 people?'

'About that,' Ralph said.

'And now there is no security any more, no guarantee of what succeeding years will bring. They are knocking down Sophiatown, and Elim may be next.'

'Where will they put the people?' Anna said.

'Ah, this is the essence of the apartheid policy, my dear. The government wishes to return them to their tribal areas.' Turning his head again, he spoke with grave, weary courtesy, as if he were addressing the President himself, and giving him all the credit he could muster for a foolish scheme. 'Well, you will grasp the situation better when you arrive there. But you must understand that for the people you are going to live among everything has become hazardous, impermanent. It is hardly possible for them to step out of doors without wondering if they are falling foul of some new law. And they feel that their futures have been taken away.'

'I hardly feel equal to it,' Ralph said. 'To such a situation.'

'Then why did you come?'

He didn't know what to say. He couldn't say, to get away from my family. 'I thought it was my duty to try to do something. We both thought so. But we have so little experience.'

'Oh, you have youth,' the archbishop said, 'therefore you have resilience. That is the pious hope, at least. May I advise you? In your work, try to relate everything to God. Try to work on the scale of eternity. Do you see? Otherwise you will be fettered by trivia. The daily frustrations will cripple you.'

'That seems excellent advice,' Ralph said. 'Good advice in any circumstances. If one could follow it.'

Anna said, 'If I were a black person in this country, I'm not sure I would believe in God. Particularly.'

The archbishop frowned.

Ralph said, 'People may think that when they are so oppressed, when they are told that their nature is somehow inferior, when they have suffered so many misfortunes, that they no longer matter to God. It would be a natural thing for them to think.'

At this the archbishop gave vent to his sentiments, in short bursts of rhetoric, like barks. He referred to 'feeble secular humanism' (which he supposed to be a temptation to Ralph) and to the Christian faith as 'the charter of man's greatness'. It was clear that these were phrases from a sermon he was writing, or from one which he had already delivered. Anna looked sideways at Ralph, from under her eyelashes. She didn't know how either of them had dared say what they had said. They would do anything, she supposed, now that they were so far from home.

When the archbishop had finished barking, she put in a feeble, conciliatory word. It was only that they were inexperienced, she said. They were apprehensive – here in a new country, in their first real jobs.

'Do you also not feel equal to it?' the archbishop inquired.

'I am not sure anyone could be.'

This was a good answer. 'Well, I know I am not,' the archbishop said. 'There are two things – no, three things – I ask of you, particularly. Try not to despise your opponents; try not to hate them. It will probably be quite difficult for you, but for a Christian the effort is necessary. And try not to break the law. You have not been sent here to get yourselves into the newspapers or the magistrate's court. I hope you can remember that.'

'The third thing?' Ralph said.

'Oh yes. When you write home to England, ask your people not to make hasty judgements. It is a complicated country, this. I comfort myself that there is little real wickedness in it. But there is so much fear, fear on all sides. Fear paralyses the sympathies, and the power of reasoning. So it becomes a kind of wickedness, in the end.' The archbishop looked up, nodded. The interview was over. They rose. Unexpectedly he smiled, and patted at his leg, lying before him painful and inert. 'Do you know what I did last year? I went to Tristan da Cunha. I expect you did not know my diocese ran so far. They had to tie me into a chair and run me down the side of the frigate on ropes. Then I had to lie in a little boat with a canvas bottom, and they paddled me ashore. Your Uncle James wouldn't have believed his eyes. But you know, I don't think I'll go again. I hardly think I'd weather it, do you?'

He didn't expect an answer. A secretary ushered them out. He was picking up papers to read as they left the room.

Outside Anna said, 'The Winston Churchill imitation, do you think it's deliberate? Do you think he's studied from recordings?'

'I'm sure.'

'He practically accused us of not being Christians.'

'We are, though,' Ralph said. 'Despite provocation.'

'His heart's in the right place,' Anna said.

'His heart's irrelevant, I'm afraid.'

At Cape Town Station, the signs said *Slegs vir Blankes*. The non-European carriages were tacked like an afterthought on to the end of the train.

At stations up the line, children gathered around the carriage doors, their hands cupped for small coins.

At Johannesburg, the station was bustling with black men in

slick suits with cardboard briefcases, and with florid white farmers come to town. Their hair seemed insufficient to cover their great heads. Their bellies threatened to burst the buttons of their shirts. Great rufous knees, exposed beneath khaki shorts, butted at the future. Beneath the pavements, Ralph said, were diamonds and gold.

It was cooler than Anna had expected, and the air seemed thin. She shrank away from the hooting and snarling of the traffic and the mosaic of faces in the street. At midnight a noise brought her to the window of their modest hotel. Hailstones – frozen chips of ice, an inch and a half across – rattled at the glass. The bombardment lasted for five minutes. It stopped as suddenly as it began. For an hour, deep in the watches of the night, the city was quiet, as if holding its breath.

The Mission House stood on Flower Street. It was set back from the road, in a kitchen garden in which grew mealies, potatoes, cabbage, pumpkins and carrots. There were three steps up to the veranda, which was netted in against flies. There had been shade at one time, but the big trees had been cut down. Inside the rooms were small and hot.

Everything had been refurbished, Lucy Moyo said, refurbished in anticipation of their arrival. The linoleum on the floor, polished till it gleamed, was offensively vivid: irrepressibly jazzy, zigzagged, sick-making. No expense had been spared – or so Lucy claimed – on providing for the sitting room nylon-fur cushions with buttoned centres, and a coffee-table which splayed its legs, like a bitch passing water. With all the vicarious pride of careful stewardship, Lucy showed off a magazine rack of bent gold wire, tapping with the cushion of her finger at its little rubber feet. In the kitchen was an acid-yellow table with a chromium trim and white tubular legs. There were chairs to match.

The town was set on a height; every day there was a breeze. On clear days you could see the prosperous suburbs of Pretoria – white houses sprawling across green lawns, avenues lined with jacaranda trees. Down there, public monuments, Boer pride: up here, *swart gevaar*, the black peril. Yet what unfolded to the view, at Elim's centre, but a vision of clipped, cold-water respectability: wide roads on a grid plan, well-fenced playing fields, neat brick houses? The houses, true, differed as to the state of their repair. The best were freshly painted; and outside them, in regular rows, grew pot-plants in old paint tins. They were not exactly pot-plants, not strictly. They were things that would have grown just as well, and more naturally, in the soil. But these sprigs had been singled out for special treatment. They bespoke ownership. They were nature tamed. They were a form of civic pride. Everyone seemed proud in Elim. 'We live here as neighbours,' Lucy explained. 'Not as tribespeople. We all agree together.' This was not quite true, of course. But it was a pleasant idea, and could be entertained for some of the time.

In their first few days they were shepherded from house to house, welcomed in the homes of churchgoers and parish workers. Cups of tea were provided; there were needlepoint footstools, framed photos, lace curtains. There was no artefact that did not rest upon its little crocheted mat.

The price of this fussiness, in labour, was clear at once. Water was fetched in buckets, cement floors scrubbed every day on hands and knees. By a servant, perhaps; even the poverty-stricken can afford to employ the destitute. Every morning, in the backyards, clothes were slapped and wrung in tin tubs.

But on the fringes of Elim the houses were overflowing. There were families living in sheds, in less space than a farmer would give an animal. Lucy explained all this; rents were high in the neighbouring locations and when families could not pay them and were turned out they came to Elim. And then, relatives came from the bundu all the time, and you couldn't turn them away, people had to live somehow; perhaps you might build a lean-to at the back, with whatever came to hand, and hope it would withstand the wind and rain; if not, build it again. She indicated dwellings constructed of sheets of tin leaning against a wall. Naked children – naked except for a string of beads around the waist – played in the dust. Lucy stood before them, cajoling till they answered her, her bag matching her shoes, and her Sunday petal hat planted on her close-curled head. Sanitary arrangements? Better not to think about them. Even the Mission House, after all, had only its huts and buckets, emptied every day by Jakob Malajane, also employed as the gardener.

The Indian and Chinese shops were well-stocked and orderly, Lucy pointed out. There were several where she knew the proprietors, they were not bad types all of them, they would sometimes put things under the counter for you till you could pay. Every so often, though, the bad boys with knives and coshes came in, left the proprietor bleeding and took what they wanted. 'Not all these tsotsis are boys whom you can discipline,' Lucy said. 'Some of them are grown men.' She shrugged; she wanted to warn the Eldreds, whom she thought pitiful children, but she did not want to dwell upon this side of life. There was no need either to mention brothels and shebeens. After all, Mr and Mrs Standish had got by without talking about them.

So she marched them off to meet church-choir contraltos, a saxophonist in Elim's jazz band, a neat-waisted coloured woman who ran a Girl Guide troop: all good people, she said, all family people. Down the road walked a stately, very black man, robed and bearing a crozier. His wife walked arm in arm with him, her purple frock sweeping the dust; she wore a necklace of bones. 'Oh, Mr and Mrs Bishop Kwakwa,' Lucy said. 'Zionist Mount Carmel Gospel of Africa. Not at all a real church.'

*

The day in Flower Street began at six o'clock; but they woke earlier. The bedroom curtains were thin. Their background colour was tan, with a design of purple sunbursts. They did not quite meet across the glass. Each morning a shaft of sunlight, thin as an axe-blade, struck across their pillows and their eyes.

Already the kitchen was busy, the mealie-porridge bubbling on the range. Jakob chopped the wood, then ambled to his garden duties. He was a country boy: his face was battered like a boxer's. He had, Lucy told them, the falling sickness. The people of his village used to throw stones at him when he fell down in a fit, to drive the devil out. They were illiterate people, Lucy explained, in her lofty way.

They would walk to Matins: the church was five minutes away. Father Alfred would shake their hands, though he would be seeing them perhaps twice before lunch, most days, and twice after lunch, and whenever he felt the need. Father Alfred was a little, anxious man. He smiled perpetually. His eyes in his brown face had an air of faded surprise.

After Matins it was time for Anna to talk to the cook, Rosinah, about the day's meals. Quantities must be approximate, they must stretch to accommodate whoever might come by. No one could say what the day would bring.

There were a large number of servants at the mission, none of them overworked. They were people with spectacular bad-luck stories, and they were engaged on the basis of these, rather than of any aptitude or proficiency for their work. Jakob, who slept under a tree for most of the day, had an assistant, a young boy with no parents, seemingly no kin of any kind except some shadowy relatives in Durban who could not be traced. He passed his day listlessly raking the ground, and manufacturing elaborate besoms. He was permanently in rags, a disgrace to the mission. Whenever Ralph gave him any clothes, he would sell them. It seemed that his ambition was to be a walking sign, a symbol of wretchedness.

The cook Rosinah sat with her chair wedged into a corner near the stove. The back door was always open, so that her cronies could drift in and out. There was a constant procession of them, rolling through the kitchen and out again, squatting on the floor to exchange gossip. When Anna passed, she smiled and greeted them, but she could not help noticing that they were usually eating something. It disturbed her that the half of Elim that claimed acquaintance with Rosinah was better fed than the half that did not.

Rosinah had been known to chase people out of the kitchen and across the yard, with some offensive kitchen weapon: sometimes a thing so relatively benign as a wooden spoon, but once at least a small meat-cleaver. There seemed no reason for these outbursts of hers, nothing especially which brought them on. The victims would be back after a few days, squatting nervously on the threshold, drawn by the chance of a handout of a bowl of porridge or the heel of a loaf.

No one knew Rosinah's own particular bad-luck story. She never spoke of her past, but something must have soured her temper, something out of the ordinary run of fire and disease and sudden death. Day to day the chief victim of her wrath was a girl called Dearie, her assistant. Dearie was a frail young woman with rickety legs; pregnant, and with a sick baby bound always on her back.

Dearie's babies died, Anna was told. This was the third or maybe the fourth, and each one was weaker than the last. Anna decided that this current infant would not die on her: she would fathom the mystery, she would keep Dearie under her eye. She suggested the doctor; Dearie, head bowed, suggested in her monosyllabic way that she saw a doctor of her own.

Anna did not dare insist. She provided powdered milk and rusks, peered anxiously at the small wizened face. The babies slipped away in the night, breathed out the last of their lives while everyone else slept. At least, that was how it appeared to be; Rosinah, in her rages, suggested that Dearie murdered them. There was no husband, and it seemed there never had been. Lucy Moyo said, for one slip you can forgive a girl, but that Dearie, she is a walking outrage. Anna said, I thought we were supposed to forgive seventy times seven? Lucy glared at her. Anna thought, perhaps I have got my Scripture wrong. Perhaps it is God who does that.

A woman called Clara cleaned the house and washed the clothes. She was a mission girl, had passed her junior certificate. She was ashamed to do such work, and Ralph and Anna saw that it was demeaning for her. Whenever she asked them, they wrote her a glowing reference, recommending her for some job in a store, or a post as a hospital orderly. But employers turned her away. She came back to the house, stony-eyed, and picked up her brush to sweep the rooms out.

Clara had once had a husband, but he had disappeared, leaving her with four small children. Her expectations of these mild babies were ferociously high: silence, industry, a useful occupation at all times. Each evening she called them to recite Bible verses; if they failed, she told them to bring her the cane. Their little cries, like the mewing of cats, punctuated the evenings. But who could tell Clara not to do it? They must not be like their father; and she believed that only the weals on their legs stood between them and a life of drink and misery, with hell at the end of it.

It was not difficult to understand why employers turned Clara away, but it was difficult to put into words. She had some quality that stirred unease. It was not an overt violence, as in Rosinah's case. It was an emptiness; you did not care to think how it might be filled up.

Each morning at Flower Street, Ralph went into the cubbyhole he called his office to deal with letters and the accounts –

84

recording minutely, faithfully, the futile expenditure of tiny sums. Anna went to the nursery school to supervise the local helpers. It was not a small enterprise; there were a hundred and fifty children, organized by twenty or thirty volunteers, who came and went by some bewildering rota that they understood and Anna did not.

Each morning they put the children into their blue overalls, smocks which fastened at the backs of their necks; this was the day's first task, feeding squirming arms into sleeves. They employed two women to wash the overalls at the end of the week, and another woman to make the mealie-porridge for midday. The children had to have their porridge scooped into their mouths; they had to be put down for an afternoon rest, supervised on the swings, slides and climbing frames; they had to be weighed and measured and told stories. There was a waiting list, bigger by far than the current enrolment.

Once the children were seven they could not keep them at the nursery. They sent them into the dangerous world, for the two and a half hours of education that the new laws allowed them. This period over, the children were at the mercy of circumstance. If their mothers managed to find any kind of work, they took it, leaving the children to the fitful and reluctant supervision of relatives, of older brothers and sisters. Where the supervision failed, they were out on the streets.

For a few of these outcasts, the mission ran what they called a 'play-group'. They gave the children soup and bread, and fruit when they could get it. They didn't give them books because that would have been breaking the law. They tried to keep them amused with games and handicrafts, making sure they did not set their feet on any path that could lead anywhere.

And were they enforced, these absurd laws? Oh yes. 'This town is full of people who will run to the police,' Lucy said calmly. 'They will do it for a few pennies. Mrs Eldred, you must understand that.'

Anna would ask for nothing for herself, but the sight of the children made her bold. She pleaded with shopkeepers in the white suburbs to help them eke out the daily ration; she petitioned vegetable stores for bruised apples, and bakers for yesterday's bread. She searched for donors to support children whose parents couldn't afford the small monthly fee. Every day she set herself a target: so many pieces of effrontery, so many crude demands. She found it hard to work in the house because people were constantly walking in from the stoep, coming to ask her foolish questions or use the telephone; an hour could go by with nothing accomplished.

One of the nursery classrooms had a storeroom – a large broom-cupboard really. She took it over. She had to edge around the trestle table that formed her desk, ease herself behind the table, squeeze her narrow body against the wall. She stabbed with two fingers at a rusty typewriter: stabbed out her begging letters.

The fact is, Ralph said, this job reduces us entirely to beggars. You can almost never just buy something, no matter how much you need it. You have to plot for it, appeal for it, arrange to borrow it, coax someone else into paying for it.

Up at the house Ralph had his office door wedged open by a stack of papers. Other papers were stacked on every surface, in dangerous sliding piles. 'Do you think the diocese would buy me a filing cabinet?' he asked Anna. 'But no ...' and he dismissed the thought at once. 'There are more urgent needs.'

Often, at the end of the day, there were nursery babies uncollected. They were forgotten – or, rather, the complicated arrangements which underpinned family life had come adrift. Anna would gather up the children, who were wailing or dumb with bewilderment; she would take them to the house, give them biscuits, comfort them, send a messenger to find out what had gone wrong at home. Sudden illness? Arrest?

At this time of day, Ralph was usually at the police station. Every morning the police appeared on the streets, picking up their quota of pass offenders, herding them together on the street corners, handcuffed two by two; then a van came to collect them. African policemen performed this chore. At first Ralph thought, how can they do it? Soon he realized that they had a living to make. A white sergeant at the station told him wearily, 'Mr Eldred, we all have a living to make.'

In the afternoon the relatives of those who had been arrested would come to the mission, telling their stories: our son, he just went out to see a neighbour, my sister, she went to buy food and left her pass at home. Ralph would go down to the station, to bail people out, pay their fines. 'Next week,' he would say to the relatives, 'you must pay me the money back, you understand?' He had to recover the money, or the mission would be out of pocket, and some other head of expenditure would have to be cut. But Ralph could only urge people to remember to take their papers, whenever they stepped out of doors.

He did not like to cooperate with the government in this way. But he was not sent to Africa to encourage people to break the law, and James' letters reminded him of this. He was not required to be a hero or a martyr, only to go on doing his best in the circumstances in which he found himself.

People are not starving, he wrote to James. The poorest can just about feed and clothe themselves. But they live on the brink of an abyss. A few days' sickness pushes them over the edge: the loss of a few pence in the week. Women struggle to bring up their children clean and with good manners, literate. They hope there is a future for them, but from the children's eyes you can see they are wiser than their parents to the drift of events.

Naught for your comfort, Anna thought. Only a long little-ness consoles you – putting another stitch, then another row, into a blanket square. As winter approached, the women's knitting became zealous and purposeful. On Wednesdays there was a sewing circle, too, and Anna felt she must put in an appearance; Lucy Moyo, or some other woman with a strong voice, read from the New Testament while their fingers flew, and faith stiffened their spines. Compare them to these people, and the Norfolk families were atheists; the Martins of East Dereham were godless hedonists, the Eldreds of Norwich were heathens, and debauched.

Thursdays was the day for the women's church meetings. The Mothers' Union wore starched white blouses and black skirts, with their special brooch pinned to their blouses and black cotton kerchiefs on their heads. Unmarried mothers – if they were penitent – could wear the uniform. But never, ever, the brooch.

The Methodist ladies wore red blouses and black skirts. The Dutch Reformed wore black skirts and white blouses with broad black collars. They made the Methodists look skittish.

Dearie, every Sunday, went missing for hours. Anna was concerned. 'Don't fret, Mrs Eldred,' Lucy Moyo told her. 'She is attending Bishop Kwakwa's church, all day singing and dancing. She is going there for wearing a uniform with braid, and whooping and making an unseemly spectacle. And their tom-fool pastor going about with blessed water in a bucket.'

In the afternoons at Flower Street, there were meetings of various welfare committees. These concluded, Anna and Ralph went out together to see people who were sick, bouncing over the rutted roads in the mission's car. Four o'clock, sinuous shapes melted into the walls; the young boys, who had run wild on the veld all day, had come back to town.

By five o'clock they had taken up their station, these boys: they lounged outside the cafés, sometimes passing a cigarette from hand to hand. They gave off a palpable air of dis-ease; they were waiting for dark. It would be sunset when Ralph and Anna arrived home. As they rattled along to the corner of the street, as they approached the corner that would bring the Mission House within view, Ralph felt Anna in the passenger seat grow pale and still with tension. In summer she would be hot and dusty, in winter chilled to the bone. She wanted to wash and eat her supper, just that; but she could not know, until they turned the corner, what was waiting to frustrate her.

What she dreaded was the sight of a half-dozen men collected on the stoep, waiting for them with some problem they would not be able to solve. The only worse sight was that of a whole family, waiting with a problem they would not be able to solve. If it was a group of men, possibly Ralph and Anna would have to climb back into the car and jolt to the police station for some verbal conciliation and a pay-out; but if it was a family, they would need food, and they would need shelter for the night, at the very least. When Anna saw that the stoep was occupied, that they were expected, she felt her pulse rate rise, and a bitter taste, like bile, swim into her mouth.

Evening at Flower Street: Anna had hardly any time with Ralph. They never sat down to a meal alone; Father Alfred would be in, or some of the nursery teachers, or committee people with unfinished business. By bedtime they were often too exhausted to make love, and always too exhausted to talk; sometimes they had no thoughts they cared to voice. And the nights were often broken. A woman had been taken ill, or there had been an accident, or a young man had been hurt in a drunken fight.

When night fell, there were beatings, stabbings, robberies, rapes. Each of these incidents caused the men in the Department of Native Administration to shake their heads and talk of 'a trouble-spot', and 'the breakdown of law and order'. They did not see the Mothers' Union, in their starched blouses; they saw only gallows-bait. The vogue weapon of the gangs was the sharpened bicycle spoke. Approaching their victim from behind, they would stab the spoke into his thigh, and empty his pockets while he was frozen with shock and pain.

It was onerous, the nightly routine of locking up the Mission House: keys, bolts, bars, clanking from room to room. Futile, really, because if anyone comes knocking you have to let them in. You can shout through the door for their name but if their name means nothing to you that isn't a reason to keep them outside.

On Saturday mornings Ralph and Anna gave out supplies from the back porch: vegetables, sacks of mealie meal, sugar poured from sacks and bagged up, and whatever tinned food and clothing had been donated by the white charities in the last week. They trusted that no one would come for food who did not need it, but they knew they trusted in vain; they must endure Lucy Moyo's impatient clucking, the turning up of her eyes to her God. On Saturday afternoons there were funerals; hymn-singing, ululation. Charity filled the grumbling stomachs of the mourners.

Ralph would say:

> 'But who hath seen the grocer
> Treat housemaids to his teas
> Or crack a bottle of fish sauce
> Or stand a man a cheese?'

Saturday at sunset, funerals and parties merged. Enamel mugs of sorghum beer were passed from hand to hand: beer that looked like baby-vomit. The hosts played gramophones in their yard. There was drumming and dancing far into the night. When the guests had had enough they rolled up in their blankets, and slept on the ground.

Sunday mornings there were church processions, the women in their uniforms, their sons in suits with polished faces. Later the small girls tripped into Sunday school, their hair braided and tied up in ribbons. Their frocks were from the Indian store, and had stiff net skirts, with which they scratched each other's shins and calves. They had white gloves, and pochettes hanging over their skinny wrists. In a year or two they'd be saving up for skin-lightening cream. They'd be begging their parents, for a birthday treat, to find the money to send them to the hairdressers to get their hair straightened. 'When you are older,' parents say. 'Wait till you are fifteen, then we will see.'

On Sunday mornings, after church, the men of Elim visited the barbers who set up shop under the trees. On Sunday afternoons there were football matches. Anna and Ralph entertained Father Alfred to tea, and the Sunday-school workers too. Anna could see in her face what opinion Lucy Moyo held of her baking; her scones were flat, and fizzed in the mouth, unlike the scones of Mrs Standish.

After the tea party was over, they were, briefly, alone. Ralph held her in his arms as she swayed with fatigue, whimpering against his shoulder. 'I shouldn't have brought you,' he whispered to her. 'But we can't go home now.'

Only weeks, months had passed; they were sealed so securely inside Elim's bitter routines that they could not imagine any other kind of life.

Anna forgot sometimes what lay beneath the surface. She saw the baked soil and red cement floors, the ant-trail and the cockroaches' path. But Ralph was there to remind her of the truth: she was walking on diamonds and gold.

Every evening, at dusk, the women lit braziers. The smoke

rose into the darkening sky, and lay over the township in a haze: blue and fine, like the breath of frigid angels. Every evening, when the women lit the braziers, some two-year-old would fall into them.

There were hospitals in Elim, but casualties came to the mission: walking, or carried in their mother's arms, or limping between two friends and dripping blood. Mrs Standish had been a nurse, and people could not grasp that Anna had not the same skill. 'We have to know our limitations,' Anna said. 'I'd feel easier in my mind if we had a doctor on call.'

Ralph said, 'Koos is on call. In effect.'

Koos had his surgery on Victoria Street, in a dusty single-storey building with a tin roof. There was a waiting room and a consulting room, and another room at the back where Koos slept on a camp-bed. In the yard were two shacks, one for cooking and the other fitted out as the laboratory and sometime cat-house of Koos' dispenser, Luke Mbatha.

Koos might have been thirty, might have been forty. He had straw-coloured hair and a worried face; his smile was rare though his general disposition must, one supposed, be benevolent. He wore stone-coloured shorts; his legs were mottled and stringy, his knee-joints large and starved. His face and arms were red from scrubbing with a fierce antiseptic soap. Ralph washed his hands once at Koos' place, and felt that the skin had been taken off them.

Koos had a vast number of patients. He treated them for a few coppers. 'But they must pay,' he told Ralph. 'If they don't pay for their treatment they don't believe in it, you know? If you just give them the medicine, they think, this thing must be rubbish, if he is *giving* it to me. They go out and pour it in the road.'

Ralph said, 'Anna's trying to persuade our kitchen girl Dearie to bring the new baby down. Anna's worried about him, she says he's not gaining weight. Dearie won't admit there's anything wrong, but I suppose she must care, mustn't she? We can't work out what she's up to. She's got coloured strings tied round his wrists and his ankles. Yesterday, Anna thought he'd been dropped and got a big bruise on his head, but it turned out to be some ash he'd been rubbed with.'

Koos said, 'She's been to see one of my rivals.'

'No harm, I suppose,' Ralph said.

'Except it makes for delay.' Koos shrugged. 'Then, you see, perhaps she thinks it's some African disease.'

'Are there such things?'

'In people's minds,' Koos said. 'They think there are diseases that white people can't understand. It's right, up to a point. If I get a woman in here complains of palpitations, fainting, short of breath, I can listen to her chest and send off a blood sample, but sooner or later I have to say to her, look, what's your church that you go to? Have you been dancing at your church? Have you got possessed by a spirit?'

'They're not barbarians,' Ralph said, needled.

Koos' sandy eyebrows shot up. 'No? So quick to learn, man. Do you know what I think? I think we're all barbarians.'

Ralph always wanted to ask Koos, why are you here? It was like meeting a man with only one leg: you feel desperate to know what has happened to him. Accident? Illness? You want to ask, but you can only hope he'll tell you.

Six months in Elim. Ralph wrote to his Uncle James:

We could manage better if there were thirty hours in a day and nine days in a week, and yet I wonder if we are usefully employed at all. We don't have much time to stop and think, and I don't know whether that's bad or good. But every week we have to make some decision which seems a matter of principle rather than of procedure, and there's no one we can go to when we want to talk things over. My nearest approach to a friend is our Afrikaner doctor, but though I think he is a good man and he has a lot of experience he looks at the world so differently from us that I can't go to him for advice, because I probably wouldn't understand the advice he gives me.

Most of these matters of principle we call 'blanket problems' – this is our shorthand for anything that derails us, in the ethical line. Now that the cold weather is here, some of the poorest people come to the door every day to ask for blankets. We have or can get or can knit blankets, but it seems that Mr and Mrs Standish, after they had given them out, would visit the recipients in their homes to check that the blankets were really needed and that they had not been sold. Anna and I, we feel terrible about this. It seems demeaning to all concerned. Yet Lucy Moyo says that if we don't do it, it will be widely understood that we are fools.

What should I do? I feel that, if I had had some training in England, I would have been aware that I would meet such problems of conscience – or am I dignifying them, are they indeed just problems of procedure? I keep saying it: I wasn't ready to come to Africa. Anna says, what is the use of all this effort? There is nothing an individual can do against a political system which, it seems to us, becomes more regressive and savage by the day. I try to urge people to think ahead, to show initiative, to help themselves, but what's the point when we know that in five years' time our town will no longer exist?

Lucy Moyo explained Koos, in her usual easy manner: 'The doctor went with some bad type of coloured girl.' She laughed. 'She thought it was for payment. He thought it was for romance.'

Anna reported it to Ralph. 'The coloured girl had a baby. A

small-town scandal, you know?' She had picked up some Afrikaans now, and her voice had taken on the local accent, the lilt. When she saw something pretty and helpless – a child, a kitten – she spoke in chorus with Lucy and Rosinah: 'Ag, shame!'

'Yes, I think I do know,' Ralph said. 'And I suppose that it happened in the days when it was only a disgrace, not a crime.' He shook his head. 'What happened to the woman and the child, does Lucy know?'

Anna was back to herself, her English tone: 'Oh, Lucy wouldn't stoop to know a thing like that.'

He thought of the doctor scrubbing himself, scouring his hands with the blistering soap. Had Koos a home, other than the back room with the camp-bed? Seemingly not; not any more.

Uncle James wrote back:

My dear Ralph, of course you were not ready to go to Africa. You went out of your own need, not out of the need of the people you were supposed to serve. Don't blame yourselves for that. It is the usual European way. When we find we lack a sense of purpose at home, we export our doubts; I have known people who – misguidedly, in my view – have gone to China to save their marriage.

The problems of our own country seem so complicated, that intelligent people wonder if it can be right to take a stance. It seems a thing only professional politicians can do – as we pay them, they can bear the burden of being simple-minded. But when we think of other countries, we imagine their problems are easy to solve – they are clear-cut, and we are so sure of the right moral line. Why do they make such a muddle of it? It is so obvious what ought to be done.

How clear-sighted we are – how benevolent! Until we arrive, of course, and see the reality.

Men and women working in the mission field are supposed to sort out their own notions before they try to foist them on others. But in my experience, when they arrive at their posting, they become – if they are worth anything – more confused than anyone else around them.

So do try, Ralph, not to burden yourself with a compulsion to be better than other people. Just do your best, can't you? I am aware that this sounds like a nursery nostrum, but it is the only advice I can give. You say you doubt (or Anna doubts) the power of the individual to achieve anything. But what if all the individuals give up? There will be precious little then for the people you are trying to serve. God will not provide, you know. You need not think it. His method is never so direct.

Every day brings a fresh problem to solve. Some people might argue that if you had a settled faith, you would not experience such turmoil. Myself, I have never believed in settled faith; there is always some emergency, God-given or otherwise, to undermine whatever certainties you have established for yourself. You could not take on, uncritically, your father's beliefs. You have had to find your own way. Conflict is not, in itself, a sign of lack of faith. It may be a sign of – dare I say it – spiritual insight, development. And at the very least – if what faces you is only a mental conflict, and an administrative problem – it shows you are beyond thinking of the world as a simple place, where good intentions are enough.

As for your problem about the blankets – of course you must go and see the people in their own houses. Has it occurred to you that the blankets may be a pretext? The people who apply to you may need far more than blankets, but find it difficult to draw your attention to this fact. And it may be that not all their needs are material.

Yes, Ralph thought, laying the letter aside; but who am I to diagnose these needs?

Anna came in. 'Am I interrupting you?'

'No. A letter from James.'

'I'll read it when I've a minute.' She wanted to tell him the news. The play-group children were going to give a concert. A ladies' charity from Jo'burg had donated a secondhand sewing-machine, and Anna would make costumes. She had been already to beg remnants from Mr Ahmed, on Nile Street.

For the next week, the machine's whine cut through his evening. Rain drummed on the roof, and the streets ran with red-brown water.

One week on, he found Anna running her hand, covetously, across a roll of cloth: it was a soft, limp fabric, a paisley pattern in a faded, near-mud green. 'Mr Ahmed sent this,' she said. 'It's got a big flaw in it. But I wouldn't mind – I could make wonderful curtains, if I could get some thick lining material. I mean,' she added, 'if I could persuade Mr Ahmed to give me some.'

'Why don't you do it? You've nearly finished the costumes now. You could start after supper, if you're not too tired.'

Anna shook her head. 'We have curtains already, don't we? Lucy Moyo sewed them with her own hands, those purple efforts with the sunbursts. The Sunday-school teachers had a collection among themselves to buy the material.' She looked up. 'Is it wicked to care about the way things look?'

'Of course not.'

'But the way people feel is more important, I suppose.'

So that was the end of the paisley curtains. Anna cut three yards off the bale, where the flaw showed least, and made herself a flowing calf-length skirt, gathered softly into the waist. 'Oh, Mrs Eldred,' Lucy said. 'Such a good seamstress you are. If you had your outfit made in Paris it couldn't fit you better. But that fabric – shame, so dull! Still, we must use what the Lord provides.'

Anna smiled. The weather cleared. Each morning the sun woke them, slashing through the inch where the curtains didn't meet.

Ralph wrote to James:

> How do you live? What is the proper way? The idea is gaining ground – and I find it is not without its appeal – that you should live like the people you work among, that for a Christian that is the only way. Why should you have more money and more comforts than they do? How can you mean anything to them, if you keep yourself apart?
>
> And yet, I can see that the idea might have disabling consequences.

He thought of Koos, with his dinner of mealie-pap and gravy.

> I am not sure I am brave enough to try to put it into practice.

James wrote:

> Do you have so much, Ralph, for people to envy you? Do I need to tell you that you are 7,000 miles from home? (You might, I realize, think it not much of a sacrifice – but let me tell you, if you do not miss us, we miss you, your sister and I, and we talk of you very often.) In one breath you complain to me of your life, your hardships and frustrations – and in the next you complain of your luxurious standard of living!
>
> Suppose you join the people you work amongst, and move into a lean-to in someone's backyard. What conceivable good will it do to anyone? It may make you feel better, for a week or two, but are your feelings the issue? When that life becomes unbearable – as it quickly would – you could escape. It would be, at best, only a well-intentioned experiment. The people around you cannot escape; there is no term put to their sentence. And so, you see, any gestures you might make in the direction of the equality of man are an insult to them. You are free to go, and they are not.

You have your education. You have your white skin, in a country where that means everything. Even the resources of your well-fed body mark you out as different. How dare you think you can become one of them? Privilege cannot be undone, once it has been conferred.

Ralph put his uncle's letter in the drawer. Again he thought of Koos, trying to scrub his skin away.

'I had another talk with Dearie,' Ralph said to the doctor. 'Anna had a talk too. We keep wondering if we should just grab the baby one day and bring it down to you, but that doesn't seem fair on Dearie, she's an adult after all. Or maybe you could come up to the mission. Though I don't know how we'd get him away from Dearie, for you to examine him. She keeps him fastened on her back the whole time. As far as I can see, he'll die there.'

'Promise her an injection,' Koos said. 'That's my last offer.'

'For her, or for the baby?'

'Both,' Koos said. 'Let's – what's the expression? – let's push the boat out. The people here, they love injections. Injections are the main thing with them. And I give so many, because if they don't get one from me they'll go and get jabbed with God knows what by God knows who, and pay a fat price for it.'

'It's not real medicine, is it?' Ralph was uneasy. 'Just giving your patients what they want.'

Koos tapped his forehead. 'Up here, Ralphie – that's where the battle's fought. You know, they have no confidence in me, these people. The girls want to find out if they're pregnant, and so they go to a diviner the day after they're late, and the diviner tells them what they want to hear, yes or no as it suits. If he's wrong, the girls somehow manage to forget it. But they come to me and I say, I can't tell you now, visit me again after two months. They look at me like – man, he's stupid, this Boer.'

Ralph glanced up at him. Koos wanted to talk; there was so much that he bottled up inside himself every day, and he would talk about anything, anything except what ailed him. 'Your girl, Dearie,' he said. 'You need to find out why she thinks her babies are always sick. You know, in this part of the world, we don't have misfortunes plain and simple. If something goes wrong you need somebody to blame. Who's done this to me, you ask? Who's put this sickness on me? It might be, you see, your ancestors. It might be some enemy of yours. But it's not just plain fate. It's not the hand of God.'

'I suppose that's comforting, in a way,' Ralph said.

'Is it?'

They both wondered, whether it was comforting or not: in the silence, cattle-flies buzzed and dashed against the wire-mesh window. Koos said, 'It sounds to me that what your girl needs is to call on Luke Mbatha, my dispenser. You've met Luke? You've seen Luke, Saturday night, in his zoot suit, with some Jo'burg shebeen queen on his arm? You think he bought that on what I pay him?'

'What, the suit or the woman?'

Koos was bowed by his amusement; his red hand knuckled his head. 'Both cost, Ralphie, suit and cunt. No, Luke – he does a good trade in cats' livers and lizard skins and python fat. You ought to go and see him in the backyard there. A lot of his mixtures you don't swallow, thank Christ, you just put the bottle on a string and hang it round your neck. Might suit your girl Dearie. He does business by mail, too. Love potions. Maybe other kind of potions – murder ones – but I don't ask him. A man came in last week and said he had beetles in his bowels. I sent him straight through to the back. If he believes that, it's Luke he needs, not me.'

Ralph no longer bothered to get on his high horse; to say, they're not barbarians. He knew Koos was not passing judgement. He was implying that there is another view of the world that you could entertain: and that he did not entirely despise it. 'Still,' he said, 'you have to keep your eye on Luke, I suppose. To see that he's not harming anyone.'

'He does less harm than some. Have you seen these things the blacks use?' Koos took a little box out of his desk drawer and skimmed it across at Ralph. *Extra Strong Native Pills*, he read. 'Extra Strong is an understatement,' Koos said. 'Almost, if you had beetles, you'd blast them out. And worms – I tell you, man, they're always deworming themselves, and killing themselves in the process. I've seen it – I've had people crawl in here and die on me slowly. Certified worm-free, but unluckily for them their blerry worm-free liver's packed up – and you need to see people dying at that speed, Ralphie, because when the liver's gone, a person's life continues three days, and the only pain-relief's a bullet in the brain.' Koos shifted in his chair. 'So I let Luke get on with it. It's like these churches, isn't it? You wish your mission servants would come to your church – but you know they go to more exciting types of services. What I do is, I go in there every month or so, have a look around among Luke's stock. Just make sure there's nothing human, that's all. Anything human, and – I've warned him – I go to the police.'

'What do you mean, human?'

'People disappear, you know? We always say, they're lost into Johannesburg, but sometimes they've gone a lot further than that. There is a trade, you can't deny it. In bodies, live ones. They take the eyes, the tongue, whatever they need for medicine at that time. It's a big problem for the police as to who's guilty – and of course they feel they shouldn't have to handle it, it's a native problem. The reason why it's so difficult to pin blame is that gangs do these things, networks, and how can you pick out who's responsible – who can you say is the killer, if a person's been cut up by different hands? And of course, if you cut people to pieces, they do die in the end.' Koos looked up, and saw the expression on Ralph's face. 'All right, don't believe me,' he said. 'I don't like to think about it either. Who wants to admit such things go on?' He jerked his thumb in the general direction of Pretoria. 'It gives encouragement to *them*.'

When the new year came, the bus fares went up, and the bus boycott started. Ralph got up at four each morning to pack the mission's car with more people than it should hold, and to edge the complaining vehicle out of Elim, downhill towards Pretoria. The people who had permits to work in the city needed to keep their jobs; every taxi in Elim was commandeered, but still they passed silent convoys of men and women, walking downhill in the smoky dawn. The headlights of other cars, going uphill, crept by theirs; there was some sympathy in the liberal suburbs of Johannesburg, and there were men and women willing to drive through the night to help the people from the townships. Ralph had his name noted, at road-blocks. He was questioned, roughly, in Afrikaans. His lack of understanding drove the policemen into a fury. 'We've got your number, man,' they said. 'You must be a communist, eh?'

I want, he thought, to put into practice a different kind of Christianity from my father's: one in which I don't pass judgement on people. I don't judge Lucy Moyo, or Koos, or (without evidence) Luke the dispenser whose trade is so dark; I don't judge the President, or the police sergeant who has just cursed me out. 'But if you don't judge,' Anna said, 'you certainly institute some stiff inquiries into people's motives. I am not sure that is always quite separate from the process of passing judgement.'

She knew him better, by now. That kindness of his, which she had taken so personally, was essentially impersonal, she saw.

That morning at the road-block, the policeman said to Ralph, *kaffirboetie*. Black man's brother, or dear friend. 'I would like to be,' Ralph said. 'But I wouldn't make the claim.' The policeman spat into the roadway. Only his upbringing prevented him from spitting in Ralph's face.

On the day of the public meeting, the day of the baton charge, Koos opened his hospital in the nursery school's hall, rolling up his shocked and bloodied patients in blankets, speaking in five languages to ban the hot sweet tea and ask for water, just water; for bandages – anything, any rags; for anyone with a steady hand to help him swab and clean.

Ralph gave a thought to a dusty office in London, an eyrie in Clerkenwell, the headquarters of the organization that had sent him here; and he thought of the churchgoers of Norfolk, passing the collection plate; he heard them say to him, you have no right to misappropriate funds in this way, misuse mission property: to press the blue smock of a nursery-school angel to the bleeding mouth of a township whore who has been smashed in the face by a baton. It was the cook, Rosinah, who of all the mission staff had witnessed the police charge; Rosinah, who seemed to have no life outside her dictatorial kitchen practices. Now she rocked herself in a stupor of grief, telling how it was peaceful, baas, hymn-singing, a speech, and now the police have chased the young women and beaten them on their breasts, they have done that thing, they know where young women are weak.

Ralph knew that on the scale of atrocity it was small. It was not, for example, Treblinka. Koos showed him what a sjambok cut looked like, administered by an experienced, determined hand. He learned something about himself; that the presence of evil made him shake, like an invalid or octogenarian.

Next day he was able to piece together a little more of the

story. It had been a peaceful meeting, as Rosinah said, on a patch of waste ground he knew, a mile away from Flower Street; but this was a typical thing in Elim, that there was no line of communication except an underground one, there was no knowledge, a mile away, of what was occurring on the waste ground; there was no mechanism by which he and Anna could have been warned and told to stand by for casualties. The meeting was to decide strategy for the bus boycott. At the last minute the police had demanded it be called off. A few children had started throwing stones, and the police had charged before the crowd could disperse. A great number of those injured appeared to be passers-by. They were dazed and weeping, their shaved and stitched scalps still oozing blood and clear fluid; they said that they had not known anything, not known there was a meeting at all.

Ralph walked over the site of the catastrophe. A few odd shoes had been left behind in the scramble to escape the batons and whips. He saw a straw shopping-bag, decorated with a swelling, pink straw rose; it lay on its side, and its contents were by now on someone else's shelf. The ground had been picked over pretty well, he saw; he thought it was a strange form of looting. It was hard to know who was worse; the policemen who had done what they said was their duty, or the scavengers who had taken from the housemaid's bag the half-loaf, the two ounces of green tripe, perhaps the soap-ends or old cardigan some Madam had given, some well-meaning idiot woman down in the white houses, the jacaranda groves.

'Can you do anything, Mr Eldred?' Lucy Moyo said. 'Anything to help us?'

'I can try,' Ralph said.

He went back to his office and rifled through his papers for the list he had been compiling: the names, addresses, telephone numbers of the senior policemen within a hundred miles. He picked up the telephone receiver and began to work his way through the list. These calls did not last long, in most cases; when the policemen heard his English accent, and learned that he lived in Elim, they put the phone down on him.

He sat up for most of the night, writing to the newspapers. 'You saw the casualties,' he said to Koos. 'You know what happened here, better than anybody. Put your name on these letters with me.'

Koos shook his head. 'Better not, Ralph. I have my patients to think about. What would they do without me?' He shrugged. 'A lot better, maybe.'

After the baton charge, their situation changed. They were invited to houses in Elim they had never entered before. People who were not churchgoers came to the Mission House. The local organizer of the ANC called on them; and on the same day came a man from Sophiatown, a black journalist from *Drum* magazine. He sat leaning back on one of the metal-legged kitchen chairs, so that its front feet were in the air. He found things to laugh about.

Rosinah's apprentice served him tea in an enamel mug. Anna said sharply, 'The cups and saucers, please, Dearie.' Dearie brought a cup and slapped it down on the table. She scowled. Cups were for whites, enamel mugs were for Africans; this Madam had instituted different practices, which proved she knew nothing. She thought this black man was above himself, putting on airs, in his lightweight blue suit with the sharp creases in the trousers. Trouble came of it: in her opinion.

'Pretoria wants to grow, grow, grow,' the handsome boy said, lolling back on his chair. 'The Nats want this place cleared. They will find these people somewhere else, some piece of the veld where they can put them and forget them. Some place with no water and no roads. So that their children can grow back into savages.' The young man laughed, a satirical laugh. His eyes were distant already, and it could be seen that he was on his way to a scholarship abroad: Moscow, perhaps, and who could blame him? 'I can tell you, Mrs Eldred,' he said, 'it is hardly possible for an African to live and breathe and be on the right side of the law.' He looked deeply into Anna's eyes; indicating, one, that she attracted him and two, that he would not think to take any trouble over her.

It was after midnight when the handsome boy left. Next afternoon, a white police sergeant sat on the same chair: its legs now foursquare and grounded. 'Makes a change, Mr Eldred, for me to come and see you. Usually it's you comes to see us.'

The sergeant was fair-haired, meagre, not a big man. But he sat like a true Afrikaner: legs splayed, as if to indicate that in no other way could he ease his bull-like endowment. Ralph did not, at once, dislike him, perhaps because he was of the same familiar, freckled, physical type as Koos, and anxious too, nervously smiling; his nails were bitten down to the quick.

The sergeant had not refused tea. Dearie gave him a cup, of course, and a saucer too. He just wanted Ralph to know, he said, as he helped himself to sugar, that the police were aware what kind of visitors he'd been getting. 'You're a stranger here,' the policeman complained. 'You're new to South Africa. You ought to make *nice* friends.'

In passing, Ralph felt sorry for him. He was nervous, a chain-smoker, offering his pack each time to Anna; sometimes a fleeting spasm crossed his face, as if he were in pain.

'I didn't catch your name,' Ralph said, when the sergeant wiped his mouth and stood up to go. 'Why don't you just call me Quintus,' the man said. 'Because I expect we'll be getting to know each other.'

'I think he must have beetles in the bowels,' Ralph said after he'd gone. 'Needs to go to Luke Mbatha for some python fat.'

Ralph told Koos that the more stupid the white policemen were, the worse they treated him – except maybe this Quintus, who was well-intentioned in his way.

Koos rubbed his red hands through his scrubby pale hair; and Ralph, who had been learning anatomy among other things, felt he could see afternoon light flash between radius and ulna. 'Be over to his braai, soon, Ralphie. You drink his beer, man, you eat up his scorched flesh-meat.'

'No. I don't see we'll be on those terms.'

'Ah,' Koos said. 'But you soon learn to like those motherfuck-ers. You like me, don't you? And I'm one of them. Something sweet and simple about us, isn't there? Something pathetic? Always trying to be liked. Well, there's this thing we have, a kind of – hospitality. If a man comes by you make him comfortable; it's an African thing, the blacks have it and so do we. Do you think that while you've been in this township you have learned anything at all about what goes on here? Because if you do, man, you're more imbecilic than I took you for.'

Later, in a more sober mood, Koos said: 'You have to try to understand these – my lot, I mean. The British put their women and children in concentration camps. The Zulu smashed the skulls of their babies against their waggon wheels. They have long memories, Afrikaners. Memory is their speciality.'

Ralph was struck by how he said 'these people'. Just as Lucy Moyo did, when she talked about her friends and neighbours.

'All I hope,' Ralph said, 'and it's a fairly faint hope, I know – is that the country will grind to a halt under the weight of its own ludicrous bureaucracy. You can hardly see a gap where a man can slip though.'

'There's no slipping through,' Koos said. 'Everybody's watch-ing everyone else. This country is like that. My home town, my people – Jesus, man, you can't imagine.'

'I think I can,' Ralph said.

'My father believes the world was made in seven days. It's in the Bible, he says.' Koos laughed.

In the new year the early-morning raids began. They happened over three days. On the first morning, the police entered the township at five o'clock. They had armoured vehicles, and they came in force. They cordoned off the area they had chosen and went from house to house, kicking in the doors. Next day, when people came down to the mission to give their accounts, this as much as anything gave rise to indignation: that they had shouted out that they were police, that the doors must be opened, but then they had given no time for the householders to obey them. 'As if we were animals,' a woman said, 'who would not understand.'

They were looking for liquor, the police said, for evidence of illicit stills. They were also looking for arms; there was a rumour current, which Ralph wished he had not heard, that *matériel* had been brought into Elim by night, and stowed away against a braver age.

Since the riot – the so-called riot – the atmosphere had been restless and strained, and the corner boys had a sullen, knowing look. He no longer allowed Anna to go out alone. Where people knew them, they were safe enough. Where they were unknown, a white face had become a provocation.

Those nights of the raids, Ralph found it impossible to sleep. There was the fear that some wider kind of trouble would blow up; that forewarned of the police action a crowd would gather, young boys heedless of the consequences, with sticks and bottles and, God knows, perhaps these mysterious arms; then there would be a replay of the baton charge, or perhaps much worse, perhaps bullets. He felt foolish, helpless, inconsequential, as he lay on his back staring up at the ceiling, an orange light insinuating itself through the gap in the curtains.

It had become necessary to fix these lights around the mission compound. A week ago, the nursery school had been broken into. There was no money for the thieves to take, no food; they had kicked the little tables about, torn up some books, ransacked Anna's broom-cupboard office and made a small fire in there. It could, of course, have burned down the building, if Father Alfred had not seen the flames from his bedroom window.

Then, on Sunday, when the mission workers were at their various services, a sneak-thief had entered Rosinah's single-room house, taken her clothing, including a woollen hat which belonged to Dearie and which Rosinah had extracted from her on a forced loan. The cook's retching sobs had been out of all proportion to the loss. They had – himself and Anna, Dearie, the gardeners – spent an hour trying to coax her to stop crying. Clara, the educated washerwoman, stood by the door not speaking. There was no expression on her face. She looked like a woman who might have lost everything, many times over.

Hence the security lights. Their sleep had been broken since. His wife's tension seemed to communicate itself to Ralph through the sagging springs of the bed. Towards dawn he dozed. Phrases ran through his head, the phrases that he lived with each day: *Thirty shillings or ten days. My husband, baas, is whereabouts unknown.*

And towards dawn on the third day the police came to the mission. It was almost a relief to hear them pounding at the door. He and Anna were both out of bed in a moment; their faces peaked in the grey light, they understood the extent of each other's wakefulness. Ralph pulled on the trousers and shirt he had left folded by the bed. Anna belted her dressing-gown over her long nightdress. What was the point of rushing? The police would break the door down anyway.

In the event, the police checked themselves; as if, here on the mission steps, some notion of civility still held sway. 'It's you,'

Ralph said, opening the door; Quintus stood there. He had feared unknown faces, Special Branch perhaps. Half a dozen men trooped in. Quintus introduced his colleague, Sergeant van Zyl. They had hardly got through the pleasantries when the men began to stomp through the house, looking in the cupboards and under the bed. 'Of course, Sergeant,' Ralph said, 'you spotted at once that I'm the type to run a still. Me and my wife, aren't we just your typical shebeen-owners?'

Sergeant van Zyl said, 'We are looking for a person we have reason to believe may be on your premises.'

'What person? Dr Verwoerd? Mickey Mouse?'

Van Zyl looked baleful. He was a big man; hitching his thumbs into his belt, he moved the burden of his belly a little. 'You wrote a letter to the *Pretoria News*, Mr Eldred. Don't do that again.'

Let's stay calm, Ralph said to himself. 'My letter was only to tell people what really happened the day of your baton charge. I wrote to invite people to come up here and look at Elim for themselves. To look at our churches and our schools, and ask themselves if we are the hotbed of vice and crime they are constantly told that we are. To look at what we do here, and ask themselves if we deserve to be destroyed.'

'We know what your letter said,' van Zyl told him. 'We have read it ourselves in the newspaper. The brigadier doesn't like your tone, Mr Eldred.'

'Well, if it's only my tone,' Ralph said easily. 'The content doesn't trouble him?'

'You'd have more idea about crime,' van Zyl said, 'if you spent some time with us at the police station.'

'But I do spend time. I could hardly spend any more. Unless I moved in with you.'

'I suppose that might be arranged,' van Zyl said.

The police had given up on the mysterious person, whoever

he was. They were in Ralph's office, rummaging through his papers. Sergeant van Zyl settled on his desk. Again he twitched at his belt, settling his bulk comfortably, as if his gut were something apart from him, a pet animal he kept.

'If I knew what you wanted,' Ralph said, 'I could perhaps help you out.'

'Help yourself out, man,' van Zyl said. 'Keep out of our way.'

Quintus attempted covert signals. He looked sick. Ralph would not meet his eyes. His clear meaning was, be careful, for van Zyl is not your decent type of policeman. And that was evident; there was no need to collude on it. If Quintus felt bad, let him quit; he, Ralph, was not going to do anything to ease a policeman's conscience.

The search was a perfunctory one, but as messy as could be contrived. They had done it for the nuisance value, Ralph thought. Even so, he knew that Anna, standing against the wall, was trembling. He would have liked to turn to her, hold her in his arms, but he did not want to take his eyes from van Zyl's eyes. He would not be the one to look away first.

Quintus ushered them from the office, grumbling. 'I don't know how you find anything in this place.'

'We've always managed,' Anna said. 'But I don't suppose we'll manage now.'

Her voice was cool. Quintus shook his head. He spoke in Afrikaans to his colleague. Enough's enough, he seemed to be saying. The men trooped out. They were left alone, with their papers scattered about the Mission House, as if a gale had blown through, or some apocalyptic wind.

The same day, late afternoon, Quintus turned up with a truck. 'Got something for you,' he said, smiling as if he had not seen them earlier that day.

Two black boys leapt down from the back of the truck, and manoeuvred on to the stoep a large filing cabinet, battered and scratched, dark green in colour. 'Just what you need, eh?' Quintus said.

'Oh, Quintus, a donation,' Anna said. She smiled, as if deeply touched.

Quintus did not know the difference between affectation and reality. 'No need to thank me, man,' he said modestly. 'It's just scrap metal. We were throwing it out. A drawer fell out and broke the brigadier's toe, that's why.' He addressed Ralph. 'So you take care and don't be rough when you pull it out.'

'Cup of coffee?' Anna said. Like Ralph, she felt a sneaking pity for the man. Quintus sat down at the kitchen table. He said, 'I know you don't like me coming round here. But we've been told to keep an eye on you. Look, there are worse people in the force.'

'I know. We've met him,' Ralph said.

The sergeant sat brooding over his cup. 'Hell, man, you think I *like* my job? A man's got to earn a living.'

'I get tired of hearing that,' Anna said. 'There are other ways, surely?'

The sergeant reached into a pocket of his uniform, took out his wallet. To Ralph's deep embarrassment, he drew from it a family snapshot. 'My girls,' he said.

Ralph looked at it. Three daughters. Twelve, ten and eight they might be. Graded by height, the arms of one sister around the waist of the next, blonde heads leaning back on to the shoulder of a woman slighter, more modest than they, scarcely taller than the eldest girl. Filaments of hair escaped from their plaits, and stood out like haloes as they smiled into the sun. Hitler's wet-dreams, he thought. He handed the photograph to Anna. 'Beauties,' he said. 'Your wife, Quintus, she looks a lovely girl.'

'When you're a family man you'll understand a lot you don't understand now,' the policeman promised. 'You think about them all the time, Jesus, you *worry*. What sort of a world are they going to grow up in? Are they going to marry kaffirs?'

'We don't use that word here.'

'Oh, words,' the sergeant said. 'That's what gets to me about you people. Words.'

He didn't explain his objection; he stood up, said he must be going. 'Next time we come,' he said, indicating the filing cabinet, 'you'll have everything in the one place for us?' Tentatively, he touched his uniformed chest and winced. 'Mrs Eldred, could I trouble you? Have you got anything to take the acid off my stomach?'

'Quintus wants to be human,' Anna said, when he left.

'He must get another job then.'

That evening Koos came to the back door. Just for a few minutes; he wouldn't eat with them. Couldn't, really, he said. His jaw was swollen. He had lost two teeth. The police had called on him too. They had smashed their way through the front of his surgery, smashed in the windows – though everybody knew he slept in the room at the back. They said they wanted to talk to Luke Mbatha, the dispenser. They'd given Luke's shack a going-over, and taken Luke away in a van.

Koos wanted Ralph to come down to the station, bringing what money he had by him, to try and bail Luke out. 'God knows he's no innocent,' Koos said. 'But you know what happens to black men in police cells.' He had, he explained, no money of his own. The matter was urgent, he said, looking away. Otherwise he would not have come. They might have taken Luke Mbatha down the hill to Pretoria by now, and perhaps they would never find him again.

'Why didn't you come before?' Ralph said.

'Because I can't walk when I'm unconscious,' Koos said. His

pale eyes were bloodshot, and his hands shook. One of the policemen had hit him in the face with a pistol butt, and then presumably hit him on the head, because he had come to at the house of one of his patients, lying on a pallet and covered with one of Anna's knitted blankets. 'A good blanket,' he said. 'Very warm. Thank you, Anna.' He couldn't remember much of what had happened. The policeman who hit him had called him a white kaffir. That sergeant, he said – not van Zyl. The thin one. The other. Quintus Brink.

They realized, over the next few days, that it was no longer safe to make telephone calls. They knew there was nothing seditious in their conversation. But anything could be twisted, and would be, and they knew that there were listeners on the line.

Van Zyl came by again – just visiting, he said – and it went badly. He stared at the filing cabinet as if he knew it from somewhere. 'Any visitors last night?' he said.

'No.'

'You surprise me. You're sure no visitors after dark?'

'I'm quite sure.'

'Any visitors in your servants' quarters?'

'I can't help you there. But I'm sure no one was on the compound whom you would be interested in.'

'Luke Mbatha has given them the slip,' Anna said from the doorway. She spoke derisively. Van Zyl was not pleased.

'Where did you hear that rubbish?'

'It's not rubbish. I heard it on the street. Everybody knows it. How did he get away, Sergeant? Did he bewitch you? Did he bewitch the brigadier?'

Van Zyl got up from his chair, and tossed his paunch threateningly. 'Tell your woman to watch her mouth,' he said. 'Or she'll feel my hand across it.'

'Out,' Ralph said. '*Voetsak*, Sergeant. Out of this house.'

It is the word you use to a dog, and only then if it is a dog of bad character. But van Zyl would not hesitate to use it, to a man of inferior race; Ralph believed now that there were inferior races, distinguished not by culture or genes, but by some missing faculty of pity. '*Voetsak*, Sergeant,' he said again, and moved towards him as if to push him out of the front door, across the stoep and down the steps into the yard.

Sergeant van Zyl knew he should not fight; he had received warnings about his excess of zeal. He attempted some sort of lumbering side-step – so when Ralph did push him, he was not truly on course for the door. 'You must be a stinking Jew,' the policeman told Ralph. 'In my opinion, Hitler was right.' Ralph's fists against his belly, he careered backwards. His right arm flailed out, swept to the floor the papers from Anna's temporary desk. He backed his calves into the wastepaper basket, overturned it: and, attempting to regain his balance, trod in it. Ralph would never forget the feeling of his hands sinking into the sergeant's flesh. It gave him a shock, how easy it was to topple that great bulk.

The Special Branch came at three the following morning, and took them both away.

FIVE

Anna heard Ralph talking on the telephone. '. . . I do grasp,' he was saying, 'that you raised £132 from the harvest supper and gave the same amount to the Mission to Seamen, but I'm afraid you will confuse the auditor if you don't show them in separate columns. Leave aside for the moment the question of the rector's expenses . . .'

Anna swore mildly under her breath as she side-stepped through the bales of newspapers stacked up in the hall. When Ralph came out of his office she said, 'There are more papers here than when I went out. People are delivering these bundles at all hours of the day and night.'

'Not quite,' Ralph said, frowning.

'Couldn't you ask them to call between set hours?'

'It might put people off. I'm relying on their goodwill. Why don't you get the boys to carry them up to the attics?'

'What's the point? They'll only have to come down again. And when you try to move them the bundles fall apart and the damn things are all over the place.'

'It's true,' Ralph said. 'People don't seem to know how to tie up bundles.'

'Perhaps it's a lost art,' Anna said, 'like broadcast sowing. Can't they go in the bike shed?'

'No, nor in any other shed. They might get damp.'

Anna sighed. The newspapers benefited the parish church's restoration fund in some way: clearly only if they were dry, not if they were damp.

'I have to go out,' Ralph said.

'But Kit will be here soon. I was hoping –'

'It's the new committee. For the homeless in Norwich.'

'I hardly knew there were homeless in Norwich,' Anna said. 'There seem to be enough council estates.' Ralph vanished back into his office. Anna was left with her bad mood. 'Perhaps,' she muttered, 'some of them could come and live in our hall-stand.'

Ralph had almost finished his letters for the day. He had been interrupted by several telephone calls from elderly people within a ten-mile radius, all of them complaining about their Meals-on-Wheels; he had nothing to do with this service, but found it hard to convince them of that. Mobile libraries, too, had been much on his mind. He had received a request for the Trust to support a Good News Van, which planned to jolt around the countryside taking the latest Christian paperbacks to the housebound. 'We have known people who have not read a book in years,' the letter told him, 'but whose lives have been transformed by thrilling new stories of what God is doing all over the world.' Ralph gave the letter a file number, and scribbled on it, 'I suggest we turn this one down. The housebound have enough to put up with.' He dropped it in the box for the next meeting of the Trust committee.

The Trust was not rich any more, and it was necessary to be selective; need seemed always to increase. He had his procedures: he tried to avoid subsidizing anything too doctrinaire, or anything involving volunteers playing the guitar. Initiatives for the young attracted his interest, but he rejected applications from any group with 'Kids' in the title.

The hostel in the East End had changed its character now. Some time in the sixties it had stopped being St Walstan's and become Crucible House. In those far-off days when Ralph had reported each weekend to count the laundry out and returned mid-week to count it back in, the task had been shovelling old men up off the street and drying them out and sending them on their way a week or two later with a new overcoat and a hot breakfast inside them. Or finding a bed for an old lag who was between prison sentences: or a quiet corner for somebody who'd gone berserk and smashed all the crockery in the Salvation Army canteen. But nowadays the clients were young. They were runaways, some of them, who had fetched up at a railway terminus with a few pounds in their pockets, played in the amusement arcades till their money ran out, and then slept on the streets. Some of them had been 'in care' – you would think that was a complete misnomer, Ralph would say, if you could see the state of them.

These young people, boys and girls, had something in common, a certain look about them: hard to define but, after a little experience, easy to spot. They were often unhealthily fat: puffed up with cheap carbohydrates, with the salt from bags of crisps. When they were spoken to they answered slowly, if at all; they focused their eyes at some point in the middle distance, beyond their questioner's shoulder. Large bottles of prescription drugs clanked in their pitiful luggage, which was often made up of Tesco bags – though Ralph always wondered where they got the means to go to Tesco.

The volunteers who staffed the hostel had changed too. The present director, Richard, was an intense young man with a higher degree. Before his time, in the days when the last of the old men used to shuffle in and out, the volunteers had been clean-cut young men in crew-neck sweaters, and girls with good accents, who had a way of talking to the clients as if they were recalcitrant beagles or pointers. But now it was hard to tell the workers and the clients apart. They had a lost air, these modern volunteers: children filling in a year before university, lured by the promise of pocket-money and full board in a room of their own in London. They wore clothes from charity shops. They read no books. They seldom spoke, except to each other.

Ralph invited them to Norfolk sometimes, for a week's country air. He would bring the clients too, packing them carefully into his car with their Tesco bags and driving them through Essex and Suffolk towards a warm family home – though because of the state of the central heating, 'warm' was only a figure of speech. Anna, he believed, liked to see new faces. The children were used to what they called Visitors. But nowadays they would look at the arrivals, and affect a greater bewilderment than they felt: 'Is she a Sad Case, or a Good Soul?'

There were nights when Ralph sat up till dawn, talking on the telephone to some suicidal adolescent in London; there were nights when he would jump into the car and roar off – this too being a qualified term, considering the state of the Citroën – to deal with some catastrophe that Richard's jargon was not equal to. Ralph had a plainer way of doing things than Richard could imagine. He was calm and patient, he expected the best from people, he never gave up on them. They recognized this; and often, from plain weariness in the face of his implacable optimism, they would decide to live, and to behave better.

Sometimes, rude questioners would ask him why the Trust didn't move its entire operation to London, since the need was such a crying need. Then Ralph would talk about the glum, silent forms of rural deprivation: the bored teenagers kicking their heels at a bus stop waiting for a bus that never came; the pensioners in isolated cottages by overgrown railway lines, without telephone and heat and mains drainage. He would talk so long and hard about branch-line closures that his questioner would wish he had never opened his mouth.

The fact was – he was the first to admit it – Ralph and the dwindling resources he could command were wanted in too many places. He was torn, divided. The demands of the world dragged on his conscience; but did he do enough for his own family? Sometimes he felt a strange physical force – little hands pulling at him, invisible hands plucking at his clothes.

So, today – he had just one more letter to do: Church of England Children's Society. Then Norwich for the committee – and then he would race back for dinner, because Kit was coming home, and Anna was cooking a big meal, and Julian would be bringing his girl over from her farm near the sea.

He applied stamps to his letters. Yawned. But, he told himself, don't despise these little things; they add up. A tiny series of actions, of small duties well performed, eventually does some good in the world.

That's the theory, anyway.

Mid-afternoon, Emma collected her niece Kit from the station in Norwich. Kit ran across the forecourt with her bag; an Easter breeze lifted her hair, fanned it out around her head. Jumping into the car, she shook it like a lion shaking his mane. She kissed her aunt, squeezed her shoulders. Her eyes were leonine: wide, golden and vigilant. How handsome she's become, Emma thought: a heartbreaker. She remembered Ralph in his National Service days, coming home on leave. Ralph had been too remote to break hearts.

'You can have tea with me,' Emma said. 'Then I'll take you home. Oh, don't worry, I've bought a shop cake. I haven't launched myself on anything ambitious.'

Emma lived in a neat, double-fronted, red-brick cottage, which stood on the High Street in Foulsham. Foulsham is not a town, by the standards of the rest of England: it has a few small shops, a post office, a church, a Baptist Chapel and a number of public houses. It has a war memorial and a parish magazine, a village hall, a Playing Fields Committee, a Women's Institute and a mobile wet-fish van. A hundred yards from Emma's house was the school Kit attended when she was five; fifty yards away was the shop where she used to buy sweets after school on her way to her aunt's house.

In those days Emma seldom held an afternoon surgery; she put in the hours at other times, evenings and weekends when her partners wanted to get away. At four o'clock she had been there to open her front door to the children, to bring them in, listen to the news of their day and give them lemonade and a plain bun and then drive them home. Often Mr Palmer the Estate Agent was leaving just as Kit arrived. He was, she knew, a very great friend of Aunt Emma's; she suspected him of getting there before them, to eat buns with icing, have treats that children were denied. Sometimes Mr Palmer was exceptionally happy. He would throw her up in the air, toss her – giggling, hair flying – to the ceiling, and then give her a two-shilling piece. She'd got quite rich, out of Mr Palmer. Her small brother Robin, when he started school, complained he didn't get the same money. Mr Palmer would ruffle his hair and give him sixpence. Well, she said to Robin: you don't know, perhaps he's fallen into poverty. People do. It's in books.

Now fifteen years had passed, and she put make-up on and went out to eat oysters with Mr Palmer's son.

Emma, though not fifty, now described herself as 'semi-retired'. You'd want to steal away, she said to Ralph, after a lifetime of pallid pregnant wives, and screaming mites with measles spots, and old men wheezing in: 'Missus, the old chest – I'm bronical.' She filled in for holidays and weekends off, kept up with the medical literature, and took the occasional family-planning session. This last had always been her interest. She would turn up at outlying cottages, and talk in blunt terms. They would call her in to attend to shingles or lumbago, and she would leave them with some rubber device. Robin had once introduced her to a schoolfriend as 'My Aunt Emma, who has done so much to depopulate East Anglia'. She was in demand these days for talks in schools and colleges throughout the county. Heads liked her because she talked straight, but did not embarrass their young people. After all, she was old. They did not have to think of her *doing it*.

Emma's house was warm and tidy. 'Make yourself comfortable,' she said. Kit threw herself at a chair. What a lot of energy she had – but then, just as suddenly, it would seem to drain out of her.

'I went to Walsingham,' Emma said. 'To pray about Felix. Wasn't that odd of me?'

'Did you go to the wells?'

'No, just to the shrine.'

'There's one well, you know, the round one – I used to know a girl who believed that if you drank the water you'd have a secret wish come true within a year and a day.'

'A secret wish?' Emma said. 'Secret from the rest of the world, or secret from yourself, I wonder.'

Kit smiled. 'That's the trouble, isn't it? It's like – didn't somebody say there's no such thing as unanswered prayers? All prayers are answered, but not in the way that you notice.'

Emma filled the teapot and brought in plates. She had managed to mash the shop cake, somehow, in getting it out of its packet. She had always described herself as a free-thinker in matters of nutrition. Her house guests were fed at uncertain intervals, at unorthodox hours and on strange combinations of food.

I wonder, Kit thought now, how much of that was because of Felix; because she never knew when he'd turn up, and perhaps sometimes she'd cook him a meal and he'd say, no, I'm expected home, and then hours later she'd heat it up for herself . . .

'Cake that bad?' Emma inquired.

'The cake? No, it's fine.' Kit cultivated a hedge of yellow

crumbs at the side of her plate. 'Emma, can I ask you something? Tell me to mind my own business if you like. Only I try, you know, to fit the past together these days. I was thinking about you and Felix. I wondered if you ever talked about him leaving Ginny, and moving in with you.'

'Oh, there was a lot of talk. There always is in these affairs.' Emma ran her hand back through her hair. 'I knew him before, you know, before he took up with Ginny. We used to hang around together, when we were sixteen, seventeen, and then when I was away doing my training he'd come to London to see me. I suppose I had my chance then. But I told him to push off. He used to get on my nerves. His waistcoats, mainly. Yellow waistcoats. So it was my own fault, wasn't it?'

'But later he didn't get on your nerves, did he?'

'No, I learned to put up with him. He persisted. But Felix had children, remember.'

'Perhaps he shouldn't have done.'

'Oh, Ginny was never one to avail herself of my devices. The babies were born before we got together again. Or at least, before we got together again in any way that seemed likely to last. Yes, of course, we should have married in the first place, I see that now ... but it was done, it was done. He wouldn't have wanted to leave Daniel and the little girl.'

'You could have had his children. I would have liked it if you'd had children, Emma. There'd have been more of us.'

'But then perhaps there wouldn't have been any Daniel.'

'Well, I don't know ... I think I would trade Daniel for cousins. They wouldn't have been like cousins, they'd have been like brothers and sisters.'

'You mustn't be greedy, Kit,' Emma said. 'The truth is, Felix wouldn't have left Ginny, even if there'd been no children. Ginny's not the sort of woman that men leave. And what we had was enough, Felix and me. And what you have is enough.'

'I suppose so,' Kit said.

A ray of grace shone through Emma, from some long-ago Sunday-school afternoon. She said it again, gently: 'You mustn't be greedy, Kit.'

Emma had tried to stop Ralph's children calling her 'Aunt'. What you are called you become, she said; she did not want to become something out of P. G. Wodehouse. She had tried to make their lives easier for them, but it was not easy being Ralph's children.

His standards were high, but different from other people's. When they were small the children had played with their friends from the row of council houses that straggled up the lane beyond the church, a quarter of a mile from the Red House. Ralph's children had better manners, Emma thought; but the council-house children were better dressed.

It was lucky that the young Eldreds had schoolmates in similar plights, or they would have thought themselves hard done-by. Kit, for instance, had a friend whose father wouldn't let a television set in the house. Robin knew a boy whose mother knitted his trousers to her own design. Norfolk breeds such people; huddling indoors out of the wind, they give birth to strange notions.

Emma had been a refuge for the children once; they still liked to be at her house, even if she could not assemble a sandwich without the filling dropping out. She thoroughly understood her practical value to them. She provided money for heart's desires – for vital clothes and sudden causes, and treats that Ralph disdained. Poor Ralph, she thought. He made them all have music lessons, but they were neither musical nor grateful. Robin had said last year, 'Dad's supposed to be good with young people, but it's other young people he's good with. Not us.'

Emma and Kit finished their tea, drove the three miles to the Red House. As they pulled up, Kit said, 'Is Dad still on Julian's back – about doing a year for the Trust?'

'I think he's given up on it. Julian wouldn't do in London, would he? He'd be back within days.' Emma leaned across to kiss her niece. 'I'm not coming in. The partners are going to the King's Arms tonight, we're going to paint the town red.'

'Have a good time.' Kit put her head in at the car window. 'Maybe I'll do it, instead. Do a year . . . it wouldn't hurt. Or would it?'

Emma was surprised. 'I thought you were doing post-grad? I thought it was all fixed?'

Kit shook her head. Her face was placid, almost sad. 'Nothing's fixed. I had this idea – I wrote home to Dad – I said I didn't want to be in London . . . but I suppose I could face it, if it were for the Trust, if I could be any use there.' She looked away. 'I don't know what to think, though. I've lost my . . . no, I don't know what I've lost.'

Your virginity? Emma wondered. The thought must have shown on her face. 'It's not Daniel,' Kit said. 'I wouldn't stay around here for Daniel. Though if I needed an excuse, I suppose he could be one.'

Emma drove away. The door of the house was thrown open and Julian came out, pretending to peer into the bushes, and calling 'Come in for your dinner, kitty kitty kitty.'

Rebecca, behind him, said, 'Kate of Kate Hall.'

Her brother looked well, Kit thought at once, he looked happy. He straightened up to his impressive height, put his arms around her and hugged her. Behind him was his red-haired girlfriend, Sandra Glasse.

Kit found Daniel Palmer in the kitchen with the rest of the family. All of them were watching carefully, to assess how pleased she was to see him.

'Hello,' Kit said. 'I didn't expect you, where's your car?'

'I put it under cover.' Daniel did not know his status with Kit; did not know her mood; wondered what the family thought his status was. 'Welcome home,' he said. He picked up a strand of Kit's hair and touched the end of it to his lips.

'He's got a new car, you see,' Julian said. 'He's afraid rain will fall on it.'

'It's my Morgan,' Daniel said. Amazed delight showed on his face. Kit retrieved her hair and tucked it back, among those strands romance had not distinguished. 'Hand-built,' Daniel said. 'I've been waiting four years for it.'

'Goodness,' Kit said. She wondered how desire could last so long.

Ralph said, 'I'd be afraid to drive it, I think.'

Becky said, 'It pretends to be old, but it's not.'

'Where's Robin?'

Ralph said, 'He's playing in it.'

Daniel displayed the car's keys, holding them as if diamonds trickled from his fingers. 'Don't worry. He won't get far.'

Sandra Glasse had not spoken at all. She did not seem to know what the others were talking about. She had just arrived, Kit saw: she had a paper bag in her hand, which she cradled against her old jersey. 'Oh, Mrs Eldred,' she said, 'I've brought you some hen's eggs.'

Daniel, who had not met Sandra before, looked around at her with a quizzical smile. It seemed to him she must have dropped in from another world.

They had decided to eat in the kitchen as usual, because the evenings were cold and the central heating was playing up again. Earlier Ralph had met Anna dragging into the boiler room with a scuttle of coal. 'Anna,' he had said, 'with two sons in the house, I don't expect to see you –'

'This effort is voluntary,' Anna said. 'I'm doing it to warm myself up.'

By the time they had fought a bout with the boiler, they were both warm. 'The poor desperate thing,' Ralph said. 'I suppose it would be a mercy to knock it out and send it wherever boilers go to die. Still, I can't see us changing over to oil. Not this year. Besides, with oil, it's so political, the prices shoot up, they hold you to ransom.'

'Daniel explained to me once,' Anna said, 'that when the price of one sort of fuel goes up, the price of all the others goes up soon after.'

'But the installation . . .' Ralph said. 'Honestly, the bills just at the moment . . . the telephone bill alone.'

'Yes,' Anna said. 'Yet when anyone comes by and says "Can I use your phone?" you say, "Of course, go ahead," and when they offer to pay for the call you say, "No, I won't hear of it." You remember that volunteer – Abigail, was it? – the one who said could she phone her boyfriend? And it turned out he'd gone to be a jackaroo for a year?'

'An extreme case. Anyway, it stopped her fretting.'

'People should have less expensive emotions,' Anna said. 'They should have them when it's cheap-rate.' Then she said, 'By the way – while we've got a private moment – what do you think of Daniel these days?'

He was all right really, was Ralph's opinion. He had always felt comfortable with Felix's son. Daniel wore the same clothes as he did – corduroy trousers, old tweed jackets, Fair Isle and lambswool from September through to May. Only recently had he become aware that Daniel's clothes were not, like his, organic developments. Daniel went to London to get them at vast expense, it seemed. They looked old because they were made that way. Ralph wore his clothes because they were what was in the wardrobe. Daniel wore them for another reason – to become someone. To become a country gentleman, Robin said; it was a pose.

Robin knew these things. Still, he was enthusiastic about the two-seater, the Morgan, could hardly be dragged inside to eat. Later Ralph went out too, to pass a hand over its gleaming body and murmur its praises. Daniel was like a child at Christmas, beside himself with glee; it would have been churlish not to admire. But he felt uneasy about the car and what it might mean. Modern mechanics purred beneath its bonnet; as Rebecca said, it purported to be what it was not.

All the same, he thought, if Daniel was Kit's choice, you wouldn't find him raising objections. Daniel would look after her. There was nothing fake about his bank balance, and the architects of the county were coming men. He could afford the car and he could afford Kit. He would design them a house, no doubt, and build it on a prime site, and Kit would have a cleaning lady and hot water whenever she wanted it, and . . .

An awful spasm of grief took hold of Ralph; he stood in the outhouse with Daniel and Robin, an old mac around his shoulders, rain and blue evening air gusting in at the door, and felt grief take him by the windpipe, grief shake him like a mugger. He turned away; no one must see his face.

This happened sometimes. More, lately. And trying to separate himself from the emotion, to pull away from it, he wondered: why is this? He went back into the house. In the kitchen, Sandra was washing up; Becky was drying; Anna was decanting the leftovers into boxes for the fridge. A usual kind of family: 1980, and all's well.

It was a year now since Julian had met Sandra Glasse.

It was a Sunday in April; Julian could not mistake the date, because the Scouts in North Walsham had been holding their St

George's Day parade. And what was he doing in North Walsham? He had wanted to get out of the house. There were some particularly nasty Visitors, Sad Cases. Robin had the excuse of some sporting fixture or other; he always had a means of escape.

His mother, who was sensitive about the Visitors, had seen Julian's plight. 'Would you go to North Walsham for me? I have a bundle of clothes for the church jumble sale, which includes some things of your father's that I particularly wish to see the back of. If you could just drop them in at this address I'll give you — leave them in the garage if they're out — then you could have the car for the afternoon. How would that be?'

Nothing doing in North Walsham; nothing doing, in a little market town on a Sunday afternoon. Only the Scouts marching down the street with their band, and a gang of bike boys jeering at them. He parked the car, delivered the bundle to a house near the church, walked up the empty street in fitful sunshine. He stopped to stare for no good reason into the window of Boots the Chemist. There was a razzmatazz of vitamin supplements and glucose tablets, and a come-and-get-'em pyramid of Kodak films, and an alluring display of hot-water bottles, for pessimists who might be buying them in for the summer ahead.

The bike boys had gathered around the Market Cross, their machines at rest, and they in their leather jackets pushing and shoving about its venerable dome. Julian always liked to see the Market Cross, but he shied away from approaching them. He was not afraid — or he did not want to think so; but like the Scouts he would have been an incitement to them. He was tidily dressed, like a good schoolboy at weekend, in a loose cream cotton shirt and well-ironed denims — no one could stop his mother pressing clothes. His hair was the colour called dishwater-blond; still, it was too blond, and conspicuously shiny and clean. He knew his own features: his unformed face, his large unclouded blue eyes. He knew what they represented – provoking innocence. It did not seem to matter that he was physically stronger than most people. Strength's not much good without permission to use it.

The boys leaning on the columns of the Market Cross had leather jackets with studs and hair shaved off to stubble. The girls with them had long metal earrings and aggrieved faces. They sprawled against the machines or pawed at the boys' jackets, keeping up a braying cackling conversation of sorts. One girl hitched up her thin skirt and threw a leg over one of the bikes; she slithered across the saddle and rode it in seesaw movements, in a mimicry of copulation.

Another girl stood slightly apart from the group. She was with them, but didn't seem to belong to them at all. She had a shaggy head of thick, dark red hair; he could hardly see her face or shape, and it was the oddity of her that made him give her a second look. She wore a black-and-white tweed jacket that was several sizes too big; it was well-worn, and the kind of thing that a settled Norfolk matron of fifty might call 'my old gardening coat'. No pretence at fashion in it, or even anti-fashion. She had lace-up school shoes: also not a rebel's possessions. Someone spoke to her, and she shook her red head violently, and started across the road, cantering off, like an animal, in the direction of the church.

Julian turned and put the car keys in his pocket. He crossed the road too, followed her into the church grounds. She stood beneath the broken, collapsed tower, whose craggy top overbore the streets, the Market Cross, the bike boys. Seeing him, she seemed to shake herself inside the vast stiff jacket, and trotted further off, to the far side of the churchyard. There she sat down on a bench (put there by the Old Folks' Welfare Committee) and waited for him to catch her up.

At first he hardly dared sit down beside her, in case she took fright and hurtled off again. Her animal quality seemed pronounced, and he wished he had something to offer, a sugar lump or even a piece of bread, to show that he meant well. As if reading his mind, she reached into the jacket and took out an apple, then a second. She offered one to him, holding it out at arm's length, without a smile.

'Do you always carry your supplies with you?' he asked.

She said, 'Yes, certainly.'

He tossed his head back towards the market-place. 'Do you know that lot?'

'Not really.'

'I thought you were with them.'

'I picked up with them this morning. I'd nothing else to do. I went to Cromer with them. Nobody had any money. We came on here. They fetched me.'

He took the apple and sat down on the bench beside her. She wiped the fruit on the sleeve of her jacket and bit into it. She chewed gloomily, reflectively, eyes on gravestones and the church's ancient walls.

'Are you going back with them?'

'No.' She was angry. 'They're senseless.'

'Where do you live?'

'In the Burnhams. You know it round there?'

'You're a fair way from home.'

'You can get a fair way when you go on the motor bikes, that's one thing about them. Still, I don't care for it. I ought to be getting back.' She threw her apple core on the ground, but didn't move, just huddled into her jacket. It began to drizzle. 'I'll take shelter in the church,' she said.

Later, it seemed to him that Sandra knew all the county's churches, great and small. She treated them as other people treated bus shelters and waiting rooms. He had to stride to keep up with her, as she bolted for the porch. 'If you're not going to eat your apple,' she said, 'I'll have it back, I might need it later.'

He said, 'I could take you home.'

'Have you got a car?'

'Yes.'

'You're young to have a car.'

'It's my mother's car. I don't mind taking you. You'll never get back any other way, and this rain's setting in.'

'All right,' she said. They stood in the church porch for a minute and watched the rain fall. 'Sanctuary,' she said, unexpectedly.

'Do you know about this church?' Julian looked sideways at her, into her face. Such pale eyes. 'When they were building it, it was the Peasants' Revolt. There was a battle near here. It was the last battle, I think. Some of the rebels came in here begging sanctuary, but the church wasn't finished, so it didn't count. The Bishop of Norwich came after them and killed them all.'

The girl blinked at him. 'I never heard that,' she said.

He loathed himself, spouting semi-facts. Why had he done it? He laughed and said, 'Didn't they tell you about it at school?' He loathed himself more. What had made him go on about the Peasants' Revolt, for God's sake? She unnerved him, that was it. She had not told him her name. Her sandy-gilt lashes drooped on to her cheek.

'I don't recall anything about it,' she said. But then, very kindly, 'I'm always glad to know anything about old places, so if you've anything to tell me you needn't be afraid I won't like it.'

It seemed she expected a long acquaintance. The rain slackened a little. Julian took her jacket by its bulky sleeve and hurried her to the car. The bike boys had scattered. She was his responsibility.

*

A fine drizzle hit the windscreen. The sea, on their right as they drove, was obliterated by a rising mist. The Sheringham caravan sites loomed out of it, and the wind plucked at the blossom on the cherry trees in the bungalow gardens. The trees looked as if they had been left outside by mistake, or transported from some softer country.

Between Cley and Weybourne, the heathland melted invisibly into the marshes. Bird-watchers, hung about like pedlars with the tools of their trade, strode towards the invisible sea. There were sheep in the fields; among their ambling forms they saw the necks of resting swans, as hard and clear as marble, startlingly white in the thick air. By the roadside, signs – crudely chalked blackboards, or painted boards – advertised FRESH SEA BAIT, SHRIMPS, COCKLES, FRESH CRABS, DRESSED CRABS, KIPPERS. The tourist season was beginning.

They drove in what seemed to be a companionable silence. At Blakeney – the salt marshes a nebulous blend of earth, sea, air – Sandra turned in her seat. 'I'm sorry if I was angry back there. I'm not usually angry.'

What Julian saw, from the tail of his eye, was a face set on placid lines; a face with a translucent pallor, and those pale eyes. She seemed strong, composed; she held her white hands on her lap, the one reposing confidingly in the other.

'What did the bikers say to you, to make you run off like that?'

Sandra thought, then said, 'They criticized my garment.'

After a moment, they both yelled with laughter, the noise filling the shabby body of Anna's car. A gust of wind, blowing inland, peppered the rain against the glass.

'Well, I admit . . .' Julian said. 'Why do you wear it?'

'We got it donated,' Sandra said. 'I can't afford clothes like they've got. It's funny, I always think – when you've got a bit of money you can afford cheap clothes, you can throw them away when they fall apart. But if you're poor your clothes go on for ever. You get given things the Queen would be proud to wear.'

'Who was it gave it you?'

'Some church. My mum has her contacts. She used to clean for a churchwarden's wife. So we get remembered when it's jumble sales.' She paused. 'It's just our size she forgets.'

They began to laugh again. The windscreen wipers swished; ahead of them, towards Wells, the horizon had the pearl sheen of brighter weather. 'I dare say it'll outlast me, this old jacket,' Sandra said. 'I once ran through a hedge in it, and it didn't flinch.'

By the time they reached Holkham, the mist was clearing. Flashes of light struck from the dwarves' windows of flint cottages, little houses tumbling towards the coast; flint sparkled like gemstones in the wall of a round-towered church. 'Turn off here,' Sandra said, directing him towards the sea. They turned between high hedgerows, leaving behind a wide view of windmills and the red roofs of distant barns. The road narrowed. 'I live down this track,' Sandra said. 'Do you want to come in? You could have a cup of tea.'

The car bumped down an incline. 'My mother calls this "one of the foremost hills in Norfolk",' Sandra said. 'OK – stop here.'

They came to a halt in front of a huddle of low buildings, the doors facing inwards, out of the wind. There was a pear tree on a sheltered wall, geese on a pond, a vegetable plot screened off by an amateur windbreak. There were some rotting hen-houses, an old cartwheel leaning on a fence, and by the front door a wheelbarrow filled with something shrouded in polythene. They got out of the car. A woman came to the door. 'That's my mother,' Sandra said.

Mrs Glasse seemed taller than Sandra, not very old. She wore patched jeans and two shapeless pullovers, the one underneath longer than the one on top. She had red hair too, longer than her daughter's, scooped up with pins. Julian saw that bits of it straggled down her back as she turned to lead the way inside. For the first time, he wondered how his own mother managed to keep her hair fixed in its dark cloudy shapes, arrested in its whirls and coils. There must be an art to it.

Mrs Glasse had been working outside. Her muddy gumboots stood by the door. There was a wide lobby, full of swirling air – peg rugs on the floor, an accumulation of dark furniture.

'You're not one of the bike boys,' Mrs Glasse said. 'Come through, I've got the kettle on.'

He followed her to the kitchen. It was a big room, light, square, tiled underfoot. Two hard chairs stood by an old-fashioned range, in front of which some clothes were drying. There was a smell of burning wood and wet wool. Mrs Glasse hoisted the clothes away, and dragged up a third chair, manipulating it with an agile foot in a fisherman's sock. 'Where d'you find him, Sandra?'

Expecting no answer, she gave him a mug of tea, the sugar already stirred into it. Julian could not think of anything to say. Mrs Glasse did not make small-talk, or ask again where her daughter had been. He sat facing the back of the house, watching the light fade. Through an arched doorway, down steps, he caught a glimpse of a small dairy, with its deep stone shelves and recessed windows. Feeling the draught, Mrs Glasse leapt up and closed the door. He snapped his gaze away. He had wanted to step into the dairy, and run a hand over the icy, ecclesiastical curves of the walls.

As he left the house and drove away, he noticed a glasshouse, its panes shattered; a gate, off its hinges. He felt like stopping the car, going back, offering his services. But then he thought, you can't ask people to rely on you, if you're going away at the end of the summer. Between now and October I couldn't make much of an impression on that place. It would only break my heart.

After this, Julian did not see Sandra for some weeks. But in June, driving back from a friend's house in Hunstanton on a bright windy day, he saw by the roadside two women selling vegetables from a trestle table. He knew them at once, with their white faces and long flapping scarves. He pulled over and climbed out of the car. 'Hello there, Julian,' Mrs Glasse said. She had a bag of money slung about her waist, like a market trader. Sandra pulled her woollen hat further over her brows, and smiled shyly at him.

'We'll have strawberries shortly,' Mrs Glasse said. 'That fetches 'em.'

'Is there a lot of trade?'

'Passing trade,' Mrs Glasse said. 'Golfers on their way home, full of golf courses this place is.' The wind ripped the words out of her mouth. 'In high season we get the self-caterings. I do vegetables, peeled and quartered, slice the carrots, whatever, put them in polythene bags, if they don't sell we have to eat them. I do samphire, not that the self-caterings know what that is. We make bread when we've got the oven going, when we're in the mood. I'm learning from a book to make bread into patterns. I can do plaited loaves, wheatsheafs, prehistoric monsters, frogs and armadillos. The armadillos get a lot of admiration – but all you do is make a monster, and squash it, and bake the top in points.'

'It must be hard work,' Julian said.

'Labour-intensive,' Sandra said. 'Of me.'

'We get bird-watchers, I make them sandwiches. We get that lot going to Brancaster and Burnham Thorpe, studying the haunts of Lord Nelson.'

'Early haunts,' Sandra said. 'Birthplace.'

'We do goats' milk, duck eggs. Sandra pushes it all up in the wheelbarrow. This table's a bugger, though. We have to carry it up between us.'

'Up the foremost hill,' Sandra said. 'We tried putting it on the barrow but it barged our legs.'

'Couldn't you leave it up here?' Julian said. He looked around. 'By the wall?'

'Self-caterings steal it,' Mrs Glasse said. She clapped her hands together, to warm them, hopped from foot to foot. 'Summer coming on,' she observed.

'I'm sure I could fix up something,' Julian said. 'I could drive a post in behind that wall, nobody would see it, I could chain the table to it. Wrap a chain around the legs and get a padlock.'

'We never thought of that, did we?' Sandra said to her mother. 'Well, we did actually, but we're busy, we didn't get round to it yet. It'd have to be weather-proofed, though. We couldn't have our table rotting.'

'Perhaps Julian could build it a house,' Mrs Glasse said. 'Seems cruel to leave it out in the open air, chained up like something dangerous.'

The two women exchanged a glance. They laughed; comfortably enough. Julian felt almost comforted.

The following day, Julian went back to the Glasses' farm. The women were very busy; Mrs Glasse sitting by the stove, knitting in an effortful fury, and Sandra, after she had let him in, returning to her task of stuffing dozens of sisal doormats into black plastic bin-liners.

'For the market at Hunstanton,' Mrs Glasse said. 'We're going tomorrow, we have a stall. Doormats do well, because people live amid such a quantity of mud. And basketwork of all types.'

'Where do you get the doormats?' Julian asked.

'I buy them cheap from a fool.'

'Baskets we make ourselves,' Sandra said. 'She taught me. We do it in the winter when the weather keeps us in.'

'How do you get to Hunstanton?'

Mrs Glasse rolled her eyes. 'He do ask questions,' she said.

'Do you like her verb?' Sandra asked. 'She does it for the tourists.'

'I only thought, with all your stuff –'

'We have a vehicle,' Mrs Glasse said. 'Of sorts. We try not to take it out more than once a week because of the summonses.'

'She got done for no tax,' Sandra said.

'We have to hide the bloody thing,' Mrs Glasse said. 'The police come down from time to time, sniffing, seeing what they can do us for. We used to have a dog, Billy, they didn't care for him, weren't so keen then. But he died.'

'You should get another dog,' Julian said, 'if that's what keeps you safe. I'm sure I could get you a dog.'

'No,' Mrs Glasse said. He was sitting facing her, and he saw that her large light eyes filled with tears. She was pretty, he thought, might have been pretty, must have been. As if angry with herself, she gave the weighty knitting a push and watched it slither off her lap. 'Billy wanted meat,' she said. 'I used to feel sorry for him, you can't expect a dog to get by on carrot and turnip.' She stood up. 'That's enough doormats,' she said. 'We'll bag up the baskets later on, we'll just have a sit now and a cup of tea.'

Julian said, 'I'll come with you when you do the market. Do you have to take the table? I'll help you load and unload.'

'You needn't,' Sandra said. 'We've always managed.'

'I can do anything you want,' Julian said. 'I can patch up the roof if you've got a ladder, you've got some tiles off. I can do carpentry. I could put you on some new wallpaper if you want. I could lift your potatoes for you.'

Mrs Glasse said, 'Sit down, boy. There's no need to do anything.'

Julian sat down and drank his tea. He could never remember a time when he had been commanded to do nothing – when it had been enjoined on him.

That summer, it seemed to Ralph, Sandra became a fixture in his house. She was to be found in the kitchen, occupying the rocking chair, her hands folded together, her legs tucked beneath the chair, her ankles crossed. He liked to talk to her if he found her sitting there. She had her wits about her, he told Anna, despite her quaint way of talking; she had a native clarity of mind which the educative process had not succeeded in clouding. School had been an interruption to Sandra's life. She had left as soon as she could. 'I didn't see the point of it,' she told Ralph. 'It was such a long way, it took hours getting there. It used to be dark by the time I got home.'

Sandra never turned up empty-handed. She brought perhaps a modest present of a lettuce, or some fresh bread; once, when they had not baked, a can of peaches from their store cupboard.

Anna was touched, then exasperated. 'Sandra,' she said, 'you don't have to bring us presents. You're welcome to come here and eat every day and stay as long as you like, nobody who comes here has ever had to pay for their keep.' No one else has ever offered, she thought.

Sometimes Sandra brought a cake; but they baked cakes only as a last resort, when they had nothing else to take to market. They only had to get their fingers amid the eggy stretch and cascading currants, to start cursing and swearing; they were fair set, Sandra said, to slap each other with their wooden spoons. Mrs Glasse's cakes had something sad and flat about them, a melancholy Fenlands quality. Sandra's cakes rose, but in a violent, volcanic way: then cracked on top. How two cakes containing opposite faults could come out of an oven at the same (albeit unreliable) temperature was, Sandra said, one of the mysteries of East Anglia.

But despite their appearance, the cakes sold well enough. People like to buy the fruits of other people's labour; they like to put the small coin into the very hand that has toiled. Julian thought that it was not the wares that drew the customers, but the women's full, grey, mesmeric eyes.

That summer he spent market days at Hunstanton, behind the Glasses' stall; flapping canvas divided him from neighbouring stalls, from the shiny acrylic clothing, the check workshirts, the nylon leopard-skin car-seat covers and rubber mats, the cheap lace tablecloths, the bright plastic kitchen gadgets, the inflatable toys for the beach. He felt himself grow an inch taller, his hair tousled, his face sunburned, a canvas bag of change thrown across his body in ammunition-belt style. As summer ended the sea turned to the colour of mud, and soon came the wind that cut through the clothes, cut to the bone, propelling the shoppers inland towards the teashops and the amusement arcades.

Ralph said to him: 'Look, I know you're old enough to make up your own mind, but don't get too involved, will you? Remember you're off to university in October. You've worked hard for it, I don't want you to be upset by anything, to have any, you know, regrets, or things pulling you back.'

Julian went over to the Glasses' farm most days. He oversaw the vegetable plots, sawed logs and mended fences. He thought about reglazing the greenhouse, but did not get around to it before it was autumn, and he had to go away.

Ralph worried. Possibly Anna worried, too; but he did not ask her to talk about it. He remembered Julian as a little boy at his first school, unable to tie his shoelaces or learn his times tables or do up his tie. Tears had been shed, about the tie. Julian did not mind that his mum or dad put it on for him, every morning; but there would be PE lessons, and he would have to take it off. Then he would not be able to put it back, he sobbed. And this was the problem: he would have to scramble it into some knot of his own devising, he could not manage the knot that society required; he would have to stretch and mangle it and treat it like a piece of string. Then, he wailed each morning, they would all know he was a spastic.

'You're not a spastic,' Ralph said. 'Is that what they say? It's very naughty of them to call you that.' Ralph felt, when he placed the length of cloth around his child's neck each day, that he was snaring him in a noose.

Then one tear-stained Wednesday afternoon, Kit had taken the situation in hand. She had re-formed the tangled mess which Julian had created, into its approved shape; then simply loosened it, eased it from beneath his collar, and lifted it over his head still knotted. She hung it on the end of his bed. 'There,' she had said. 'Now, in the morning, you see, just put it over your head.'

'Oh yes.' Julian's face lit up. 'Then all I have to do is –'

'Just pull the knot up,' Kit said. 'Here you go.' She fastened his fingers around the short end of the tie. 'Gentle, now – not too tight. That's it. Lovely. Just you wait and see. They'll all be copying you soon.'

Years later, Julian remembered Kit's good idea with a pathetic gratitude. Even now when he was grown up, he said, no one had ever taught him anything so useful. Ralph wished he had thought of it.

He had not known how to help Julian; ordinary patience did not seem to be enough. He was slow to learn to read, slow to tell the time; when he tried to learn to write he seemed to be using a foreign alphabet. Even when he had mastered the letter shapes his progress was slow. He was always stopping to rub out what he had written and start again. His collection of erasers was something he prized. Robin sneaked to his mother that he had names for each one: Mouse and Cat and Mother Bear. Julian fell asleep over his reading books, exhausted by the effort of trying to comprehend them.

They took him for an eye test but his sight was perfect. Anna thought of him as a baby: his eyes always on their way from his mother's face to somewhere else.

Julian had a long memory, longer than seemed possible. One day when he was six he said, where did the cat go, Emma?

'I haven't got a cat,' Emma said.

'But you had, you had Freddie.'

He described the ancient tabby, vast and slow like a sofa on the move, its lop ear, its tail without a tip. Emma was astonished. Freddie had died long ago, before Julian could walk or talk. It was a prodigious feat of memory, truly extraordinary: Emma reported it to Anna and Ralph. Anna said, 'He must have heard him described. I'm sure we've often talked about Freddie.'

Kit was listening. 'Julian does have lots of memories,' she said. 'And so do I. We can remember from before we were born.'

'Don't be silly,' Anna said. 'You know better. No one can do that.'

They plucked Julian out of the village school, saying that they had got him a place in a prep, weathering the scepticism of the headmistress. They kept him at home for a term, feeling guilty about it, and tried to teach him themselves. Mostly he played with bricks, building houses then knocking them down. But he started to look at books, just for the pictures. His fright diminished. Imperceptibly, very slowly and cautiously, he began to read.

The problems were not over; at least, his new teachers did not think so. Hard not to nag such a child, at home and at school. Julian was unpunctual, dreamy, sweetly polite but deeply uncaring. His conversation was intelligent but elliptical. He was seldom on time for anything; he did not seem to see the point of punctuality. Even when he reached his teens, he never wore a watch. 'He's a natural animal,' Kit said. 'He goes by the sun.'

Julian was wary of surfaces, it seemed. When he drew a house he began with its contents. Pots and pans came first, objects in cupboards. Then beds and chairs; only then, walls and doors and windows. When he drew a tree he drew not just the trunk and leaves and branches but the roots, running deep under the soil, beyond the range of normal vision.

By the time he reached his teens Julian had adapted to the world, learned to fit in. Sporadically attentive, he passed just enough exams, with just the grades he needed; and passed them doggedly, until the prospect of university loomed – if that was what he wanted. Ralph tried to interest him in geology, thinking that the strenuous, outdoor aspect of it might appeal. But Julian associated the subject with the wrapped, labelled specimens which Ralph still kept in boxes in the attics. He seemed to have a peculiar horror of them: their broken traces, their dead-and-gone lives. Then Rebecca began to have her nightmares about the fossils. 'You might get rid of them, give them to a museum,' Anna suggested. 'You never look at them.'

True, he thought. I never do. He went up there one weekend, spent a bit of time unwrapping them, labelling them in his mind. There was the devil's toenail, fresh and horrible and impressive as ever, lying cold in his palm and smelling of the sea. Phylum: Mollusca. Class: Pelecypoda. Order: Pterioida. Family: Gryphaeidae. Genus: *Gryphaea*. Species: *arcuata*. Old Nick's remnant ... he knew people, or his father had known people, who maintained that all fossils were planted in the rocks by Satan, to tempt scholars into scientific hypotheses, which led them from the knowledge of God.

He put *arcuata* into his pocket and, downstairs, transferred it to the drawer of his desk. Why not keep it to hand? It was his trophy, taken in the battle for reason.

As soon as he arrived at his university, Julian wrote a long letter to Sandra Glasse. He received a picture postcard two weeks later, showing countryside views, clouds and church towers. He wrote again, asking her to visit him. She didn't answer. He thought that probably she did not have the money for a train ticket; but if he sent the money, would she answer even then? Perhaps his letters were not arriving: perhaps the postman couldn't be bothered to turn down the track.

He wrote to his father: would he consider driving over to the farm to see if everything was all right? His father wrote back in surprise, to say that of course everything was all right; Sandra had been over a couple of times, turned up unexpectedly, hitched lifts, coast road to Fakenham, Fakenham to Bawdeswell, then walked to the house. He didn't like her hitching lifts, in fact he was very upset, but she wouldn't be told. Julian should write to her on that topic. He shouldn't expect much by way of reply, she said she wasn't used to writing letters.

Just before Christmas Julian wrote another letter, to his head of department. Then he packed his bags and took the train to Norwich; then hitched lifts and, changing his suitcase from hand to hand, walked the last few miles from the main road to the Red House. There he had stayed, ever since.

When he was not at the market, or working on the Glasses' small-holding, he was underneath his new car; his old car that is, the one Emma had given him the money to buy. He coaxed it along; it got him to the coast and back. His new skills were undeniably useful; Anna's car was now a barely coherent as-semblage of rattles and squeaks, and the Citroën caused oily boys at garages to titter and roll their eyes and cast their rags to the ground.

144

Then there was the Glasses' Morris Traveller to be rescued from its decrepitude and illegality. He told Ralph about the tax and insurance problem; Ralph immediately handed over some cash that had been earmarked for a new vacuum cleaner and some school clothes for Rebecca. Julian promised to mend the old Hoover; it had value as a technological curiosity, Ralph said, in a year or two they might be able to take it to London and flog it to the Science Museum. Rebecca did not really need new clothes – she would, on the whole, fit into her old ones. With school uniform, it is often heartening if you look a little different from the other girls.

Julian gave the money to Mrs Glasse. No question of paying it back, he said, it wasn't like that. 'I just don't want to think about you being pulled up,' he said, 'or about the police coming round when I'm not here.'

'They'll still come if they want,' Mrs Glasse said. 'You'd be surprised how many offences there are, that a person can commit just without thinking about it. You know, I don't want to take your money. But I can see that you want to give it.'

Even now they were legal, she would only take the car out on market days, she said. There was the problem of money for petrol. 'You can't knit petrol,' she said. 'And they won't let you barter for it.'

He did not tell Sandra about his sister's school uniform, or about the row his parents had when the story came out. Privately, he agreed with his father; it was Anna's fault, it was the fault of her habit of saving bits of money in pots and jars around the house, like some old granny in a cottage. It was too tempting for other people, when they had a prior need.

He did not tell Sandra because he knew she would think the row was ridiculous. She thought his family was rich; she said so.

'Oh, come on,' Julian said. 'There's four of us and none of us has earned anything yet. My mum's a teacher but she had an illness and she hasn't been able to work for years. My dad works for a charity, he doesn't draw a big stipend, he just draws enough to keep us solvent.'

'There you are,' Sandra said. 'Stipend. Solvent. Of course, we're mostly solvent, because we never buy anything if we can help it. Money doesn't enter into our calculations. I learned it in geography, it's the only thing I recall. We're a subsistence economy.'

'I think you're proud of being poor,' Julian said.

'No, we're not proud. We just don't think about it. We just go along.'

'You could get benefits,' Julian said. 'Other people do it.'

'Oh, we know all about that. My mum's been to offices appealing for benefits. Sometimes you get things, other times you don't. The trouble is, they keep you sitting in a waiting room for hours when you could be out trying to earn something. You get coughs and colds from the other people. Last time my mum went they asked her if she had a man friend. She said, better eat turnips all winter than talk to bureaucrats of romance.'

After Julian's own household, constantly full of Visitors and their noisy upsets, the silence and peace of the Glasses' farm was like a convalescence. Only one thing had changed: during his term away, somebody had given them a black-and-white television set. They watched all the soap operas, and discussed them in terms of gentle surprise, as if the characters were people they knew. They explained the characters to him, and he sat with them and watched, predicting the plot developments out loud, as they did. It was something new for him. There was a television set at home, but it was kept in the cold back sitting room, like an impoverished relative whom it was best not to encourage.

Also, they had discovered a big enthusiasm for story-books. When Sandra had been over at the house one day Anna had

146

taken her into Dereham to help with the weekly shopping, and at the secondhand bookstall Sandra had bought a book called *Middlemarch*, with the back off, priced 20p. They called this book 'the book we're reading', and talked about Dorothea all the time, with the same mild interest, the same mild censoriousness. 'That's it,' Mrs Glasse said. 'When you're young you just don't know what you want in life. You've messed everything up before you find out.'

'The die is cast,' said Sandra.

Julian was confused by them. He was only a geographer; that, at least, had been his subject before he ran away. People from other faculties claimed that geography was a subject studied by slightly dim, marginal students, who enjoyed superfluous good health. It might be true: among those few people in his year with whom he had casual conversation, three or four said they were going to be schoolteachers, teach geography and games. He could not imagine teaching children anything – least of all, to kick footballs about or swing from ropes. If he was going to be healthy and stupid, he could do that at home.

So he reasoned. It didn't seem to convince his mother. His father didn't ask him any questions; strangely, though, this seemed to make him like his mother more and his father less. He's not bothered about me, he said to Robin. He can't get me to be a Good Soul, and I'm not enough of a Sad Case. He's only worried about those spotty kids with carrier bags.

Not yet, you're not enough of a Sad Case, Robin said.

One day in February, he went to bed with Sandra, upstairs in her large brass bed. Mrs Glasse, downstairs, carried on knitting. Sandra bled all over the sheets.

'He's drifting – that's all.' Anna said. 'When I ask him what he wants to do with his life, he changes the subject.'

Ralph said, 'He's always been like that. Anyway – is there any point in knowing what you want to do with your life? There are so many things that can go wrong.'

Anna's voice was strained. 'So you just drift with the tide?'

'Remember when he was little,' Ralph said. 'We thought he would never learn to read, never do anything. But we cured him just by letting him be. Those few weeks of peace cured him. If we'd have left him at school, with ignorant infant teachers bawling at him, he'd never have made anything. As it is, he got to university –'

'And passed up his chance,' Anna said. 'And what will happen to him if he gets tied up with Sandra?'

'He could do worse.'

'I'm aware,' Anna said, 'that Sandra is a charity case of yours.'

Ralph said gently, 'I hope we can be charitable. Now that the need exists.'

'Hasn't it always?'

'I mean, in our own family.'

'I suppose I'm not charitable,' Anna said.

Ralph didn't answer. But he thought, I will never be party to bullying and hectoring my children as my father bullied and hectored me.

Julian explained to Sandra and to Mrs Glasse what he had not felt able to explain at home. As he talked, he remembered the place in which he had been stranded, this Midlands place, where mean slivers of sky showed between tower blocks. 'Homesick,' Sandra said. 'Wouldn't you get over it in time?'

She was not vain; it did not seem to enter her head that – partly, anyway – he might have come back for her.

'You don't know anything about it, Sandra,' Mrs Glasse said. 'You've never been away. It's like an illness, that's why it's called homesickness. People don't realize. Are they blaming you, your mum and dad?'

'I couldn't give a reason like homesickness,' Julian said. 'They'd think it was feeble. They weren't that old when they went to South Africa.'

'Did they?' Sandra said. 'I didn't know that.'

'Some people just aren't cut out for travelling,' Mrs Glasse said.

Ralph said to Anna, 'You are right, of course. About Julian. I apologize.' She stared at the spectacle: this sudden attack of public humility. 'I probably ought to find out more about the whole thing,' he said. 'I think, after Easter, I'll go over and see Mrs Glasse.'

SIX

The week after Easter the winds were so violent that they seemed likely to tear up small trees by the roots. There was never a moment, day or night, when the world was quiet.

Mrs Glasse had no telephone, so Ralph couldn't contact her to arrange a time to meet. 'Should I drive over with you?' Anna said.

'No. It would look like a deputation. As if we'd come to complain about her.'

'You wonder what sort of woman she can be,' Anna said. 'Strange life they lead.'

His car joined the coast road at Wells. The sky was patchy, clouds moving fast, rushing above him as he skirted the dusky red walls of Holkham Hall: parting now and then to reveal a pacific blue. The sea was not visible at once; but as the road turned he saw on the broken line of the horizon a strip of grey, indefinite, opaque.

It was ten o'clock when he rattled down the stony incline to the Glasses' house. The door opened before he had switched off the engine. Mrs Glasse stood waiting in the doorway.

His first thought: how young she is, she can't be more than thirty-five, thirty-six. She was pale, straight-backed, red-haired: the hair a deeper red than her daughter's, long and fine. The wind ripped at his clothes as he stepped out of the car, billowing out his jacket like a cloak. 'This weather!' Mrs Glasse said. She smiled at him. 'Hello, Julian's dad.'

It was a low house, old; its bones protested, creaked under the onslaught of the weather. He heard its various sounds, as she stood hesitating inside the door; he thought, it is a house like a ship, everything in movement, a ship breasting a storm. 'On your left there,' Mrs Glasse said. 'Go in the parlour. There's a fire lit, and the kettle's on.'

'You might have been expecting me,' he said.

He sat by the fire, in a Windsor chair, waiting for her to bring them tea. The wind dropped; it was as if a noisy lout had left the room. In the sudden silence he heard the mantel clock ticking. She returned. Handed him a mug. 'I didn't put sugar in. Did you want it? No, I didn't think you were the sugar sort.'

'Goodness,' he said. 'What does that mean?'

She pushed her hair back. 'Sugar's for comfort,' she said.

'You think I don't need comfort?'

Mrs Glasse didn't reply. She pulled up a stool to the fire. Ralph half-rose from his chair; 'Thanks, I'm comfortable here,' she said.

'That clock up there.' Ralph shook his head. 'We had one just like it at home when I was a boy. It was my father's. His pride and joy. He wouldn't let anybody else touch it.'

'You're not going to tell me,' Mrs Glasse said drily, 'that it stopped the day he died?'

'No, not exactly. My mother threw it out.'

'That was extreme.'

'For her, yes, it was. She couldn't stand the chime.'

'Did she ever mention it? In his lifetime, I mean?'

'I shouldn't think so. She was a self-effacing woman. At least, she effaced herself before him.'

She had fine hands, Mrs Glasse; the calloused hands of a woman used to outdoor work, but still white, long-fingered. They were hands that rings might adorn, and that one did adorn: a plain red-gold wedding band, an old ring, one that might have been in a family for generations. Her skin had begun to line a little round the eyes: so many years of looking into the wind. All this he saw in the vibrant light that spilled into the room, morning light: sliding over the cream walls, turning them the colour of butter.

He said, 'We have a problem about Julian. Well, not a problem.'

'A problem, but not a problem,' Mrs Glasse said.

'We thought, Anna and I – Anna, that's my wife – that perhaps he talked to you. He doesn't talk to us.'

'Do you see a reason for that?'

'There's no reason, I hope. It's just his nature.'

'Well then,' Mrs Glasse said placidly. 'If it's his nature, what is there to be done?'

Ralph leaned forward, to engage her attention. 'You see, Julian's never been communicative. And a bit of a drifter – you could call him that. Still, we believe in letting him work things through for himself, at his own pace – we always have pursued that policy.'

'Sandra is the same,' Mrs Glasse said. 'Resistant to direction. Not that I try.'

'Yes . . . so we wondered, Anna and I, if he had said anything to you, about his plans.'

'Plans,' Mrs Glasse said: as if the word were new to her. 'He's not mentioned any. He's done a lot for me, around the place. I don't ask him, he just does it. You can't say he's not industrious. He fills his time.'

'But where's it leading?' Ralph said. 'I can't help but worry.'

There was a pause. They looked into the fire; the flames now were pale as air, the sun drawing their colour out. Only the flicker held their eyes. Tinny, grating, the clock struck the quarter hour. Ralph looked up at it in wonder. The sound seemed to tremble in the air. She laughed. 'You can have it,' she said, 'if it means so much to you.'

He shook his head. 'It's very kind. But no – on the whole I think I share my mother's opinion.'

'Was he a Norfolk man, your father?'

'Oh, yes. From Swaffham originally – but we moved to Norwich when I was a child.'

'A city boy,' Mrs Glasse said. 'Imagine. I've never moved much.'

'Did it belong in your family, this house?'

'Oh, no.' She seemed puzzled. 'Nothing like that.'

'It is a very nice house. Very peaceful. I'm not surprised Julian wants to spend his time here. The dairy, he said –'

'Yes – would you like to look around?' Ralph protested, politely. She got to her feet, put her mug down on the mantelpiece by the clock. She led him into the kitchen, where she and Sandra spent most of their leisure time, their chairs set one either side of the range; led him from there to the dairy, its chaste stone slabs, its chill. The tiles were cracked, and the turning world had stopped beneath their glaze; cows trod forever through squares of blue grass, through fields of blue blossom. She turned to him and smiled. 'Make our own butter is one thing we don't do,' she said, 'but I did have a cow, at one time. Daisy, she was called – that was original, wasn't it? I'd sell milk up at the top of the track there. It's against all the rules, so I had to stop.'

'You're very enterprising,' Ralph said.

'I have a couple of ponies in my top field now, look after them for weekenders. We didn't know anything about horses when we took them on. But they couldn't, we thought, be as complicated as people.'

'And it's worked out?'

'Yes – Sandra has her talents.' She took him back through the hall, up the low-rising stairs. There were four bedrooms, each of them square and neat, each with the same cream walls; and the furniture of dark wood, chests and tallboys, massive and claw-footed. 'All this furniture was my grandmother's,' she said. 'This is Sandra's room.'

'It's like a room in a picture book,' he said. 'Do you know what I mean? The bed.'

'Yes, Sandra made that quilt for herself, it was the first she ever made, I taught her. She's a careful worker, she's slow but she's neat enough. The trouble is, people don't want them. Or they want them, but they won't pay the price, there's months of work in a quilt, People go for something cheap, something run up on a machine. They can't tell the difference. But there is a difference, if you look.'

Downstairs she put the kettle on again. They sat in the kitchen waiting for it; 'I'm a woman who drinks a lot of tea,' she said, as if in apology.

'It occurs to me,' Ralph said, 'it must be worth a bit, this place.'

'I'd never thought about it.'

'Prices are rocketing. You'd be amazed. Would you be interested? I know a good firm of estate agents, old friend of mine but he's dead now. If you follow me.'

'Of course,' she said. 'He'd give me a price from beyond the grave?' She turned her head to him: such pale eyes.

'Actually, he has a son – Daniel, he's an architect, a nice lad, he sees a bit of my daughter Kit. He'd probably come out here for nothing, give you a rough figure, he knows the market as well as anybody. He'd be interested to see the place.'

'But then where would we live?' Mrs Glasse said.

'I thought . . . well, I don't want to intrude, of course, but I know money's a problem. You could buy yourselves a cottage, and you'd have a tidy sum left to invest, and it would give you an income.'

'I could live like a duchess,' Mrs Glasse suggested.

'Well, not quite that.'

'If I had a cottage, I might have to get rid of my ducks and hens. I wouldn't have eggs to sell. Not to mention vegetables.'

'You could get jobs. It would be more secure for you.'

'Oh, we do get jobs sometimes. In the high season. Hunstanton, Burnham Market. We might go and waitress for a week or two. Not that we're good waitresses. We're not used to it.'

He was struck by the slow and thoughtful way in which she spoke, as if she weighed every word. Struck too by how she spoke of her daughter and herself as if they were of the same generation; as if they had one opinion between them, and what one felt, the other felt. She said, 'Sandra and me, we don't mind hard work, nobody could say that. But we prefer to keep each other company at home.'

'You're very close.'

'Aren't you close to your children?'

'I don't know. I like to think I am. But there are so many other things I have to do.'

'I think that parents ought to take care of their children, and that children ought to take care of their parents. That's the main thing, that's what comes first.'

'I've said too much,' he said. 'I didn't mean to interfere. I'm sorry.'

'No, that's all right, you can't help it. You're used to putting people's lives to rights, aren't you, and giving them advice?' She looked up, full into his face. 'God knows, nobody has ever advised me, it might have been better if they had. The thing is, me and Sandra, we manage. Hand to mouth, I know. But there's always something you can do. Sometimes we've gone out house-cleaning. And I know where the best blackberries are. At Brancaster – I could get you some this year. We get basketfuls, we bake pies, blackberry and apple, use our own apples, sell them up there on the road.' She shrugged. 'There's always something.'

'I admire you, Mrs Glasse,' Ralph said. 'You live the kind of life you believe in.'

She looked down, and blushed. 'What is it, Ralph? Don't you?'

The Easter holidays ended. Kit went back to London for her last few weeks. Robin began the term at his day school in Norwich; early mornings still so chilly, getting up in blue light to walk a mile to the crossroads and wait for the first bus. His efforts would be rewarded, his parents thought. Robin wanted a place at medical school, and would get it. Yet he seemed to have no humanitarian concerns. He marked off the seasons by a change of games kit; now, spring having arrived, he tossed his hockey stick up in the attics and packed his cricket bag. Weekends saw him bussed about the county, playing away. Sunday nights he bounced, or trailed, back: sad tales of full-length balls on the off-stump, or glory sagas that put colour in his cheeks and made him look like his father when his father was young: sixty-five off the first twenty overs, he would say, and then we accelerated, run-a-ball, finished it off just after tea with five wickets in hand. 'Do you know what Robin's talking about?' Anna would say – deriving a pale routine gratification from the child's health and simplicity, from his resemblance to the other boy she had once known.

'Good God, I was nothing like Robin,' Ralph would say. 'My father thought cricket was High Church. Do you think he'll ever do any work when he goes away? Suppose he became a heart surgeon, and he had to do a transplant, and there was a Test Match on?'

But Emma would say, speaking from experience, 'Robin will make a good doctor. Only half his mind will be on his work. That will limit the damage he can do.'

And Rebecca? She rode off on her bike, on the first day of term, to her school two or three miles away; a flouncy, sulky, pretty little girl, who had reached the stage when her family embarrassed her. Soon her embarrassment was to be compounded.

On the Monday morning, the week after term began, Julian came down to the kitchen with his car keys in his hand. 'I'll run you,' he said to her. 'Put your bike in the shed.'

Rebecca dropped her spoon into her cornflakes, spattering milk on the table. 'Suddenly so kind,' she said. 'But how will I get home, sir?'

'I'll collect you.'

'In your so-called car?'

'Yes.'

'But I don't want you to.'

'Beks, life's not just a matter of what you want.'

Rebecca sat up and looked pert. 'Yours seems to be.'

Julian was not drawn. 'Hurry up now, finish your breakfast,' he said. 'Don't argue.'

'What will my friends say when they see me turn up in that thing?' She popped her eyes and pointed, to show what her friends would do. 'They'll take the piss all week. I'll be a social outcast, a – what is it? Not a parishioner – you know what I mean.'

'A pariah,' Julian said. 'Come on now, girl.'

Rebecca saw that he was serious; about what, she didn't know. She turned to her mother, wailing. 'Mum, I don't have to go with him, do I?'

Anna was loading towels from a basket into her temperamental and aged twin-tub washing machine. 'Let Julian take you. It's kind of him. It's a nasty morning, very cold.'

Sulking, Rebecca zipped herself into her anorak and picked up her lunchbox and followed him out. 'When we get there you can stop round the corner, out of sight . . .' she was saying, as the back door slammed behind them.

When Julian got back, Ralph was on the phone to London, defusing the latest crisis at the hostel. The office door was ajar, and Julian could hear snatches of the conversation. 'What occurs to me,' Ralph was saying, 'is that she won't be able to buy much with our petty cash, with the street price what it is, so what will she do to get the rest of the money?' An anxious babbling came back down the line. In the kitchen the washing machine rocked and danced over the flagstones, in a creaking thumping gavotte.

Anna was sitting at the kitchen table. She looked up from the *Eastern Daily Press*. 'What was all that, Julian?'

Julian began to cut himself a slice of bread to make toast. 'It's been on my mind,' he said abruptly. 'That little girl in Devon, Genette Tate – do you remember, it was in the papers?'

'The child who disappeared?'

'They found her bike in a lane. She was thirteen. Some man took her away. They think she's dead.'

Ralph came in. 'Going to be one of those days,' he said. 'That child, Melanie – do you remember I mentioned her? Swallows every banned substance she can lay her hands on, ran away from her foster parents, absconded from the children's home?'

'What's new?' Anna said tiredly. 'Don't they all do that?'

'Just got her off a shoplifting charge last week. Now she's run away and taken our petty cash. Not that she'll get far on it. So I was thinking . . . could we have her here for part of the summer?'

'That's not really a question, is it?' Anna said. 'It's a command.'

'She really needs, you see, to be part of a normal family for a while.'

'And this is normal?' She rested her forehead on her hand, smiling. 'Yes, Ralph, of course we can have her, we must have her, poor little thing.'

'I heard what you were saying just now,' Ralph said to Julian. He put his hand on his son's head, lightly. 'What's sparked this off?'

'I told you. Well, I told Mum. This little girl in the West Country. I keep thinking about it.'

'But it was Devon. It's miles away.'

'Use your imagination,' Julian said. 'Crimes breed other crimes. People copy them.'

'Rebecca rides to school in a crowd. And back in a crowd. You ought to get behind them in a car, then you'd see.'

'Yes, but when she turns off the main road, she's on her own for half a mile, isn't she? It's not fair, it's not safe.' He moved his head irritably, pulling away from his father. 'So I've made up my mind. If either of you will drive her, odd days, that's OK. Otherwise I will. She's my sister. I'm not prepared to take a chance.'

Anna looked up. 'And will you be her escort for life, Julian? Thirteen-year-olds are at risk, but then so are eighteen-year-olds. So are forty-year-olds. You hear of battered grannies, don't you?'

'Anna,' Ralph said, 'there's no reason to be sarcastic. It's just, the trouble is, Julian, if everyone thought like you no one would ever let their children out of the house.'

'OK,' Julian said. 'So you think it's unreasonable? Look, let me tell you something. Ten years ago a boy vanished near Fakenham, he was eleven, he went up the road to see his friend and he never came back. The same year a girl was riding her bike along a track near Cromer – what do you think, is that close enough to home? April, she was called, and she was Rebecca's age exactly. She set off to go to her sister's house at Roughton. A man driving a tractor saw her, four hundred yards from her house, six minutes past two in the afternoon. At a quarter past two, three men who were mapping for the Ordnance Survey saw her bike in a field. There was no trace of her. She was six hundred yards from home. Nobody's seen her since.'

His face set, he waited for their protests to begin. But his father only said, barely audible, his eyes on the table: 'You've been studying these cases. Why is that?'

'I can't explain any more than I have.'

'I can't say you're wrong. It is a dangerous world, of course.'

'There'll be an argument every morning,' Anna said. 'I don't know what to say. I don't know what to say to you, Julian.'

'I'm going over to Sandra's now.' He glanced back from the doorway. Anna was gathering plates, noisily.

'Help me, please, Ralph.' Her tone was wounded, ragged. Ralph scraped his chair back. He began to clear the table slowly, with deliberation, his eyes on a plate, then a cup: anywhere, but not on Anna's face.

Two days later Ralph went back to see Mrs Glasse. His frame of mind was exhausted, distressed; he found it difficult to be in the same room with Anna.

Rebecca moaned and squalled; her social life was being ruined, she said. Julian explained patiently that he would drive her wherever she wanted to go; he would pick up her friends too, and see them all safe home. 'I don't want you on my back,' she snapped; Anna watched her without speaking, her face set and tense. Rain slashed against the windows; the air was thin, green, shivering towards summer. I must give the family a breathing space: that was the excuse Ralph made to himself.

And besides, he had been thinking of Amy Glasse. She was continually on his mind; she had established a hold over it, he felt, and he needed to see her again to break the hold, reduce her to an ordinary woman, naive, limited, down-at-heel. He remembered her in the doorway of the farmhouse, those white long-fingered hands flying up to drag back her hair. He thought of the dull gleam of her red-gold wedding ring, and of the curve of her mouth.

It was a finer day than on his last visit: a verdant dampness, a fresh breeze, the promise of a fine afternoon. The holiday caravans were beginning to take to the roads, and behind their flowered curtains, caught back coyly, you could catch glimpses of the owners and their miniaturized lives. Soon the coast road would be nose to tail with cars, each one with its freight of fractious children bawling, elbowing each other, complaining of hunger and boredom and heat.

Again, Mrs Glasse was waiting for him in the doorway. 'I heard the car,' she explained.

'Yes, it does have a distinctive note.'

He stood looking up at the sky. 'Good day to be alive.'

'Yes. When you consider the alternative.'

'I was passing,' he said. 'I thought, it's lunchtime. I wondered if I could take you out, you and Sandra.'

'Sandra's not here. She's gone cleaning out some holiday flats in Wells, getting them ready for the visitors starting.'

'Well then – just you?'

She dropped back from the doorway. 'Come in.' She glanced down at her jeans. 'I'd better have a word with my fairy godmother, hadn't I?'

'You don't need to dress up – I thought, just a pub lunch or something?'

'Give me five minutes.'

When she came back she was wearing a different pair of

jeans, faded but clean and pressed, and a white shirt open at the neck. She had let down her hair and brushed it out; it fell over her shoulders to the small of her back. The sunlight made it liquid. It was the colour of the cream sherry that his father's friends, with guilty abandon, had sipped each Christmas: 'Just half a glass for me, Mr Eldred.' He picked up a strand of it, ran it through his fingers; she stood passive, like a kindly animal. 'It reminds me of something,' he said.

'Something good?'

'Something sad.'

They drove along the coast. Past Brancaster the sea encroached on their view, its grey line fattening. They stopped at a small hotel he knew, whose windows looked out over the reedbeds and marshes. They were the first lunchers. A girl brought them a menu. 'Drink?' she asked.

'I'll have whisky,' Mrs Glasse decided. Two tumblers were fetched, set side by side by considerate fingers. A small wood fire burned in a stone hearth, sighing with its own life; its heart palely burning, but the logs at its margins charred from ash-grey to white, from wood to dust. Parrot tulips stood on a dresser; their stems drooped, and the vivid flowerheads seemed to swarm away from the vase, hurtling into the air.

'They have lobster today,' Ralph said. 'Would you like that?'

'Thank you, but I couldn't touch it,' Mrs Glasse said. 'I have an ingrained dislike of animals with shells. My husband was a crab fisherman, he worked out of Sheringham. Well, the life must have palled. I haven't seen him for sixteen years.'

'Sandra would have been — how old, two?'

She nodded. 'But he wasn't Sandra's father.' She looked up. 'Are you shocked?'

'Oh, God, Amy — it would take a lot more than that to shock me. I don't lead a sheltered life, you know.'

'When Sandra told me about you at first I thought you did. I

162

said to her, what does Julian's father do for a living? She said, "He goes about doing good." I thought you were a clergyman.'

'I would have been, I suppose, if things had been a bit different. It would have pleased my family. But I wasn't concerned to please them, when I was a boy.'

'But you were a missionary, weren't you? It just shows how ignorant I am – until Julian explained to me I thought all missionaries were clergymen.'

'Oh no, you get doctors, teachers – just people who are generally useful. We didn't go around converting people.'

'They'd been converted already, I suppose.'

'Yes, largely. But we weren't like missionaries in cartoons. We didn't have a portable organ, and shout "Praise the Lord!"'

'I'm glad not to have to picture it.' Her smile faded. 'But Julian told me, you know – about you being put in prison.'

Ralph nodded. 'It was nothing,' he said: writing off the second worst thing that had ever happened to him.

'Julian's very proud of you.'

'Is he? We never talk about it.'

'No. He said you don't like to.'

'All that part of our lives, we prefer to forget it, Anna and me. It's – we've closed the door on it.'

'Did they treat you very badly, when you were in prison?'

'No. I told you, it was nothing. If it had been very bad we would have come home after we were released, but we didn't, you see, we went north, we went up to Bechuanaland. We stayed on.'

'It's a bit of a mystery. To Julian. He wonders why you won't talk about it. He builds reasons, in his head.'

'Kit went through a phase, you know how children do – she wanted to make us into heroes. She couldn't understand why I didn't go on marches, join Anti-Apartheid, sit down in the road in front of the South African Embassy.'

163

'And why don't you?'

'Because it's more complicated than they think, witless people parading around with their banners. I get sick of them using South Africa to make themselves feel good. Being so bloody moral about a country they've never seen, about the lives of people of whom they know nothing. Especially when there is so little morality in their own lives.'

'I didn't mean to upset you.'

Ralph shook his head. 'Sorry, I get – well, I lose my patience. I'm sure it is a mystery, to the children.'

'You've not been open with them, have you?'

'No.' He picked up his glass and drank off his whisky and asked for another.

They ate their ham and chicken and baked potatoes, and he turned the conversation, from past to the present, parents to children. He was curious about her life but he could not expect her to reveal anything, when he had been so obstinately unrevealing himself. They ordered some chocolate mousse and some coffee and another whisky, and then she said, 'Better get on with the day, I suppose.'

He drove her home. As he prepared to turn down the incline to the house a police car pushed its snout into the road. Its two occupants, carefully expressionless, turned to look at Mrs Glasse. One of them spoke to the other. Ralph waited for them to pull out. After a moment they did so, and drove away.

'It's a good thing I don't have a gun,' Amy said, 'or I'd probably have shot that pair by now. They're always grubbing about round here. They made sure they took a good look at you.'

'Is it because you had that trouble with your tax disc?'

She looked sideways at him. 'Ralph, you gave me the money. Thank you.'

'No, I – no, forget it, I wasn't trying to remind you or anything.'

'What it is, it's because we do the markets, me and Sandra. They think we're receiving. Stolen goods, I mean.'

'And are you?'

'Would I tell you if I were?'

'I would like to know.'

'For your son's sake,' Amy said, finishing his thought for him. 'Well, I can understand that. But you can put your mind at rest. Do you think I'm stupid? I know they watch me. Do you think I want to see Sandra dragged in front of a court?'

'No. I'm sorry.'

'I couldn't go to gaol. Not like you. Anna must be a very brave woman, it seems to me. I'd bash my head against the bars until they let me out or it killed me.'

'If they're harassing you, you must tell me. I can make a complaint.'

'And where would you be when the complaint came home to roost?' She smiled, to take the offence out of the words. 'Come in. I'll make us another cup of coffee.'

'Better not. I ought to get on.'

If she'd said, do come, do, it will only take five minutes, he would have agreed. He wanted to be persuaded. But she said, 'OK, I know you must be busy.' She opened the car door. 'I did like that, it was a treat for me, a change. Nobody ever takes me out.' She leaned back into the car, kissed his cheek. 'Thanks, Ralph.'

He said nothing. Drove away.

Three weeks passed, in which he sometimes returned. On each occasion, he made sure his son was somewhere else.

Ten o'clock, a blustery morning, Daniel Palmer at the back door: he did not like to turn up uninvited, but this morning he had prepared an excuse. 'Hello, Kit. So you're home for good.'

'I'm home for the summer,' she said.

'How did the finals go?'

She shrugged. He followed her into the kitchen. 'Me and Jule have just put the kettle on,' Kit said; not ungraciously, but so that Daniel would realize that no special effort was to be made on his behalf.

'How are you, Julian?' Julian nodded. Daniel began to take off his new acquisition, his riding mac; it was a complex coat, with many flaps and buckles, and pockets in unlikely places. 'Been over to Wood Dalling to look at that barn,' he said, 'you know the one? For a conversion. Get four beds out of it.'

'If you must,' Julian said.

Kit raised her eyebrows at him.

Julian said, 'They put in windows where no windows should be, and doors where no doors should be.'

'What do you expect people to do?' Kit said. 'Go in and out of the big doors, as if they were cart-horses? And live in the dark?'

'Of course, you would side with your boyfriend,' Julian said.

'He's not my boyfriend.'

'Look,' Daniel said easily, 'I take your point, but the alternative to conversion is to let the barn fall down.'

'At least that would be honest.'

'I don't understand it,' Daniel said, 'this reverence for the original. Because it's not, you see. I've looked into it, its history. The whole roof pitch was altered sometime in the 1880s. Probably that's when it began to fall down. For the last hundred years it's been patched up anyhow.'

Julian thought of this crumbling barn, of its roof: lichened, sway-backed, with its many mottled and graduated shades. 'It seems right,' he said, 'however it got that way. It's been that way as long as I've been seeing it.'

'I suppose we tend to exaggerate antiquity,' Kit said. 'Take, for instance, Daniel's coat.'

'Make sure you do it properly, then,' Julian said.

'Are you setting up as a vigilante, Julian? A barn warden?'

'Something like that.' He turned to Kit. 'I'm off to Sandra's now.'

'Where else?' Kit said.

Daniel said, when he'd gone, 'He doesn't like me much, your brother.'

'Oh, he likes you all right. He thinks you're a visually illiterate money-grubbing poseur, but he likes you. More coffee? Ginger nut?' Kit rattled the biscuit tin at him, aggressively. 'Come on, don't take it to heart. None of us likes any of us at the moment. Julian insists on taking Becky to school every day and fetching her back, because he's decided there are kidnappers about.'

'Kidnappers? What, the mafia or something?' Daniel smiled. 'After robbing Becky's pencil case, are they?'

'Nobody can talk sense into him. Becky's driven mad with it. She calls his car his "so-called car", and says she'd rather he walked her to school in those reins they put on toddlers. She keeps on at Mum and Dad to call him off but they won't. The more tantrums she throws, the more silent they go. We think, me and Robin, that they must have had a big row about something, but we can't work it out, because they never have a row, never.'

'All couples do. Surely.'

'That's what you read in magazines,' Kit said. 'But my parents are the exception to the rule. My father is so bloody saintly it would make you sick, but the trouble is it's real, it's all real. My mother has bad tempers but they're over in a minute. You can see her, you know, getting worked up – and then she has second thoughts, and then she's saintly too.'

'Well – how can you live up to it?' Daniel said.

'Precisely. That is what I ask myself.'

'Is that why you're so depressed?'

'Am I? I suppose I am.'

'You haven't made any plans yet? About going away?'

'No.' She put down her coffee mug. 'I'm getting like Julian,' she said. '*Mañana*. Couldn't give a toss.'

'It would suit me if you stayed around,' Daniel said. 'But you know that, Kit.'

He waited for some cross-patch response: I'm not here to suit you, am I? Instead she said, 'Suppose – well, I've sent off for forms – suppose I went to Africa?'

'Like your parents?'

'Yes, but I wouldn't go for a church group.'

'Too many strings attached?'

'Yes. And also I don't believe in anything.'

'I see. You pretend, do you?'

She pushed her hair back, restless and bothered. 'It doesn't arise. I'd not like to hurt people.'

'You don't feel you should stand up and be counted?'

'What – in the cause of atheism? Not much of a cause, is it? Better be a barn warden. It means more.'

'Yes, I see that. But you'd go as a volunteer, would you?'

'I could offer. They might not want me. I think they only want qualified people, engineers and well-diggers and so on. I could teach English, perhaps.'

'You've never mentioned this before.'

'No.' She looked at him balefully. 'I don't mention every thought in my head.'

'Have you talked to your parents?'

'I've talked to nobody, except you. Oh, and Robin, I did mention it to Robin, but he was practising his forward defensive in front of the wardrobe mirror, and I don't think he heard me.'

Daniel smiled, flicked a hand at his head. 'He's out of it, Robin.'

'Still, you can try your thoughts on him. Voice them. Feel

them on the air. See if they sound too unreasonable before you present them to the rest of the human race.'

'To me it doesn't seem unreasonable, though naturally I . . . from the purely selfish point of view . . . the thing is, why do you want to go?'

'Because I dream about it,' Kit said. 'Most nights, now. Sorry if that sounds stupid. But there's really no other reason I can give.'

He frowned. 'Good or bad dreams?'

'Neither. They have atmosphere. They don't have events. You know that kind?'

'Not really,' Daniel lied. 'I seldom remember my dreams.'

'Oh, bloody men!' Kit said. 'I think they're a lower form of life. They exist in an eternal present, like dogs and cats.'

'Look, I think I ought to get on.' Daniel moved to the edge of his chair and began to do something with one of his flaps and buckles.

'Of course,' Kit said. 'Don't pause for ostentatious consulta-tion of your Cartier. Good God, a woman may be about to speak of her feelings! Gosh, it must be late! Better run!'

Daniel smiled: meekly, sheepishly. Bowed a little, at the kitchen door. 'May I call again, Miss Katherine?'

Kit shook her hair, made a low growling noise. Daniel clicked the door shut as he went. Kit sat back in her chair, her arms around herself. She found she had tears in her eyes. She did not understand this.

Kit had been at home for many days now. It had been the usual arrangement – Emma collected her at the station at Norwich. It was a way of easing herself back into the family, her tea with Emma. But Emma seemed preoccupied and in low spirits. 'What's the matter?' Kit asked. She misses Felix, she thought; she must be lonely.

When she walked into the Red House, the atmosphere hit her at once. 'Hit' was the wrong word; seeped into her, that was more like it. It was a cold fog of dismay; her first impression was that something was happening, slowly and stupidly, which the people concerned could not comprehend.

It sapped her strength, whatever it was; she was tired, desperately tired. She had left London healthy enough, only dogged by that usual feeling of anti-climax the end of exams brings. After this, you think, after my papers are over, I will do, and I will do . . . and then you don't. You are a shell, enclosing outworn effort. You expect a sense of freedom, and yet you feel trapped in the same old body, the same drab routines; you expect exhilaration, and you only feel a kind of habitual dullness, a let-down, a perverse longing for the days when you read and made notes and sat up all night.

But now, she had gone beyond this disappointed state. A new exhaustion made her shake at any effort, mental or physical. She discovered the curious, unsung, regressive pleasure of going to bed while it is still light. She moved her bed, so that it faced the window. She found herself two extra pillows, and composed herself against them. Eyes open, she watched the sky rush past, and the birds wheel and swoop.

Anna brought her food on trays: a boiled egg, an orange carefully peeled and divided, thin cinnamon biscuits warm from the oven. 'Don't,' Kit said. 'Don't bother. Really.' It was a strange comfort to her to go past the point of hunger; she had never been a thin girl, particularly, so she knew she wasn't going to waste away.

But it pleased her to push her situation to extremes. She fantasized that she was dying. She was old, very feeble, very weak. Her life was draining from her. But she had *lived*. She had no regrets, her will was made, and nothing was left undone. She was dying in the odour of sanctity. And indeed she was more and more tired, as if a lifetime's fatigue had banked up behind her eyes ... perhaps, she thought, I have glandular fever, some special disease suited to my time of life ...

She slept then, only to be roused by the sounds of the house below as it woke up for the evening: the shrilling of the telephone, the crunch and scrape as the family cars ground home, the slamming of doors and clattering of pans for dinner, the hard stony shower of coal going into the range; and Robin's feet stampeding upstairs to the next floor, Julian after him, sometimes Sandra Glasse's high clear voice from the kitchen: 'Shall I scrape the carrots, Anna?'

Home life. Sandra had been the first person she saw when her aunt dropped her at the gate. The girl was by the side of the house, with a laundry basket. As Kit stepped out of the car she saw Sandra stretch up to peg on the washing line the white nightdress – chaste, elaborately pin-tucked – which Daniel had given her as a present the previous Christmas. Sandra's cheeks were flushed from exertion and the wind. She looked very pretty. 'Your mother lent it,' she said. 'I stayed over. I hope you don't mind. I'll iron it and it will be just as nice as you left it. I'm a good ironer.'

Kit's brows had drawn together. 'Have it, if you want,' she said. 'Another bit of Daniel's ersatz tat.'

She'd hauled her bags into the house, and then sat in the kitchen for an hour, brushing off Sandra's attempts to look after her, to scramble some eggs, to drag luggage upstairs; not even making tea for herself, or going to the lavatory, or washing the metropolitan grime off her face. She seemed unable to do anything to bridge this gap between her former life and the life that was to come.

Then the days passed; she felt ill, a vague, nameless malaise. A white space seemed to grow around her, a vacancy. She felt that it was she who should be able to diagnose and treat the unease in the house, the sudden deficit of happiness, its draining away.

In time, as she knew he would, her father made occasion for a talk. He wanted a talk; she had nothing to say. But she had to decide soon whether she would go back to London to work for the Trust. Live in the hostel: get on democratically with all sections of society: not use expressions like 'ersatz tat'. Not make judgements on people.

'I don't want to push you,' her father said. 'We've given Julian leeway – I don't want you to think that we're discriminating against you. But you see, I have a list of applications from people who want a job, they want the experience before they do social-work courses –'

'Yes,' Kit said. 'I'm being selfish.' She combed her fingers through her long hair. He remembered Emma doing that, years ago, in Norwich. 'You see, Dad, up to a point it's easy. You go to school. You go to university. You don't have any thoughts, from day to day. You just do what's expected of you. Then somebody asks you to make a choice and you find yourself . . . slowly . . . grinding . . . to a halt. That's how I am.' She started to plait her hair now, loosely winding, looping. 'I'm a mechanism winding down.'

'A life crisis,' Ralph said.

'Yes, I should have known there'd be some jargon for it.'

'I'm sorry. But that's what it is.'

'Have you ever had one?'

'Oh, several, I'd say. The first when I was seventeen or so . . .'

'When you had the row with Granny and Grandad.'

'Yes . . . well, you know all about that. For months after it I felt as if I were walking around in fog. It was a kind of depression, suffocation – very disabling, because all the time I wasn't taking decisions for myself other people were taking them for me. That's how I ended up in teaching, for which, God knows, by temperament I am not suited.'

'Aren't you? I'd have thought you'd have been a good teacher.'

'No . . . Teachers need all sorts of large certainties.'

She looked at him in arrogant disbelief. 'And you don't have them?'

'Good God, do you think of me as a person who would have?'

'It's the impression you've given. I mean, you seem to believe in your work, for instance. And in, well, family life, and God, and the Labour Party by and large – the whole package, really.'

'The package.' He thought about it. 'I'd not deny that my own father believed in a package. But I dare hope his package seems more stupid than mine?'

She smiled. 'Yes, to be a creationist and to have family rows about Darwinism . . . yes, it does seem stupid. Victorian.'

'So it seemed to me. Even then. But we've always been behind the times in Norfolk.'

'You should have stood up to them,' she said.

'Not that easy, Kit. There were penalties they could impose. People bullied other people, in those days.'

It was his oblique way of telling her that she had nothing to fear; not from him, anyway. 'You must rest,' he said. 'Then when you have rested, think. And then you will know how you want to go on with your life.'

She didn't mention Africa, this idea she had. Better not; she was afraid of touching some well-spring of unhappiness. One night lately, walking the house in the small hours, she had found Robin alone in the cold back sitting room where the television skulked.

'Test Match highlights,' he explained. 'Just finished. I was off to bed. Want a coffee?'

She nodded; sat down on a chair, picked at its upholstery,

173

said, 'Do you know, in any other family this chair would be put out for the dustmen to take.'

'I'd never noticed it,' Robin said.

'You're just like your father. Don't you ever see how shabby we are? How poor?'

'We're not poor.' Robin was indignant. 'Mrs Glasse and Sandra, they're poor. Beks was laughing at Sandra because she said, "Do you like my skirt, I got it in a charity shop."'

'Beks is a brat. She knows nothing. When you're that age you think you're sensitive – well, I did, I remember. But you're about as sensitive as a bouncer in a nightclub.'

'What would you know about nightclubs?'

'As much as a child of two saints should know.' She looked up. 'What about that coffee?'

When Robin brought it back – modern coffee, grey and tepid and sugarless – she asked him, 'But do you know what I mean? Mum works so hard to keep the house going, with that furnace to be fed, and that demented twin-tub, and that antique Hoover. All Dad does is bring home hulking great hall-stands from Yarmouth, and then beam on us like Jehovah and think he's done his duty by us. Don't you ever wonder why we have to be good all the time, why we have to have such tender consciences, why we have to have these Visitors every summer?'

'We'll be getting some new Visitors soon,' Robin said. 'Morlocks, Yahoos, slags and tarts.'

'Why can't we be normal, and self-absorbed, and acquisitive?'

Robin's eyes were fixed on the blank television screen. 'Haynes 184,' he said thoughtfully. 'Hit out to all parts of the ground. Viv Richards 145. God help England. I don't know, Kit. If you want to be acquisitive, why don't you marry Daniel?'

'He hasn't asked me, and I don't want to get married. Anyway, it's not a career. What do you think this is, the era of W. G. Grace?'

'I wish it were.' Robin sighed. 'So . . . what are you going to do then? Slope about getting on everybody's nerves?'

'Do I do that?'

'No, but fuck it – there's Julian living out his rustic fantasies, and Becky with a mental age of seven, and nobody but me with any sense of purpose these days.'

'Oh, sure,' Kit said. 'Jack the Lad, aren't you? On with the hockey pads. On with the cricket pads. Why don't you take up schoolboy boxing and then you can get a padded helmet too? With that on you'd be totally impervious to life.'

They sat in silence, Robin slumped on the sofa, Kit curled into the chair, her legs drawn up into the skirt of her chain-store nightdress, which was too tight under the arms, and neither short nor long. 'All these questions, Robin. I've never had a sensible discussion with you before.'

'And you aren't now.'

'But you do have thoughts?'

'Yes.'

'Such as?'

'Such as why are we so miserable these days? Creeping around Julian and his obsessions.'

'You'd think Dad would laugh him out of it.'

'He doesn't seem disposed to laugh.' Robin turned his head back to the TV screen. 'West Indies 518.' He looked glum. 'Only rain can save us now. What was that you were saying the other day, about going to Africa?'

'Yes. I mean it.'

'Do you want to do what they did, is that it?'

'Perhaps.'

'Why, do you admire it?'

'How can I? I have no information, do I? I don't have a basis, to admire or not admire. Oh, I know about them going to prison – but even Emma won't say much, and so you wonder what really happened and whether they . . .'

'Were tortured,' Robin said.

She gazed at her brother. 'I've never been able to say it.'

'It is hard to say. I've practised.'

'But then again I ask myself, why were they there in the first place? It was only a kind of colonialism. I put that to Dad once, but he said, we did what seemed right at the time. And I know he is good, he is practical, he does help people now and I expect he helped them then. But what use would I be?'

'If you go off to some place in Africa,' Robin said, 'it won't be to do something for the country, it will be to do something for yourself.'

'Do you know what frustrates me?' she said. 'That I was born there, in Bechuanaland – Botswana, it is now – but I don't have any memories.'

When she thought of Africa she thought of a clean place, full of light and air, the sun so hot that everything was sterilized, scoured clean by its glare. When she saw the pitiful babies on the famine posters it damaged the image she held inside. She did not know what to think when she saw the pictures from South Africa: glum men in suit jackets and woollen hats, trudging by railway tracks, and smoke blowing into a granite sky.

'I do remember one thing,' she said. 'No, two things really. The first thing I remember is the feeling of heat.'

'Hardly strange,' Robin said.

'Yes, it seems obvious – but do you think that your body has memories that your mind doesn't have access to?' She thought, heat seemed knitted into me; it was as if the sun were moulded into my flesh. 'Even now, I'm surprised if I'm cold. It seems unnatural, it doesn't seem right.' She paused, looking up at him to see if he was following her. 'There is another thing, a little thing – we had a nurse, I asked Mum and she said her name was

Felicia. She used to carry me on her back. I remember my cheek pressed between her shoulder-blades, the feel of it, the heat of her skin through her dress. Isn't that funny? I must have been very small. And then I remember Julian – I must have been older then, and I must have been in my cot or somewhere – I remember seeing Julian on her back, being carried the same way, with his head turned sideways, and fat legs dangling down. And knowing exactly what he felt – your head skewed against her spine, the bone at your . . .' she hesitated, 'your temple, I suppose, though you didn't have such words, that feeling of each separate bone in her spine, and skin against hot skin, just this layer of cotton between.'

'That's odd,' Robin said.

'Yes.'

'I mean – because Julian wasn't born in Africa.'

'Surely,' Kit said. 'Because I saw him.'

'No. You can't have. Add it up. Count on your fingers. Julian was born after they came home.'

'Who then? Who do I remember?'

A silence. They turned it over in their minds. Kit thought, I do remember Felicia: her skin smelled of onions and harsh soap. Robin said, 'Perhaps you remember wrong. You were a baby yourself. Perhaps you think you remember, but you've made it up.'

She shook her head. 'No, I'm not wrong. Could it have been a neighbour's child? That must have been it. But what neighbours? I've asked them, you know, what was it like? They've always said, it was very remote, there was only us.'

'Insofar as they've said anything.' Robin yawned, threw out his arms; but she had his attention, he was listening to her now, and this was an act, which said, I wish to distract myself from the thought in my head. 'Don't you think it must have been Felicia's child?' he asked. 'Her own baby?'

'No,' she said. 'Not Felicia's child, a white child. It was Julian. Surely?'

Again, a silence. Then Robin got up and went to the kitchen and made more coffee for them, and brought it back, cool and comfortless as the first mug had been, put it into Kit's hands. Kit said, 'Do you remember Joan? That woman who cut her wrists in the kitchen?'

'No. When was that?'

'You'd be six, maybe seven.'

'There, you see,' Robin said cautiously. 'I ought to remember. Memory's odd, it doesn't work like it should. It's unreliable.'

'I think they kept it from you,' Kit said. 'You'd be out playing somewhere.'

'What happened?'

'I bandaged her up. Then she disappeared – took her things and went. I often wondered where she ended up.'

'Dad probably knows.'

'Yes.' Kit sighed. 'We labour in his shadow. At least, that's what I was telling Daniel. Or something of that sort.'

They sat on until it was three o'clock and they were stiff with cold, Kit sunk into her own thoughts, and Robin into his; then without a word they stirred, stretched, rose from their chairs. At the top of the stairs, Kit said, 'Robin, another area of mystery is this. The heart complaint. Mum's heart complaint that she's supposed to have. I used to wonder why, if she had heart trouble, she never seemed ill. But do you think it might have been the other kind of heart complaint? Like when people say "she has a broken heart"?'

Robin shivered, not from cold. 'Surely, not that bad?'

'No.' Kit's face was sombre. 'But of that order.'

Robin kissed his sister on the cheek. They parted without a word, crept into cold beds, slept at once.

*

Afternoon: on the beach at Brancaster, Ralph stretched out a hand to Amy Glasse, as if without his help she could not stand in the wind. 'I used to bring Billy here,' she called. 'Billy, my dog.' Stones and pebbles flew from under their feet.

It was high summer now. The sky was an inverted lapis bowl. Away from the sea, below the dunes and marram grass, a few families huddled behind wind-breaks. Family dogs trembled by them, constrained by habit of obedience, quivering with a passion for the stones and air and waves. 'Imagine when the seas were warm.' Ralph pulled her to his side. 'There were tropical reefs. But in those days, there were no people to enjoy the sun.'

On the beach at Cromer they have found the bones of bison, the antlers of wild deer, the skeletal remains of wild horses. There were elephants at East Runton, bears at Overstrand; there were wild boars living at West Runton. Think of this, he tells her, as you watch the caravans roaming over the hills, as you catch the reek of onions from the sea-front hot-dog stalls.

'I found something as a boy,' he said. She pressed close to his side to catch his words. 'A fossil. *Gryphaea*.'

'What's that?'

He traced the curve into her palm. He did not tell her what the balaclava man had called it; didn't want the devil to come between them.

'A shell. Very old?' Pale eyes looked into his. 'Will we find one today?'

'It wasn't here – it was near Whitby. I never found anything as good again.'

'It's luck,' she said.

She put her hand in his. He felt her loose wedding ring snag against his palm. His son had made a kite and flown it that weekend on the heath near Holt; the kite was called 'The

Sandra Glasse'. But Sandra was a child, and trifles amused her, and you cannot give a woman wood and canvas and the slight prospect of rising above the weather. Amy belonged to this coast; its jewels are jasper, moss agate, chalcedony. She should have jet from striped cliffs, to make a mourning ring for the life that was. And amber, next March; it is washed ashore, it waits for the lucky, it is tangled with the seaweed thrown up by the spring gales.

'Enough,' she said. She wrapped her arms about herself, a parody of the athlete in pain. 'I've walked far enough.' He held her upright, gathering her hair into one hand and holding it away from her face, sweeping it back into an unravelling topknot. He fitted her arm into his. They turned, and the wind was against them. It was a warm wind, and peppered their skin with sand. Through narrowed eyes they could see the sand swirling before them, like smoke. Sometimes they had to stop, and shield their faces. The sand blew into their mouths, between their teeth. It was like biting on diamonds.

He drove her home. They stopped at a store and bought peaches. They sat together in the kitchen. Amy Glasse took a sharp knife from the dresser and brought it to the table. She gave the knife to Ralph. He took one of the peaches and cut into it. It was a yellow-fleshed peach, its skin as rough as a cat's tongue, and its ripeness spread out from the stone like a bloody graze.

Later still they went upstairs and lay in the double bed, under a quilt — the second — that Sandra Glasse had made. Amy put her long white arms around him and locked his body into hers. It was as if there were a key and she had found it: a code, and she had broken it. Afterwards she cried for a moment, almost without a sound, her head turned into the pillow. He did not know what he felt: not guilt, not yet. Love, certainly; yes, he felt that. Her hair spread over her shoulders like a fan of feathers; her spine seemed dipped into her flesh, like a shallow channel scraped through wax.

That afternoon, Kit was at her aunt's house in Foulsham. They sat together in the kitchen, the half-door open to admit the sunshine, elbows propped on the table and a pot of tea cooling between them. 'So what are you asking me?' Emma said. 'About Daniel?'

'For your advice.'

'Kit! Come on now! You know I never give advice!'

'Make an exception.' Kit looked at the table top. Absently she scraped at it: delicately, with her fingernail. 'Emma, what is this disgusting thing? It looks like the remnant of a squashed baked bean.'

'Quite likely.' Emma grinned. 'You know they say every cloud has a silver lining, and the only good thing about losing Felix is that I no longer have to concoct a delicious little *dîner à deux* every time we fall out of bed. Baked beans are very nutritious, let me tell you.' The light faded in her face; Kit watched her eyes fade, sharp blue to grey. 'One thing about Felix, though, was how he was made happy with strong drink. Two big gins with a waft of vermouth and he'd be off back to Blakeney to dine *à deux* with Ginny, and some appetite still left. You know, Kit, they write all sorts of rubbish about people having affairs. Their tortured souls, and so on. But how is a man to eat two dinners? That's the question they should look into.'

Kit's hand lay on the table: large, white, capable. She wanted to place it over her aunt's, but taste restrained her. Emma fitted her knuckles into her eye-sockets, and ground them around, carefully. 'Sorry, sweetheart. All I can say about Daniel is this – ask yourself, how will you feel if he goes off and marries someone like Ginny?'

Kit paused. 'OK, I think.'

'Then that's not the real question, is it?'

She shook her head. 'It's home, you know. And me, me myself. I'm asking you for information, Emma.'

Emma looked up. 'For information or knowledge?'

'Are they different?'

Emma didn't reply.

SEVEN

At midnight the train stopped. Anna raised herself on one elbow, then scrambled from the top berth, reaching out with her bare toes for a foothold. She swung herself to the floor, pulled down her nightdress, and put her head out of the window. A man was walking by the side of the track. She could not see him, but she could hear the crunch of his boots. She could see the tip of his lighted cigarette, bobbing and dipping with each step.

Ralph said, 'What time is it?' He eased himself from the lower berth, put out his head in turn. A moonless night. Not a breath of wind. Useless to ask, why have we stopped, when will we go again? Best just to wait. They had crossed the border. They were in Bechuanaland, moving north through the night. Not moving now: becalmed. They had been late at Mafeking, late at Lobatsi; 'I'll give you a bed,' the conductor had told them. 'You can try sleeping two hours, three. You'll reach your station before dawn.' He brought two flat pillows and two railway blankets, and four sheets that were as white and crisp as paper.

'There must be a village.' Ralph had picked out the glow of a fire, far to their left. If there had been a wind, it might have brought voices to them. Closer at hand, a baby was crying, ignored, from some outlying hut: Anna heard the thin insistent wail.

She climbed back to her bed. She had wanted the top berth because she felt there was more air, with no other body stacked above hers. It was December now, midsummer; sunset brought some relief from the heat, but it was best if you kept moving. Ralph passed up their bottle of water. It was tepid and stale. She closed her eyes, and disposed her body carefully so that no part of it touched any other part. But the berth was narrow; she folded her hands across her ribs, till the heat and weight of them became unbearable.

The night settled about her like a black quilt. Lucy Moyo had packed a bag for her in Elim, and handed it to her at the prison gate; her cotton nightdress had been starched and smelled of the iron, but now it was a sodden rag. The sheets the guard had given them were rucked damply beneath her hips. Her hair stuck to her neck; she put her arms by her sides again, looked up at the roof of the train. It was a metal coffin-lid, a coffin in the air. Hands folded, she made a decorous corpse.

She imagined her voice, floating down to earth. 'I think I am pregnant, Ralph.'

What then? What if she said it? What would they do? Lurch from the train at some desert halt, and begin to navigate their passage back to civilization? How would they do it? The South Africans might not let them back over the border. They had been given the choice: take the plane home, or the train north.

She thought of herself decanted into the winter at East Dereham, her trunks bumping up the stairs of her parents' house for storage in the attics; she imagined rubbing together her blue hands, while she tried to explain their situation. *You've been in prison, Anna? A daughter of ours, in gaol?* And they would have no place in the world, no future mapped out for them; they would be like fish hauled out of the water, gasping in a strange element, writhing on the hooks of expectation unfulfilled.

No, she thought. My lips are sealed.

She dozed. The train began to move. It carried her onwards, into a world of dust.

★

The Security Branch had come for them before dawn: parking their vehicles outside the compound, and knocking politely, persistently, on the front door of the Mission House until Ralph admitted them. 'Will you get dressed, Mrs Eldred, please? And pack a bag?'

They began another search. They emptied the contents of the wastepaper baskets into bags to take away, and noted the titles of the books on the shelves. They went through the out-tray and read the addresses on the envelopes waiting for the mail. 'Who is Dr Eldred, please?'

'My sister,' Ralph said.

The letter was laid down again. It would go all the way to Norwich, greased by a policeman's fingertips.

When one of the men approached the filing cabinet, Ralph and Anna exchanged a glance. One impatient pull . . . they waited for the top drawer to sail from its runners and break the policeman's toes. But these officers were circumspect, almost reverential. 'We give a receipt for anything we take away,' one explained. The drawer remained anchored, innocuous. The policemen went about their work quietly, as if not to injure or alarm the incriminating evidence. The mission staff – Rosinah, Dearie, Clara the washerwoman, Jakob and his boy assistant – had been brought from their beds to stand in a line outside the back door. Their quarters were being searched. With the same creepy-fingered care? Ralph doubted that. 'Let me speak to them,' he said. 'Just to reassure them.'

'That won't be necessary, Mr Eldred,' said the officer in charge. 'My men will do all the reassuring that is needed.'

'Mrs Eldred?' They had brought a female officer; she touched Anna's arm. 'I must come with you while you get your things together.'

'Things?' Anna said.

'For a time away from home,' the young woman said.

'Where do you think you are taking me?'

'You have to . . .' The girl looked aside. She had a tender skin, a North European skin, and blushed easily; she was not hardened to her trade. 'To prison, Mrs Eldred.'

'To prison.' Anna digested it. The pause made her sound cool. 'To prison for how long? And why? On what charge?'

The female officer glanced at her superior. She didn't know the answer. An expression of impatience crossed the man's face. 'Just take her,' he said.

In the bedroom Anna pulled drawers open, aimless and distracted. She could not stop her hands from trembling. The female officer sat on the bed. 'You hurry up now,' she said, not unkindly. 'Bring your nightie. Bring soap and your toothbrush. And your sanitary protection if you think you might need it.'

When her bag was packed the woman stood up and took it from her. She ushered her back to the sitting room. The double doors to the front stoep stood wide open. The two officers had gone, and taken Ralph with them.

It was only then that Anna understood that she and Ralph would be separated. She broke away. The woman officer leapt after her, catching at her arm. A man standing outside on the steps slammed the wire door of the stoep back into her face. She heard a car drive away. She put her fingers against the netting of the stoep, as if to force them through.

There was an iron bedstead and a stained mattress; traces of vomit, menstrual blood. She had to force herself to sit down on it, but she thought it was a good sign that they had not given her sheets and blankets. Perhaps they would ask some questions, and release her before the day was out. Dawn came, her first dawn in prison. She listened to the morning sounds, still and attentive: her hands in her lap, her spine sagging slightly. They had taken away her watch, but she estimated that it was about seven o'clock when the door was unlocked. A wardress brought in a tin tray, and put it down on the metal locker by the bed. She went out again without speaking. The key turned in the lock. She heard the stout shoes squeak away.

Left alone again, she investigated the tray. There was a bowl of mealie-porridge. The spoon seemed encrusted with the remains of other, long-ago breakfasts. Quelling her revulsion she brought a spoonful of the food to her mouth, but before she tasted it she gagged, and a wash of nausea lapped over her. It ebbed, left her shivering and light-headed. She dropped the spoon into the porridge and put the bowl back on the tray.

There was a beaker of coffee; it was no longer hot, but she held it between her hands for comfort. She took a sip; it tasted of nothing. Comfort receded.

The third item on the tray was a cob of brown bread. She broke some off and put it into her mouth. It stuck there, un-negotiable, like a stone. Last night at Flower Street, she had complained it was too hot to eat. She had meant to get up early, boil an egg pre-dawn.

Some time later – perhaps an hour – the unspeaking wardress returned. She brought a water jug with a cover, and stood holding it while she waited for Anna to move the tray. In her other hand was a bucket. She put it down by the bed. 'Is that what I must use?' Anna said; looking up, without belligerence, wanting nothing but to learn the rules.

The wardress indicated the tray. 'You don't want that?' She picked it up without waiting for an answer.

'Can I have my bag?' Anna said. 'Can I have my watch?'

The door clicked shut. The key grated. She was alone again. Her hands returned to her lap. She examined the crack in the cell's wall. From the base it ran a meandering course, to a height of four feet. Then other cracks seemed to spring from it, creeping wide of their source. It was like the delta of some great river. Anna took her handkerchief from her pocket and dabbed its corner into the water jug. She laid the damp linen first against one eyelid, then against the other. Don't cry, don't cry, she said to herself. Let this be in place of tears.

At intervals, the spy-hole in the door would flick open. She would raise her face to it: let them see that I have nothing to hide, she thought, not even a covert expression. She wondered if they came to stare at her on the hour; she began to count. She thought, by the heat in the cell and what she could see of the sunlight, that it might be midday when the door opened again.

A different wardress. '*Kom.*'

'Where?'

'Fingerprints.'

They took her along the corridor to a room furnished only with a table and two chairs. A second wardress took her flinching hand, straightened her fingers and pressed them into the pad of black grease. On the waiting paper, she saw loops, whirls, smudges like ape-prints. It was hard to believe they belonged to her.

They let her wash her hands then, but she could not get the slime from under her fingernails.

When she came out into the corridor, an African woman in a prison dress was kneeling, scrubbing brush in hand, a scum of soapy water widening around her in a pool. She was singing a hymn, her voice strong, unwavering. When she saw Anna she stopped singing. She sat back on her haunches to watch her pass. Anna looked down into her face; then over her shoulder, to see the woman bend her back again. The soles of her bare feet were a greyish-white, hard as hooves. The hymn followed her as they swung open the cell door:

'How dearly God must love us,
And this poor world of ours,
To spread blue skies above us,
And deck the earth with flowers.'

When the light began to fail, they tossed two blankets into the cell, and brought in her bag. She had packed her hairbrush and a comb but she had no mirror. She could not think why it seemed so important to see her own face. She said to the wardress, 'You haven't got a mirror in your pocket, have you? That I could borrow just for a minute?'

'What do you think, that I'm a beauty queen?' the woman said. She laughed at her own joke. 'It's against the rules,' she said. 'You might hurt yourself, you see? Try and sleep now.'

Early in the afternoon there had been another tin tray, with a bowl of broth this time. She had stirred the ingredients without much hope, disturbing cabbage and root vegetables and what might be scraps of meat. Globules of fat lay on the surface, and when she brought the spoon to her mouth the morning's reaction repeated itself, and she thought she would vomit. The last meal of the day had been another beaker of weak coffee and a hunk of bread. She regretted now that she had let them take away the bread untasted. She was so hungry that her stomach seemed to be folding in on itself, curling into a hollowness above her navel. 'Can you help me?' she said to the wardress. 'I couldn't eat earlier, I was feeling sick. Can I have some bread?'

The woman hesitated. 'I'll see,' she said.

She went out, banging the door, rattling her keys. An electric light flicked on overhead, taking Anna by surprise. Anna waited, unmoving, under its glare.

She'll not come back, she thought. But after some time the woman did return, with bread on a plate and a smear of margarine.

'I can't let you have a knife,' she said. 'You'll have to do the best you can.'

Anna took the plate. 'I'm grateful.'

Then the woman took an apple out of her pocket. 'Don't tell anybody.' She put it down on the metal locker.

Anna said, 'Do you know what is going to happen to me? Can you tell me where my husband is?'

'Don't take advantage,' the wardress said.

'I want to write a letter. I have things to do. I work at a mission you see, in Elim, Flower Street, and there are things I have to take care of. I have to give instructions, or nothing will be done.'

'I dare say they got on all right before you came,' the woman said.

'I ought to be given access to a lawyer.'

'You must take that up with the colonel.'

'When can I see him?'

'In time.'

It was the least hopeful sentence she had heard that day. When the wardress had gone she broke open the cob of bread and tore out the middle, wiping it into the margarine and forcing it into her mouth. She held the apple for a long time before she ate it, running her fingers over its shape, admiring its innocence, its cleanness. She ate it in mouse-like nibbles, and wrapped the core carefully in her handkerchief, so that tomorrow morning she would at least be able to taste the juice on her tongue. She held off using the bucket for as long as she could, but in the end she had to squat over it, the metal rim cold against her thighs. She felt debased by the dribble of urine that would be her companion all night, and would be there for her when she woke in the morning.

They did not take her to see the colonel the next day, but the wardress who had given her the apple brought in a pillow, a pillow case and a pair of sheets. At least one more night then, Anna thought.

'Did you eat your breakfast this morning?' the woman asked.

'No, I couldn't.'

'You ought to try.'

'Will you get me another apple? I'd be so grateful.'

'Yes, I dare say you would.'

'Do you think they would let me have something to read?'

'That's for the colonel to decide. I couldn't decide that.'

'Would it be possible for someone to go to my house and get me a change of clothes?'

She knew the answer: the colonel will decide. But this is what prison life must be, she thought: a series of endless requests, some great, some small, repeated and repeated, until one day – in the face of all expectation – one of them, great or small, is granted. Can you arrange for me to send a message to my husband? Can I have a bowl of hot water, I cannot get the fingerprint ink from under my nails? Can I have a newspaper, can I have a mirror? Can you assure me that God loves me and that I am his child?

The next day, after the mealie-porridge but before the broth, another wardress came in. 'You want to comb your hair, Mrs Eldred? The colonel is waiting to see you in his office.'

She jumped up from her bed. 'Never mind my hair.'

The woman stood back to let her pass out of the cell. To her surprise, two more wardresses were stationed outside the door, and they trod a pace behind her along the corridor. They treat me as if I'm dangerous, she thought. Perhaps I am.

The colonel was a man of fifty, with pepper-and-salt hair shorn above his ears. The regulation belly strained at his uniform belt, but the rest of him was hard and fit looking. He motioned her to a chair. A ceiling fan creaked over her head; she lifted her face to it. Round and round it churned, the same stagnant air.

'I must apologize for not seeing you sooner, Mrs Eldred. There were some incidents in the men's prison that have been taking up my time.'

'What incidents?'

'Nothing that should bother you.'

'Is my husband in there, in the men's prison?'

'You'll have news of Mr Eldred very soon – in fact, you'll be seeing him soon, all we want is that you talk to us a little bit.' The colonel sat down opposite her. 'You've been to political meetings, Mrs Eldred?'

'No. Never.'

'You've been to protest meetings? About the bus boycott, for example?'

'Yes.'

'So, isn't that the same thing?'

'I didn't think so, at the time.'

'We have photographs of you at these meetings. We know you have held political meetings at your house.'

'Never.'

'You have had people from the ANC at your house. Agitators.'

'It's not illegal to have visitors.'

'So what were you doing, Mrs Eldred, if you weren't having a political meeting? Just having tea and cake, were you? Perhaps reading the Bible together?'

Anna didn't answer.

'We have the names of everyone who has visited you.'

'Yes. I know you have your spies everywhere.'

'It's necessary,' the colonel said. 'Believe me, Mrs Eldred. We have to keep control.'

Anna pushed her hair back, smoothing it with her hand. It

felt lank and greasy; the cell was an oven by mid-morning, and she was not given enough water to wash properly. 'Can I ask you a question, Colonel? Just one? All I want to know is if any of the mission staff are on your payroll. Has anyone been informing against us?'

'If you were innocent, Mrs Eldred, you wouldn't have to ask me that question.'

'Oh, I'm innocent, Colonel.' She felt colour rise in her face. She was not afraid. Since they had brought her to the prison she had felt every emotion, but not fear. 'I am perfectly innocent, and so is my husband, and I am quite sure that the mission society who sent us out here have been informed of what has happened, and that they will be making representations to your government on our behalf.'

'I'm sure that is so,' the colonel said, 'and I am sure their representations will be listened to with the greatest of respect.' He ran a hand over his bristly head. 'But you must understand, Mrs Eldred, that my government takes exception to people such as yourself coming out here to tell us how to run our country, coming out here in the guise of mission workers and then turning political and interfering in affairs that you don't understand.'

'I do understand,' Anna said. 'You can't expect that line to succeed with me. I've seen everything, with my own eyes.'

'With respect, Mrs Eldred, you have seen nothing and you know nothing. When you've been here twenty, thirty years, tell me then.' The colonel looked up at the ceiling, as if self-control reposed there. When he spoke again it was in a flat voice, with his former quite meaningless courtesy. 'Can I offer you a cigarette, Mrs Eldred?'

'No, thank you.'

'You don't mind if I smoke myself?'

'Feel free.'

'Do you have any complaints, Mrs Eldred?'

She looked at him wonderingly. 'If I began on my complaints . . .'

'About your treatment, I mean.'

'Could I be allowed some fresh air?'

'I'm afraid there is nowhere suitable for you to take exercise.'

'I can hear other women outside. I can hear their voices.' And laughter. Songs.

'That will be from the courtyard. The blacks go out there to do their washing.'

'I expect I shall need to do washing.'

'It will be done for you, Mrs Eldred.'

'I should like a change of clothes from home, and some books. Is that possible?'

'I will send someone to see about your clothes.'

Relief washed over her; she had not thought about it until now, but for the first time it occurred to her that they might put her into a prison dress. 'And the books?'

'You can have a Bible for now. Will that do?'

'Thank you.'

He inclined his head. 'You're a well-mannered woman, Mrs Eldred. I'd like to see you keep it that way.'

'I hope I can, Colonel.' Whatever you say, she thought, I shall have the last word. 'Could I have the light on for longer, so that I can read? I couldn't sleep last night. I never can sleep much before midnight.'

The colonel hesitated. 'For one hour, perhaps. Till nine o'clock.'

She had gained a piece of information. She had a sense of petty triumph.

'Can I have my watch back?'

'Yes, that is possible. I didn't know it had been taken away.'

'And this bucket, this so-called sanitary bucket – it's disgusting. When they brought me down the corridor I saw some buckets standing in a corner, a kind with lids. Can I have one of those?'

The colonel looked stricken. He flung himself from his chair, and chopped the wardress to pieces in blunt Afrikaans. The wardress shrugged, talked back; then became abject. 'Mrs Eldred,' he said, turning to her, 'we owe you an apology. I do not know how this can have happened. You've been given a native-type bucket. All coloured and white prisoners are automatically allocated buckets with lids, that is the rule. Your bucket will be changed immediately.'

Anna stared at him. The colonel had the last word after all.

That night, her legs began to ache; sleep was fitful, but before dawn she plunged into a dreamless stupor. When she woke she was shivering, and her scalp was sore: a vast headache lay behind it. She felt it was difficult to breathe, let alone eat. She had wrapped herself in her blanket, but it didn't help.

They came for her at nine.

'The colonel again?'

'Ag, Mrs Eldred, he must be in love with you.'

He was pacing his office; stopped pacing when he saw her. 'Good morning, Mrs Eldred, please sit down.' He looked at her closely. 'So it's a hunger strike?'

'No, it's not a hunger strike. I just prefer not to eat.'

'You don't like the food you are given?'

'How could anyone like it? It's not fit for pigs.'

'So if we were to supplement your diet, you would eat?'

Anna didn't answer. She didn't want to give him the satisfaction; didn't want to allow herself the temptation. Since that first time, there had been no apple. The skin on the back of her hands seemed greyish, as if the colour of her blood had altered.

'Come, Mrs Eldred,' the colonel said. 'What would you like? Some fruit?'

She didn't speak. The headache had gone now, but its ghost remained, and the back of her neck was stiff.

'I'd like to go home,' she said in a low voice. 'I'd like to see my husband. I'd like to know why you are keeping me here.'

'In good time,' the colonel said. 'You must understand that whatever you decide, we have to send in the prison rations. That's the rule.'

She nodded, head bowing painfully on the stem of her neck. He seemed to have made up his mind that she was on a hunger strike, even though she had denied it. Well, let him think so. Let it be so. The black woman who scrubbed the corridor, who would supplement her diet? She imagined her own body: saw herself fading, growing meeker, thinner, thinner . . . For the first time fear touched her. I am not made for this, she thought. Emma, now . . . Emma could bear it. Bear it? It would be an ornament to Emma. And yet, the fear was almost a relief to her. So I am human, she thought. If I had been in prison, and not afraid, how would I have lived the rest of my life? How could I be allowed the luxury of everyday, ordinary fears, if I were not afraid now? She said, 'Colonel, for pity's sake, tell me what you have done with my husband. All I want is to know that he is safe.'

'We should be able to arrange for you to see him.'

'When? Today?'

The colonel exhaled gustily. 'Have patience, Mrs Eldred.' She saw him struggle to quell his exasperation with her. 'Look, Mrs Eldred, I'm sorry if you think you've been treated badly, but the fact is that we are not used to prisoners like you. This situation is unprecedented for me. And for the staff, it is unprecedented for them. That is why we had the mistake about the buckets, and maybe – maybe we have committed other mistakes. No one wants to keep you here for any longer than necessary.'

'But why are you keeping me at all? You've hardly asked me any questions.'

'No one wants to harass you, Mrs Eldred. What you've done, you've done.'

'Are you asking my husband questions?'

The colonel shook his head. 'Not in the way you mean, Mrs Eldred. Why should you think such things? No one has hurt you, have they?'

'No.'

'Just so – no one has hurt your husband either.'

'I don't believe you.'

'What can I do then? Except to assure you that you are here as much for your own protection as anything else?'

'Protection from whom?'

The colonel looked weary. 'From yourself.'

'You haven't brought any charge. I don't think there's any charge you can bring. Why don't you let me go?'

'That is not possible, I'm afraid.'

'Why isn't it?'

Keep asking questions, questions: just once you might get an answer.

'I am waiting on a higher authority, Mrs Eldred.'

'Are you, Colonel? Waiting for your God to speak?'

'No.' He half-smiled. 'A telephone call from Pretoria will do for me.'

'And when do you expect that?'

He shifted in his chair, ground out his cigarette in the ashtray. 'I no longer *expect*, Mrs Eldred. I've learned patience. May I commend it to you?'

She looked up into his face. 'We might grow old together, Colonel, you and I.'

That evening, unprecedentedly, they brought her a bowl of hot water and a clean dry towel. Until now she had been allowed to wash only once a day. They brought some fruit and a bar of chocolate. 'Not all at once or you'll be ill,' the wardress said. Her face showed her disapproval of this special treatment.

Anna unwrapped the chocolate and inhaled its fragrance, its deep cheap sweetness: sugar and oil. She despised herself. The colonel saw through me, she thought, he knew I was weak. The emulsion slid over her tongue, into her bloodstream. Her heart raced. She sat back on her bed, drawing up her feet. I shall always hate myself, she thought, I shall never forgive myself for this, I shall suffer for it hereafter. She flicked her tongue around her teeth, like a cat cleaning its whiskers: collecting the last taste. Took her pulse, one thumb fitted into the fine skin of her wrist. Its speed alarmed her. But I am alive, she thought.

Then she thought, but perhaps this is only a trick. Perhaps tomorrow they will bring back the porridge and the encrusted spoon, and the native bucket. And I shall not be able to bear it.

Next day they told her that she had a visitor. 'A kaffir,' the wardress said, turning down the corners of her mouth. 'The colonel has given permission.'

Lucy Moyo was seated in the room where the fingerprints were taken. Her handbag rested on her vast knees. She wore one of her ensembles: a plum-coloured dress, a pink petal hat to tone with it. Her handkerchief was folded and secured under the band of her wristwatch. She smelled of lily of the valley.

Anna flew towards her, her arms outstretched. But Lucy Moyo took her by the shoulders and held her off, in a brutal grip. 'Brace up, brace up now, Mrs Eldred.' Her voice was fierce. 'Do not let these people see you cry.'

Tears flooded Anna's face. Letting go of her for a moment, Lucy twitched her handkerchief from under her watch-strap. She took Anna by one shoulder and began to dab and scrub at her face, just as if she were one of the nursery children who had taken a tumble into the dust. Anna's tears continued to flow, and Lucy to wipe them away, all the time talking to her in the same tone, brisk and firm and no-nonsense, as if she knew that sympathy and tenderness would break her spirit.

'Mrs Eldred, listen to me. Everything is in hand, everyone has been informed. We have telegraphed to London – Father Alfred has done it, that man is not such a fool as he sometimes appears. The High Commissioner is sending someone from Cape Town. Everyone is praying, Mrs Eldred. Do you hear me?'

'Yes, yes, I understand – Lucy, have you seen my husband? Is there any news?'

'Father Alfred has seen him. He is well and in good spirits and saying not to worry. At the mission we are all well, we are all in good spirits, the monthly accounts are done, the wages are paid, you must have no fear, everything is in good order.'

'Five minutes,' the wardress said. Her face was set into a grimace of distaste. She held out her arm, showing her watch, as if Lucy might not understand.

Lucy looked at her hard. 'Are you a Christian woman?' she asked. She let Anna go. She fell against the table, limp as a rag doll. Lucy opened her handbag. 'They said one book, no more. I have brought you this. I know this book is dear to you because you have brought it from your home in England, and as you once told me, given to you by your mother.' Lucy put into Anna's hand her copy of *The Sun-Drenched Veld*. She kissed Anna on both cheeks, shook off the wardress's arm, and sailed from the room, her bag over her wrist. She left her perfume behind her, lying heavy on the air.

Back in her cell Anna sat with the book on her knees. She heard her mother's voice: 'One of the *Windows on the World* series, Anna.' She flicked through the pages. 'There is no fruit more refreshing than the golden pulp of paw-paw . . . natives often reverence their ancestors . . . Today ostrich-keepers look back with wistful eyes at those days when fashion favoured their wares.' She closed the book, and stared at the purple-blue mountains on the cover. The hills of heaven, she thought. Another night gathered in the corners of the room.

Lucy's visit seemed to Anna to indicate that release might be at hand. Don't raise your hopes, she said to herself; but she hardly slept.

In the morning she made no attempt to eat. She had developed a disgust for the tepid water in its metal jug, and had to make an effort of will – tip her head back, hold her throat open – to pour it into herself. She was thirsty all the time, and once again shaky and cold, her nerves taut.

She wanted peace from her own thoughts, from their relentless, spinning nature. She realized that not once since she had been in prison had she prayed. It had not crossed her mind to do it. She looked into her heart, on this sixth morning of her imprisonment, and found a void where the faith should be.

At ten o'clock the cell door was unlocked and the colonel came in. 'How are you today, Mrs Eldred?'

'I want a bath,' she said instantly. 'I want news of my husband. I want you to let me go.'

The colonel held up his hand: peace, peace. 'Mrs Eldred, your husband is here. I have come to escort you to my office, where you will find both Mr Eldred and a representative of the High Commissioner. Will that do for you, for now?'

Ralph rose from his chair when he saw her, his face dismayed. 'Anna! Good God, what has happened?'

For a moment she thought she might faint. She saw that Ralph's face was puffy and bruised, his lip was cut. Her stomach tightened and churned; a spasm of physical and moral disgust shook her, and she felt suddenly raw, as if her skin had been peeled; I can't bear it, she thought. She loved him, he was her child, and it made her light-headed with rage to think that he had suffered a moment's pain, and from these swine ... The room swam and shivered, the ceiling fan churned the air, the colonel put his hand under her elbow, and a stranger wedged into the corner of the office bobbed up from his chair and said, 'Cooper from Cape Town.'

She found herself sitting. She grasped Cooper's damp, extended hand, not seeming to realize what it was for. 'She's been a silly girl,' the colonel said. 'Refusing food.'

'And you let her?' Ralph said.

'What would you have preferred, Mr Eldred, did you want me to force-feed her?'

'It would be better if you sat down, Mr Eldred,' Cooper from Cape Town said, 'so that we can conduct our business in a seemly and civilized manner.'

'We're in the wrong country for that,' Ralph said.

But he did sit; took Anna's hand and touched her dry lips with his.

'May I begin?' Cooper said. Too young a man, ill at ease, sweating inside his businessman's suit. He cleared his throat. 'To be frank, this is turning into something of an embarrassment.'

Ralph leapt from his chair again. 'Embarrassment? We are taken away in the middle of the night and detained without charge, I am threatened with violence and my wife is starved, the mission staff are terrorized, and you call it an embarrassment?'

'Mr Eldred, you are not helping your case,' Cooper said. 'Of course you are aggrieved, but as Her Majesty's representative my duty is to extract you from the unfortunate situation in which you have placed yourself, and to do this without damage to the relations of our two governments.'

'What do you mean?' Anna swooped forward to the edge of her chair. 'What do you mean, the situation in which we have placed ourselves?'

'Please, Mrs Eldred,' the colonel said mildly. 'Listen to the man. He's come a long way to talk to you.'

'Thank you, Colonel,' Cooper said. 'Now, the situation roughly speaking is this; you can as I understand it be released almost immediately, but there are certain conditions with which you must comply.' Cooper took out his handkerchief and swabbed his forehead. His no-colour eyes travelled from side to side.

'I think it would be easier for you,' the colonel said, 'if I left you alone with your nationals.'

'Properly speaking,' Cooper said, 'that is what should occur.'

The colonel smiled slightly. 'You are not afraid of Mr Eldred?' Cooper didn't reply. 'If I hear the sound of your skull being pounded on the floor, Mr Cooper, I shall come right away to your relief. Depend upon it.'

The colonel went out, closing the door on them. There was a moment's silence. 'It will be easiest if you resign,' Cooper said.

'Never,' Ralph said. 'Let them throw me out, if that's what they want. I'm not going to do anything to make their lives easier.'

'We have been in constant touch with your employers in Clerkenwell. Your mission society.'

'So they know exactly what's happened?'

'They do, and they are less than delighted. With you, I mean, Mr Eldred. I am assured they have forsworn any political involvement, any whatever.'

'It's easy,' Anna said. 'From Clerkenwell.'

'There is a suggestion . . .' the man hesitated. 'That is, I am empowered to put to you a suggestion –'

'Yes?'

'That it would, as it were, save face –'

'For whom?'

'– for all concerned . . . if you were to leave voluntarily rather than be deported . . .'

'We've been through this,' Ralph said.

'. . . but without altogether quitting, as it were, your field of mission endeavour.'

'Do you speak English, Mr Cooper?' Anna asked.

The man swallowed. 'Do I understand that you have no wish to return to the United Kingdom as of this time?'

'No wish,' Ralph said. 'No intention.'

'Mrs Eldred?'

'I want to go home to Flower Street,' Anna said. 'That's what I want.'

'You know that is impossible.' A note of scolding entered the official's voice. 'The South African government will no longer have you on its territory. But I am directed to put to you, on behalf of your mission society, a proposal that you should take up a post, possibly a temporary one, in Bechuanaland, in the Bechuanaland Protectorate.'

'Clerkenwell is proposing this?'

'I am only the intermediary.'

'What do you mean by temporary?'

'They mean three months, probably,' Anna said. 'Until the fuss dies down and the newspapers have forgotten about us and they can sneak us back into England and then sack us.'

'Oh, I hardly think –' Cooper began.

'Shut up, Cooper,' Ralph said. 'No one is interested in what you think.'

A silence. They seemed to have reached an impasse. 'My husband means,' Anna said, leaning forward, 'that it would be better if you just gave us the facts. Where is this post they're offering?'

'It is at a place called Mosadinyana. Remote, I understand.'

'That makes sense,' Ralph said. 'Get us well out of the way.'

Anna put her hand on his arm. 'Let's listen to him.'

'As I understand it,' Cooper said, 'the couple who ran the mission station have been repatriated on medical grounds. It is not a place of any size. There is a small school, I am told.' He looked at Anna. 'There is a requirement for one teacher –'

'And what would I do?' Ralph said.

'Administer, Mr Eldred. You would administer.'

'I've never heard of this place,' Anna said.

'Your Society describe it to me as a toehold,' Cooper said. 'A toehold in the desert.' He seemed pleased with the phrase. 'There is the possibility that in the years to come it may grow into something larger.'

'A foothold,' Ralph said.

'Is it on the railway line?'

'Not exactly,' Cooper said.

'What is there besides the school?'

'There might be a trading store,' Cooper said, frowning. 'I could look into that.'

'If I went up there,' Ralph said, 'do you think there is any possibility that at a later date I might be able to return to Elim?'

Cooper favoured them with a thin smile. 'Not unless there is a change of government, Mr Eldred.'

'You are putting us in a very difficult position,' Anna said. 'You are asking us to go up-country, to a place we know nothing about –'

'I am required to encourage you to regard it as temporary,' Cooper said. 'I am required to assure you that should the posting prove unsuitable you can be replaced. Really, Mrs Eldred, there is nothing to fear. The South African government –' he hesitated – 'that is, it has been indicated to me – the South African government would have no objection to your travelling through their territory to take up this post. But should you refuse the opportunity, they have reserved two seats on a flight to London departing tomorrow.'

Ralph and Anna looked at each other. 'Tomorrow,' Anna said. 'That's ludicrous. We couldn't possibly leave at that sort of notice. We have to put everything in order at Flower Street, it will take a month at least to hand over to someone else.'

'I'm afraid you don't grasp the situation, Mrs Eldred. You can never return to Elim, as I imagined I had made adequately clear. After all, there is no one who could give a guarantee as to your conduct.'

'You make us sound like schoolchildren,' Ralph said.

'You are little more, Mr Eldred.' The man closed his eyes. 'Little more.'

Ralph took Anna's hand. 'We must decide.'

'Yes.'

'Anna, you look ill. Perhaps to go home would be best.'

'I'm not ill.'

'I can't risk you. I love you, Anna.' Cooper looked away in distress.

'If we go home now we will have failed.'

'Oh God,' Ralph said. 'I wish we had never seen this bloody country. I wish we'd gone to Dar.'

'No,' Anna said. 'I wouldn't have missed Elim, Ralph.' It will always be the place where we grew up, she thought. I shall never forget Flower Street. She looked up at Cooper. 'All right, we'll go.'

'I congratulate you on a brave decision.' Cooper put his hand out. Ralph ignored it.

In the small hours, the train set them down on an empty platform. Their two bags – their trunks would be packed for them, and sent on later – were placed at their feet; then the train gathered itself for the next haul, and steamed away up the line.

The darkness was total. They heard footsteps approach, shockingly loud. A railway employee called out a curt greeting in Afrikaans. Anna answered him. 'We are late. There's no one to meet us, where can we stay?'

The railway employee was a man of few words. 'He says there's only the waiting room. And it's here behind us. And he says that everyone knows the train is late. Everyone concerned.'

'They won't abandon us,' Ralph said. The footsteps retreated.

The waiting room had a cement floor and two wooden benches. It seemed to offer no more comfort than the platform, so they took up their station on the single bench outside. Though it was midsummer, the starlight was cold. They leaned together, their heads touching. 'We're nowhere now,' Anna whispered.

Ralph said, 'We are in the heart of Africa.'

'Yes. Nowhere.'

She lay down on the bench, her head on his knees, a cardigan draped over her. His head drooping, he dozed.

Ralph woke to a touch on his shoulder. A torch beam flashed into his face. As soon as he looked up the torch was switched off. An African voice, a man's, said, 'Mr Eldred, sir. Come, baas, come, madam.'

Hands reached for their bags. Anna stood up, stiff from sleep, disoriented, chilled. Beyond the station compound they saw the lights of a truck. 'This is yours?' Ralph asked.

'No, baas.' A silence. Ralph thought, how can I stop them calling me that? I never want to hear that word again. The man said, 'It is mine and my brother's truck, and his brother's also. Mrs Pilane, the clinic nurse, has asked me to lift you to the mission.'

'Thank you,' Ralph said. 'The train is very late. We thought no one was coming.'

'I was coming,' the man said calmly.

As they approached the truck, they saw by torchlight a half-dozen figures rise from the ground, draped in blankets. No one spoke. One by one, the half-dozen climbed into the back of the truck, handing up to each other parcels and sacks. 'Who are these?' Ralph said.

The man replied, 'They are people who are travelling.'

Ralph pushed Anna into the cab of the truck and scrambled in beside her. 'Do you work for the mission?' Ralph asked.

'No. There is only Salome. And there is Enock.'

The man did not enlarge on this. He kept his own name to himself, a private possession. They drove on in silence. The track was rough, and stones clattered away from their wheels; ruts jolted their spines. Small branches brushed the sides of the truck with a metallic click-click-click. Sometimes branches lashed across the windscreen; the glass protected them, but instinct made them duck. Anna leaned against Ralph, her head on his shoulder. The metal shell filled with their quiet, ragged breathing.

Almost imperceptibly, the sky began to lighten. The road became less bumpy. 'We are arriving,' the driver said. The village of Mosadinyana took shape about them: the cattle kraals of plaited thorns, the shaggy thatched roofs of the rondavels, the mud walls which enclosed each yard. The driver pulled up. There was a moment's stillness; Anna looked at the walls; a pattern was set into them, striped and zigzagged, ochre and dun. The travellers melted away, wrapping their blankets more tightly around them; the women balanced their parcels on their head.

The sun was almost up now, but the pale light could have been dawn or dusk. Anna looked up beyond the village. Her vision filled with low brown hills, an interminable range of hills: like the mountains of the moon. Around the borehole, donkeys bent their necks and plucked at the scrubby ground.

They jolted up to the Mission House a few minutes later. The driver dismounted to take down their bags. 'You may give me three shillings,' he said.

'Gladly,' Ralph said. 'I am very grateful to you.'

Money changed hands. The Mission House was a low building, its walls gleaming white in the half-light. There was a candle burning on a table on the front stoep. As they watched, it was extinguished. The sun burst over the hills, born fully armed: a great disc of searing gold.

They found inside the house the sticks of furniture left behind by their predecessors, Mr and Mrs Instow. There were dusty, sagging armchairs, the upholstery worn by long use to an indeterminate shiny grey. There were some scarred tables, a couple of bookcases, indecently empty: a solitary picture on the wall, of Highland cattle splashing through a stream. Their bedroom was furnished with a bulky dressing-table with a spotted mirror, and with wardrobes whose doors creaked and swung open when anyone entered the room, disclosing their dark interiors. Their ancient mothball reek lay on the air.

At once, their new routine began. There were new problems, new dilemmas, both human and ethical. There was no time for reflection, no period of induction. It was a month before a letter from Clerkenwell came. It was not an accusing letter, but it was huffy and vague. It wished them success in their new post. 'Cooper said it would be temporary,' Ralph said. 'But here they say nothing about moving us on. Still –' His eyes rested on his wife. Her pregnancy showed now, more evident because she was thin.

'Better the devil you know,' Anna said. 'The thought of packing my bags again – it's too much.' She came over to him and put her hand on his head, stroked his curly hair. 'It's all right. We'll get used to it.' And that would not be difficult, she thought. There were routine panics: a scorpion in the kitchen, a thorn under a nail. Otherwise, every day was the same.

Enock, a man with no family, dug the garden and raked it: he was aimless, erratic, prone to disappearances. Salome, in the kitchen, presided over their monotonous diet: stringy meat and mealie-pap, small bitter oranges from their own trees. After breakfast each day she washed the clothes and polished the red cement floors. Salome was shapeless, like most of the women who had passed their youth. She wore a lilac overall which she had been given by Mr and Mrs Instow: of whom she seldom spoke. She wore gaping bedroom slippers and a woollen hat; each morning by six o'clock she was in the kitchen, stoking up the cooking range, putting the kettle on the hob.

A second month passed, and already their memories were fading. Their time in Flower Street seemed to be an episode in other people's lives. What has happened to Koos, Anna sometimes wondered, did the police take him? What has happened to Dearie and Rosinah? Was there an informer? If so, who was it? Her mind recoiled from this topic. Even the better memories were soured. She could not think of Flower Street without knowing that they had been betrayed.

Each morning by eight Anna was in the little schoolroom. She had a floating and variable number of pupils: some tots who could barely grip a pencil, some big bold girls who sat knitting and gossiping at the back. Anna did not try to stop them; she had no doubt they needed whatever it was they were knitting. The boys would go off for weeks at a time, herding cattle. Months on the battered schoolroom benches; then months on the trail.

Her aim was not high: just that they should be able to count, add up, subtract, and not be cheated when they went to the store with small coins. They should be able to write their names and read from primers meant for children in English suburbs: children with lawns to play on, and pet dogs, and strawberry jam for tea. There were no lawns here, for each blade of vegetation had to pit itself against God to survive. There was mealie-porridge for tea, and for breakfast and dinner too. And if they saw a dog, her pupils threw stones at it.

They were incurious, apathetic children; impossible to know whether or not they took in what she was trying to teach them. They were, she guessed, often hungry: not with the sharp hunger that goads the mind and makes the hand shake, but with a chronic hunger, grumbling and unappeasable. There was no starvation at this date: not in the village, not in the country. There was, rather, a malnourishment which bred lethargy, which bred an unfitness for any effort beyond the minimum. The Afrikaner farmers had the best land; they sweated it and made it pay. The desert produced thorn bushes and scrub, and in spring, after rain had fallen, a sudden, shocking carpet of strange flowers.

By eleven each day, the sun high in the sky, her pupils slept, nodding and slumping at their benches. Her voice dried in her throat. By one o'clock school was over. The children pressed around her. 'Goodbye, and go well,' she would say, in her awkward, minimal Setswana.

'Stay well, madam,' they would say. And enclose her. Their hot bodies to hers. Hands patting. She felt herself shrink inside.

Why? Her own reaction disgusted her. The village men were meagre, spiritless and skinny. The women were great tubes of fat, blown out with carbohydrates. They carried vacant-faced infants, strapped tightly to their backs. Too many babies died. The clinic nurse Mrs Pilane could not cure measles. When the women spoke, they seemed to shout and sneer. Their voices were harsh, monotonous, somehow triumphal. God help me, Anna thought: but I don't like them, perhaps I fear them. These feelings were a violation of everything she expected from herself, of all her principles and habits of mind.

News came patchily from the outside world; the mail arrived twice a week, and a newspaper sometimes. Bechuanaland, the obscure protectorate, was making news itself. Seretse Khama had returned home, the young tribal leader with his white wife; ten years earlier, a bar student alone in London, he had chosen for himself this trim lady-like blonde, to the fury and dismay of his relatives and of the South African government. 'MARRIAGE THAT ROCKS AFRICA' the *Daily Mail* had bellowed. For a few weeks the world had turned its eyes on the protectorate. Frozen out, banned by the British from his own country, the chief had now returned, to the ululations of tribeswomen and the pop of flashbulbs. Ralph said, 'In the news again, think of it. James and Emma and our parents, reading about us in Norwich. It makes you feel we live in a real place, after all.'

They had been in the newspapers themselves, of course. Emma had sent the cuttings. Their story had run for a day or two, then been dropped as soon as they were let out of gaol. The papers had used photographs from their wedding; it seemed no one had been able to find any other pictures of them. In their strange ritual garments they stared into the lens, startled and shy; they looked like children, playing at weddings to pass a rainy day.

News came from Cape Town, too. The archbishop was dead. It was the government that had killed him in the end, Ralph believed. Another apartheid measure had been proposed, with a clause giving the government the power to exclude Africans from churches in white areas; and this brought the old man to his sticking point.

The archbishop drafted a letter: if this becomes law, his letter said, the church and its clergy and its people will be unable to obey it.

The battle-lines were drawn at last. Late at night, the archbishop's secretary came into his study, bringing the final version of the letter for his signature. The old man lay on the carpet. He had fallen by his desk, and his heart had stopped.

Receiving this news, Ralph felt more alone.

Within a week or two of their arrival it became clear that the mission did not provide a job for two people. And Mosadinyana would never grow, as Cooper had purported. The mission was a fossil, a relic; its time was past, and the focus of effort and activity had moved elsewhere. Ralph imagined their lives and careers filed away, in Clerkenwell's dustiest, lowest drawer.

He was angry. 'It is so stupid. They are treating us as if we have committed some horrible crime, as if we are disgraced. But the truth is that there are people in England who would not only sympathize with us but applaud us.'

'We're not heroes,' Anna said. 'We didn't do anything really. We just got in the way. We were an inconvenience.'

'At least that's something to be.'

Clerkenwell sent their small salary every month. There was nothing to spend it on.

'There's one thing to be grateful for,' Ralph said. 'When the baby's born, I can take over the teaching and you need do nothing. We can get a nurse from the village, Salome will find someone for us. Then if we have broken nights, you can get some rest during the day.'

The thought of the baby made him proud, worried, indefinably sad. That it would be born here, in Mosadinyana, in the heart of Africa. Anna's body was swollen, but her face was gaunt, and her arms were stick-thin. In those few days in prison the flesh had simply peeled away from her frame; her bones seemed larger now, and her wide-open eyes made her look sad and frail.

When they stepped out of their front door, in the morning or at evening, the go-away birds wheeled overhead, mocking and barracking, swooping and squawking their single, unvaried message; the only words which nature had given them. They were insistent companions, like someone you pick up with on a journey: someone who claims better knowledge of the terrain, who tries to persuade you to vary your planned route.

Ralph drove Anna to the Lutheran mission hospital, over roads that shook the bones and viscera. The doctor was an elderly Dutchman, worn and faded by the sun; he received her with kindly concern. All would be well, he assured her, passing his hand over the mound of her belly. There was no need for her to think of travelling down the railway line when her time came; he had delivered a hundred babies, and he had plenty of experience if anything, God forbid, should go wrong. He saw, he said, that she was a sensible young woman, stronger than she looked; and after the event, all she would need would be the most simple precautions of hygiene, the common-sense measures any mother would take. 'Think what your baby will have,' he said. 'God's blessed sun, almost every day of the year. Quiet nights under the stars and moon.'

Anna looked up at his outbreak of lyricism, half-raising herself on the examination couch. Had he been drinking? He laid a hand on her forehead, easing her back. 'Mrs Eldred,' he said, 'I have heard of your troubles in the Republic. You and your husband, you are young people who deserve the happiness that will come to you. It will be a pleasure and an honour to me to put your first child safe in your arms.'

Each night, by the light of lamps and candles, they sat over their Setswana grammars. Outside, the darkness rustled and croaked; inside, the only sound was a moth's wingbeat. And yet they were not alone; there was a settlement out there, lightless, invisible, ragged night-breathing its only sound. In the first week, a parade of blanket-wrapped men and women had come to the door, asking for work. Anna was bewildered. She did not know how to turn them away, and it seemed there was no end to them. Ralph and Anna had made little progress in the language; when they tried to speak, people grinned at them. 'You may take on anyone you need to help you,' Anna told Salome. 'But not people we don't need, not people who will just sit around doing nothing. Because it is not fair to choose some and not the others, to pay some and not the others. But Salome, listen, anyone who is hungry, you never, never turn them away.'

Did she turn them away? Anna was afraid that she did – on a whim, or according to the dictates of her own judgement. They had to acknowledge that her judgement might be sounder than theirs. She was their mediatrix, their mainstay. Her English was hybrid, sometimes sliding into Afrikaans. Once she did speak memorably, her hands folded together, her eyes resting unseeingly on something through the window, in the dusty yard: spoke with rhythm and fluency, with perfect confidence that she would be understood. 'In the days of our grandmothers, madam, there were many women to divide the task of carrying the water and grinding the millet and sweeping the house. Now there is only one woman. She must work all day in the heat of the sun until she drops.'

'An exaggeration,' Anna said, 'but, you see, she was speaking of the advantages of polygamy.'

'What will you think of next?' Ralph said.

'I think we have denatured these people,' Anna said. 'Everything old is condemned, everything of their own. Everything new and imported is held up to them as better.'

'Soap and civilization,' Ralph said. 'That was the idea. Oh, and God.'

'Oh, and God,' Anna said. 'I begin to wonder what Christianity has to offer to women. Besides a series of insults, that is.'

There were quarters on the mission compound for three servants. Two of these whitewashed rooms were already claimed, one by Salome, one by the gardener Enock. But the people Anna could not employ did not go away. The other hut was soon taken by a large family of mother and children whose origin no one knew; other families camped out in the vicinity, built themselves lean-tos even frailer than the shacks on the outskirts of Elim. They were hanging around, it seemed, in expectation; you could not say in hope, for nothing so lively as hope could ever be discerned in the expressions of these visitors of theirs. That was what Ralph called them: our visitors. Their faces showed, rather, an awesome patience, a faith; a faith that one day the beatitudes would be fulfilled, and the meek and the poor in spirit would come into their kingdom. Or into a job, at least. One day Anna would wake up, and find her ambitions quite different; she would need as many servants as Blenheim, or Buckingham Palace on a garden-party day.

Anna wrote home, in cautious terms, about her condition. Her mother's reply came, two months on: 'Last week you were in the minds of our whole congregation. Everyone keeps you in their prayers and thoughts. The people around you, though primitive, are no doubt very kind.'

The cooler weather brought relief. She breathed more easily then, above the arch of her ribs. Only one thing had sickened her, and its season had been brief: the guava tree, riotously fertile, diffusing through the air the scent of eau-de-cologne slapped on to decaying flesh.

Anna said, 'Ralph, in my grandmother's generation . . .' Her voice tailed off. She hadn't meant to sound so biblical; she must be catching it from Salome. She began again. 'In our family, some years back . . . there were twins.' She waited. He looked up. She glanced away from the shock on his face. 'The doctor can't be sure, of course, but he says to keep the possibility in mind. He thinks it will be all right.'

'Thinking's not enough,' Ralph said. He put his head in his hands. 'Oh God, if we were in Elim now . . . If you could get to Jo'burg or Pretoria there would be no problems, every facility would be there for us. We should go south, Anna. Surely they wouldn't refuse us? It's your first child, you've not been well . . . Surely they'd make a gesture, a humanitarian gesture?'

'No, they wouldn't,' Anna said. 'If we turned up in Jo'burg or Pretoria they'd put us back in gaol.'

'Me, perhaps – not you, surely?'

'Why not? They put me in gaol before.' Anna shook her head. 'Forget it, Ralph. I don't want to set foot on that soil. I don't want that kind of compassion.'

Three weeks before the birth she did go south, but only to Lobatsi, a small town on the railway line. She had booked herself in at the Athlone Hospital; if something went wrong, she and the babies had a better chance here than they would have up-country. She believed in the twins, they were no longer a subject for conjecture; she imagined she could feel the two new hearts beating below her own. While she waited to be proved correct, she passed her days sitting at her window in the Lobatsi Hotel, watching the populace pushing into the Indian trading stores, wanting buckets and sacks of sugar and sewing cotton and beer. Men who had called at the butchers dragged up the dusty road, carrying sticky parcels from which grey intestines flopped. Women sat on the hotel steps and sold knitted hats; when evening came their daughters sat there and sold their bodies, elbowing each other and shrieking while they waited for trade, passing from hand to hand a cigarette, a plastic comb, a mirror encrusted with glass jewels.

The weather was cool, blue and still, the mornings sharp with frost. There were few white faces in the street. She listened every day for the call of the train, from the track beyond the eucalyptus trees; she saw the procession that trailed to the station, women hauling sacks of onions and laden with boxes and bags, and boys with oranges running to sell them to the travellers. When the train drew in, the passengers mobbed it, swinging from its sides and swaying from it, as if it were a steer that must be wrestled to earth. Sometimes it seemed to her that the whole country was on the move; yet she became stiller, heavier, more acquiescent to the strangeness and the pain that lay ahead.

In the depth of winter, and before dawn, her babies were born. Her own Dutch doctor had intended to be there with her, but he had been delayed, impeded somehow – broken axle, perhaps, or sudden minor epidemic – and she felt some protection had been withdrawn. She heard strange voices in the corridors, and the moans of another woman in labour; and this sound seemed to come to her now from her left, now from her right, now from the hospital gardens beyond her window and once perhaps from her own throat. When her daughter was born she held out her arms for the child, but when her son was born she had become an object, leaden with fatigue, her arms no longer hers to command. She heard him cry, and turned her head with difficulty, very slowly, to see him in a nurse's hands, his body transfixed by a shaft of early light. Ralph stood by her bed, and held her hand as if it were a stone. They had already chosen a girl's name, Katherine. 'The boy after your father,' Anna whispered. 'Because it will heal . . . because it will heal . . .'

Because it will heal all wounds. She left him suddenly, hurtling into sleep like an unstrung climber from a cliff face.

The doctor took Ralph by the arm and led him from the room. His heart felt small, very heavy, a pebble in his chest, contracted with shock and fear at the sight of the bloody streaked beings his wife's body had produced. Later that day, after he had slept for a couple of hours, he went to see the babies again. He saw that there was no reason to be afraid. The twins were small, but healthy. They had curls of black hair, and eyes of black-grey: hard but melting, like the eyes of puppies.

The months that followed were months of a lulling calm, shot through by the small emergencies of infant illness and ill-temper, by the vagaries of life in the wasteland; and these months, when Ralph and Anna looked back on their time in the protectorate, would seem like years. They were years of air so dry it seemed to burn the lungs; years of thorn and scrub, of a fine dust that covers every surface. The country's spectrum was narrow: rose-red, through brick, through lion-colour, to stone. In summer, under the sun's unclosing eye, the landscape seemed flattened, two-dimensional, as if it were always noon. Mosquitoes whined in the darkness, plunging unseen at swollen ankle veins, and ticks bit and clung and swelled fat with blood, engorged like blue-grey peas. About the place early one morning, inhaling a hot dawn mist, Ralph saw baboons in the garden, stripping the fig tree, handling the wormy fruit with murmurs of appreciation. Still as death, he watched them from the back stoep; it was as if he were watching someone else's dream, or the re-enactment of a myth. It puzzled him; he could not say what myth it was.

In summer the sky was violet, sullen; when storms came, the downpour whipped garden snakes from their heat-trances. Green mamba, boomslang, spitting cobra: after the rains, the ground seethed like a living carpet. Six legs, eight legs, no legs: everything moved.

Salome found a woman called Felicia, to be the children's nanny. Felicia must have her own home; the mother and children who had taken over the third servants' hut moved out, and Felicia moved in. She would have a bed in the twins' room, but she must have privacy, a place for her possessions; and I, Anna thought, wish sometimes to be alone in my house. The displaced family built themselves a lean-to. They seemed to accept the situation. Still they waited, week after week, to be called to Anna's service.

Felicia was a tall erect woman with a smooth face and thin, almost Hamitic features. She was twenty-three years old, she said, was a mission girl herself, and had two children, who stayed with their grandmother in Kanye, in another part of the country. It was Matthew she liked best to carry on her back, but – as if in compensation – she placed on Katherine's wrist a bracelet of tiny blue beads. When the babies were tiny, she wafted the cattle-flies from their faces, and soothed one while Anna fed the other; when they grew she taught them to sit up and clap their hands and sing a song. She was scrupulous and clean, diligent and polite, but she spoke when she was spoken to, and then just barely. Her thoughts, she reserved to herself.

In winter there were porcupine quills on the paths, and the nights were as sharp as the blade of a knife. The waterless months brought wild animals to the edge of settlements, and once again the baboons crept down at dawn, shadowing the compound families, waiting to seize a porridge-pot left unwatched. Once, early in the morning and from a distance, Anna saw a leopard, an area of clouded darkness covering his chest. The darkness was fresh blood, she supposed; she imagined how the sun would dry it, and the spotted fur stiffen into points.

Anna spoke now in an arbitrary blend of English, Setswana, Afrikaans – any language which served. She loved her children with an intemperate blend of fear and desire; fear of insects and snakes, desire for their essence, for their shackled twin souls to be made free. She placed the brother beside the sister, watched them creep together, entwine limbs; she wished for them to grow and speak, to separate, to announce themselves as persons. An only child, she envied them and found them strange. When she prayed, which was almost never, it was only for Ralph: God preserve his innocence, and protect him from the consequences of it. She felt it was a dangerous thing, his bewilderment in the face of human wickedness; she felt that it left them exposed. She had been told as a child that you could not strike bargains with God, but she had never understood why not; surely God, if he had once been Man, would retain a human desire for advantage? Where simple strength is required, she bargained, let Ralph provide it; but where there are complexities, give them to me. Alone in her schoolroom and her house, below the tropic of Capricorn, she saw her path in life tangled, choked, thorny, like one of the cut-lines that ran through the bush and melted away into the desert.

Later, of course, she wondered at herself; how could she not have seen the road ahead? Even in the early days – before the wisdom conferred by the event – any trouble, any possible trouble, seemed to settle around the sullen, fugitive form of Enock, the man who was nominally in charge of the garden.

Enock, like them, was a refugee from the south. So they understood; asked where he came from, he nodded his head indifferently towards the border, and said, 'Over that side.' Ralph tried to talk to him: look, whatever you've done there, whatever happened, it doesn't matter, that was there and this is a different country. Ralph suspected that Enock had been in prison, for some petty criminality rather than for some offence against the race laws; though they make sure you can't distinguish, he said, between a criminal act and an act of protest, and God knows, he said, if a man like Enock were to cheat or steal, should we make a judgement? Who can say what I would do, in his shoes, in the shoes of a black man in South Africa today?

But then Ralph would come back, from another dragging, weary quarter hour with Enock, and say, well, we never get anywhere. I'm just a white man to him.

Anna nodded. 'And isn't he just a black man to you?'

'I try not to think like that.'

'How can you not? You have to make him into something. A victim. Or a hero. One or the other.'

'Yes. Perhaps you're right.'

'But it's not like that. He's just an individual.' She considered. 'And I think as an individual he's a waste of time.'

Ralph shook his head; he wouldn't have it. 'We can't know what his life has been. How can you know? You are talking to him and he walks away.'

'And yet he understands you. He understands what you say.'

'Oh yes, that's not his problem. He reminds me of Clara sometimes – do you remember how she would freeze you out? I used to wonder if something so terrible had happened to her that she just couldn't bring herself to speak about it – she seemed numb. And Enock's like that. Oh well,' Ralph said. 'If I think I can help him, I must be patient and persist.'

Enock was about thirty years old, a handsome and composed man, with the same thin features as Felicia, an even, impassive face. He wore tattered khaki shorts and the cast-off jacket of a European-style suit. Ralph wondered about the original owner – who would have bought such a thing? The jacket was tan, and it was tight under his arms, and shiny from wear. Sometimes, when he went about his tasks, he would take it off and hang it on the branch of a tree. One day, the puppy took it down and worried it; Anna dragged it from his jaws in a state not too far from the original, but she felt that this was one more grievance for the gardener to chalk up on his soul.

This dog of theirs; *your* dog, she said to Ralph, when it ate books and dragged blankets outside into the dust. Ralph had brought the puppy home from a trip to Palapye, a settlement on the railway line; he had climbed out of the truck dazzled by the sun, thirsty, weary, coated in dust, and put into her hands a baffling fur bundle, an indecipherable animal like a tiny bear, with boot-button eyes and a dense, lemon-coloured coat. 'Whatever is it?' she had said, alarmed, and Ralph had said, reassuringly, just a dog. The McPhersons gave him to me; they said, this is what you need, a dog about the place.

'What a strange thought for them to have,' Anna said. 'Don't they think two babies are enough?'

'The babies don't bark,' Ralph said. 'That's what he's for, a watchdog, not a pet.'

'I suppose he can be both.'

'When I was a child I was never allowed to have a dog.'

'Nor me,' Anna said. 'I had a goldfish once, but it died. Just as well. I always thought that my papa would usher some customers through from the shop, and tell them he could get two fillets out of it.'

'So,' Ralph said. 'So, you see, the twins, they'll have a dog, and we didn't have.'

'What is it, anyway, what breed?'

'The McPhersons claim its mother is a pure-bred Alsatian, and they did – Anna, give me another glass of water – they did show her to me, and she looked authentic – but then they say his father is a yellow labrador, also of good pedigree. I can't believe that. I think his mum climbed out of the compound and took potluck.'

That was what they called the dog: Potluck. Potluck, as

young things do, passed through a phase of great beauty. His button eyes grew large and lustrous, and his lemon fur turned to the colour of butterscotch. His temperament was mild, and when the twins were fractious and unrewarding Anna would pick him up and kiss the velvet, benign space between his ears. Even Salome and Felicia, who did not see the point of dogs, would sometimes take time to speak to him, and caress him in a gingerly way.

At the age of eight months Potluck grew ugly. His head was huge, his muzzle blunt, his ears pointed different ways; he developed brusque, selective barking, like an old colonel suddenly moved to write to the papers. Almost grown now, he shambled around the mission compound, winning friends and giving offence. 'It is a horrible, English trait,' Ralph said, 'to despise people who are afraid of dogs.'

'Enoch's not afraid,' Anna said. 'He just affects to be.'

'I like to think well of Enoch,' Ralph said, 'and in fact I make it my policy, but it has to be said that he's becoming a bloody nuisance.'

It was Salome who had begun the complaints. 'He has stolen from me,' she said. 'My straw hat.'

'Do you think so?' Anna said. 'What would Enoch do with your straw hat?'

'Sell it,' Salome said. Anna almost asked, sarcastically, and what do you think it would be worth? She checked herself. These people negotiate in pennies, rather than shillings, so perhaps it's true, perhaps Enoch has sold her hat.

She said to Ralph, 'Salome is always complaining about Enoch, and now she says he's raiding her wardrobe.'

'Then I must have a word with him. We can't have Salome upset. Do you think she's telling the truth?

Anna frowned. 'Hard to know. She has a preoccupation with clothes at the moment. She thinks she should be given dresses, cast-offs. But I have a difficulty here, because I can't manufacture cast-offs, no one can. I could make her a dress, that would be no problem, but it wouldn't be the same, it's *my* clothes she wants.'

'Nothing of yours would fit her,' Ralph said. 'Even if you wore your clothes out, which you don't.'

'I gave a skirt to Felicia – that one I made in Elim, out of the roll Mr Ahmed gave me. That grey-green paisley skirt, do you remember?'

'Yes,' Ralph said, lying.

'I was pleased with that skirt, it was the nicest thing I'd ever made for myself. Now I'm an inch too big for it, so I thought I'd give it to Felicia, she's so smart and neat.' Anna smiled. 'She doesn't like it much. She thinks it's drab. Still, I like to see her wearing it. It hangs well.'

'So Salome is jealous?'

'More than that. Jealous and aggrieved.'

'Perhaps Mrs Instow used to give her clothes. The best Paris labels.'

They laughed. In the back of a drawer, they had found a photograph of the Instows, the kind of fading snap that people describe as 'taken with my old Box Brownie'. A little, huddled, sexless couple they were, false teeth bared in haunted smiles. Where were they now? The mission society's pension arrangements were not generous. A bed-sitting room and kitchenette, Ralph thought, somewhere like Leamington Spa. God save us. Sometimes now his thoughts turned to what he would do when they left Mosadinyana. His father would be seventy in three years' time, and his mother's letters hinted that the work of the Trust was getting too much for him. The Trust had grown a good deal, from its original local foundation; and Uncle James, still toiling among the London derelicts, was approaching what would normally be thought of as retirement age. I should be putting my mind to taking over from them, Ralph thought, going home and finding us a house and beginning the next phase in life. I can face them now, he thought, my mother and father, because I have done and seen things they have never dreamed of. And I have children of my own, now.

Anna seemed disinclined to speculate about the future. She had too many petty day-to-day concerns. A kind of kitchen war had broken out. Someone had taken a whole sack of sugar, just brought in from the store; it must be Salome, Anna thought, because sugar was one of her perquisites, she took it for granted that no one would prevent her from carrying it away by the pound, under her apron. 'But a whole sack, Salome,' Anna said, turning on her disappointed eyes. 'So that I go to the pantry and there is none – none – not a spoonful for Felicia's tea.'

Salome said nothing, but a peevish expression crossed her face. Later that day she began her ritual complaints about Enock. 'He is not doing his work properly. Always at a beer-drink when he says he is going to a funeral.'

Beer-drink, Anna said under her breath; yes indeed, there are plenty of beer-drinks, with beer brewed by you, madam, brewed with my sugar. Later that day, Salome came back for another attack: 'All my vegetables I have planted, they are dying and dead.'

Anna considered. There was some truth in this. What she did not like about Enock was his attitude to the poor things that tried to grow in the earth. It seemed to her that he had chosen his trade specially so that he could be destructive. When things grew, he cut them down. You might call it pruning, she supposed, but he liked to cut until you could see plant-blood; she felt for the stunted, cropped-back plants, and remembered how when she had been a small child her mother had in the name of hygiene pared her nails to the quick; five years old, she saw her little fingers, sore and blunt and red, turning the pages of her first reading book. And again and again her mother had done it, and so did Enock, and you could not argue, for they thought it was a thing they were morally obliged to do. What flourished, Enock left unwatered. He killed with his sharp blades, and he killed by neglect.

'Ralph will take over looking after the vegetables,' Anna said. 'And I will look after them too when the babies are bigger.'

Salome looked shocked. 'No, madam,' she said. And for the first time referred to precedent: Mr and Mrs Instow would never have done such a thing.

Ralph said, 'They're against Enock because he is an outsider.'

'He is not an outsider,' Anna said. 'He has plenty of friends.'

'Where?'

'I don't know. Somewhere. On the railway line. He's always sneaking off, you know that. Salome says we should give his job to one of the visitors.'

'Give him another chance,' Ralph said. 'Please, Anna? There must be some story that he's not telling us. There must be some reason he's like he is.'

Must there? Anna had the feeling a row was building up.

The next thing to occur was the loss of most of Ralph's clothes. Ralph had gone to Palapye for the day, and she must have been in the schoolroom when it happened; classes were over, but she was making a coloured chart for the wall, a coloured chart with the nine-times table. The babies had been put down for their afternoon sleep, and Felicia took her own siesta beside them. Anna finished her work, put away the scissors and the big paste-pot; closed the schoolroom door behind her, shutting in its heat; trailed into the house, washed her hands and face, and made for her own bedroom, hoping to rest for an hour. The wardrobe door gaped as usual, but the camphor-scented interior was nothing but an area of darkness.

Enock's disappearance could not be entirely coincidental. Odd items had gone missing before; Ralph's wardrobe was not so extensive that she did not notice the loss. She would not have minded so much if Enock himself had seemed to profit from either the theft or the sale. But he still wore the tight tan jacket, sweat stained: the same ragged shirts and broken shoes.

'This time he's gone too far,' she said. What bothered her was the thought of Enock in the house, pawing their few possessions. She imagined herself confronting him, and could see already the arrogance of his expression, his superiority; at the back of her mind she heard Ralph saying, well, perhaps he is entitled to his expression, perhaps he is indeed superior to us, but she did not believe it, she thought Enock was just one of those people you find everywhere in the world and in all cultures, one of those people who spread disaffection and unease, who sneer at the best efforts of other people and who make them restless and unhappy and filled with self-doubt.

'Let it go,' Ralph said. 'We've no proof it was him. Where was Potluck, anyway?'

'Asleep under a bush. Besides, he knows Enock, doesn't he? I've had to teach him to leave Enock alone.'

'It could have been one of the visitors. Anyone could have come in.'

'Don't be simple-minded,' she said. 'It's Enock, he has his trading routes, everybody tells me about it. He takes things and puts them on the train and his pals take them off in Francistown.'

Ralph looked miserable. 'We'll have to start locking the doors, I suppose.'

Anna thought of Elim: the great bunch of keys that Lucy Moyo had put into her hand on her first day at Flower Street.

'Yes, we will,' she said. 'And I'll have to start locking the larder and counting the supplies and giving things out only when they're asked for. Goddammit, Ralph, are we going to let ourselves be robbed blind?'

'It hardly matters,' Ralph said. 'My clothes weren't that good.'

Then, two days later, Felicia came crying that her skirt had gone, her best skirt, the one that madam had given her. She looked dangerous; she wanted to make an issue out of it.

Anna thought: oh, the bare-faced cheek of the man! She had done as Ralph told her, she had said nothing, but now she was not going to consult Ralph, she was going to sack Enock that afternoon and be done with him. Her patience was at an end. Felicia had been a good girl, she was careful with the babies, it was against their interests to have her upset.

She called to Enock from the back stoep. He sauntered towards her with his corner-boy's gait. Salome stood by, swollen with self-righteousness.

Anna looked out over her parched, devastated garden: 'Enock, what has happened to Felicia's skirt?'

Enock's lip curled. 'Ask that woman,' he said, barely indicating Salome with his eyes.

'You skelm,' Salome said, furious. 'God will strike you.'

'Don't be stupid,' Anna said. 'Salome does not steal.'

'Sugar,' Enock suggested.

Anna conceded it. 'Maybe.' Her eyes travelled sideways to Salome. 'I don't mind sugar, or anything within reason. But it is you who steal clothes and sell them, Enock. It is a bad thing to steal from my husband, bad enough, but it is worse to steal a skirt from Felicia, who is poorer than you are.'

'I did not see this skirt,' Enock said.

'Rubbish,' Anna said. 'That's rubbish, Enock, and you know it.'

And into the sentence she put contempt; what she meant to say was, Enock, I don't hate you, I just despise you, you're in my way and I want to clear you out, and get something better.

228

The man looked straight at her, into her face. Their eyes locked. She tried to face him down, and was determined to do it. The moment drew itself out. A voice inside her said, it is ridiculous, that you should engage in a battle of wills – you who have everything, you who have an education, a husband, twin babies, you who have God's love – with this poor wanderer, this gardener, this man with no home. A further voice said, it is ridiculous in itself, this battle of the gaze, perhaps it is some convention that we have in Europe, yet how does he know of it? Perhaps all people know it, perhaps animals even. And perhaps, thought Anna, it is one of the battles that I am equipped to fight.

So it proved. Enock, his mouth moving around words unspoken, dropped his gaze and turned, his head down, and moved hunch-shouldered towards his own quarters.

There was a silence. Anna looked down at her dusty sandals, as if her eyes were worn out from the effort. Salome spoke, taking her own time, and her voice had a sick gladness in it. 'Oh, Mrs Eldred, oh, madam. You know it is a thing you must not say, you must not say to a person, you are rubbish.'

'What?' Anna said. She looked up again. 'I didn't say that. I didn't say he was rubbish. I said his excuses were rubbish.'

'It is the same,' Salome said complacently.

Anna felt a quiver of doubt inside. There were, she knew, these forbidden phrases in every language; phrases that seemed harmless in themselves, but contained some deadly insult. Uncertainly, she asked, 'I've said something bad?'

Salome nodded. 'Enock will go away now,' she said.

'Good,' Anna said. 'That is what I want. I don't like to sack him, you understand? But if he goes because I have spoken the truth, I can hardly be responsible for that. We can have another gardener now. One of the people who lives in the huts may come.' She heard her strange, stilted speech, but didn't regard it. That was how she talked these days.

That morning would always stay in her mind. It was many months since rain had fallen. There were bush fires on the hills, ringing the village and the settlements near by. They smouldered, sometimes flared: at night you could see them moving slowly, like an affliction in the blood.

It was just as Salome had predicted; Enock was gone by nightfall. His room had been cleared, and there was nothing left of him but his distinctive footprints dragged through the dust. Anna found them next morning on the cement steps of the back stoep, outside the kitchen. Perhaps he had come to make amends, to plead his case? If so he had thought better of it, and turned away, and vanished into the bush. By afternoon they had engaged another gardener from among the visitors, and the whitewashed room was occupied. Enock had taken the curtains with him, and Anna sat down at her sewing machine to make another pair.

She brooded while she worked: so much unpleasantness, over so little. She was reluctant to have perpetrated even the smallest injustice, though she tended to be practical in these matters; to be brisk about other people's squabbles, as schoolteachers are. Nothing would ever be taught or learned, if you stopped the lesson every two minutes, to hold a court of inquiry: *Madam, madam, Moses is stealing my pencil, Tebogo is sitting in my chair, Effat is hitting me and calling me a cat.* It seemed to her that this was a case of the schoolroom kind. Perhaps Salome had taken the skirt, out of spite. It was possible. And Salome herself had been claiming for the past month or more that she had seen the gardener leaving Felicia's room in the early morning. Would Enock steal from his mistress?

Yes, quite likely, Ralph said, when she put it to him. He seemed to have grown tired suddenly. Or tired of this situation, anyway. 'You were right,' he said. 'We should have sacked

Enock long ago. Anyway, he's out of our hair now. Not that you have much,' he said to his son. He lifted Matthew above his head. 'Up to the roof,' he said. 'Up to the roof and up to the moon. What a big strong boy! But when will you get a head of hair like your sister?'

Kit watched from her cot, a finger in her mouth, her face dubious. 'Up to the moon,' Ralph said. 'Up to the moon, baby. And down again.'

Next day Salome said, 'Storms tonight, madam. The weather is coming up.'

It was August now, and not warm; there were clouds blowing over the hills. 'Good,' Anna said. 'We need the rain.'

Let it be a good storm, she thought, one that fills the water tanks. I don't mind tomorrow's cold and the damp, even tomorrow's snakes, as long as we have water to see us through the winter.

Early in the afternoon, just after school was over, Potluck came in from the garden – plodding, poor dog, as if his feet were lead. It was not like him; usually he bounded and bounced. 'What is it, Potluck?' He staggered towards Anna, falling against her legs. 'What's the matter, chicken?' His great butter-coloured head drooped, nuzzling her shin. Then suddenly his body contorted. He seemed to shiver all over, in a violent spasm or fit; then his ribs arched, and he began to vomit.

Anna watched him, stepping back in shock, calling out to Ralph to come and see; but Ralph was not in the house. Potluck's body seemed to shrink, as if his bones were contracted by his efforts. And yet there was no effort, because a stinking liquid seemed to flow from him as if a tap had been turned on inside. Yellow-green, viscous, the fluid pooled about his feet, washed across the carpet, widened about the room. Its stench rose up; it hit Anna like a fist. She herself gagged; it was like nothing she had smelled before, a hellish compound of rotting plant-life and burnt rubber, a smell of panic and morbidity and flesh revolted against itself. On and on it went, a ceaseless flow. She had heard of cancers, of malignities that are so foul that even the most Christian of nurses must enter the rooms with masks. Was that what she was inhaling now? She wanted to turn and run, skitter down the steps of the front stoep and out into the air. But pity for the creature gripped her; it held her to the spot. She saw the dog's ribs heave, saw his eyes turn up into his skull; hand over her mouth, she saw his whipped crouch, his buckling joints. Potluck fell, lurching stiffly on to his side; but still that revolting fluid pumped on, and on. How could his body contain so much? She moaned his name; oh, Potluck, my little dog, what has happened to you? She crouched beside him and put her hands on him. His fur was wet, and a thousand pulses seemed to jump at her through his side.

But as she touched him, the flow stopped. The feculent pool ceased to grow. With a final expulsive effort the dog heaved his body clear of the floor, like an animal galvanized in an experiment. He dropped back, thudding against the floorboards. He drew a great breath, shuddering as a human being might. His whole body twitched, and his lips curled back from his teeth. He closed his eyes.

But Potluck was not dead. When she put her hand on his head, his tail moved, once. It beat the floor, spreading the hideous efflux to her skirt. She looked up, saw Ralph in the doorway, staring down at them. 'Poisoned?' he whispered.

They said nothing further. They were afraid to speak. They picked up the dog and carried him to the veranda next to their bedroom; they sponged the filth from his coat, wrapped him in blankets, and dabbed water on to his dry muzzle, hoping he would lick. Anna sat by him while Ralph dragged the ruined carpet into the air, and threw buckets of water and disinfectant on to the floor, and swept out the froth and scum.

When he finished, and returned to Anna, Potluck was licking water from her fingers. His eyes were still closed, and the orbs danced and jerked under his lids. 'I think he's saved himself,' Ralph said. 'God knows what it was, but no doubt if it had been in his system another hour it would have killed him.'

Potluck is a big dog, Anna thought. The poison for a dog would kill a child, kill two babies. A horrible rush of fear swept over her, left her nauseous, weak, clinging to the windowsill. 'What can it have been?' Her voice shook. 'What can he have eaten?'

'Something left for him,' Ralph said. 'Bait.' He dropped his head. 'I'm sorry, Anna. Enock's final act of spite, I think. He never liked Potluck and he knew that we loved him, I have seen his lip curl when he has heard me talk to him. You were quite right about the man, I should have listened, you were completely right and I was completely wrong.' He held out his hand. She took it. 'Anyway, he's failed.' He stooped, patted the animal's side. He looked vindicated, as if good had won out. As if it had prevailed. As if it always would.

For the rest of the day Anna checked Potluck at intervals, first every ten minutes, then every half-hour, then on the hour; keeping a fearful vigil, as she had for the twins in their first months. She would have brought him to a more convenient place, but he was an outdoor dog, and did not understand carpets and furniture; to lie on the stoep was as much as he could tolerate. By dusk he had heaved himself from his side into a more alert position, and his strange swivel-mounted ears had begun to move in accordance with the sounds of the household and the compound. But he was half-hearted about his vigilance, and when he tried a bark he had to ponder it; the sound was muffled, and afterwards he looked bemused and exhausted. 'Never mind, Potluck,' Anna said, rubbing his head. 'You're off-duty tonight.'

'He'll be all right now, won't he?' Ralph said. 'I would have cried, I think, if we'd lost Potluck. I love him for his simple and greedy character.'

'He's like the twins,' Anna said. 'That is their character, exactly.'

He took Anna in his arms, pressing her head against his shoulder, feeling her shiver from the stresses of the day. He stroked her back, murmuring meaningless, reassuring words, pet-names; but he was shot through by self-doubt, shaken inside by it. This business with the gardener, it had bothered him, disturbed him a good deal. Anna would say, oh, of course there are injustices, there are miscalculations: they all even out. But he did not believe that. He did not say so to his wife, but he thought her attitude faintly repulsive; it is fatalistic, he thought, it releases us from the responsibility which we should properly take. We should do our best, he felt, always our best – consult our consciences, consult our capabilities, then, whenever we can, push out against unjust circumstance.

Enock was a crook, a petty criminal, perhaps accused of the one crime he didn't commit; all acts of injustice are magnified in the victim's eyes. The error may be irretrievable, Ralph thought; we have made a choice about him, perhaps the wrong one, but what can we do now? The situation could not stand still. We had to choose.

Lying awake sometimes, listening to the sounds of the bush, he brooded on the larger thoughts that routine keeps at bay. This I could do, or that . . . Each action contains its opposite. Each action contains the shadow-trace of the choice not made, the seeds of infinite variation. Each choice, once made, trips contingencies, alternatives; each choice breeds its own universe. If in the course of his life he had done one thing differently, one tiny thing, perhaps he would not be where he is now; his frail wife in his arms, his twins on the knee of their dark nanny, his convalescent dog at his feet, ribs heaving with delight at mere survival. Everything in the universe declines to chaos and waste; he knows this, he is not so poor a scientist. But he believes that his choices have been the right ones, that this is where he wishes to be; believes it simply, as he believed in Bible stories when he was a child. If his choices have led to this, have brought him to this moment, they have an intrinsic rightness; as for those other worlds, the alternative universes, he will not inquire. And surely, in the end, he says, my will is free? The world is not as Anna says. There is no dispensation that guarantees or provides for an evening-up of the score. If we are not to be mere animals, or babies, we must always choose, and choose to do good. In choosing evil we collude with the principle of decay, we become mere vehicles of chaos, we become subject to the laws of a universe which tends back towards dissolution, the universe the devil owns. In choosing to do good we show we have free will, that we are God-designed creatures who stand against all such laws.

So I will be good, Ralph thought. That is all I have to do.

The storm broke that night, around nine o'clock. Ralph and Anna had lit a fire in the twins' room, and left them, warm and drowsy, under Felicia's eye. The twins did not wake much at night now, and Anna was happy to attend to them when they did; so usually the nanny would have been back in her own quarters. But the rain was heavy, unrelenting, cold like frozen metal and falling like metal rods. On her haunches before the fire, Felicia rubbed her shins and indicated that she would stay; and her own bedstead, with its two plump pillows and crocheted blanket, was more inviting than the battering wind outside.

The world was full of noise, you had to raise your voice against it; the metal rain drummed the roof, and the wind moaned. Anna stood at the window, watching sheet lightning illuminate the garden, the fig tree, the mutilated fig tree that was part of Enock's legacy. It lit up the straggling boundary fence of the mission compound, the shacks of their visitors – lighting them as they had never been lit before, because there were people in those shacks who could not afford candles. The inhabitants would be awash in brown water and mud, their roofs carried off perhaps, their cooking fires dowsed, their cardboard suitcases spoiled and their bundles and blankets and Sunday clothes now sodden. Tomorrow, she thought, we will tackle everything. Nothing can be done tonight, nothing can be done while this rain is still falling. She shivered. Ralph put into her hand a glass half-full of Cape brandy. She stood sipping it, still at the window; behind her the paraffin lamp guttered and flared. The coarse spirit warmed her. 'Fetch Potluck,' she said to Ralph. 'Carry him in. We could put him by the fire, it would do him good, I know he doesn't like to be inside but he might like the fire. Besides, if the wind veers round, that stoep will be awash within a minute.'

Ralph went out, a torch in his hand, down the passage to the back of the house. No respite; still the wind howled, the rain slashed in its rhythm against roof and wall and window. He heard the dog lift his head and whimper. Ralph clicked his tongue at him. 'Come on, Potluck.'

Potluck tried to get to his feet, his paws scraping on the polished floor. But the effort was beyond him; he fell back and lay miserably on his side. Ralph put down his torch, squatted by him, heaved him into his arms; his legs thrust out stiffly, Potluck grunted, half in indignation and half in relief.

It was dark in the house's central corridor, and Ralph guided himself by letting his shoulder brush the wall; he was on his way back to the sitting room, to Anna standing by the fire with her brandy. Now Potluck kicked his legs, as if he would like to make efforts for himself – so outside the kitchen Ralph lowered him gently on to his feet. Wagging his tail feebly, the dog crawled away under the kitchen table. 'Come to the fire,' Ralph said to him. 'Come on with me, Potluck.'

From outside the back door, Ralph heard a little noise, a scrape, a cry. It was a woman's voice, very small: *Baas, let us in*. He thought, it is our visitors, the poor people in their shacks; they are panic-stricken, their houses are carried off, they want shelter. The thought crossed his mind: your dog has been poisoned today, there is a man with a grudge against you, you are not entirely safe. Then he heard the voice again, little and pleading: baas, we are washed away, we are frightened, let us in.

And so, without more thought, he made his choice; he turned the key, stepped back, and drew the stiff bolt. As he swung open the broad, heavy back door, he felt it pushed, smashed back into his face; and he was not then surprised that Enock stood there, his face mild, curious, composed. Enock reached inside his jacket. As calmly as a man takes out his wallet – as calmly as a man in a grocer's shop, offering to pay – Enock took from inside his coat a small hatchet.

At once, Ralph smashed it from his hand. He had time to think, and he thought at once of his superior strength; so many years of full-cream milk, of lean beef, of muscle-building protein, and beneath his hand this poor felon, whose cloth jacket tore under his hand, ripping at the seam. Enock slid along the wall, his hands thrown up in front of his face.

Ralph smashed his fist into the man's jaw. He felt the intricate resistance of tooth and bone, felt pain in his own hand; and as he closed in on the man to throttle him he felt the slithering resistance of his sinews, of his stringy muscles and green bones. He had ripped away not just the jacket but the familiar sweat-soaked third-hand shirt, and he pushed against the wall clammy hairless flesh, pounding his fist above the man's heart as if that would stop it, adding this rhythm, thump, thump, to the drumming of the rain. He wanted nothing but death, nothing but to feel Enock wilt and stagger, droop, retch, fall, and then his feet would do the rest; and already in a kind of red-out of thought, a bloody dream, he saw his booted foot kicking in the delicate skull, splintering bone, scattering teeth, thudding and rebounding, thudding and rebounding like a machine, until the creature was dead.

He saw this in his mind; yet at the same time sensed movement in the darkness behind him. He heard the dog stir, try to get to his feet, fall back. Then a dull blow, very hard, between his shoulder-blades. He believed he had been hit with some huge, blunt object, like a fence pole. His mind filled with a picture of damage, of a huge bruise like a black sun. He turned around on this presence behind him, moving more slowly than before, and put the palm of his hand against a looming face, and shoved it away. It was a stranger's face, and though later he would think and think about it he would never be able to identify it. He also wondered, later, at how long it had taken him to realize that he was bleeding. The dull blow was a knife-wound, a wound between his ribs; and as his blood began to flow, he fell against the kitchen wall.

The next moments were lost, would always be lost. He had a vague consciousness of his own heart, an organ he had given no thought before. Unregarded, unpraised, heart beats and beats: but heart jibs now.

He lay down, passively, curiously tired. He was waiting to die. Let me die, his mind said, dying is not too bad. It is too much trouble to stay alive. I am warm now. This easy emission of blood is to be desired; flow on, and on. I am warm now, and soon I will be safe.

When the stranger entered the room where she stood by the

fireplace, her drink in her hand, Anna did not scream, because she found she had no voice; she knew the essence of fear, which is like a kind of orgasm, and she was numb and white and still as she listened to the man's demand for money, as she took the keys from the top drawer of the sideboard, opened up the mission cash-box and gave him what was inside. Without looking at them, the man thrust the notes into his pockets with his free hand. He spilled some coins; he did not seem to care about them, and yet those coins too were money, a lot of money. She watched them roll away, under the furniture. The man kept his eyes on her face. So, she thought, have they come here to kill us?

She saw a torn shape creep into the room. 'Enock!' she said. The strange man closed in on her, took her by the arm. But rage made her strong enough to tear her arm from his grip – to pick up the bottle of brandy from which Ralph had poured her drink, to smash it against the sideboard, that ghastly piece of furniture the Instows had so loved. Let them turn it on me, she thought, let them take it out of my hand, let them blind me, but let me blind them first.

A moment later she was alone. They had gone. The alcohol fumes rose into the room. Shattered glass lay about her feet. The neck of the bottle was sealed in her palm, as if it were fused to the bone. She was alone, the storm still battering the house; within her was a small dangerous silence, like a chip of ice in her heart.

She must move from the spot, and find out what hideous thing had occurred; the splintered bottle in one hand, the lamp held high in the other. She must walk from the room to the kitchen, see her husband slumped in death's narcotic embrace; she must walk from the kitchen to the room where her children were left sleeping. In that room she will receive her own death-blow; the one that will leave no mark on her skin, but will peel and scalp her, part the flesh of joy from the bone of grief. Let her move from this room, and she will be impaled to suffer slowly, to suffer as much when she is a woman of eighty as she will suffer now – a little pale English girl with black hair, footsteps pattering down a black corridor, running into an abandoned, empty room.

Dawn came late. Felicia had gone, and taken everything from her hut, all her possessions; she had packed and flitted, in an orderly and premeditated way. There was blood on the kitchen walls, and less noticeable blood, dark and slippery, on the red cement floors. Ralph, white as a bandage, lay cocooned in other bandages. The light was splintered, refracted, full of water; the grass moved, the bush moved, the earth seemed to shiver and shift.

Anna walked, tottering, between Salome and an Englishman who appeared to be an official, perhaps a kind of policeman. Everything will be done, she was told; for, Mrs Eldred, this is unprecedented, we have never before in the history of this country recorded the abduction of a white child, of two white babies, and from their family's compound at night – no, Mrs Eldred, there has been nothing like it.

She thought, because there is no precedent, they wish to believe it cannot be true. They wish me to say that, finding myself alone, finding this shattered bottle welded to my palm, I ventured out, saw my husband half-dead on the floor, saw by the light of my lamp the blood on the walls; that I proceeded then into my children's room, saw that their nurse was gone, saw the doors open, saw all the doors of the house open, saw the wind and rain flying in – saw my children's beds empty, but no: no, there I was mistaken, for there is no precedent for it, it has never been heard of, such monstrosities cannot be entertained. I was mistaken when I thought my twins were gone; my son Matthew, my daughter Kit. They were safe all the time, dear policeman. My husband's life-blood had to be washed from the walls, and I am the woman who did it; but no, in this matter of my twin children, I was mistaken. I must be. You cannot bear it, otherwise, your official burden is too great. For if they are really missing, you must track them now, in the fractured light of the day after the storm: the country awash, the mud sliding, the fords in flood . . . Anna broke away from them, from the supporting restraining hands, and walked alone in the gardens, red mud caking her bare legs, her arms wrapped across her chest, walking, walking, while living creatures scattered from her feet.

It was nine o'clock that morning when Anna found her daughter. The party on the stoep saw her stumble towards them, holding in her arms what they believed to be a baby's corpse. They saw her approach them through a shivering silver light: like a woman breaking through sheets of glass, like a woman ploughing through mirrors. One child in her arms, but only one: plucked from the snake-seething ditch, plucked from muddy-brown water, blood-caked, rigid, frozen. Hands reached out again – to pull into the circle of humanity the bereft woman, the tiny carcass.

'Oh, Mrs Eldred,' Salome moaned. 'That God in all his goodness should send this trouble to you.'

But then the child began to utter: not to cry, but to make a jarring, convulsive, sucking sound, louder and louder with each breath, as if her tiny ribcage were an uncoiling spring.

EIGHT

After a month Ralph wrote to his Uncle James:

There is no news. If in two weeks there is still no news we are to return to England. After all, they say, they can carry on the search without us – and they will carry it on, and thoroughly, I have confidence in that, if in nothing else. Still, I dread the thought of leaving here, because the day we leave we will be admitting to ourselves that there is no hope.

I am much better than when I wrote last. I was 'lucky', the doctor said. I'm afraid I laughed in his face. Anna and I, we dislike being in different rooms now, and we never let Kit out of our sight. The same doctor who told me I was lucky said that this was a shock reaction and it would wear off, and that we must expect to find in ourselves certain oddities of behaviour, jump at any noise, suffer nightmares and so on. I don't suffer nightmares, because I don't sleep.

I feel I am living in an alien world now. I know that is one of those phrases that your brain reaches for when it's tired, but I can't think of any other way to express it. To be more exact I feel that I am suspended, that I am like someone hanged, that the ground has been dug out from under me, or my support kicked away. This woman, Felicia, the children's nanny, how could she do it? There is no doubt that it was planned. I must have told you in my earlier letter that Felicia had packed her clothes – everything in her room was gone. The two men brought a truck – the police found the tyre tracks. And Felicia stayed in the house that night, whereas for some months she had been in the habit of going back to her own room as soon as the twins were settled. I thought it was the storm that made her want to stay by the fire – but she was staying for another purpose. If I had not let the men in, she would have let them in. I suppose that might be some comfort to me. But then, it isn't. There is no comfort. I am the one who opened the door to them. They said they wanted shelter. I decided to do a good action, and by it my life has been split open and destroyed.

James, can you please explain to my mother and father and to Emma what we think has happened – I mean, can you explain to them that it is not likely Matthew has been taken for ransom? I can't write it in a letter. Besides, people in England wouldn't believe that crimes of such a nature occur. I would not have believed it myself, but when we were in Elim our doctor, Koos, told me one day about medicine murders. So when I asked the police why anyone would take my boy – and they told me – I knew I should believe them. They don't know how many children are stolen in a year and sold to the witch doctors. Sometimes children, older children, wander into the bush. The disappearance is not reported because there is no one to report it to. These children never come back. Perhaps animals kill them, or they starve. That is possible, of course.

Anna believes that Matthew may still be alive, and that is what she fears most. She says 'If he is dead, he is not suffering now.' But she is not sure. There is not a moment when we can be sure of anything.

There is of course a hope, a possibility, that the police will arrest these people. After all, we can identify Felicia and Enock, though I could not swear to recognize the man who stabbed me. If they are caught, perhaps they will tell us what happened to Matthew, but I am given every reason to doubt it. When these cases come to court no one will ever give evidence. They are too afraid of the witch doctors, I am told. If they are caught, they will probably be hanged. That matters nothing to me, one way or the other. I have no feelings about it. I would only want them to speak – so that I can know, so that we can know our little boy is dead, so that we can mourn for him. It is hard to mourn when there is no body to bury. I think – I try to imagine – how many people have said that in the history of the world. But most of them have entertained some hope, I suppose, whereas we must accept that there probably never will be a funeral. In these cases the police never find an identifiable victim. One man said to me, 'Sometimes we find traces.' I asked him what he meant by traces, and he said, 'Substances, in bottles and jars.'

Why was Kit spared? They wanted the boy, that's clear. They could have taken and killed her too, but perhaps there would have been no money in it for them. It seems a strange impulse of grace, to lay a baby down in a ditch, with a storm raging. She could have drowned in that ditch, or have died of cold before we found her, or have been savaged by an animal. It seems to me that she has been selected for life, and her brother for death. I shall always have to think about this. And I do not think the years that pass will make it easier to understand. Do you?

Kit is a strong child. She cries a lot now – for her brother, we suppose – but she is too little for us to explain anything to her. It is a blessing, in a way – you see that I am looking very hard for blessings, James. She will never remember what has happened. We mean never to tell her. Because how, in God's name, would we begin? I want you to impress this, to impress this very strongly, on my mother and father and on Emma, that as Kit grows up she must be protected from knowledge of this horrible thing. If she learns about it, it will contaminate her life.

I wish we had never left England. I do not believe that any good we have done here can compensate for a hundredth part of what we have suffered, and for what we will suffer as our lives go on. It seems to me impossible that we will ever lead lives like other people, or that anything ordinary and normal and safe will ever be within our reach again.

Don't advise me to pray, because I don't feel that prayers meet the case. I wonder about the nature of what I have been praying to. Before now I have looked at the world and I have seen no compelling evidence of the goodness of God, but I chose to believe in it, because I thought it was more constructive to do so. I thought that not to believe in it was a vote for chaos. I thought there was order in the world, at least – a kind of progress, a meaning, a pattern. But where is the pattern now? We've tried blaming ourselves, but we are not very convincing at it. If I had dealt earlier with this man Enock, if Anna had not insulted him . . . if I had not opened the door. I accept that I made choices and they were wrong, but then I think, too, that our lives have been ruined by malign chance. I do not see any pattern here, any sense, any reason why this had to happen.

James, in his office in the hostel in the East End, turned over the letter. On its back he wrote, 'If it is chance, can it be malign? If it is malign, can it be chance?'

From beyond the flimsy partition he heard the broken and shabby men in his care, going about their evening routine. He heard the thump and scrape of furniture, the clink of spoon against tin mug. He heard the reiterated wild shout of a frequent customer of his, a tramp with pre-senile dementia: 'Tommy didn't do it. Tommy didn't do it, Tommy didn't . . . he never.'

Tommy didn't do it, he thought. No, no, he pushes off the blame, he places it elsewhere. And Enock didn't do it? God did it. Ralph will think so, anyway. How not – if God made us, if God made us as we are, if he is all powerful, all knowing – could he not have stretched out his arm? In Ralph's mind, God works through Enock now, just as once God worked through Hitler. He will think it is God that plunged the knife into his back and took his child and cut him into pieces, dissected his child alive.

A wash of bile and saliva rose into James' mouth. He struggled not to vomit. He rose from his chair, gripping the arms. Let no one come in; he cannot face them, cannot meet human eyes.

Animals are better than we are, he thought; they do what they must. Pounce, tear, suck the blood; it is their nature, God has made them so and given them no choice.

He moved heavily across the room to the small window, which was barred against thieves. He looked out at an East End evening: waste paper scudding in autumn gutters, and cabbage leaves from some street market, white veins shining in the dusk. Early darkness: months ahead of rain and fog, slush and thaw. God had to permit his creations to do evil; it was the penalty of giving them a choice. Animals have no choice; it is why they are different from us. If we could not choose to do evil, we would not be human. I will tell him this, he thought, tell his poor wife. I will not say what I have often thought: that animals, who have no choice and so commit no crime, may have a guarantee of heaven, but that we, who are God's apes, may be shut out for eternity in the cold and the dark.

From beyond the office door the banging and clattering grew louder. He heard cursing. No doubt there was a fight about to break out; perhaps one of the old men had fallen over, or pulled out a knife. James turned from the window, caught sight of himself in a square of dusty mirror that hung on the opposite wall; saw a spare and desiccated old man, worn by humility, sucked dry by the constant effort of belief. He spoke aloud for a moment, as if Ralph and his wife were in the room with him. 'Anna, there is nothing, there is nothing worse, there is nothing so burdensome . . . there is nothing so appallingly hard . . . as the business of being human . . .' His voice died in his throat. I should take that mirror down, he thought, I have often meant to do it, glass is a danger in a place like this.

When Ralph and Anna returned to England they began at once upon the business of finding a house. Practical considerations would not go away; there were decisions to make. Anna had talked only briefly, grudgingly, about her missing child. What was the point of talking? she asked. No one could share her feelings. No one could enter into them.

'Anna, don't injure yourself more,' James said. 'There is a thing people do – when they have been hurt, they hurt themselves again, they compound the damage. Don't become bitter. That's all I ask.'

'It's a great deal to ask,' Ralph said.

'Next, James,' Anna said, 'you'll be asking me to forgive.' A kind of hard jauntiness had entered her voice; it was her usual tone now.

'No, I wouldn't ask that. Not yet.'

'Good,' Anna said. 'I am not up to the effort.'

'If you could think,' James said, 'that there are some things that God does not control or will, then you could ask God for comfort . . . but it's very difficult, Anna.'

'It's impossible,' she said. 'I asked God for comfort when I came home to Elim every night, and saw these beaten people waiting for me on the stoep – but God kept very quiet, James. God did nothing. It was up to me to do something, but I acted within constraints – I tried to be good, you see, I felt the love of God biting into my wrists like a pair of handcuffs. So what did I offer these people? Bandages and platitudes. Suppose my training had been different? I might have stepped on the train to Cape Town with a revolver in my bag, I might have shot Dr Verwoerd – then I might have done some good in the world. Now, James – when I had in the room with me the man who was going to kill my child – when I had in my hand a broken bottle, suppose I had drawn the edges across his eyes? Suppose I had sliced his eyes to ribbons, suppose I had severed his veins and made him bleed to death? Then I would have done some good in the world.'

'Anna –' he said.

She saw the fear in his face. 'Don't worry,' she said. 'You leave me alone, James, and I'll leave you alone. You don't come at me with your theology, and I won't stop Ralph doing his job. It was planned that he should take over the Trust, yes? So there's no reason to change the plan. It doesn't matter what I think, inside myself. Nobody could imagine or know what I think, inside myself. But I promise you I won't stand up in church and bawl out that it's all a sham. We're professional Christians, aren't we, Ralph and me? That's how we make our living. Why should we be poor, when every hypocrite is rich?'

No one had seen her cry, not once; not from the beginning. Emma knew right away, when she met them at the airport: 'Anna is too angry to cry. She is almost too angry to breathe.'

They found a house quite easily. Emma's friend Felix drove them through the country lanes, away from the bustle of Norwich: which seemed to them, after their time in the wilderness, like some vast metropolis. Felix stopped his car under a tree by a red-brick, rambling, ill-proportioned house: 'It needs work,' he said. 'But it will accommodate both your office and your family.'

He looked over his shoulder at Anna, in the back seat. No point trying to avoid the word. Anna was expecting another baby. Everyone said it was the best thing that could have happened.

They went inside. 'The drawing room,' Felix said.

They moved into the light of the long windows. Anna noticed how they were liberally bespattered with mud; Ralph noticed the panelled shutters of old pine. He admired the wide staircase, the lofty ceilings; she breathed the house's air, the compound of strange moulds and the trapped smoke of long-dead fires. 'We must have it,' he said. Anna shook her head. But then she felt – or thought she felt – the child move inside her.

She registered its claims. She thought of having more children, many children, to fill the aching void of grief.

They moved into the house three months before Julian's birth; two months after the birth, Ralph's father died. It was a shock, because he had seemed a fit man; but last year's news from abroad, the news carried in Ralph's first incomprehensible and distressing letter, had dealt him a terrible blow. The whole business perplexed and maddened him; he was used to taking control of life, but now here was a problem without a solution, the theft of a child he had not seen in a country he could not imagine. When his son came home he seemed unable to speak to him, barely able to be in the same room. James said, 'To some people, great grief is an indecency. They cannot look at it. They blame the bereaved.'

Matthew became, more than ever, subject to sudden outbursts of temper, to seizures of indignation about the state of the world. The sight of Julian – his second grandson – made him want his first; it made him rage with disbelief and dismay. 'Why did you go?' he said to Ralph one day. 'You didn't need to go. The missions must be staffed, but you needn't have gone, you shouldn't have gone, there were plenty more experienced people to go. Pride made you do it, I think – pride, and being above yourself, knowing better than other people. That's always been your fault, boy.'

Ralph said, 'You want to know why I went to Africa? I'll tell you. I went to get away from you.'

The day after the quarrel, Matthew suffered a stroke. Ralph never spoke to him again – or rather, he spoke, but the old man gave no sign of hearing or comprehending, though somehow Ralph believed he did both. Ralph whispered to him: forgive me, for the things I have done that hurt you, and for the things that hurt you that I didn't know I had done.

By his father's deathbed he felt himself begin to grow up. He said, after all, my father was not so old himself in the days when he treated me so badly. He was still learning the world, he felt responsibility heavy on his back. It is hard to be a father; no doubt he was not malicious, no doubt he did the best he could. 'Please forgive me, because I forgive you,' he whispered. His father died after three days, the pardon ungranted.

What to do now, with ordinary grief, ordinary guilt? All emotions seem attenuated in the wake of the one great disaster. 'Nothing can hurt you worse,' Ralph's mother said. 'Nothing can hurt you worse than you have been hurt already. I don't expect you to cry for him, Ralphie. Let's just get him buried.'

After this, Dorcas moved in with them, a carpet-slippered presence in the draughty hall of their new house.

It's not so easy to return from Africa, even when circumstances are favourable and the return is planned. Hostilities against the cockroach and the ant cease only gradually. A mark on the wall converts itself into a crawling tick, and there is effort and vigilance all the time – it is hard to sit in the fitful English sunshine, in the heat without threat, harmless insects brushing your bare arms. It was more than a year before Anna could bring herself to leave a plate or a cup on a table; after it had been used, she would snatch it away and wash it, to thwart the advancing carpet of crawling greed. 'Poor Anna,' people said. 'She's always on the go. She'll wear herself out, that girl.' The words used about her, the trite kindnesses, had a sting of their own. There had been a tragedy in her life, and no one here had the terms for it. In winter the weight of her clothes oppressed her; wool and shoe-leather chafed and cramped and squeezed.

And how England looks like itself! After the white light, the sun that bleaches out colour and destroys perspective, here are the discrete, exclusive Old Master tints, sienna, burnt umber, indigo: the dense conifers in shadowed ranks, the tan flash of stripped bark, the flush on the trunk of silver birch at sunset; breath on the raw air, and owls calling at dead of night. Another spring will come, and summer: green layered on green, the mossy wall, the lichened fence: and drowsing horses beneath an elm, flanks fly-buzzed, necks bowed, dreaming of George Stubbs.

So now, where should they begin? How should they coordinate their slow crawl back from the desert? What should they say? What could they tell people? Who was entitled to the whole story, and who could be kept at a distance with a half-truth?

Anna's parents knew the facts – knew the probabilities, that is – but they settled for not talking about them. They pretended that they were sparing their daughter's feelings, but really they were sparing their own. Nothing in their lives had prepared them for catastrophe. They worshipped routine; *events* were dubious matters, and often in bad taste. It was a form of showing off, to have things happen to you. 'Of course, it's terrible, a horrible thing, dreadful,' Mrs Martin said, 'but although I don't say so, of course, I blame him for taking her there in the first place. He could have had a nice job with his father, there was no need to trail half-way across the globe.'

The Martins had spent much of their lives beating the drum for the Christian faith, getting up jumble sales and flower shows so that the dark races could have the benefit of the company of brisk young Englishmen who were familiar with the Psalms and (among other Books) the Book of Job. But they did not expect to have one of these young Englishmen in their back parlour behind the shop, frozen and speechless with misery. They did not expect the Book of Job to have any practical application.

And friends of the families – what to tell them? They

flinched from detail, and Ralph flinched more than Anna. He thought, if we tell them what we think has happened, we will pander to their filthy prejudices, we will seem to traduce a whole nation: savages, they will say.

It was possible to say, 'We lost our son.' That covered everything. Few people inquired further. Rather, they would shy away, as if the bereaved might break down in front of them, lie on the floor and howl. It was surprising how vague people were, even the people who claimed they had been praying for them every Sunday. I thought the young Eldreds had two children, people would say, didn't I hear from somewhere that they had twins? Unease would cross their faces; was there some story about it, an accident perhaps, or was it just that the child succumbed to a tropical fever? Ralph had feared intrusive questions, but instead there was an indifference that he felt as an insult. He made a discovery, common to those who expatriate themselves and then return: that when he and Anna went abroad they had ceased to be regarded as real people. Out of sight, out of mind. Nobody, even the most generous donor to mission appeals, wanted to hear anything about Africa.

In the early years after their return, huge areas of reference were excluded by their family, their close friends. They were surrounded by acres laid waste, acres of silence. Slowly, cautiously, normality tiptoed back; the family no longer censored themselves, guarding conversation from all mention of Africa. After a while they ceased to flinch when a picture of a lost child appeared in the newspapers. Finally the dimensions of the tragedy shrunk; there was a little barbed area in which no one trod, in which the secret was sequestered and locked away. Was it less potent, confined? No: it was more potent, Ralph felt. He dreamt of scrubbing blood away, scrubbing his own blood off a cement floor; but the stain always returned, like the blood in Bluebeard's room. He understood, then, what the fairy-tale means; blood is never wiped out. No bad action goes away. Evil is energy, and perpetuates itself; only its form changes.

Over the next few years Ralph made himself busy, burying the past under a weight of daily preoccupation. Anna watched him change, cultivate a sort of shallow and effortless bonhomie – beneath which, she imagined, his real thoughts teemed on, guilty and seething and defrauded. In daily life he became an exacting, demanding man, who gave her only glimpses of the gentleness of those early years; she had to look at his sons, as they grew up, to see the kind of man Ralph had once been. She had realized very early, when they lived in Elim, that his kindness had a detachment about it, that his care for people was studied and willed; now it became a hard-driving virtue, combative.

During the 1970s the Trust became one of the better-funded small charities, and attracted a member of the royal family as patron. Ralph was contemptuous of the young man, but he would put up with anyone's company to further his aims. He must see progress everywhere; he must see improvement. All day there must be action, or the simulation of it; letters in every direction, telephone calls, driving about the county and up and down to London; there must be advertising and exhortation, press campaigns and fund-raising drives. He took charge of policy, of the broader picture, engaged the services of a freelance public-relations expert; he rebuilt the hostel, updated its aims and methods. He granted an interview to the *Guardian* and one to *New Society* and was sometimes called into television studios to engage in futile scraps with those who thought differently about drugs, housing policy, education. At the hostel he was available to oversee the minutest detail, the supply of paper-clips and pillow cases; he spent a lot of time sitting with the sullen, inarticulate, unlikeable children who found themselves in his care. In Norfolk, too, he became well-known as one of those men who you telephone if you want something done; sometimes the novelty of his ideas outraged the *Eastern Daily Press*. The power of his will, he seemed to think, could pull the world into a better shape. Underneath, Anna thought, he must know it is all an illusion. A futility.

For a year or so after their return from Bechuanaland, she fought to keep her hold on the past, on every detail of it. She had been afraid to forget anything; to forget seemed a betrayal of her child who might – it was possible – still be alive. She rehearsed constantly in her mind the incidents of their life at Mosadinyana: from their arrival on the station platform under the stars, to their final exit, bags packed for them by commiserating strangers. But though the pain remained fresh, specific memories staled and faded; they receded from her, the little events of this day and that. The one night remained in her mind, indelible – the thunder snarling overhead, the hammering of the rain on the roof, Ralph's blood coating her hands to the wrist. But after two years, three, her inner narrative slipped, became disjointed. What remained as memories were a series of pictures, some hard and sharp, some merely cross-hatched blurs of light and sound.

On the day Julian was born, Anna had no interest in resisting pain, or behaving well, or making the process pleasant for those who attended her. When a medical fist squashed a mask on to her face, she gulped oblivion; and she would not allow herself to come back. She wanted the gas and not the air; oblivion informed her, it was what she craved. When Julian was first placed in her arms – a neat, clean, pink little baby, held by the unfeeling hands of nurses, scrubbed and sanitized before they gave him to her – she felt a certain flinching, a pull away from him; she hated to place any burden of expectation on this fragile scrap of being wrapped in a shawl. She saw the tight folds of his lashless eyes, his sea-sponge mouth, forming and re-forming, the stiff mottled fingers that thrust through the cobweb knitting of the shawl: she tried to pretend she had no other son, that she was seeing a son for the first time. Julian had fair curls and soft eyes; he lay in his father's arms and trusted him. He did not remind her unnecessarily of her sharp, small, dark child, his fragile skull still showing when she lost him, the pulses visible, beating beneath that fluttering baby skin.

Ralph's mother Dorcas was a friend to her, in those early years; a close-mouthed, uncommunicative old woman, but always there, always attentive, always to be relied on. Anna shrank from her sister-in-law at first; bossy young GP, driving over from Norwich every other Saturday, full of specious knowledge, worldliness, vitality. She shrank from the world, indeed; there were days when she wouldn't go out of the house, couldn't go out, when a word from a stranger would make her blush and shake, when she could not bear to lift her head to meet another person's eyes.

Sometimes she woke with her right hand contracted, clenched, as if she were still holding the neck of the bottle she had broken against the Instows' sideboard. For a year and a half she kept Julian's cot in her room, and only when Robin was born, and she had something frailer to concern her, did she cease to wake and check his breathing many times during the night. When Kit went to school, she could hardly be persuaded from the school gate.

Of course, people noticed her behaviour. They said, Anna, you're a trained teacher, you've got your mother-in-law to look after the children for you, why don't you go back to work? You need an interest, it would take you out of yourself. They wondered why she was seen so seldom, outside her own house; why she did not take what her mother called 'an active interest in charity work'.

After a year or two of this – the searing gaffs of other

people's demands — Ralph's sister Emma took her aside and spoke to her, just in time to save her life. She saved it by small, usual words, trite in themselves, but very important if you were dying.

'Anna,' she had said, 'you don't seem well to me, you seem out of breath, shall I listen to your chest? I wouldn't treat my own family, of course — but I could just tell you if there was anything obviously wrong.'

'It's nothing,' Anna said, 'it's the cold weather, you know, it puts me out of breath — besides, I've always been like it.'

'Have you?' Emma said, interested.

'Oh yes . . . I'm strong enough, in myself, but I could never run much. Even when I was little. Don't you notice me, when I dash upstairs?'

'No, what do you do?'

'My heart pounds.' She frowned. 'I've always been like it. I told you. It was easier when we went to Africa. There were no stairs.'

'I never realized,' Emma said. 'What an idiot I am.'

She was able to tell Ralph, after investigations, that Anna had a slight defect in a heart valve: nothing that required surgery, nothing that was going to kill her, nothing that would ever give her more than the minor inconvenience she had suffered all her life, and which she had never thought to speak of. 'It's common enough,' Emma said, trying to create the proper balance between reassurance and alarm. 'But you must give her a quiet time, Ralph. She has enough with the house and the babies, you mustn't let anyone try to prod her and pester her into supporting amateur dramatics and doing these damn flower festivals and calling on old gossips who are fitter than she is. You must protect her, you see. When people want her to do something, you can sit back in your chair, and frown, and say, well now, my wife, didn't you know she is not precisely well?'

Not precisely well. Ralph wondered if it was fear that impeded Anna's breathing, fear that stuck in her throat.

'It's difficult,' Emma said, 'to disentangle the causes and effects. Certainly, Anna has anxiety attacks. I've seen them, I've seen it happen. It's not surprising at all that she has them, when you think what she's gone through. After some great upset in your life you may think you're coping, in your mind – you may feel you're on top of life. Very well – the mind has strategies. But the body needs different ones. It has a memory of its own.'

'But this defect, in her heart, the valve – that's not to do with anxiety attacks, it's something in itself, you're saying?'

Emma hesitated. 'Yes, it's something in itself – something and nothing. But Ralph, people are very ignorant and cruel, and they won't accept mental suffering as an excuse to avoid anything. They say, "Pull yourself together." I am afraid I couldn't bear to hear anyone say that to Anna – and we are not far off the day when they will. But – trust me, I know what people are like – they'll respect a heart complaint. A heart complaint is very respectable, very respectable indeed.'

Ralph said, 'Sometimes I feel panic too. And a . . .' he put his hand to his throat, 'something here, a heaviness, it won't move. Still, I . . . I keep going.'

'That's what men do,' Emma said. 'Keep going. Often at the expense, don't you think, of the people around them?' They shout at the news on the television, she thought, and call politicians fools – that's a release for them. They lose their temper and hit people, and are admired for doing it. They sit on committees, or enforce laws. Whatever is wrong inside them they project to the outside, they find somebody out there to stick the blame on. But women – women turn inwards. 'Men make decisions,' she said, 'and women fall ill.'

'That seems a gross simplification.'

'Of course it is,' Emma said. 'Of course it is. But you can help your wife now, can't you? Why do you want precision reasoning? I've given you something, Ralph – won't it do?'

'Thank you, Emma,' he said. 'You may have saved her life.'

'Oh, she wouldn't die of it –' Emma began; but then she stopped because she saw the extent of his fear. Impenetrable, delicate, dry-eyed Anna: she had been near that cutting edge? 'Oh, Ralph,' his sister said. 'I didn't know. I'd have come up with something before. Doesn't she want to *live*, for the children she has?'

'It is the one we don't have that dominates our life,' Ralph said. 'It's what is missing that shapes everything we do. Sometimes she smiles, but have you noticed, Emma, she never laughs. She is crippled inside. She has no joy.'

'Joy,' Emma said. She smiled her twisted smile. 'A word to be kept for Christmas carols, don't you think, Ralph? Don't expect joy. Survival, that's all – survival should be the ambition.'

There was some surprise when – after Kit, Julian, Robin – Anna Eldred became pregnant for a fourth time. People said, Anna, I thought you'd stopped; three is enough in this day and age, and I heard you had heart trouble. Yes, I've got heart trouble, Anna said. Yes, I've stopped now. The world had moved on by the time Rebecca was born. There were people who knew nothing of what had happened to them in Bechuanaland, and people who had known but had contrived to forget. There came a time when she didn't think, every minute, about her stolen child.

But the grief waited in the thickets of daily life, in unoccupied hours, ready to bludgeon her again, to drag her down: drag her under like a woman drowned, a woman sewn in a sack.

One day Dorcas had a fall in the kitchen, broke her wrist. They took her in to hospital, to casualty, but it was a Friday night, and they had to wait, and the wait and the pain and the other clients distressed Dorcas beyond bearing. There were young men with springing scalp wounds, blood leaking and pumping out of them as if blood were as cheap as water; there was a woman brought in after a road accident, dumped in a wheelchair waiting for attention. One eyelid was cut, puffing and oozing; she had lost one high-heeled shoe, and in the twenty minutes she waited for attention she never stopped sobbing and asking for her husband.

In time Dorcas was led away, curtained off, her arm manipulated; she was wheeled through cold corridors to X-ray. The hospital offered a bed. 'No,' Anna said, 'this place has frightened her, I'll take her home.' The doctor seemed relieved. 'Call your GP in the morning,' he said.

'Keep her wrapped up,' their GP advised, 'keep her in bed, don't let her get worked up about things.' When Emma came to see her late that afternoon she was dismayed by the old woman's low spirits; she seemed in pain, could not rest, would not eat. 'You know what I think?' Emma said. 'I think she's had enough.'

When a chest infection developed their GP arranged for Dorcas to go back into hospital. But because she fretted, and still would not eat, the hospital sent her home. She insisted that Ralph stay by her, then; she began to hold his hand tightly with her good hand, and to talk to him, talk with a grim fluency, about her girlhood, her courtship, her marriage, her husband. It was as if, on what she acknowledged to be her deathbed, she was giving birth to a new version of her life.

'You thought he didn't believe in science, didn't you, Ralph?' Her face was very small against the pillows. 'But he broke my spirit, scientifically. I wasn't always the carpet under his feet, I wasn't born like that. No, I had a life, when I was a young girl – my family weren't so strict. I used to go to dances.'

259

'Mum, don't cry,' Ralph said.

'Let her,' Emma said. 'Crying does no harm. It might ease her chest.'

'That Palmer boy, young Felix – that friend of yours, Emma – I knew his father. He was a good dancer, very light on his feet. And a gentleman. He'd buy me ginger-beer.'

Emma sat on the bed. She lifted her mother's hand and rubbed it between her own. 'Was he sweet on you, Mum?'

'Oh yes.' Dorcas smiled, painfully. She seemed to sleep for a moment. But then she continued quite smoothly, just where she had left off. 'The thing was though, your father came along, and I thought he was more of a man, really. His father was a lay preacher,' she said, as if they hadn't known it, 'and he had a fine voice.'

'Ah,' Emma said. 'So you gave up Mr Palmer?'

'Yes,' Dorcas said, 'I did, I did give him up, I told him he should look elsewhere. He was a snappy dresser, you know, I'll say that much for him – and oh, could he make you laugh! Still, that's not life, is it . . . laughing, that's not life. He married a bottle-blonde from Cromer, went into the building trade, he did well I always heard, that's how little Felix got his airs and graces. Your father was a serious man. We never went to a dance.'

'Mum, you're tired,' Ralph said. 'Why don't you have a sleep now?'

'Don't try to shut her up, or I'll never forgive you,' Emma said mildly. 'This is my mother, and –' she turned to him, and whispered – 'and I've got to my present age without ever hearing her say anything of interest. So don't you try to stop her now.'

Dorcas looked up. 'You see, I always had to please him, Ralph. I was a good girl and went to church, but six months after I was married I gave up fearing God and started fearing your father. I mean that, you know. I don't mean it as a blasphemy. He always seemed to me like a person from another age. Abraham. A patriarch. He wasn't fair to you, Ralph, and the worst thing, you know – he made me take part in it. Oh, you hated me then. That night when I came into your room and said to you, you have to fall in with him, Ralph, or you'll see your sister suffer for it.' She closed her eyes. 'He knew you loved your sister.'

Emma said, 'What does she mean?'

'Nothing,' Ralph said.

'What is it? Come on, Ralph! If you won't tell me, she will.'

Ralph glanced at Dorcas; she seemed to be sleeping, but he had a feeling she was listening still. He reached out for his sister's arm. 'Emma, come with me, come, let's get out a bit, let's go and walk, or let's make tea, do something, go and sit by ourselves . . . this is such old ground, I didn't think I'd ever have to go over it.'

Emma seemed stunned. 'But Ralph, why didn't you tell me? All these years have gone by, events making no sense or partial sense . . . I used to say to you, why did you let him bully you?'

'Yes, you did.'

'How did you bear it?'

'There was no alternative.'

'I thought you were spineless. Weak.' Emma looked very young, as if layers had peeled away. 'He'd have done it, you know – he'd have kept me at home to punish you. With most fathers it would have been bluster, but with him – no, he meant every word he said.' She shook her head. 'Imagine – it would have been a better revenge than anything he could have done to you directly. If you'd have insisted on your path in life, I'd have been turned off mine. And think of the hook of guilt it would have put into your flesh.'

'Yes.' He remembered a thorn that had once, at Mosadinyana, embedded itself in the pad of his middle finger, and made his arm numb to the elbow: an intricate thorn, like a medieval battle-weapon, designed by man to do its worst. 'But she, Mum – she's no saint. She colluded with him.'

'She was frightened, Ralph.'

'Can't you overcome fear?'

'You ask too much of people,' Emma said sadly.

They did not speak for a while. Then Ralph asked, 'Will she live?'

His sister said, with professional accuracy, 'She'll die the day after tomorrow.'

It is a pity that she cannot, with similar accuracy, put a term to the after-life of the missing child. It would be possible, if one were harsh, to regard this lost child not as an innocent, but as a malign half-presence, a destroyer, a consumer of hope. Katherine grows up; they search her face for signs of what her brother would have been. As babies, they were not much alike. So no consolation there; but no further suffering, either. Except you cannot help but mark out the course of the shadow-life . . . he would be six years old, he would be seven years old, he would be seventeen. He has all we lack, he is everything we are not; we have our gross appetites, but he is the opposite of flesh. Somewhere in Africa the little heart rots, the bird-bones crumble or – alternatively – the traces dry in their jar; their child becomes a bush-ghost, powder on the wind.

Norfolk, 1980: midsummer. Cyclists take to the road, with flapping shirts and fluorescent saddle-bags. Women in loud print dresses, their cardigans over their arms, pad downhill in seaside streets, with wide feet like the feet of waders. There are fathers in cars, lost in country lanes: irate metropolitan faces behind glass, and wives tearfully slapping at maps that won't fold.

There are poppies in the verges – indecent splashes, as if blood were welling up beneath the landscape. In every vegetable garden in the county, cabbage-whites hover dangerously over the brassicas. Those hedges that remain are towering walls, walls of deep green; lemonade bottles perch in them, chucked out from passing cars. Small animals are smashed into the tarmac of the A149 – so flattened, so thoroughly dead, that they look like animals in cartoons, who will instantly spring back into their old shape.

Sandra and Amy Glasse are selling samphire, cauliflower, lettuces, beans and new potatoes. They are selling large fleshy tomatoes, because last winter Julian reglazed their greenhouse. Ralph is now in love with Mrs Glasse, and sees her once a week, twice a week, three times if he can contrive it. Contriving is hard and goes against his nature; but when has his nature ever been what it should be?

Summer visitors came to Ralph's house, children from the hostel. Ralph's own children treated them with the usual distant tolerance. Kit had not resolved her future; she drifted around the house, and bickered with Daniel, who found himself in the neighbourhood every other day.

The Visitors exhibited their customary bewilderment. They had grown up in cities, and spent a lot of their lives standing about in the street. Here, there was no street worth standing in – just a lane, its high verges choked with thistle and fern, cow-parsley and rose-bay willow herb. They did not go out of the house much, because they did not like to walk anywhere or ride bicycles. Sometimes they begged lifts to Reepham, the nearest market town. They would swagger across the market square, then lean on the railings outside the Old Brewery, looking hopeless; stare into the butcher's window, to see if the lamb chops were doing anything exciting; shove and barge into the post office, which sold stationery and newspapers and picture postcards of Norwich, and there shoplift packets of paper doilies, and marble-swirl pencils with erasers on the end. Then they would vandalize a few hanging baskets, and beg a lift back to the house again.

'If this goes on,' Kit said to Robin, 'the people in Reepham will start complaining. They'll get up a petition.'

'They'll get up a mob, I should think.' Robin lurched unsteadily across the kitchen, pulling his forelock and pretending to be a vampire's manservant. 'My lord, the villagers are advancing, armed with staves.'

'No, seriously,' Kit said. 'The Visitors seem worse than ever this year.'

'It's you that's changing. Getting old and mean.'

'And where's Julian? He's no help. He's always over at Sandra's house, you'd think he'd decided to leave home. When he's here he doesn't speak.'

'Well, he's gone mad, hasn't he?' Robin said. 'Round the twist. I thought we'd established that. What I want to know is, how is he going to keep a grip on Becky now it's the school holidays? He can't be over there screwing Sandra and here guarding his little sister, not both at the same time.'

'No,' Kit said. 'Think how he must be torn.'

'Very odd, our family,'

'I said that. A few weeks ago. You seemed to disagree. You seemed to think they were normal.'

'I've changed my mind.'

'A man's privilege.'

'But Kit – can you make sense of it? Don't watch television, it contaminates your brain. Don't hang around with smart kids with money, or you might contract that fearful disease material-

264

ism. So what do we get instead, for entertainment and company? Child prostitutes from Brixton. Heroin addicts. Thieves.'

'We're supposed to be proof against it,' Kit said. 'We've been so well brought up that they're not going to influence us, or do us any harm.'

'That's the theory,' Robin said.

'It works, doesn't it? I don't see you shooting up, or selling your body.'

'True,' Robin said guardedly. 'But Kit, isn't it time you got away? Once I go off to medical school you won't catch me hanging around here in summer. Not if summers are like this one. All this snapping and snarling, and creeping about.'

'Yes.' Kit turned away. She had been thinking a lot, since her midnight conversation with Robin, and she was uncomfortable with her thoughts. She didn't want to risk having them exposed. 'Anyway,' she said, changing the subject. 'Anyway. The Visitors will have gone soon. All except this Melanie.'

'Oh yes, Melanie – when does she get here?'

'Tomorrow, I think.'

'Kit,' Ralph said, as the family sat down to eat, 'do you have any nail-polish remover?'

'Why, Dad, do you want to do yourself a re-varnish?'

'Christ,' Robin said. 'Dad's a transvestite. He's got a secret life.'

'Don't worry,' Kit said. 'There's probably a self-help group we can join.'

'Yes,' Robin said. 'Ask Dad. He'll know.'

'For goodness sake,' Anna said. 'Listen to your father and stop being so slick.'

'Ah,' Kit said. 'Mum doesn't like the thought that he's got a secret life.'

'My problem is this,' Ralph said. 'Melanie. She might inhale it.'

'Dad, look.' Kit held up her hands, 'I am a stranger to the manicurist's art.'

'Oh, good,' her father said.

'Not very observant, are you?' Robin put his chin on his hand and watched his father.

'I'm not,' Ralph said. 'It's a fault of mine.'

'People are just problems to you,' Kit said. 'Problems on two legs. That's why you don't notice things.'

'Well, I — you may be right, but in my line of work — if you think about it — I don't meet people without problems.'

'That's not my point,' Kit said. 'My point is that you don't see — what's her name, Melanie — you see "persistent absconder, multiple addictions" — whatever the jargon is at the time.'

'Do I? Well, I yield to you in charity, you are my superior. The problem is that the nature of what I do is so contentious, so risky — wading into children's lives and trying to put them right — that I'm always glad if I can identify a pattern of behaviour. And there are such patterns, you see.'

'Everyone is unique,' Kit said. 'Surely.'

'I used to think so. But then I see how they — my clients — behave or react in the same way as others who have gone before — or, let's say, they have a small range of possible reactions.'

'Don't they have free will?'

Ralph looked at his daughter appraisingly, as if to judge her seriousness. 'I used to think that was the single question,' he said. 'I used to think, of course they have free will. But then after a few years I saw these patterns repeat themselves, as if people were born into them. I read case files all the time, and sometimes, quite often really, I get one client's story mixed up with another. People use certain drugs, perhaps, or drink, or whatever — they are as they are, and that is much as their parents were — they beat their children or neglect them, they go into prison and come out and go in again, and you feel that you could write the next page in the file, you know what their future is going to be, and their children's future too. Nine times out of ten you'd be right. It depresses me, how seldom people do the unexpected. They start off down a path and they stick to it.'

'In my opinion,' Robin said, 'stupidity has a lot to do with it. I know people can't help being thick, but if they're so thick that they can't control their lives properly I don't see how it matters if they have free will or not. That's just theory. In practice they don't have choices.'

Rebecca kicked her brother's shin, under the table. 'I asked you half an hour ago to pass the sweetcorn.'

'Shut up, Becky,' Kit said. 'But Robin, you can be quite bright and not have choices. Take love, for instance.'

Anna sat back in her chair, putting her fork down. 'Take love?' she said.

'Sorry,' Kit said, 'I know I'm contradicting what I said earlier, but I do see your point, Dad. Love, you know, it's a chemical thing. When people say they're in love it's just a set of physical reactions, there are all these substances whizzing around your brain, and hormones making you obsessed –'

'Very scientific,' Robin said.

'– and that's why although everybody thinks that nobody in the world has ever felt like they do, they all listen to these schmaltzy songs and write poems and feel at one with the universe. They're all going through the same process. We're programmed for it.'

'You may be right,' Ralph said. 'Are you in love, Kit?'

'No. I'm sure that if I were, I wouldn't talk about it with such a lack of respect.'

'You'd be like everyone else,' Robin said. 'You'd think you were unique.'

267

Kit made coffee. As if on cue, Daniel came to the front door. 'How are you, young man?' Ralph said. He liked Daniel, he had decided, because he seemed to have evolved; in the present casual optimist, in his new stiff tweeds, you could seem to see his grandfather, the snappy dresser so slick on the dance floor and free with ginger-beer.

'I came to thank Julian,' Daniel said. 'Shame he's not here. Peace is much better than war, isn't it? Oh,' he looked around, 'don't you know what I've been up to?'

'Barn conversions?' Ralph suggested. 'That's the usual bone of contention, isn't it?'

'Not any more. You know Julian's girlfriend? I've been over to their farm. Mrs Glasse has this outbuilding that Julian wants to demolish because it's falling down anyway. Mrs Glasse was very mysterious about it and made objections, she said, "I use it to keep buckets in." Anyway, when I had a look at it, I came in and told her what I would pay for the roof-tiles, which are beautiful, absolutely beautiful — and she said, quick, Sandra, let's all go and lean on the bugger, it can't come down soon enough for me. I said, "What about the buckets?" and she said, "They can be rehoused. Or get foster-homes. Ralph knows all about it. He'll get them a social worker if I ask him."'

'Oh,' Kit said, 'so you're best mates now, you and Jule?'

'He still says I'm a vandal, but I think he's glad to find a way of reducing the damage. By the way,' he said to Anna, 'have you met Sandra's mother? She'd interest you.'

'In what respect?'

'She's not what I expected — quite a clever woman, I'd think, very sharp, very, what's the word, droll — but just absolutely content to stay on her patch. No wider ambitions, none at all.'

'You mean she's like me?' Anna said.

'Oh no — I didn't mean that.'

'You needn't blush. She sounds an admirable type.'

'She's so young,' Daniel said. 'Of course, you know her, Ralph. I was amazed, she's so attractive – I mean, Sandra's not much to look at – don't mention to Jule I said so – but Mrs Glasse is quite stunning, in her way.'

'Did you tell her so?' Anna said.

'God, no,' Daniel said. 'Mrs Glasse? I wouldn't dare.'

'I don't see why not. She leads a solitary life, from what I hear. She probably goes short of compliments.'

There was a fine disgust in Anna's voice. Ralph's pulse-rate rose when he heard it. Daniel looked covertly at Kit, to see if he had made her jealous. But Kit only smiled her placid smile.

It was a chilly evening, for August. Daniel's pullover had a suggestion of cashmere, a certain Burlington Arcade air about it. Ralph was wearing an army-style sweater, with fabric elbow and shoulder patches, which Rebecca had given him last Christmas. Ralph disliked it, because it was shoddy, militaristic and already fraying; but Becky had saved up for it, and thought it dashing, so he wore it to please her. Daniel seemed to be eyeing it – not covetously, Ralph thought. 'How's your car running, Daniel?' he asked. He lunged into the conversation as if at a runaway horse, trying to catch it and lead it away from Amy Glasse.

Ten o'clock – Daniel on his way home, Kit washing up – he went out to attend to the boiler. This brute occupied its own hot little room – in the depth of winter, it was a popular meeting place for the family. The air was dry, calcified, osseous. He would have let it go out in the summer, except that it supplied the family's hot water too. When the children were babies it had seemed quite natural to dunk them in and out of each other's bath water; when they were older, he had expected them to exercise economy. One Easter holiday long ago, Kit had a friend to stay. 'You can have first bath,' Kit had said, 'but leave me your water.' Her friend had stared at her. It's like the middle ages here, she'd said. And telephoned her parents to be collected next day.

All these thoughts were running through Ralph's mind – to block out certain other thoughts – as he drove the scuttle vengefully at the coal, felt the coal rattle in, felt the dust fly up and sully his cuffs. He straightened up, and Julian was there, in the doorway, leaning against it.

'What do you think you're doing?' Julian said.

'The boiler,' Ralph said.

'Don't be funny. It's not funny,' Julian said. 'I've just come from Sandra's. I've been covering up for you so far, but why should I go on doing it? Why should I? You're going to wreck up everything for me and Sandra, and that's only the beginning of the damage you're going to do.'

Ralph said, 'This is neither the time nor the place, is it?'

Julian leaned forward and took a handful of his father's sweater, somewhere around the shoulder patch. He shifted his grip, seemed uncertain whether he had his father or not. 'Look, what the hell are you doing?' he said.

Ralph said, 'Give me an inch of space, Julian. What am I doing? I don't know.'

Melanie, their Visitor from London, arrived next day. The children always hung around to see a new arrival, but they were disappointed by this one. She was wearing an ordinary pair of jeans, black lace-up boots with domed toe-caps, and a leopard-skin print T-shirt with a hole in it. 'Very conventional,' Kit said. 'Almost Sloane Square.'

'Boring,' Rebecca agreed.

Melanie had a nylon hold-all, but it seemed to be empty. 'What's happened to her clothes?' Anna said.

'She burned them,' Ralph said shortly. It was clear that he didn't mean to enlarge on this.

Anna sighed. 'We'll have to get her kitted out, then. That will be a battle.'

She took Melanie upstairs to settle her in her room. 'Have you got any tablets, my dear?' Anna said. 'Anything you shouldn't have? Needles?'

Melanie shook her cropped orange head. Anna felt that she was lying, but balked at a body-search. The girl slumped down on the bed and stared hard at the wall. She was here against her wishes and she meant to make this clear. Anna looked out of the window, over the fields. Fields, fields on every hand, all choked with snares for the urban young. To Melanie – who had broken out, sooner or later, from everywhere she had ever lived – it must feel like a Siberian labour camp. The permafrost on every side; searchlights and razor wire. As if catching her thought, the girl said, 'Is there bulls?'

'In the fields? No, not usually. We don't have that kind of farming. In the fields we grow things.'

'What, like bloody grass?' the girl said.

'Oh, sweetheart,' Anna said. 'Don't swear at me. It won't make you any happier.'

'But it does,' Melanie said balefully.

Anna went downstairs, and checked that anything Melanie might inhale or swallow was locked away. Not many women have to padlock their oven-cleaner, Anna thought. They had tried to exclude from the house any substance with a potential for abuse, but you could never be sure; a boy who'd stayed last year had a predilection for a certain brand of suede-cleaner, and had ransacked the kitchen cupboards and her dressing-table drawers on the off-chance that she might have some lying about. Again, these children were given to what are known as 'suicidal gestures' – drinking bleach, for instance. Some of their experiments were so unlikely that it was only later, when they got out of hospital, that you could find out from them whether they'd been in search of euphoria or oblivion – a temporary exit, or a permanent one.

'Ralph,' Anna said. 'I'm afraid Melanie is a Sad Case, a very sad one indeed. You're not going to leave me with her this afternoon, are you?'

'I have to go out,' Ralph said, 'for three hours.'

'Can't you cancel? I don't think I can be responsible.'

Ralph wavered. 'I'm expected,' he said. He thought, how easy it is to lie. 'Robin's locked the bikes away. She'll not run off, I don't think. Nowhere to run to. She seems dazed, doesn't she? It's odd, because she was all right at Norwich station when the volunteer handed her over. But then as soon as we got out of town she seemed to go rigid. In the end she shut her eyes and wouldn't look out of the window.'

'I'm not worried about her running away,' Anna said. 'I'm worried about what she might do if she stays here.'

'We've had worse than Melanie.'

'I know – but Ralph, I know we've done this for years, had these poor things here in summer, but I'm beginning to wonder if it's fair on them – they hate it so much. And we hate it, too.'

'We've had this out before,' Ralph said. 'And I really do believe it does some good. They get good food, they get at least a bit of fresh air, they see something different from what they've seen all their lives – and there are people around who are willing to spend time with them and sit and listen if they want to talk.'

'Let's hope she doesn't want to talk this afternoon, then. Because you've gone and fixed some meeting, which will probably go on into the evening.'

'No. I'll be back for five. I promise.' He was already on his way out of the back door. I have to see Amy, he was thinking, *I have to*. He felt nauseous at the lies he was telling, at the thought of his duties neglected; felt almost sick enough to turn back. But *I promised I'd see Amy, I have to*. He drove away, cherishing the comforting belief that he was under a compulsion.

Anna was annoyed with herself; she hadn't meant to get involved in a debate about the philosophy of Visitors, she'd really meant to get a phone number from him, so that if there was any crisis with Melanie she could get him out of his meeting. She went into his office. His diary was in its usual place, top right-hand drawer. From his pewter frame Matthew Eldred frowned at her, hand on his watch-chain; Uncle James, in his tropical kit, squinted into the sun. And Ralph was there, too; Ralph on the stoep at Flower Street, one hand in his pocket, leaning against the wall. It was the only photograph they displayed, of their life in Africa. It was there because Rebecca, a couple of years ago, had begged to see some; she had taken a fancy to this, saying, 'Oh, Dad, weren't you handsome, you're not a bit like you are now.' Ralph had decided the picture should go on his bureau, to remind him of his present imperfections. It was a photograph devoid of associations; he did not remember it being taken. He saw a smiling, insouciant boy, a lounger with curly hair; a broad-shouldered boy, who looked – if only momentarily – at ease with the world.

Anna took out the diary, found the week, page, day.

'9 a.m.: Meet Red Cross about Home-from-Hospital scheme. DON'T FORGET – ring the bishop.

11 a.m.: Collect Melanie Burgess from station.'

Then nothing. So he had left the afternoon free, and something had come up at the last minute. Why didn't he say so? Anna put the diary back in the drawer. She thought no more about it.

Ralph left Amy's house at half-past four. As he reached the top of the track he saw a police car, apparently waiting for him. He stopped the engine and waited in his turn. He recognized the officer who got out first; it was one of the men he had seen previously at the same spot, one of those who, Amy said, were always watching the house.

Ralph wound his window down. 'What do you want?'

'Could I have your name, sir?'

'Eldred, Ralph Eldred.'

'And your address?'

He gave it.

'Is this your car?'

'Yes. Unfortunately.'

'Can you tell me the registration number?'

He told it.

'Would you have your driving licence on you?'

He took it out of his pocket. The policeman looked at it, handed it back; clean, not a penalty point, nothing to be done there. 'We've seen you round here before.'

'Yes. I've seen you.'

'Been calling at the farm down there?'

'Yes.'

'Reason for visiting, have you?'

'No,' Ralph said. 'I just drive about Norfolk at random, calling at farmhouses whenever I feel like it.' He swung open his door and stepped out. 'What is it you want? To look in the boot, is that it?' He walked around and unlocked it. 'OK. There you go. Get on with it.'

The officer didn't know what he wanted, really; but he ferreted about in the boot of the Citroën, found a pair of wellingtons, a jack, a tool box, a bundle of old newspapers. 'All right?' Ralph said. 'It doesn't make much sense, this, does it? If you think I'm supplying stolen goods to the people down there, why didn't you search the car on the way down?'

'We might just go and check out the farm, now,' said the other constable, who was leaning against the police car.

'You are harassing Mrs Glasse,' Ralph said. 'You know perfectly well that all her market-trading is legal and above-board, but you like the thought of tormenting two women who can't torment you back. But I can, and I will, because I know the procedure for making a complaint against the police, and I know when to make one and I know how to make it stick.'

'Had many dealings with the law, have you?'

'God's my witness,' Ralph said, 'I don't know how you blokes keep your front teeth. Finished with me, have you?'

'Oh yes, sir. We've got your name and address.'

'Oh no, sir, you mean.' Ralph got back into his car, slammed the door, spoke through the window. 'Right, so we'll be seeing each other again, will we?'

'Look forward to it,' one of the policemen said.

At the Red House next morning, Melanie did not appear for her breakfast. 'Leave her,' Ralph said. 'Let her get some rest.' He sat at the breakfast table, trying to argue sensitivity into his younger daughter. 'Be kind to Melanie,' he said.

'Why?' Rebecca asked.

Ralph looked at her in exasperation. 'Because it might achieve something. And the opposite won't.'

'Melanie,' Rebecca said, 'is filthy and foul.'

'Perhaps,' Ralph said. 'Maybe. But how will she get any better unless people treat her kindly? And you must ask yourself, before you start, if any of it is her fault. Melanie has what we call a personality disorder.'

'Oh, come off it,' Robin said. 'She can't have. She hasn't got a personality. She just sits there with her mouth half-open, staring at her boots.'

'If that were true,' Ralph said, 'there wouldn't be a problem. But I'm afraid she's not really like that. Come on, Robin, I don't expect much of your sister, but you ought to have some sense at your age. Melanie has barely been under this roof for twenty-four hours, you can't know anything about her. Don't tease her and don't provoke her, because she can be violent.'

'Oh, we won't stand for violence,' Kit said. 'Robin will bring her to the ground with a flying tackle.'

'You don't understand,' Ralph said mildly. 'The violence would be against herself.' He paused. 'When she comes downstairs, look carefully at her arms, the inside of her arms. You'll see she has old scars there.'

'She cut herself,' Anna said. 'Did she use a razor blade? Or something else?

'You noticed, did you?'

'Of course I noticed,' Anna said, annoyed. 'Do you think I'm as heedless as the children?'

'I'm sorry,' Ralph said.

'So you should be. You went out and left me with her yesterday afternoon, and you warned me about things she might sniff or inhale but you didn't warn me about knives and scissors. When I noticed her arms I had to slide away, and then run around the house hiding anything sharp.'

'You're right,' Ralph said, 'I should have warned you, but it was a long time ago she did the cutting, she seems to have other means now of relieving the stress. She was bullied at school, that's where it started, and so she played truant and then she got in with a gang of older girls, and they took her shoplifting.'

'The usual story,' Robin said.

'True,' Ralph said. 'But with one piquant variation. She was taken into care, and after three months she was allowed back home. Her parents had sold her record player and her records, and they'd given away the toys she'd had as a baby, and her clothes. Anything they couldn't sell or give away they'd just put out with the rubbish. Maybe the social workers hadn't done their job properly, or maybe the family hadn't listened, maybe they didn't take in what they were told, because it was quite obvious that they never expected to see her again.'

The children were quiet. 'So what did she do?' Robin said in the end; his tone respectful now.

'There's some waste ground near her family's council flat – she found some of her clothes there. In a black dustbin bag, she told me. She went around for a bit trying to find out who they'd sold her things to, and knocking at their doors trying to persuade them to give them back, but naturally as they'd parted with cash they thought they had a good title, as the lawyers would say. After that I don't know what happened, it's a blank, she won't tell anybody. She turned up in London about ten days later. She hadn't a penny on her when they brought her to the hostel. She had the dustbin bag, though.' He sighed. 'We bought her some clothes, but she wouldn't wear them. She wanted the originals, I suppose. She went out at the back and had a bonfire.'

Kit had stopped eating. 'It seems a terrible thing,' she said. 'That a child could be worth so little to its parents.'

'What do you expect?' Anna pushed her plate away. 'We live in a world where children are aborted every day.'

'Hush,' Ralph said. He did not want Rebecca to start asking questions. Or anybody to start asking questions, really. He had not seen Julian since their confrontation two nights ago. His son had gone back to the coast and not returned. He, Ralph, wanted so badly to see Amy Glasse that it was like a physical pain. He didn't want to drive to the farmhouse and run into Julian again, but what could he do? I am going to have to speak, he thought, tell Anna – or break this off – break it off now, because it's already too serious – how could it not be? All these years I have never looked at another woman, never thought of one, my life in that direction was closed, there was no other woman in my calculations.

If only Julian would come home, he thought. Then I should make some excuse, get into the car, drive.

He looked up. Melanie was standing in the kitchen doorway, staring at them. 'Come on, my dear,' Anna said. 'There's plenty of food left. Pull up a chair.'

Melanie recoiled: as if she had been asked to sit down with tribesmen, and dine on sheep's eyes. For another minute she studied them, poised as if for flight; then her big boots pounded up the stairs again, and her bedroom door slammed.

Summer heat had built up. White sky and a smear of sun. No wind. Heaven and earth met imperceptibly in a straw-coloured haze, and the outlines of trees were indistinct. Through this thick summer soup Julian and Sandra walked together by the footpaths, tacking inland. There was thunder in the air.

'You can come and live with us, if you want,' Sandra said. 'My mum would be glad to have you. And then – though you'd have to see Ralph – you wouldn't have to go home and face Anna.'

'My father,' Julian says, 'actually believes that you don't know what's going on.'

'There he's wrong. The first thing I noticed, he was always there when he thought I was away.' Sandra raised her hands, and tucked her red hair modestly behind her ears. 'He doesn't see me, so he thinks I don't see him. But I do see him – because you know my habit of coming home across country.'

'Through hedges and ditches.'

'If need be.' Sandra stopped, and looked directly at him. 'I brought this on you, Jule. If I'd never come to your house, this would never have happened.'

'But you did,' Julian said. 'You did come. So what's the use of talking like that?'

'I don't know. It's no use. But it's a point of interest, isn't it? If you hadn't come to North Walsham that day, when I'd gone out with the motor bikes. Or if it had rained before, five minutes before, you'd never have seen me. You'd have turned up your coat collar and gone striding off back to your car, and I'd have taken shelter in the church. And your dad would be at home with your mum, and everybody would have been happy.'

'No, not happy,' Julian said. 'That's not how I'd describe us.'

They were heading towards Burnham Market. But before they reached the village she said, 'Come in this church.'

'Why? It's not raining.'

'No, but there's a thing in it I look at. I want to show you.'

An iron gate in a grassy bank, a round tower; their shadows went faintly before them over the shorn grass. Inside, an uneven floor, cream-coloured stone; silence, except for the distant hum of some agricultural machine. Light streamed in through windows of clear glass. 'The old windows blew out in the war,' Sandra said. 'So my grandmother told me.'

'I didn't know you had a grandmother.'

'I called her my grandmother. She lived at Docking.'

'But who was she really?'

Sandra shrugged. 'My mother, she never talks about her life. I don't know who my dad was, so I'm not likely to know much about my grandmother, am I?'

The chill of the floor struck through his thin rope-soled shoes. He looked around. A square, massive ancient font, of the kind he had been dipped in, he supposed; he found it easy not to examine it. But there was something here worth attention; he saw a wine-glass pulpit, delicate and frail. 'Is this it?' he asked Sandra.

He stood before the pulpit: I should not touch it, what if

everyone touched, it would dissolve. He made himself an exception: his fingertip grazed the outlines of church fathers in their mitres and cardinals' hats, their quills inscribing scrolls: deep green and crimson scratched and flaking away to show the wood beneath, so that the faces were half of paint-flake, half of the wood's grain. On the walls he could pick out the curve of a halo, a line of colour faint as thought; he would not have seen it if Sandra had not traced it for him with her finger.

Then she touched his arm. 'But look, Julian. Come here. This is what I want to show you.'

She led him away from the pulpit to the south aisle, turned him with his back to the altar. She pointed to the flags at their feet, and to one stone, grey-black, mottled, scarred: yet each letter perfectly incised and clear. 'This one,' she said.

> In Memory of Mrs Theaophila
> Thurlow, Daughter of the
> Reverd Mr Thos Thurlow
> Rector of the Worthams in
> Suffolk, descended of the
> Thurlows of Burnham ulpe
> She departed this life 18th of
> Iune 1723 aged 24 yeares.
> And Frances Hibgame her Niece,
> Daughter of Iohn and Catherine
> Hibgame of Burnham Norton, who
> died 19th of Decemr 1736 aged
> 10 yeares, 5 months, 2 weekes and 1 day.

They stood for a moment without speaking. Then Sandra touched his arm. 'They say that people in those days didn't love their children, but it can't be true, Julian, can it?'

'No.' He dropped his head. 'Of course they must have loved her. Because they counted up every day.'

Again, silence. Sandra said. 'Listen, this thing about Becky –

you must stop. It's cruel, you see. It's cruel to your mother and father.'

'Cruel to *them*?'

Unwanted knowledge lay inside her like a stone. 'Just let it go,' she said. 'Let her grow up, will you? You talk about them being unhappy, but can't you see? What you're doing, it's like putting a knife in them.'

'Why? You mean, because I say they can't look after her?'

'Yes, just for that reason.'

'I'm frightened for her,' Julian said. 'Such evil things happen.'

'I know. I know you're frightened. But let it go now, will you?'

They walked away down the aisle to the back of the church, and again their shadows moved before them, merging and melting, their limbs like those of giant animals, their shapes outlandish; but soft, very soft, shades reflected, shadows seen through glass. The machine in the distance had cut its engine; the thunder in the air had killed the bird song, the insect hum. They touched hands as they came out of the porch – just the back of their hands brushing against each other. Sandra did not dare look into Julian's face; he did not look at her. In the distance, imaginary no doubt, the undisturbed pulse of the sea.

NINE

Julian telephoned home from a call-box in a pub on the coast road. 'Mum, is everything all right at home?'

'Where are you?'

'In the Ship,' he said, confusing her.

'When can we expect to set eyes on you?'

A pause. 'In a day or two.'

'Robin seems to think you've moved out for good.'

'He's no reason to think that.'

'Julian, is there some problem over there?'

Another pause. 'We'll have to have a talk sometime. But not just ... not just yet. Till I know what's happening here. But look, don't worry. It's just that I can't come home at the moment.'

'Julian,' she said, 'if you are trying to reassure me, stop now. All you are achieving is to alarm me wildly.'

'Mum, don't tell Dad I called, OK?'

'Why ever not?'

'I only wanted to know if you were all right.'

'Julian ...'

No answer. The line went dead. I'll drive over, she thought, see what's what. It occurred to her that she wasn't entirely certain where Mrs Glasse lived. Still, she could find it, it wasn't beyond her capacities ... but then, she thought, there's Melanie, and it's getting urgent to find some clothes for her, I ought to take her shopping; and even if I put it off for another day, I can't leave Kit at home with her while I go chasing after Julian, it's not fair. What does it matter if he doesn't come home for a few days? It's not like him to make mysteries, but perhaps it's something to do with Sandra's mother, family business, something he doesn't want to talk about. Not trouble with the police again, surely? Another thing went through her mind, that goes through the mind of every woman with a grown-up son on the loose: could Sandra be pregnant? Probably I'm being melodramatic. I wonder . . . would Ralph have time to drive over? She looked at her watch. I'll catch him at Mrs Gartree's, she thought.

Mrs Gartree was an old woman, very deaf and vague. She had been a friend of Ralph's parents, and a great churchgoer in her prime, and Ralph had taken it upon himself to call on her once a month. Mrs Gartree liked to discuss parish politics in her strident bellow, and was assiduous in filling out forms for obscure state benefits to which someone had told her she might be entitled. She had a fortune in the bank, Ralph said, but he helped her with the forms all the same; she had few pleasures left in life, he said, just this one and planning her funeral.

Mrs Gartree's voice: indignant, very loud. 'My telephone flashed at me. Who are you? What do you want?'

'It's Anna. ANNA. ANNA ELDRED. Ralph's wife.'

'Oh yes.' Mrs Gartree sounded mollified.

'Is he there?'

Mrs Gartree dwindled into vagueness. 'Oh, I don't think so.'

'Has he left?'

'What?'

'Have I missed him? Has he been and gone?'

'Missed him? Oh, I'm sure I would,' Mrs Gartree said skittishly. 'But he was here last week. I think so. Within the month.'

'But today?' I should have known better than to get into this, Anna thought. 'Today – he said he was going to call on you.'

'No,' Mrs Gartree said. 'You called me. I haven't spoken to Ralph. No, not for many a moon.'

Anna turned up her eyes. 'OK, Mrs Gartree. Sorry to have bothered you.'

'I wouldn't, except I'm deaf,' Mrs Gartree said.

'Goodbye,' Anna said.

'Toodle-oo,' said Mrs Gartree.

Anna went into Ralph's office and found his diary. He really is beginning to move in mysterious ways, she thought. In the afternoon, at two o'clock, he was due for another meeting in Norwich about the Home-from-Hospitals scheme. The Trust was funding a project to create networks of helpers for the old and chronically sick; discharged from hospital to isolated cottages, or to homes in villages with no shop or chemist, they needed failure-proof rotas of visitors if they were to be kept free from anxiety, hypothermia and the risk of falls.

She flicked through Ralph's address book; the Norwich number came to hand. 'Pat? It's Anna. Ralph's wife.'

'Oh, yes. How are you, Mrs Eldred?'

'Look, when Ralph arrives for your meeting, would you ask him to ring home? I'd like a quick word.'

There was a silence. 'Just a minute.' A pause. Then 'Mrs Eldred? I think there must be a mix-up. We haven't got a meeting today.'

'Are you sure?'

'No – yes, I mean – I've just checked my diary.'

'I'm sorry,' Anna said. 'I must have got the dates confused.'

'That's OK.' The woman sounded relieved. 'For a minute I thought I'd made some awful mistake. I'd hate to make a mistake about a meeting with Mr Eldred, he's always got so much to do.'

'Yes, hasn't he?' Anna said. She put the phone down. Well now, she thought. But she did not like what she thought. Mrs

Gartree could be discounted, as a witness; but it was strange that Pat Appleyard wasn't expecting him. It was agreed between them that he would always leave his diary for her, and update it each evening, in case there was an emergency at the hostel, in case she needed to contact him; and he had always stuck to that diary, he was known to be reliable and punctual and to save his severest strictures for people who were not.

I am not quite an innocent, Anna thought. I have read a novel or two, in my time. A disappearing husband – unless he's a drunk or a criminal – means another woman; yet there's something farcical about it, isn't there, if a disappearing husband covers his tracks so badly, or doesn't try to cover them at all? But no doubt, if Ralph took to lying, he wouldn't be very proficient at it. Not at first. As far as she knew, he'd had no practice.

Anna sat down in the hard chair at Ralph's desk. Her mind moved slowly, cautiously. Opportunity? He had plenty. He met hundreds of people in the course of his year, clients, social workers, journalists. Routine to fetter him? He had none; each week was different, and the diary was all that constrained him.

Anna tried to smile – as if there were someone in the room to see her effort. You are being ridiculous, she thought. Yes, he meets women, but so he has done for years; he meets women, but if he were interested in one of them, who in particular would it be? No answer suggested itself. I would have imagined, she thought, that though you cannot know people, not really, I would have imagined that I did know Ralph.

She felt very cold, and went upstairs to fetch a cardigan.

The day must continue, though the cardigan somehow failed to warm her. She said to Kit, 'Are you doing anything this afternoon?' Silly question; when was Kit, this summer, ever doing anything? She sat around, she slept, she made herself intermittently useful. 'Because if you're not, would you come shopping for clothes with Melanie and me? I thought, you see, as you're nearer her age –'

'Sure,' Kit said. 'We've got a lot in common.'

'Where do you think we would do best?'

'Depends what she wants. If she wants another leopard-skin print T-shirt, we could try Woolworths in Dereham.'

'Such snobs, my children.'

'OK,' Kit said grudgingly, 'I'll come. What does she need?'

'She needs a coat of some sort. And some shoes to wear in the house.'

'To spare us the clatter of the boots.'

'A sweater, as well, in case it turns cold.' She pulled her cardigan around her. 'And another pair of jeans, perhaps, and a couple of shirts or T-shirts. And underwear, I feel sure – I've not inspected, I don't feel up to it.'

'She doesn't wear any,' Kit said.

'Who says so?'

'Robin.' Kit sighed satirically. 'He's of an age to notice. Well then . . . we could go to Norwich, and catch up with Dad after his meeting. We could make him take us out for tea and iced buns, so Melanie can see us behaving like a family in a picture-book. We could have anchovy toast, and dote on each other.'

'No,' Anna said. 'Not Norwich. I tell you what we'll do – it's a nice day, let's go to the seaside. Get some fresh air. We'll go to Cromer. She might like it.'

'She'll be crying for candy-floss, and to ride on the donkeys, I suppose,' Kit said. 'Honestly, you do have a strange idea of what constitutes a treat for a person like Melanie.'

'You know what your father said. Try to be kind.'

Anna went upstairs. She stood outside the closed door for a moment, gathering herself. Then she tapped on it. No answer. Softly she turned the handle. 'Melanie?'

The curtains were drawn, and the room was dark and close and tainted; no one, so far, had seen Melanie wash. She had hauled her mattress on to the floor, and heaped the sheets and blankets and pillows into the middle of it. At first Anna thought that the bed was empty, and Melanie had somehow escaped; but then there was a slight movement at the centre of the heap, and the girl stuck her head out. 'Do you prefer to sleep on the floor?' Anna asked.

Melanie stood up amid the wreckage. Sheets fell away from her body. She was wearing a pink T-shirt that belonged to Becky. It was painfully tight under her arms, and rode up to show the frail rack of her ribs. 'Where did you get that?' Anna asked. She wondered if it had been on the washing line, but thought not. 'You shouldn't go into Becky's room without telling her, you know. She won't like it.'

'She won't like it,' the girl mocked, aping her tone.

'You're welcome to borrow anything. Anything you like. But you should ask.'

'Why?'

Because, Anna thought. Because . . . for a thousand reasons. Because it is what civilized people do. She heard the flat anthropologist's tone of the question: why? Passing no judgement: just, why?

'Besides, you're a big girl, Melanie, Becky's things won't fit you. Would you like Kit to lend you something?'

'Borrow. Lend,' the girl said. 'Snobby cows.'

'I was thinking we'd go out.' Anna tried to make her tone easy. 'Go to the seaside.'

'For kids,' Melanie said.

'Yes, but a shopping trip. To get you some clothes.'

'I had clothes.'

'Yes, but you burned them.'

'Before that. My own clothes.'

287

'I know you did. Don't pick your fingers like that.' Melanie's finger-ends were raw: the skin peeling, the nailbeds inflamed. She constantly tore at them, tormenting each one with her other nails and her teeth; it was a habit she had picked up in her amphetamine phase, it was something that these children did. And it hurt; Anna remembered – memory like a needle under the skin – her own fingernails, cropped to the quick. And then a picture flashed into her mind of Enock standing in the compound with a scythe in his hand, wasted nature at his feet: the torn-out blossom that would only have annoyed him, anyway, for a few hours before the sun killed it.

'What's the matter with you?' the girl said. Anna looked up and met her eyes. What she saw shocked her; almost evidence of humanity.

'It's nothing,' she said.

But the girl persisted, her tone cold. 'Did you think about something you shouldn't have?'

'Yes.'

'What sort of thing?'

'I can't say.'

'I can't say.' Again the imitation, cruel and strangely exact. 'A bad thing, was it?'

'Yes . . . if you like.'

'How bad?' The girl's face was intent: for once, she was asking a proper question. She needed evidence of iniquity, Anna thought, of fallibility at least. How not? She needed comparisons and juxtapositions, if she were ever to find her own place in the scale of things. 'Like killing somebody?' Melanie inquired.

'Yes.'

'Have you ever killed somebody?'

'What a question! I'd be in gaol.'

'Have you ever been in gaol?'

'Yes.' The answer surprised Anna. 'I have.'

'For nicking things?'

'No. Not that.'

'You'd have no need, would you? You've got everything.'

'You may think so.'

'You've got a house,' Melanie said.

'Yes, that's true.'

'I haven't got a house. I've been in homes.'

Anna's face softened. 'Yes . . . they shouldn't call them that, should they? Homes. Look, Melanie, your mum and dad . . . how long is it since you saw them now?'

At this question, Melanie's eyes dulled; but behind her locked-and-barred expression Anna sensed a small movement of mind, the dawn of a precarious desire for cooperation: saw the mind moving, vaguely, around the months and years. Perhaps she was trying to come to terms with an alien chronology, the dates of court orders and social inquiry reports. 'I've forgot them,' she said.

'No. You can't have.'

'I can. I have.'

'So, now . . . what about this day out we're going to have?' She smiled with a professional brightness. She had learned from Ralph, to talk in this way: to presume assent to any initiative, to state always the positive, never to consider the possibility of no for an answer.

'Are we? Us? Going out?' Melanie's eyes were like two big grey pebbles; she rocked back on her heels, as if Anna might try to haul her by force into the open air.

'Yes. Why not?'

'I like it here.'

'You do? That's something.'

Melanie saw that she had lost an inch of ground. 'And these clothes, I like these clothes, I don't want any others.'

'I'm sure you know why that is quite unreasonable,' Anna

289

said. 'You're clearly not without intelligence.' Ralph's tone was less evident; she was cool, at the end of her patience. 'You know perfectly well that you can't spend the rest of your life wearing a T-shirt that belongs to a child two or three years younger than yourself, so it's only a matter of when you get new clothes, isn't it, not whether?'

They surveyed each other: level ground. Anna calculated that Melanie might hit her: it would not be unprecedented, in a Visitor. She weighed the prospect: the pale stringy arms below the tight sleeves, arms laced with cuts, and the torn hands, the right middle finger with its cheap heart-shaped ring. She knew that she should step back a few inches, beyond Melanie's reach. The girl's arms hung at her sides, and Anna − who had seen men fight − imagined that she might jerk one fist up, straight-armed, to catch the point of her jaw. But I will not step back, she thought. I will not give way. Melanie whispered, 'Tell me what you thought.'

'What do you mean, what I thought?

'Before. When you thought about killing somebody.'

'What will you do, if I tell you?'

'Come with you. Get clothes.'

'No, you'll break your promise.'

'I won't. I'll come. But tell me.'

'All right.' Their eyes locked: Anna thought, I'll tell you something you don't know. 'I had another child once,' she said. 'A boy. A baby. He was taken from my house and murdered.'

The girl nodded. Her eyes slid away. Stayed on the floor: on the heap of crumpled bedding. 'That was hard,' she whispered.

And it was that − the very poverty of her response, the laughable poverty of her vocabulary − that made Anna speak again. 'Hard. Yes. Extremely hard. You ask me what I was thinking about − I'll tell you, Melanie, why not? I was thinking about the man who did it. About how I would kill him, if I had him.'

Melanie watched her. 'And how would you?'

'I don't know. I think about it, but I can't choose. You see, there are so many ways.'

The girl dropped her head again, and for the first time Anna saw it as a frail, living thing; half-destroyed, bruised, but a blossom on the stem of her thin neck. Her skin was white and fine, her hair, no doubt, had a colour of its own, and only parts of her body were cut and marked. She is retrievable, she thought: possibly, in some small way. But I should not have said what I did, I should have found some way to lie; I should have tried to retrieve her, but not by that method.

She moved to the door. 'You made a promise,' she said. She held the door open. 'Come on now, Melanie, you drove a bargain and you got more than you asked for. You made a promise that you'd come and buy some clothes.'

Melanie nodded. Again, there was no expression on her face now: no reaction to what she had been told. She will suppose it is a dream, Anna thought; she lives from moment to moment, perhaps, her memory constantly erased. Behind her, the big boots descended the stairs. In the strong sunlight that shone through the kitchen window, she observed the girl's flawed, bluish face, and put up her hand to touch her jaw. 'Do you not sleep, Melanie?'

'No. Cough keeps waking me.'

'Keep off the glue, and your cough will clear up,' Anna said briskly.

Anna lapsed into silence as she drove; Melanie was silent anyway. When they arrived in Cromer she lifted her feet in the big black boots and locked her arms around her knees, wrapping herself into a knot in the back seat. She didn't want to see the sunlight on the cold North Sea, or hear the ice-cream van chimes and the gulls' cries. Kit saw the birds' bodies floating and skimming, mirrored in the high windows of the old sea-front hotels: skimming the turrets and dormers and gables of the red-brick houses, wheeling inland to swoop and cry among the pines. The gulls leave an after-image, on the ear and eye, and the waves have the sound of a laboured breath; trippers tramp over mastodon bones, and plaice is fried in cafés with plastic tables.

Melanie shut her eyes tight; she wasn't getting out of the car. Anna seemed to have run out of energy to coax her.

'You know you need clothes,' she said feebly.

'I've got clothes,' Melanie said. 'I told you.'

Kit said, 'You've got what you stand up in, and some of that stolen. Come on, you silly bitch! What you're wearing has to be washed, for our sake if not for yours.'

'Why?'

'Because,' Kit said mildly, 'if you start to smell any more we'll make you go and live in one of the bike sheds.'

Surprisingly, this seemed to have an effect on Melanie. She unwrapped her body like a stiff uncurling fist, and tumbled from the car. Kit, having warned her about the sea breezes, had brought along a spare jacket of her own. She tried to put it around the child's shoulders. Melanie bellowed, 'Get off me. *Murdering* pig.'

'Not quite,' Kit said. 'Not yet, but don't try me, honeybunch, I'm bigger than you and if I wallop you round the head you'll know about it.'

Anna shivered. She had abdicated to Kit now, lost control: she was terrified by the thought of what she had said to Melanie, the ease with which it might seep from that pale inarticulate mouth.

Kit took Melanie by the arm. What a formidable wardress she would be, Anna thought; very strong and very sure, with that hand that sinks into the tender female flesh above the elbow joint. She felt that bruises might blossom out again, on her own flesh. She asked herself, have I something for which I must forgive Kit? Have I forgiven her for living?

They headed off into the town. Kit released her prisoner, and strode out smiling equably. Melanie slouched, sullen and furious, her green-twig arms whipped by the wind. Anna had made a move to pick up the coat, for use when Melanie changed her mind; but Kit, almost imperceptibly, shook her head at her, and Anna let it lie on the front seat of the car.

An hour later they had managed, after a fashion, to get Melanie equipped. They had to apologize for her rudeness to the people in the shops, and received commiserating smiles. 'They think she's my retarded little sister,' Kit whispered.

Melanie at least was willing to carry her own parcels. The day darkened, there was drizzle on the wind; now, while the trippers turned blue and rubbed their hands, the local women leaned into the squall in their quilted jackets and wool scarves. Anna swept her collar up to her throat, and glanced at Melanie's white arms. Norfolk may teach forethought, in a way London never does.

'Look!' Kit put a hand on her shoulder. 'Mum, look at that washing machine!' She arrested her before the electricity showroom. 'Sixteen programmes! Just think!'

Anna said, 'Yes ... but you know, with the twin-tub still going strong –'

'Going strong?' Kit was outraged. She glanced over her shoulder, to ask Melanie – their relationship had flourished in the last half-hour – if she'd ever heard of such a thing as a twin-tub washing machine, where you hauled the sodden shirts with tongs and rubber gloves from ... but Melanie wasn't there. Kit spun around. Her long hair flew out in the wind. 'Run,' she said. 'It's thirty seconds since I saw her, so how far can she have got?'

They gaped up and down the street. No trace, no sign. 'In a shop,' Kit said. 'Quick.'

They put their heads into the neighbouring shops, gabbling questions, apologies: 'Have you seen a young girl, short reddish hair, jeans, pink T-shirt?' The queue turning: what, your daughter is she, how old would she be? A woman behind a counter stood with her hand poised, ready to drop Norfolk shortbread into a paper bag. Blank faces. 'Sorry, my dears,' the woman said.

'We're wasting our time. Where would she go?'

'Anywhere,' Kit said. 'She doesn't know her way about, so she'd go anywhere.'

They looked into each other's faces. 'I don't want to sound like a silly film,' Kit said, 'but why don't you go that way and I'll go this way? And if you see her, grab her, don't hesitate, just hold on to her, OK?'

'Where will I meet you?'

'Here,' Kit said. 'By the washing machine. Give it ten minutes, then start walking back. I'll see you in fifteen, twenty. If we don't find her by that time we may as well give up, she'll probably have got on a bus and gone somewhere. Has she any money?'

'A fiver,' Anna said.

'Oh, right, a fiver.' Kit pounded off down the street, her head turning from side to side. Anna watched her for a moment and then skittered awkwardly in the opposite direction, high heels uncertain over the paving stones. She hadn't known it would come to this, or she'd have dressed for it.

A few minutes, and her efforts were over. She leaned against a wall. I can't run, she thought; never could. Still, she had done what her heart allowed, her ribs heaving and her chest sore, her head swivelling from side to side to see if she could catch a glimpse of Melanie's orange hair. Surely, she thought, if she tries to hitch a lift out of town, no one will give her one? She's too peculiar, she looks deranged. Unless, perhaps, they take pity on her. For people do, of course. They do the most amazing things; prisoners escape, and people give them lifts, and every runaway gets money and shelter somehow.

Fifteen minutes later, distressed, her lips almost blue, she was back with Kit before the washing-machine shop. Kit put her hands on her mother's shoulders, then under her elbows to hold her upright. 'Are you all right? I didn't say kill yourself.'

'Fine,' Anna said. 'I'm fine.' She pulled back and held her midriff, one thin hand folded protectively over the opposite wrist.

'We've lost her. I questioned bus-queues, in a melodramatic fashion. Ought we to go to the police?'

'No. She's not done anything wrong.'

'But she might. Or something might happen to her.'

Anna straightened up. Breath was coming back. 'Nobody's obliged to take their holidays with us,' she snapped.

'No, but –'

'Kit, if we get the police involved it is almost sure to land her in some sort of trouble. And what would your father say? She'd never trust us again. We should give her – I don't know – we should just stand here for a quarter of an hour. She might come back.'

'She won't be able to find her way back.' Kit rubbed her hands together, to warm them. 'OK, but we should let someone know – I don't suppose you've got Dad's number in Norwich?'

'No.'

'We can call Directory Enquiries. Get him back home. Listen, you stand here. There's a phone-box over there – Red Cross, isn't it? What's the name of the person he's meeting?'

'I don't know.'

'Never mind. I'll tell them to turn him round and send him home.'

'No, Kit.' Anna tore at her daughter's arm. She thought, if my daughter phones Pat Appleyard asking for him, that'll be twice in a day, so she'll know there's something wrong, she'll be asking questions, starting gossip ... 'Kit, he's not in Norwich.'

'Where is he then?'

'I don't know.'

'But he said he was going to Norwich! This morning!' Kit swept her hair back, then flung out her hands, exasperated. 'Robin said, bring me a *Wisden Cricket Monthly* and he said, all right, but if I can't see one, will anything else do, and Robin said no. Rebecca said, bring me something. He said, what? She said, a surprise. Dad said, OK. Robin said, you spoiled brat.'

Anna drew herself gently from her daughter's grasp and leaned back against the plate-glass window of the washing-machine shop. She covered her mouth with her hand, and a little, bitter bleat came from her; laughter?

Kit tried to pull her hand from her mouth, to claw it away, as if her mother were a baby that had eaten something it shouldn't: earth or soil or a stone. On and on it went, the little noise: the heave of the narrow ribs, the out-breath like a moan, the breath sucked in as if air were poison. Anna's ribs drew up, into a panic-stricken arch, and for a moment she was frozen, paralysed, eyes closed. Then she let out her breath – with more than a gasp, with a muffled scream heaved up from her stomach. She sucked in the air, the raw salty Norfolk air. 'I knew I should lose everything,' she said. 'I knew I should lose everything, one of these days.'

Late afternoon, someone came to the door. Anna let Kit answer it. She noticed that Kit had changed out of her jeans into a neat skirt, and had tied her hair back, as if she anticipated a sudden transition into adult affairs.

Anna sat in Ralph's study, in the old wooden swivel chair he used at his desk. It had come from Emma's surgery, this chair: given to him when it was too disreputable for the patients to see. In better times, they had joked that it was impossible to sit in it without the urge to swing around, to say, 'That sounds a very nasty cough.'

But these are worse times. Anna was exhausted by the effort of imagination chasing its own tail. I can formulate no sensible ideas about Ralph, she thought, and my head aches; Kit will never trust me again, never trust me not to break down and start screaming in the street. And the girl has gone, Melanie, and somehow I will be held responsible; screaming doesn't get me out of that one. Now with each little breath she took, the chair swayed under her, sedately. Each movement brought forth its ponderous, broken, familiar complaint.

Kit came in: two policemen followed her. She looked grave, pale, very correct. 'They've found Melanie. She made it as far as Norwich. She's in hospital, I'm afraid.'

Anna stood up. 'What's happened?'

'Mrs Eldred?' one of the policemen said.

'Yes. What's happened to her?'

'She gave us your name,' the policemen said. 'Mr Eldred's name, I should say.'

'Oh, for God's sake,' Anna said. 'Answer my question.'

'She's taken something, swallowed something maybe, that's what we've been told. Would you have any idea what it might be?'

'I told him,' Kit said. 'I've already explained how she ran off.' She turned to the policemen. 'She was fine then. I told you.'

'How is she?'

'She's comfortable.'

'Comfortable?' Anna stared at the man. 'How can she be?'

The other policemen spoke. 'The hospital won't let us interview her. She's drowsy, you understand.'

'Is she in any danger?'

'That's not for us to say.'

'We understand,' the first man said, 'that Mr Eldred would be *in loco parentis*.'

Anna nodded. The other policemen said, 'Mr Eldred not home from work yet?'

'He doesn't work. That is, he doesn't go out to work.'

The men looked confused. 'He's an invalid?' one suggested.

'My husband is an officer of a charitable trust. He works from home.'

'That's why we have Melanie,' Kit said. 'I tried to explain.'

'Would it be all right if we looked round, Mrs Eldred? Around your house?'

'No, I'm afraid I can't allow that.'

'They want to look in Melanie's room,' Kit said. 'In case there's something there that she might have taken, a bottle of pills or something.'

'Yes,' Anna said. 'I know what they want to do.'

'I'm sure it's fine,' Kit said uneasily, to the men.

Already, Anna thought, she is treating me as if I were of unsound mind, unable to speak up for myself. I must expect it, I suppose. 'Go and get the proper warrants,' she said. 'The papers. Then come back. And then you can search.'

At once the atmosphere changed; the men changed, their natural obstructiveness and obtuseness giving way to a sneering hostility. 'Why do you want to make it difficult?' the first man said.

'I don't want to make it difficult. I just want things done properly.'

'If the young girl dies,' the second said, 'you'll be to blame.'

'I thought there was no question of her dying. I thought she was comfortable.'

'Mum —' Kit said. Her face was shocked; she thinks I'm a new woman, Anna thought. 'Mum, look. It's just to help Melanie.'

'There's a principle,' Anna said to her daughter. 'There's a correct way. Once you depart from it, you leave yourself open.'

'It's not South Africa,' Kit said.

'Not yet,' Anna snapped.

Her daughter was silent. A policeman said, 'Well, madam, perhaps it would be better if we talked to your husband. What time are you expecting him?'

'No particular time.'

'Doesn't he keep regular hours?'

'By no means.'

Kit said, 'We usually know where to contact him, but today there seems to be some mix-up with his diary.'

'Oh yes?'

'So we don't know how to get hold of him, you see.'

'That's unlucky,' the second man said. 'We'll have to radio in. Say he can't be found.'

'I can come to the hospital,' Anna said.

'Yes, madam, but it's not you that's *in loco parentis*, is it? Well now, we have got a problem.'

None of their language, Anna thought, means what it says. It is a special dialect, charged with implication. One of the men was looking over her shoulder. He seemed to be staring at the wall. She turned to see what he was looking at. 'That picture there,' the policeman said. 'That photo. That wouldn't be Mr Eldred, would it?'

'Yes.' She picked up the photograph, defensive, startled: Ralph on the stoep at Flower Street. 'If you're thinking of putting out a wanted poster, I'm afraid it won't be much use to you. It's twenty years old, this picture – more.'

'Is it, now? It's not a bad likeness, not bad at all.' He turned to his colleague. 'Brancaster way? Down the track? The market-trader?' He turned back to Anna. 'We've had a few dealings with Mr Eldred. We've seen him coming and going from a small-holding, just off that loop of road before you get to Burnham Deepdale. I wouldn't be surprised if that's where we'll find him, madam.'

Each time he said this – 'madam' – it was like a kick or a blow with his fist. He meant it so; he was watching her face, waiting for her to flinch. 'Would *you* know a woman over that way, involved in market-trading?'

'A Mrs Glasse?' Anna's face seemed frozen. She nodded. 'Will you go over there now?'

'It might be worth a try.'

'Kit,' Anna said, 'when Rebecca comes home from her friend's, will you see that she has something to eat? Then take her over to Foulsham and ask Emma to put you both up for the night.'

'What for?'

'Because I don't want her here. OK?'

'Can I take your car?'

'No. I need it.' She turned to the men. 'I'll follow you,' Anna said to the men.

'We can't stop you, madam.'

Anna said to Kit, 'You can bike over, can't you? Just take your toothbrushes.'

'I'll leave Becky with Emma, and I'll come back.'

'No. Stay with your sister. Kit, look – do this one thing for me, please?'

Anna was brittle, exasperated; Kit knew the tone, it was familiar. But she saw how Anna's nerves were stretched – tight, tight. 'What shall I say to Emma?'

'I don't know. Must I think of everything? Aren't you old enough to help me?'

'No,' Kit said. 'Not really.'

Anna picked up her car keys from beside the photograph. She has been waiting for this, Kit thought, waiting to go out, her bag ready and to hand.

Anna followed the police car. They could have lost her, at this junction or that, but they preferred to dawdle and let her stick with them.

It was evening now. The sky was striated, precise overlays of colour working from regal purple to the palest blush. Amy Glasse woke and sat up in bed, stretching her arms and fingers, rippling her fingers through the liquid light like a stage pianist preparing to play. Ralph turned and reached for her as she slid from the bed; sleeping, he followed the heat-trail of her body across the sheets. His arm, empty, cupped the space from which she had moved.

From below, there was a monotonous thumping, a solid hammering, like the copulation of giants in a myth.

'Oh, God,' Amy said. 'We're back in the old routine.'

Ralph woke to see her shape against the window. Her long back, white in the dusk: 'Sweetheart, come back to bed.' He put out a hand for her, drowsy; didn't see why his peace should be disturbed.

'Sorry,' Amy said. 'I don't know, shall I go down, or shall I pretend I'm not here? Ralph, you're not awake, are you?' She cast around, snatched up the T-shirt she had taken off, and swabbed the area between her thighs. She looked around the room for something else to wear, then with a little laugh pulled the T-shirt over her head. She reached for her skirt. 'What shall I do? If I don't go down now they'll only come back later.'

'Who?' He had focused now, on that sound of fist on wood. 'Who is it?'

'Purvis and his mate,' she said. 'The constabulary, my dear. Sometimes I wish I lived in the city, then you'd get a choice of bastards. Not always the same old pair.'

He pushed back the covers. 'Ralph,' she said, 'don't go down. No, listen to me.' She was at the window, the curtain parted minutely. 'There's two cars here. Just get dressed, but stay up here and be quiet. If they come up say nothing – don't antagonize them.'

Buttoning her skirt, she flitted from the room. No one could crouch and hide, and listen to that destructive thump-thump-thumping; Amy couldn't do it, and neither could he. Panicking, he began to pull himself into his clothes. He must get there before her; feared violence. Once before he had imagined hitting Purvis. Once, a long time ago . . . his hand, clenched to pull in and fasten his belt, felt itself sink into belly-flesh: propel a bully towards ridicule and the stoep door, one foot in a wastepaper basket. The body has its own memories; muscle and bone, marching its own ghost-trail.

He put his shoes on, straightened up: randomly buttoned his shirt, skittered down the stairs after Amy. The front door was open: he went out into a September evening, a confrontation, the air a golden-rose; the past summer a memory, bloom of sea-lavender, scent of tourist tyres on narrow burning roads. Purvis said, 'Mr Eldred, isn't it?' Yes, it is, he said, yes, I do: what's happened, how is she?

Anna's car drew up behind the police car. It rattled to a halt. After a moment, Anna stepped out. She did not move away from the car, held the vehicle's door before her like a shield; but she took the time to let her eyes rest on everything. She raised one foot, tucked an ankle behind her, balancing it on the car's rusting door-sill. The policemen's eyes slid like snakes over Amy Glasse, her creased homemade cotton skirt and her breasts bouncing beneath the stained white cloth. 'Fuck off out of here, Purvis,' she said. 'You were here last week and into everything, so what the fuck do you want now?'

Ralph put his hand out, to take Amy's wrist. 'Calm down. It's nothing. They want me, not you.'

Amy's eyes travelled: to Purvis, to Ralph's face, to Anna still as a statue in the fading light.

I have lost track of the time, Ralph thought; I should have been home an hour ago. Anna, without a word, climbed back into the car and drove away.

When the police had given their news, and driven away in their turn – their eyes roaming around the farmyard and outbuildings – Ralph said to Amy, 'I must go right now. You understand, don't you? I have to go to Norwich and sort this out.'

'Of course you must go.' Her smile was twisted, bleak. 'Then you've your wife to face.'

'Yes. That will be later.'

'I'll not be seeing you, then?'

He didn't reply. 'We've seen it on the television,' she said. 'Me and Sandra. Men always go back to their wives.'

'I'll see you tomorrow.' He felt shaky, weak; was not sure whether he was lying or not. 'Unless I'm at the hospital, that is. There'll be all sorts of people I have to talk to – social workers, and her parents if she's really ill, and my own people, the Trust committee, because if there's any possible legal problem I like them to know about it. I'll be on the phone all day.'

'Anna, she's beautiful,' Amy said. 'Sandra didn't tell me. I had no idea. I thought she was some biddy in a print frock.'

'I can't talk about it. I haven't time. I'll be back as soon as I can.'

'I'll not count on it,' Amy said. Her voice was light and bright. She was fighting back tears. Ralph felt inside him a great rolling mass of nausea and cold, of apprehension and self-hatred.

At a phone-box on the outskirts of Fakenham, he stopped the car and rang his home. He calculated that Anna would just have arrived; if she were walking in, he thought, that would be best, that would be the best time to get her.

He let the phone ring for a long time. He checked his watch

again. She should be home by now. Where would she go, except the Red House?

As he was about to replace the receiver, he heard it picked up. 'Anna? Anna, are you there?' Silence. 'Please speak to me.' Silence. 'I'm going to Norwich,' he said. 'I have to. To the hospital. I'll call again from there. Anna, please . . .'

She had put the phone down. He got back in the car and drove away.

I would have spoken, she thought: I would have spoken, except that I could not think of a single thing, not one thing to say. She went into the kitchen and made herself some instant coffee. She drank it standing up, by the sink. Then she washed her cup. There was a long night ahead, and she would be alone. Robin was playing in a school match, he would not be back, he was staying over in King's Lynn. Julian, she supposed, was at the farm; and she had sent her daughters away. She dried her hands, folded the towel, laid it over the back of a chair.

It is in the nature of betrayal, she thought, that it not only changes the present, but that it reaches back with its dirty hands and changes the past.

She could not be still. She wandered through the rooms; then returned to the kitchen to make herself some more coffee. She sat at the table, trying to subdue her ragged breathing. She got up and went to the sink again. She saw from the kitchen clock that only half an hour had passed since she put the phone down on Ralph. You cannot pass the time like this, she thought: washing your cup and washing your cup.

Darkness had fallen. Autumn would choose a day like this, to announce its presence: stealthy feet, chilling the rooms. Ralph had lit the boiler this morning, but she had forgotten to attend to it. A major salvage operation would be needed now. She felt she did not have the strength for it. She took a blanket from the airing cupboard and walked downstairs with it gathered about her, African-style. She went into the sitting room. Did not put on the light. Chose herself a chair. She wrapped the blanket around her and pulled it almost over her head. She was swaddled now, like an ambulance casualty.

There had been times before, when she had thought they could not survive. There had been times when she had wished to erase her husband and children, her whole biography. There had not been a day, in twenty years, when she had not thought about her lost child. Sometimes on the television – they often watched the ten o'clock news together – they had seen the parents of missing children, shaking, bleating, heads sagging: making what was called an appeal, trying to wring some killer's heart. No such appeal had been open to her. They had left the corpse behind, in another country. The verdict was final. When you have suffered together as she had, she and Ralph, what lies between you can't be called romance. You can't talk about a marriage, in the normal terms people use: a happy marriage, a marriage under strain. You are not partners, but the survivors of a disaster. You see each other and remember, every day. So how can you live together?

But how can you not?

She fingered the blanket's satin-bound edge, and sat, apart from this fingering, without moving. When the room grew quite dark she put a hand out of her wrappings and switched on a lamp which stood by her on a round table. This table had a white cloth, on which Sandra Glasse had embroidered a scatter of daisies, violet and deep blue, their centres black like poppies: fantasy flowers, bouquets from an alternative world. Ralph said that every action contained its opposite. That nothing was fixed, nothing in creation; that cells made choices all the time. If we could rewind the tape of the universe, play it over again, we might find ourselves to be different: six-legged intelligent creatures, crawling on the seabed, and speaking like birds, in song. But no, she thought, perhaps that is not what Ralph says. Perhaps I have got it wrong, he would be talking to the children and I would not be listening properly, that is usually the case with me. Have I not imagined, often enough, a universe in which other choices were made? The girl, Felicia, we turned out of the house. Some instinct warned me, so that night I kept my son in my arms. Or, Ralph took no pity on the wanderers in the storm, kept the bolts drawn, the key turned in the lock. She shivered. She felt closer to that night, now, than she did to the light and air of this morning: to the sea wind and coastal showers, the truculent girl in the back seat of the car, Kit with her hair streaming about her as she ran calling for Melanie through the streets.

The telephone rang, in the next room. She did not stir. It would be Emma, perhaps, wanting to know what was happening. Or Ralph, calling from the hospital. She still had nothing to say to him, so what was the point of answering? She withdrew her hand into the safety of her blanket. An hour passed. The phone rang again. It was raining outside, and now the house was very cold. Anna thought of nothing at all. Her ideas seemed to have stopped, as if chilled and narrow conduits no longer carried blood to heart and brain.

Very late — it must have been towards midnight — she heard the doorbell. She sat listening; someone had a finger pressed on it, insistent. Ralph would have his key, so would the children. Emma? She pulled the blanket around her. She did not want to see Ralph's sister. Emma had a key for emergencies, but who was to know what she would consider an emergency? The person was knocking now, thudding at the door.

The police again? That's possible. She could not ignore the noise. She extricated herself from the blanket. Her legs felt stiff. She fumbled for the light switch in the hall. 'I'm coming,' she called. 'Don't break down the door.' Her voice sounded peculiar, precarious. She opened the door.

'Anna? Kit telephoned me from her aunt's.'

He was the last person she had expected. 'Daniel, come in from the night.' Rain blew in with him. 'What did Kit tell you?'

'About the young girl you have staying. And that the police came. That you had gone off after them to find Ralph. You did find him, I suppose.'

'So Kit knew.'

'Had an idea.'

'A shrewd one, I'll bet. And Julian would know of course, and Robin, I suppose. And you, now. The whole county, soon.'

'No, Anna, it's nothing like that.'

She began to fasten her hair up; saw herself dimly in the hall-stand mirror. 'I used to laugh at Ralph because he went on for years without knowing about Emma and your father. Now the laugh's on me, isn't it?'

'Believe me, I knew nothing,' Daniel said. 'Not until to-day. When Kit telephoned I found it hard to take in. Ralph, I mean . . . it doesn't seem possible.' He looked down at his shoes. How young he is, Anna thought. A boy.

'And Kit asked you to come here, did she?'

'She wants to come home herself, but she promised you she'd stay and look after Becky. Becky's asking all sorts of questions, but Emma can deal with that.'

Questions suitable to her time of life, Anna thought. Between us, we will have to come up with some suitable answers. 'Yes, I made Kit promise to stay at Foulsham . . . you see, I can't face anybody.' She looked up at him. 'I have to prepare myself, Daniel. I have to think out what I am going to say.'

'I don't think you should stay here on your own. Have you . . . I mean, Ralph, has he been in touch?'

'The phone's been ringing. I didn't answer it.'

'He's probably still at the hospital. Kit would like to know how the child is.'

'I don't care,' Anna said.

'Don't you?'

'No. I've had enough of all that.'

'Yes, I can understand. But you're doing yourself an injustice.'

'Oh, I'm not good, Daniel. I'm not a good woman. Not at all.'

Daniel hesitated. 'It – your standard of goodness, Anna – I think it would defeat most of us.'

'Oh, my standard, yes. But what I live up to, that's another question.'

Daniel became brisk. 'Have you eaten? No, of course not. The house seems very cold. I think I ought to try to track down Ralph. The hospital's number, do you have it? They could find him and bring him to a phone. You don't have to speak to him. I'll do it. Just to see what the situation is, what his immediate intentions are.'

'Don't bother.' She turned away. 'As for the child – I've told you, I don't want to know. Year after year he's inflicted these dreadful children upon me, awful, hopeless children –' She stopped. 'He will come home. Eventually.' She leaned against Daniel. He put an arm around her. She began to cry. 'I can't face him. I feel ashamed. It's as if it's me who's done something wrong. I won't be able to look him in the eye.'

'Then you don't need to stay here. Let me drive you over to Blakeney.'

'To Ginny's? Oh no, it's late . . . and besides . . .'

'She wouldn't ask you questions, you know.'

'Daniel, how can you believe that?'

'I'm an optimist.' he said. His face looked grim, as if he were ageing in a night. 'Come back to my flat, then. Just bring what you need for now. I've got a spare bed. I'll make you comfortable.'

'Yes, take me to your flat. I want to be gone before Ralph gets here. I must be.' She moved slowly back down the hall. 'I'll be five minutes.'

As she packed her toothbrush, nightdress, a change of clothes, she remembered the policewoman, standing over her in Elim: telling her what she would need. She should have a policewoman now; directionless, enfeebled, her hands moved among her possessions. She heard Daniel downstairs, talking on the telephone. 'No, Kit, I don't think she should come there to you, she'd have to think of something to say to Becky, she can't face it . . . Just you and Emma hang on for now, can you? . . . It's very late, we're all tired, tomorrow things will be . . . Yes, to Blakeney, why not? If she still feels she must keep away from Ralph.'

They are making arrangements for me behind my back, she thought. As if I were a sick or injured person. Which I am, of course. She had an image of herself and Ralph, two sick or injured animals yoked together: dragging their burden, sometimes in circles.

In the car she began to cry. The lanes were dark, the trees dripping, puddles shining in their headlights; the half-hour journey seemed a lifetime. Holt was deserted: a few shopfronts dimly lit, the pub doors bolted. Daniel parked his car, walked around it to help her out. She needed the help; slumped against him, leaned on his arm. 'It's clearing,' he said, looking up at the sky.

'Yes.' She scrubbed at her face. Tried to smile.

Daniel unlocked his door and flooded the night world with a vast, white, hard light. She climbed a steep staircase, seeing the phantom outlines of drawing boards through a glass door. 'Up to the top,' Daniel said.

'You are being very kind to me.'

'It's nothing, Anna.'

The staircase opened into a large and lofty room, sparely furnished: the walls of exposed flint, the timbers exposed, the floor bare and waxed: its expanse broken only by two dark fringed rugs, their design geometric, their colours sombre. Flying carpets, she thought. No clutter anywhere, just those matt black machines that young men have: no windows, but skylights enclosing the weather and the night. Anna stood considering it. 'Kit never told me about this.'

'A way of being outside when you're inside. Kit hardly comes here.'

'True. I know.'

'Do you like it?'

'Very much.' A life free of complexity, she thought. 'Can you keep it warm?'

'Not easily. Can't have everything. Would you like to bathe your face?' She nodded. She sat on the sofa, and he brought her a bowl of water, some cotton-wool, and a small cream towel. He sat down next to her, as if she must be supervised. 'Lukewarm water is best,' he advised. 'If you have ice, it makes your eyes swell even more.'

'I'm sorry, Daniel,' she said.

'Nothing to be sorry for. Better to cry among friends. Look, Anna – all this, with Ralph, it's ridiculous. An aberration.'

'You think so?'

'I know it is. Just one of those things that happen in marriages.'

'The marriages of middle-aged people, you mean.'

'Look, everything is easier to face in daylight.' He ventured a smile; took from her fingertips one of the sodden balls of cotton-wool. 'In the morning you can have your choice. The greengrocer will be open, so you can have cucumber slices for your eyes. Or tea-bags, if you like. I have Earl Grey, Assam or Darjeeling.'

'Goodness. What a lot you know about female grief.'

'My mother, you see.'

'Since your father died?'

'Mainly before. Years before – always, really. We'd be alone in the house and she'd cry buckets. Horse-troughs. Oceans. So,' he said, with a soft bleakness, 'I'm used to comforting.'

She looked up. 'You mean . . . this, it would be when your father was with Emma?'

'Where else?'

'She always appeared – I don't know – so self-possessed.'

'Yes. Of course, the tea-bags helped. The cucumber slices. And the fact that she's got a nice sort of flippancy, my mother, a sort of veneer of stupidity. So you wouldn't know – why should anybody know? Emma broke my mother's heart.'

She took his hand. After a while he said, 'Brandy, that's the next thing. Can you drink brandy? It will warm your heart, Anna.'

He gave her a glass. It did warm her, stealing through to feelings, levels of comprehension, she had not known were there. 'It would be nice to get drunk,' she said. 'I don't think I ever have. I see the attraction, though.'

'The bottle's at your elbow.'

'One doesn't know . . . one doesn't know other people's histories at all.'

'No, of course not. Not the half of what goes on.'

'I feel I have been stupid.'

'You were misled. People do mislead you, don't they, they have an instinct to cover up the mess. It's how we're taught to live. I've always thought, or rather my concern is, that history shouldn't repeat itself. I've thought, I don't want to marry some poor girl who I'll end up leaving for Kit.'

Anna tried to answer him, but the effort was almost beyond her. 'I'm exhausted,' she said flatly.

'It's emotion. It is exhausting. I dare say that's why we try to get by without it.'

He helped her up. Her legs were jelly. He took her into the little spare room. 'The bed's made up. Do you want anything?'

'I'll be fine.'

He touched her cheek. 'You should know, Anna, that Kit's going to Africa. She had a letter, she says, this morning. Some volunteer project has accepted her. She wants to see the place where she was born.'

Anna shuddered.

'I know,' he said. 'Emma's put me wise.'

She looked up. 'Wise. And Kit? Has Emma put her wise?'

'That's more than I can say. In the circumstances it would be very wrong of me to make assumptions about what other people know or don't know.' He paused. 'I think, Anna – for what it's worth – that you are a very brave woman.'

She shook her head. 'My heart failed me, Daniel. I had to be rescued from myself. And my kindness has failed me, many a time. I've harboured such thoughts – I couldn't tell you, thoughts that there are no ordinary words for. Only this thing – with Ralph – I don't deserve it. I know I don't.'

He left her to put on her nightdress. She promised that if she could not sleep she would come for him. We can see the dawn together, he said. She eased herself into the narrow bed. He had put two hot-water bottles in it, one for her feet and one for her to hug to herself, burning her ribs, slapping and washing itself against her. The Red House is empty, she thought: for the first time in years. And she had not slept in such a little bed since she had been in prison.

There was another skylight above her, its glass containing the night. Oh, Daniel, she breathed, I might see the stars. She was afraid she had spoken out loud; but she was past that, too tired to have a voice at all. Her heart hammered, but then lay still: obedient creature. She turned on her back. The blankets were heavy; she pushed them back a little, to free her chest with its great weight of misery. The air was clearing, it was true; still, she was looking up through a veil of water. She saw two stars, then more. Very faint, old stars: light attenuated.

Kit woke her. She brought a tray with a glass of orange juice and a pot of coffee.

'Daniel promised me cucumber slices.' Anna said.

'You need them. You look awful.'

'What do you expect?'

'It's ten o'clock. What would you like to do?'

Anna pushed herself upright in the bed. 'What are the choices?'

'You could go home. I understand if you don't want to. Daniel had to go and see a client, there was an appointment he couldn't break. You can stay here, you're welcome, he says. You can go to Emma. She's very worried about you.'

'I seem to be homeless.'

'Not at all,' Kit said. She thought, it's everyone else who is homeless, waiting for what will occur.

'Robin will be back, you know? Maybe five or six o'clock. He won't know what's happening.'

'I can intercept him. Don't worry about that.' Kit seemed impatient. 'Worry about yourself. What do you want to do?'

'What do I want to do? With the glorious prospect that stretches before me?'

'Dad rang. Last night. Said he was calling you but you wouldn't answer. He was very upset, very concerned about you.'

'A bit late for that.'

'Melanie's going to be OK, they're pretty sure, but they're keeping her for a few days, because she still won't say what it was she took. Dad spent the night at the hospital.'

'At the hospital, did he? That was blameless, at any rate.'

Kit blushed. She looked stern, set. 'How can you?'

'What?'

'Make these weak sarcastic little jokes?'

'I don't know how I can. Do you happen to know your father's programme for the day?'

'He's got a lot of calls to make.'

'He'll want his office, then. To be at home.'

Kit sat down on the bed. The tray wobbled; she put out a hand to steady it. The coffee cooled in its pot. 'You think we've let you down, don't you?' she asked. 'By not telling you?'

Anna didn't reply. Kit said, 'We would have told you. But it was too difficult. We couldn't think of the right words.'

'Yes, I understand.' Anna sounded sad, remote, resigned. 'It explains some things, though. This summer we've had.'

Some things, Kit thought, but not that uprush of strange fear. Who knows where a crisis comes from? The world should be more predictable. 'Let me pour your coffee,' she said.

'I'd be sick,' Anna said. 'How can you ask me to eat and drink?'

'Look, you must fight for him.'

'What? Like a dog with a bone?'

'No, but you must let it be known — let it be known that —' Kit pushed her hand back through her hair.

'Oh, Kit,' Anna said. 'Don't talk about what you don't understand.'

'What will you do?'

'Go and see Ginny,' she said, unexpectedly.

Ginny's house was a low, sprawling complex of buildings —

boathouses once, no doubt – by Blakeney Quay. It had been built for Ginny and Felix by a local firm, and its additions and extensions had been crafted with reverence for the vernacular; but its most startling feature was a huge picture window of staring, blank plate-glass, which looked out over the creek to the invisible sea.

This window was one of the great acts of Ginny's life. Some women die and leave only their children as memorial; but Ginny, like some anointed saint, would have a window. It represented a moral choice, an act of courage. Some would shudder at it, though secretly they would crave the vista. Questions of taste would cow them: questions of vulgarity, even. Ginny simply said, 'Why live at Blakeney, if you don't have the view?'

Mid-morning, Ginny began to issue large drinks. When her hands were unoccupied, without a glass or a cigarette, she rubbed them nervously together, so that her rings clashed and chimed: her engagement ring with its grey solitaire, her broad yellow wedding ring, the 'eternity rings', studded with chips of sapphire and ruby, that Felix had given her at a constant rate through the years. She was never without these rings; perhaps, Anna thought, she used them from time to time to deliver a scarring blow. But Felix had never appeared scarred. She remembered his handsome, bland, betraying face.

'I've heard,' Anna said, 'of women who came home to find a note on the table. Until then, they had no inkling.'

'Had you an inkling?'

Anna smoothed her hair back. It was very smooth already. Ginny thought, she seems to be the one in charge here.

'As I see it,' Ginny said, 'you have three courses before you. When you choose which to take, you must bear in mind that this affair of his will very likely not last.' Anna raised an eyebrow. 'Oh, you know my situation,' Ginny said. 'It was different with me. Felix and Emma, they were old flames.'

'You don't have to talk about it.'

'Why else are you here?' Ginny lit another cigarette. 'Really, Anna, I don't mind. I know you're here because – well, whatever did Daniel tell you?'

'He gave me a version of your life that was different from the one I knew. I'm sorry. It is an intrusion on your privacy.'

'Bugger that,' Ginny said. 'It's a relief to talk about it. More gin?'

'Why not? Ralph's not here to see me.'

'He stopped you drinking?'

'Not exactly. It was more the weight of tradition. Our families. And his uncle, Holy James, the total abstainer. Who'd seen otherwise competent missionaries go out to the tropics and be pickled in spirits within the decade.'

'Yes, I remember James – whatever happened to him?'

'He went abroad again. Back to Africa. After, you know . . . a year or two after we came home.'

'But he was old! Wasn't he?'

'Yes.'

'And then?'

'He died.'

'Of course. Well . . .' Ginny breathed smoke. 'You see, with Ralph, you've been married all these years, and now you're in a position to renegotiate. I say it won't last, because they don't – these affairs between men of fifty, and young girls.'

'She's hardly that.'

Ginny looked hard at her. 'Comparatively.'

'Oh yes – comparatively.'

'You see, there's a pattern to it. These men of fifty – they never fall for women of their own age, you notice. It's always someone who makes them feel young.'

'How comforting to be part of a pattern,' Anna said. 'I always wanted to be.' It struck her, then, that Ginny did not know the course of her life, not in any detailed way; that if she had ever known, she had forgotten it. 'But Mrs Glasse,' she said. 'I haven't an idea of what her attractions might be. And so, I have no idea how to combat them.' She picked up her drink. 'Well now, Ginny, you said there were three courses I could take.'

'Yes. Bearing in mind that it won't last, you can negotiate with him. You can ask him to live with you and let him see her when he wants. That may prolong the agony – it did for me. Or, you can let him stay with her for the while, and sit it out – keep your home and finances intact, and prepare for a return to normal on the day he says he wants to come back.' Ginny ground her cigarette out. 'Or, of course, you can give him the push.'

Anna shook her head. 'I'm not patient, Ginny. I couldn't sit it out. What do you do, while you're sitting it out?'

Ginny reached for another cigarette, flipped it into her mouth. 'This,' she said. She flicked a nail at her glass. 'And this. Alternatively, you can count your blessings. Think of people less fortunate than yourself. Cripples.' She smiled. 'Women who work in launderettes.'

TEN

The child had been scraped up off the streets. She was drowsy and confused, her speech slurred, her eyes unfocused. Her mouth was bleeding. She hadn't a penny to her name.

She remembered jabbing a fist out at some woman who leaned over her; it was a face she didn't know, and that was enough to provoke her. Then the rocking motion of a vehicle, an interval of nothing: and a rush of light and air that hit her – like a drench of cold water – as they carried her from the ambulance into casualty. She bent her arm and laid it over her eyes, to protect herself from this brightness and cold; a nurse saw the scars on her inner arm. 'What's this?' she said. 'Silly girl!'

That was how they talked to her. As if she were two years old and yet at the same time a piece of filth off the street, something they had got on their shoes. They shook her to try to keep her awake, to make her talk. They tried to keep her eyes open. This tortured her, and she didn't know why they wanted to do it. She wanted just to slump on the hard hospital trolley, to melt into it: to give way, to give way to the covering darkness, to pull over her head the blanket of death. 'What was it?' they shouted. 'Tell us what you've taken. You silly girl! Nobody can help you if you don't help yourself.'

Their voices were very loud and hard, the edges of their words shivered and blurred; but she could hear whispers too, nurses talking behind screens. 'I never could have patience with suicides.'

Her head lolled. To buy some peace for herself she gave them the address – or an idea of the address – at first able only to describe a house set in fields, with many staircases and people, many huts and sheds and small buildings around it, so that they said, 'Some kind of camp, could it be?' and for a while there was a respite. A policewoman in uniform appeared at the end of the bed. When she saw this she tried to climb out. 'Your drip!' a nurse yelled, and another nurse and the policewoman dumped her back into the bed and held her there while they rearranged the stand and the tube they had put in her arm.

'Why don't you let us help you?' the nurse said. 'Just your name, my dear.' But there was no love in the words, no my dear about it.

'Where's my clothes?' she said.

'Why? You don't want them. You're not going anywhere, are you?'

'That T-shirt's not mine,' she said. 'That pink top, it doesn't belong to me. You had no right to take it.'

She meant to say that they had done wrong, double-wrong, taking from her what she didn't even own.

But one thought disconnected itself, unplugged itself from the next, and her words slid out through bubbles of spittle that she felt at the corner of her mouth but was too weak to wipe away. One of the nurses mopped her mouth for her, with an abrupt efficient swipe: as if she were not aware that her lips were part of a living being. Suddenly, memory flooded her; this is what it is like to be a baby. You are a collection of parts, not a person, just a set of bones in flesh, your hands grasping and your mouth sucking and gaping; you are a collection of troubles, of piss and dribble and shit.

Her mouth stretched open for air. She was sick; she was sick and sick and sick. First on the blanket, which they dragged away from her legs, then in a metal bowl which she held herself, so hard that the rim dug into her fingers. The nurses stood by approving of this, of the awful corrosive fluid that poured out, the stained water and yellow bile.

For a time after that she lay back stiffly, her arms wrapped across her body. Perhaps she slept. Then the door opened, rousing her, and Mr Eldred came in. He stood at the end of her bed without speaking, just looking at her. She looked at him back for a minute, then turned her head away. There was a crack in the plaster of the wall. She studied it. Eventually he spoke. 'Oh, Melanie,' he said. 'Whatever next?'

Sometimes she woke up and the man was there. Sometimes she slept. Sometimes she woke up and he was not there. She shouted to a nurse – her voice surprising her, issuing from her mouth like some flapping, broken-winged pigeon – and asked where he had gone, and a nurse said, 'He has more than you to attend to, Miss.'

She raised her hand, the one without the drip, and scrubbed her wrist back and forth across her forehead. She looked down at her legs, lying like dead white sticks; her body was hot and clammy, so she kicked the covers off, and then, tight-lipped, they dragged them back again. 'Look, I want to talk to you,' she shouted to a nurse, but as soon as she started to talk she began to cry, a wailing sort of crying she'd never done before, which hurt her throat and made her have to blow her nose, and made her breath stick in her throat as if it were something she'd swallowed, a bone. 'Please,' the nurse said. 'Do you think you're the only patient we have to attend to? Have some consideration for others – please!'

The thing it was necessary to say was where she'd got the T-shirt from; that she'd taken it out of a basket in the bathroom, where somebody had said dirty clothes went, but that was all the same to her, all her clothes were neither clean nor dirty but just what she wore, and it seemed to her the ones in the basket were just that, clothes. When the policewoman came back, she tried to explain it to her. 'Not out of her bedroom,' she said. 'I never went in there.'

The woman frowned. 'I'm sorry, darling, I don't know what you're on about. What T-shirt is this, then?'

'Shoplifting,' a nurse breathed. 'I'll just bet you.'

'Look, just don't go on about it,' the policewoman said. 'All right? I'm sure it'll just be forgotten about, if you don't keep on.'

Behind the screens the nurse said, 'As if that were all she had to concern herself about.'

'She had a bag of clothes,' the policewoman explained. 'New ones. That'll be it. Couple of hours before she collapsed somebody saw her selling them.'

'Well, where did she get them from, you wonder? And did nobody do anything about it?'

'You see all sorts of things on the streets,' the policewoman said. 'The first thing you learn in this job is to expect no assistance from passers-by.'

Time passed; she could not guess how much. The nights were bright and full of action, full of squeaking wheels in the corridors and the squeaking of shoes as nurses ran. Days were indistinguishable. She didn't know the day of the week, not that she ever had. They put her in a side room, said, 'I should say you're privileged, Miss.' She heard diagnoses, part-diagnoses of her condition. Can't or won't eat. Can't or won't remember. Their voices were hard and bright, like knives.

She heard nurses gossiping, talking about an abortion, one that had breathed. Her own breathing became painfully tight, as if she were trying not to draw attention to herself, trying not to take up space. In the hospital there were sluices and incinerators. She lay in the ward's half-day, half-night, deciding when and how to run.

★

Ralph drove to Blakeney. Ginny let him in, twittering nervously and offering him a drink. 'I don't think so,' he said. 'I'd like to talk to Anna alone, I suppose that's all right with you?'

Ginny waved him towards her drawing room. The shock of the vast window: the grey day flooded in, its monochromes intermingled, the dun mud of the creek and the shiver of gulls' wings.

Anna sat with her back to the light. She was wearing a grey dress, and he noticed it because it was not hers; it was too short, too narrow, and even as he came in she was pulling at its neckline, straining it away from her white throat. Seeing him, she let her hand settle on her thigh. 'I hardly recognize you,' he said.

'We have that in common.' He understood that she had been crying. Her voice was coarsened, blurred, at her elbow was a glass of dissolving ice.

At first, she didn't speak. The moment spun itself out. Her eyes rested on his face. Then she spoke all at once, in a rush.

'Ralph, I want you to know that I don't want anything. The house, everything, you can have it. At first – last night – I didn't think that. I thought, this woman, whatever backwoods berry-picking life she's been leading, I don't want her to improve her position at my expense. But now I realize –'

'Anna, you're exhausted,' he said.

'Yes. But I think now, what's the point, what's the point of hanging on?'

'You give me up, Anna?'

'What choice have I?'

'Every choice.'

'Every choice? I don't think you will indulge me while I consider them.'

'It's not a matter of indulgence. You have every choice. Trust me.'

'You have no right to ask that, Ralph. Of all the things you could ask, you have least right to trust.'

He nodded. 'I see that. I suppose I meant, trust me for the sake of the past, not the present.'

'I shall have to go back home for a little while. A few weeks. To work out where I am going to go after that, and what's to happen about a school for Rebecca. So what I want – I want to make this agreement with you –'

'Anna, this is not what I meant.' Ralph was panic-stricken. 'You can't just – re-invent yourself like this, people don't do it. I thought we should sit and talk –'

'Too much of that,' Anna said. 'So much talk, but here we are.' Again her hand went to her throat, trying to pull the neckline of Ginny's dress away from her skin. 'I want to make this agreement. That you will come home and get your things and do it all at once. I mean that you should get yourself organized and move out. I don't want sordid to-ing and fro-ing with suitcases.'

'So that's the decision you have made?'

'That's the first decision I have made.'

Ralph looked away. 'I wish you would get back into your own clothes.'

'I didn't bring any.'

'Why did you come here?'

'Ginny's a friend.'

'Ginny is pernicious.'

'Oh – because she gave me a drink, and a dress to wear?'

'This is childish. A childish conversation.'

'True. And you, of course, are acting like a mature man.'

'You must not think,' Ralph said, 'you must not think that this was some stupid fling.'

'Oh, wasn't it? I see, I do see. Your emotions were engaged, were they? Your poor little emotions.' That first rush of energy had died out of Anna's voice; it was low, toneless now. 'Then let me congratulate you. You've found the love of your life, have you? Well, go to her then. Quick about it!'

'I don't want to go. I want you to forgive me, if you can. That's what I came here to ask you, but you didn't give me a chance.'

She shook her head. 'Ginny has been talking me through it, a woman's options. A woman in middle life, whose husband flits off to something more juicy. But I don't feel that I can consider these options, I feel that I'm not going to sit in the house, waiting and hoping. I have done it before, and I'm tired of it.'

Ralph sprung up from his chair. He wanted to cross the room to her, but he did not dare. 'I'm not asking you to wait. Or hope. Or anything. Just talk to me, let's talk it through. I wanted to explain my feelings –'

'Why should you think I might want them explained?'

'Because it is usual. In a marriage. To talk about feelings.'

'Oh yes. Perhaps. *In* a marriage.'

'Listen to me,' Ralph said. 'There is nothing to be gained by bandying words and freezing me out. I wanted to tell you what had happened, I wanted to be truthful with you – and if you can't forgive me now, which I well understand, I wanted to go away with the hope that you might forgive me – in time.'

'I'm no good at forgiving.' She looked down at her nails. 'Don't you know that? It doesn't matter if the action is to be deferred. I can't do it. The years pass and they don't make a difference. I know, you see. Because I've been betrayed before.'

'It's useless, then,' he said. 'If you will insist on seeing this as some kind of continuation or extension of what happened to us twenty years ago.'

'All my life has been a continuation of it.' She raised her eyes. 'I know you have put it behind you. You have been able to say, let us not hate, we are reasonable people. Even though what happened was not reasonable. Even though it was barbaric and foul.' She put her hand to her throat again. They had hanged Felicia.

'You were not the only person betrayed,' he said. 'I was betrayed too.'

'Not so much. After all, you opened the door to them.'

'Yes. Is it the action of a human being, to throw that in my face now?'

'There is no limit to what human beings will do. We know that, don't we? There is no depth to which human beings won't sink. And I've never claimed to be more than human. Though you would have appreciated it, if I had been.'

He looked as if the breath had been knocked out of him. Sat down on one of Ginny's fringed Dralon armchairs; on the edge. Wiped his hand across his face.

When evening came Anna and Ginny put on their coats and went to walk by the quay. The water was flat, motionless. The small boats were perched on it, like toys on a steel shelf.

'How are you now?' Anna asked her. 'About Felix?'

'You mean him dying?'

She really is faintly stupid, Anna thought. 'Yes, that's what I mean.'

'Well, you get to a stage where you don't think about it every day,' Ginny said. 'At least, so I'm told. I haven't reached it yet.'

Anna saw the bulk of the Blakeney Hotel, a ship of flint, bobbing at the quayside and showing its lights. She heard the evening complaints of cattle from the salt marshes, and the competing snicker of sheep. She said, 'I don't understand this thing about forgiveness, Ginny. You hear about these people in Ireland. Their husband's been shot, or their children blown apart. And you have some woman propped up before the cameras, saying oh, I forgive the terrorists. Why forgive them? I don't.'

'I thought you were religious,' Ginny said: her tone careful, distant.

'I'm barely a Christian. Never was.'

Somewhere in Ginny's mind a door opened, just a crack; was there not some story, long ago, about a dead child?

'Why don't we drop in to the hotel for a drink?' she said.

'A drink, for a change!' Anna said. 'Yes, why not?'

They sat in the bar for half an hour, sipping gin among pseudo-mariners. Evening light on blazer buttons: early diners tripping in to their shellfish and game. 'I could ask if they had a table,' Ginny said.

Anna shook her head. 'It would be a waste. I couldn't eat. And I hate to waste food.'

'I'll make us an egg then, shall I? A nice scrambled egg, or would you prefer it boiled?'

'Whatever,' Anna said. Widow's food, she thought; food for women alone, for their pale little appetites. Who cares if the flesh drops from their bones, if the light fades from their eyes?

Ginny said, 'Be careful, Anna. You're fifty.'

'Whatever do you mean, I'm fifty?'

'I mean you might lose everything, if you don't put up a fight.'

Anna sat eating peanuts from a glass dish, looking out at the mud flats. 'Tomorrow I must go back to the Red House,' she said. 'Everything must be faced.'

Foulsham: 'Both our parents have run away from home,' Rebecca said. 'I'll have to come and live with you, Emma.'

'Your mother telephoned, my dear. She'll be back in the morning. She wants you not to worry, she says she knows you're a grown-up sensible girl – and soon everything will be explained.' Somehow, Emma added under her breath.

'Till then Kit has to be a mother to me. And Robin has to be my father.'

'That's a very nice way to think of it,' Emma said admiringly. 'But it's really only for one night, you know. And you can stay with me if you like.'

'People who run away never go for long, do they?' Rebecca's face was bright, avid, sharp with fear. 'That girl who was here, Melanie. She used to run away all the time, Dad said. But people caught her. The police.'

She is too young for her age, Emma thought; they've kept her that way, her brothers and her capable sister, even with all the Visitors they get, even with all that's happened under that roof, each summer's tribulations: 'It's not the same when people are grown-up,' she said. 'You see, they have to make their own decisions about where to live. And sometimes it happens . . .' Emma shut her eyes tight. What must I tell her? She felt weary. Perhaps it is premature to say anything, she thought, perhaps in some way the row will blow over. She remembered Anna's voice on the telephone: obdurate, balanced on the steely edge of tears. They've been married for twenty-five years, Emma thought; can it fall apart in a night?

But what do I know about marriage?

Rebecca said, 'When Dad comes home I'm going to ask him if we can have a donkey to live in the garden. He'll say no, certainly not, but I'll keep following him round saying "Donkey, donkey, donkey", till he gets tired and says yes all right then if you must.'

'Is that how you usually get your way?'

'You have to ask,' Rebecca said. 'Don't ask and you don't get. Did you know Julian came home?'

'No. Did he? When?'

'He came like a highwayman at dead of night. Two nights ago, or three, I don't remember. He came climbing up – there's a way the boys get in, you know, like burglars?'

'I didn't know.'

'Oh, they've always done it. Kit says it's to show off and they could just as well come in by the door.'

'So didn't your mum and dad see Julian?'

'No. He stayed in Kit's room. Robin came down. They had a very serious talk.'

'Where were you?'

'I was sitting on the stairs with my ears flapping.'

'And what did you hear?'

'I don't know.' She jerked her head away, and began to cry. 'I couldn't understand,' she said. 'I had a dream, that I was on my own in the house.'

Emma said, 'It wasn't a dream, was it, Becky? You mean that's what you're afraid of.'

'Yes. Because what if they all go, what if everybody runs away? Jule's gone already. And Kit said she was going to go to Africa.'

Emma drew the child against her. 'Becky, put your arms around me. Take hold of me very tight. I'm here, aren't I? Don't I feel solid to you? Do I feel as if I'll run away? No one will leave you in the house alone.'

There was no more she could say. She was incoherent with love for the child and anger at Ralph and dismay at what had overtaken them. At the beginning of summer, she thought, never in my wildest dreams could I have imagined such a thing; but then that's perhaps the problem, my dreams have never been wild enough. I don't understand what drives people, who does? I don't understand the process by which our lives have unravelled. Why this year, and not other years? Because they are growing up, I suppose, and there had to be a turning point; Ralph met this woman, spoke to her no doubt of certain things, and after that everything must change. When a secret has been kept for twenty years, reality has been built around it, in a special way: it is a carapace, it is a safe house. When the walls have been pulled down and the secret has been let out, even to one person, then it's no good trying to rebuild the walls to the same plan – they are walls to hold in nothing. Life must change, it will, it has to.

She wondered about going to the coast to see this woman, Mrs Glasse. Pleading with her in some way. She would be laughed at, of course.

'We ought to be spared this scene,' Amy Glasse said.

'Yes.' Usual kinds of words came tumbling out of Ralph's mouth, lines that she could swear she had heard on the television. For the sake of the children I really feel . . . Ah yes, comedy half-hour, she thought.

She said, 'You look weary, my dear.'

'Yes. I seem to be on the road all the time, driving about between one place and another.' He had spent the best part of a night – by far the best part – sitting at Melanie's bedside, while she dipped in and out of the conversations that were held around her, picking and mixing as she liked. Nobody had filled in the missing hours, and so they would keep her in hospital till they were sure there was no delayed liver damage from anything she might have taken. What was most likely, given the limited means at her disposal, was that she had been inhaling some type of volatile solvent, enough to make her almost comatose when they fetched her in; but he was aware of her history, the range and type and peculiar dosages of the various means she had used to effect escape, and his greatest concern was that her broken and incoherent conversation, her apparent thought-disorder, should be seen as a possible consequence of drug abuse and not madness. He had witnessed this before, a heavy amphetamine user become agitated, hear voices, hallucinate – and then a cell, and then a prison doctor, and then the liquid cosh: and then the inquest.

Slowly he dragged his mind back, from that sorry afternoon in court to this date and place. 'For one thing,' he said, 'I feel I would have nothing to offer you. I would probably lose my job, you see. I would have to offer my resignation to the Trust's committee. They would be obliged to accept it.'

'Hypocrites then, aren't they?' she said.

'People aren't enlightened, you know, you think they move with the times but they don't. I suppose it's that they're always looking for a stick to beat you with . . . there's the press, if it got into the papers . . . you see it's all complicated by the fact that Sandra is my son's girlfriend and they would twist the whole story around – believe me, I know about the newspapers – into something that resembled incest.'

'Sandra is your son's mistress,' she said. 'Let's get it right.'

'Yes, I know that. I can't afford to damage the Trust, because if there is a scandal it affects our fund-raising, and then if we have less money it means we must disappoint people and turn them away.'

'Are you married to Anna, or the Trust?'

'I don't know what you mean, Amy.'

He did know what she meant, of course, but he was buying time, thinking time; surely, he thought, no one could accuse me of being one of those who love mankind in general but not persons in particular? Perhaps I incline in that direction, no doubt I do, but I try to correct my fault: I love Amy, who is easy to love, and I love my children and Sandra Glasse, and I love Anna, who is another proposition and a tougher one. What person could be harder to love than Melanie, and even there I try; I have made a study of love, a science. He thought, I cannot let them admit the child to a mental hospital, because Melanie is clearly, reluctantly, spitefully sane; stupid perhaps, self-destructive, but in possession of her faculties when she is not under the influence of some dubious tablets bought on the street, or cleaning fluid, or lighter fuel. If she is diagnosed as schizophrenic, or labelled as psychopathic, that will be the end of her, in effect, they may as well bury her now. But I can't take her out of hospital, I can't take her back to the Red House now Anna isn't there, and if I offer to take her back to London and dump her on Richard and the staff she'll run away again in hours, we can't keep her under lock and key, we have no authority to do it.

He looked up. There was a smell of baking from the kitchen; the need of income was constant, and no crisis would make Amy alter her schedule. She said, 'I think that if you leave me, Ralph, you must give me a proper reason.' Her voice shook. She put her hands to the back of her neck, raked her fingers upwards through her long hair, then let it fall. 'You came this spring, and I was lonely. I've been on my own for many years now. Since Andrew Glasse walked out of this house when Sandra was two years old, I've never let a man over this threshold, if I could help it. You came here; and you were kind, you were very kind to me, Ralph.'

He nodded. 'I see I had no right to be. Not in that way.'

'So you must give me a reason now. Don't give me some stupid reason about how it will be in the *News of the World*. Tell me you love your wife. Tell me a reason that makes sense. Tell me you love your wife and children and you have to protect them.'

'Anna says she will never forgive me. She wants me to move out of the house.'

'That's natural for her to say.'

'But she says that as soon as it can be arranged she is moving out herself. I can go back then, she says. The children – I don't know.'

I will lose them anyway, he thought. It's not a matter of who lives where, or what custody is sought and granted; I will lose them. I have taught them to discriminate, to know what is right and wrong and choose what is right. They will value the lesson now, and not the teacher. Because what I have done is so patently, so manifestly, so obviously, wrong. And not just wrong, but stupid. 'You ask me do I love Anna,' he said. 'It's not the right question. It goes beyond that. You see, when we met, we were children. We made an alliance against the world. Then what held us together –'

'Yes. You don't have to tell that story, ever again.' Her face was composed, he thought; pale, alight with pity. 'One telling is enough for a lifetime. Don't imagine I'll forget it.' She stood behind his chair. 'Ralph, listen to me. Look at any life – from the inside, I mean, from the point of view of the person who's living it. What is it but defeats? It's just knock-backs, one after the other, isn't it? Everybody remembers the things they did wrong. But what about the thousands and thousands and thousands of things they did right? You lost a child. And every day you think about it. But think of the children you didn't lose.'

'Nobody has ever said that to me before.'

She moved away and stood before the fireplace, putting her hands flat on the mantelpiece, at either side of the stupid ticking clock. 'Just tell me. When you said you loved me, was that a lie?' The careful blankness of her profile seemed to show that she was prepared for any answer.

'No,' he said. 'No, it wasn't.'

She let out her breath. 'It's a brute of a world, Ralph. A brute, isn't it?' She moved towards him. Her eyes had never been so pale and clear. 'Take your coat, my dear. It's time you left.'

'Sandra and Julian – where are they, do you know?'

She smiled. 'Last time I saw them they were sitting in a hedge like ragamuffins, eating blackberries.'

'They must come home. To you, or to us.'

'Sandra's got the key of a flat in Wells. It's one of the places she cleans. The landlord will let them have it cheap, till next season.'

'I don't see how they can afford it. Even cheap.'

'I suppose the Lord will provide.' She smiled tightly. For a moment she reminded him of Anna. 'But of course, he won't. I'll see they get through the winter.'

She turned away, presenting her shoulder to him. Before she turned, he read the coming winter in her face. As he was leaving she called, 'Ralph! Are you sure you don't want that old clock?'

'Nowhere to put it,' he said. I am houseless, he thought; I should have carried my house on my back. 'Be seeing you, Amy.'

Another night of rain; and then, fine windy weather. On the roads there were great standing pools, shattered by sunlight. The sun struck every spark of colour from the landscape, revivifying the trees with green, dazing the driver of the early bus; even dead wood, even fence poles, quivered with their own green life.

At ten o'clock, Anna returned to the Red House. She put her key in the door: thought, could there ever be a time when I will not do this?

She remembered how she had tried to sell the place, only a couple of years ago. It was a house with no centre, she had always felt, no room from which you could command other rooms. Sound travelled in its own way; from one of the attics, you could hear the downstairs telephone quite distinctly, but from nearer rooms it couldn't be heard at all. The house had its own conduits, sight-lines. Sometimes one of the children's friends had stayed overnight, without her knowing. She didn't make a practice of searching the rooms, scouring the cupboards and landings for fugitives or stowaways; the house would have its private life, whether she agreed or not. In the morning a parent would telephone, furious or distraught. She would say, 'Your child is here to be collected. I make no charge for bed and breakfast.' And then, oblivious to the babble on the line, she would put down the phone. She had not lived her life in a way that attracted sympathy. She had made sure of that.

Already – in the course of her small absence – the house had acquired an air of neglect. The vast hall-stand had a vast cobweb on it, and just off-centre sat a small brown spider, its legs folded modestly. Dirty plates and cups were piled in the sink. The boiler was out. 'Kit, couldn't you manage?' she said, exasperated.

'Is that all that's on your mind? Housework?'

Rebecca was tearful: Robin baffled: Julian absent: Kit hostile. Kit had heard – through Daniel, no doubt – that Ralph had been to Blakeney and had tried to patch things up. She propped a hand against the kitchen wall; her eyes were snapping and fiery. 'What can a person do?' she asked. 'Except say they were wrong, and try to put it right?'

Anna gazed at her. 'You know nothing, Kit.'

'I'm not claiming worldly experience. It's a general principle I'm talking about.'

Ralph and his daughter, she thought: their terrible moral energy, their relish for the large statement. She had been pre-occupied all her life with the particular, the minute; the neat stitching of a seam, the correctness of a turn of phrase. She had thought that life was governed in that way: by details. She had learned as a child, she thought, that details were what you offered God; you couldn't hope, in any larger way, to please Him.

'Oh, Kit.' She sat down on a kitchen chair. 'Will you make me something? Some coffee, with hot milk in it?'

The light of combat died in Kit's eyes. Docile, solid, efficient, her daughter moved: table to fridge, fridge to the Rayburn. 'Why should you forgive?' Anna said.

Without looking at her, Kit said, 'Because if you don't, it will kill you.'

Anna nodded. She knew such a thing was possible. Already she was becoming lighter, skeletal; her feet scarcely seemed to touch the ground. She had not been able to eat the little egg, the widow's meal. This morning there was a dizzying lightness at her centre, a space under her heart.

'I have always thought,' she said, 'that before there is forgiveness there must be restitution.'

Kit took the pan from the heat. She poured the milk carefully into the cup. 'So what do you want him to do?'

'It's not just him. You see, Kit, I've never forgiven anybody. I've had no practice. I don't know how to do it.'

She put her hand to her mouth, as if the secret might spill out. (Are you sick? Kit said. No, no, she said.) All summer she had felt the drag of it, dragging itself towards the light. But perhaps there are no words for it; it can express itself only through symbols, through shadows. And life has always been like this: something more than it appears. In safety, there is danger. In tears, the awful slicing comic edge. In moments of kindness and laughter, the murderer's fist at the door.

And year after year, Anna thought, I have occupied this room. I have sat at this table making shopping lists and writing letters, reading my daily paper, some faculty below consciousness alert for signs of disintegration: the sighing of the pipes and dripping of gutters, the malfunctioning squeak of ancient domestic machines, the boiler's cough and the squeak of old floorboards. Coal dust and mouse droppings and vegetable peelings: gas bills and school reports: bitter wrong, and bitter duty correctly performed. Year after year I have sat in the house, windows sealed against the cold, waiting for someone. Who will not come home: who will never come home now.

Ralph went back to the Red House to collect his belongings. He would stay with Emma, he supposed. Anna said she did not want the house, but of course when she had thought about it she would want it, and it would be his responsibility to support her and the children. When he thought of the possible consequences of their separation – of rent for him and rates for her, of the severing of bank accounts and the relative poverty in which they would both live – his mind sheered off and went in some other direction, towards the contemplation of his moral insufficiency. That was easier for him; he was used to abstractions. Perhaps most people are, he thought. We indulge in guilt, shame – but faced with the practical effects of these emotions, we call in a solicitor. No wonder lawyers are never out of work.

He went up to their bedroom and packed some clothes. Anna had said she did not want sordid to-ing and fro-ing – that was the expression she had used – but of course it is impossible to crush a life into two suitcases. He tried, and then gave up, and sat on the edge of their bed, his face in his hands.

He hoped Anna would come in. She would not, of course. What would she see? Nothing to lift her spirits. You wreck your family once . . . years pass . . . you wreck it twice. He had evolved very nicely, he thought: along the only possible route.

Perhaps I should leave my clothes, and take my papers, I will need to clear out my desk . . . He was conscious of Anna, moving elsewhere in the house. Wherever he was, she wasn't; they skirted and avoided each other.

In his office, he sat down in his wooden swivel chair. He looked at his photograph, the picture taken on the stoep at Flower Street. He folded the frame, laid it face down. That would be the last thing Anna would want; he should never have taken it out, it had only made the children ask questions. Sightless, his mother and father stared down at him: sepia eyes. How his father's face had coarsened, with age; the flesh swelling, the features seeming to shrink. Would he be like that? It was possible, of course, that when the picture was taken his father was no older than he was now. And surely, he thought, I'm going his way: two inches on the waist, the reading glasses, those shirts that are too small around the collar, and get put to the back of the wardrobe. I am in no shape for a new life, he thought. But, anyway. It seems I have to have one.

Will Anna just watch me go, he wondered. Or is she waiting for me to make some gesture, some sign – but how would I know what it was? She had said she meant him to go, and he must allow her to mean what she said, he must allow her that.

Everything's gone, he thought: just pride remains.

But how terrible, perhaps the worst thing in the world: to be taken at your word.

His hand crept into the first drawer of his desk. Closed around stone: Gryphaea. He held it to his cheek, and then against his mouth. A child's life; the salt and cold. He tasted it: Phylum: Mollusca. Class: Pelecypoda. Order: Pterioida. Such confidence, he'd felt as a child, about the order of the world. Family: Gryphaeidae. Genus: *Gryphaea*. Species: *arcuata*. The past doesn't change, of course: it lies behind you, petrified, immutable. What changes it is the way you see it. Perception is everything. It turns villains into heroes and victims into collaborators. He held the object up between his fingers: took a sighting, and spun it across the room into the wastepaper basket.

Anna was in the kitchen: I will do something useful, she thought. She ran the hot tap, and rinsed the crumbs out of a dishcloth. She wrung it between her hands, flapped it out, shook it and straightened it and set it to dry, carefully squaring up the corners as it hung over the draining board.

Well . . . that was marginally useful, was it not? She remembered the night Ralph had left her: washing her cup and washing her cup. A phrase from an old letter came back to her, a letter James had written: 'There is always some emergency, God-given or otherwise.' How very odd memory is: and not an ally, on the whole. She could not see how this phrase had any application to her circumstances.

In the other room, Ralph was no doubt going about his preparations.

She walked around the kitchen table, touching the back of the chairs. She had consulted their solicitor; she had better tell Ralph about this, she supposed, as a family solicitor cannot act for both parties when those parties are not to be a family any longer.

She sat down at the table, because she felt ill.

Will he go?

Surely he will not?

But what will stop him?

She felt she had set him a test, an examination; but he was not aware of it, and so he could not hope to pass.

Ralph picked up his bags. He went out into the hall. 'Anna? I'm going now.'

After a moment she appeared. She wrapped her cardigan tight across her chest. He saw the gesture: elderly, a means of defence. 'So,' she said.

'You can phone me at Emma's.'

'Yes, of course.'

'If you want me.'

'I should tell you, Ralph, that I've been up to Norwich, to see Mr Phillips. He agrees that there are grounds, advises I stay in the house, but I told him I don't want to do that. You will have to find another solicitor – I'm sorry about that, but of course Mr Phillips can't act for us both. What I mean to do is to find a flat in Norwich for myself and Becky. Then you can come back here. Kit and Julian and Robin, they won't mind. They'll stay here with you, I suppose. The kind of mothering I've given them . . . they'll probably barely miss it.'

He looked at her for a moment, considering; put down his cases. She thought, he has put down his cases, surely he will not go now? He said, 'You are indulging yourself, aren't you?'

'Oh yes, of course. Self-indulgence is my habit.'

'I mean, you are indulging a notion of failure . . .'

'Failure? How could I be a failure?' She smiled brightly. 'I mean, haven't I kept the twin-tub in trim? Haven't I managed the boiler, all these years? And the hall-stand – oh, yes, I've come to grips with the hall-stand. Say anything, but never say the Red House has beaten me.'

He clenched his hand inside his pocket, frozen around the space where he had thought *Gryphaea* would be. Then he took his hands out of his pockets and picked up his cases.

She opened the front door for him, helpfully. Unbalanced by the bags, he stepped back to kiss her cheek. He saw that she was crying. 'You don't want this to happen,' he said.

'At least acknowledge that I know my own mind.'

The door of the Red House was an old and heavy door. When it was opened the cold morning came in: a big breezy presence, filling the hall. He hesitated on the threshold, scuffing a foot, dragging the time out.

Anna touched his arm. 'Ralph . . .'

He looked away, unwilling to influence by any expression on his face the expression on hers. He glanced up, out into the garden – if garden it could be called: over the mud and the lawn churned up by bikes and neighbours' dogs that the children played with, over the pond where they'd had fish once and over the rusty swing with its sodden ropes, and over Julian's vegetable plots, and the wilderness of the dog-runs and the outbuildings beyond. Something moved – dog-height – from one of the rotting sheds. Anna said, 'What's that? What on earth is it?'

A creature moved into their view, at a distance. It came slowly over the rough ground, crawling. It was a human being: its face a mask of despair, its body half-clothed in a flapping gown, its hands and knees and feet bleeding; its strange head the colour of the sun. It progressed towards them; they saw the heaving ribs, the small transparent features, the dirt-ingrained skin.

'I must put these cases down somewhere,' Ralph said. All he could think for the moment was that they were dragging his arms out of their sockets; he did not know whether to put them inside or outside the house. He wondered which of them would move first, he or Anna, towards this jetsam, this salvage; but wondered it idly, without that spirit of competition in goodness that had animated his life. Whichever, it didn't matter . . . he put his baggage down, nowhere in particular, wedged across the threshold. 'We must take her in,' he said to Anna. 'Or she will die.'

'Yes,' Anna's face was open, astonished. They left the Red House together, stumbling over the rough grass. As they approached the child, she stopped trying to crawl. She shrank into herself, her head sunk between her shoulder-blades like some dying animal. But then, as they reached out towards her, Melanie began to breathe – painfully, slowly, deeply, sucking in the air – as if breathing were something she were learning, as if she had taken a class in it, and been taught how to get it right.

In November that year, Emma went back to Walsingham. It was seasonably cold, the light struggling against an obdurate bank of cloud. In the street she saw the pug dog and his woman; these months on, both were a little greyer, stouter, their feet and pads stepping gingerly on the cobbles.

As she walked up the flagged path of the Anglican church, Emma tried to edit her usual perception – that she was entering an extravagantly designed council house. A poor thing, but our own, she thought: noting the brick arches and brick columns, the stoup for holy water. Holy water, that's going too far – and in fact there was no need for her to go any further, no need to go inside at all.

'ALL WHOSE NAMES ARE INSCRIBED IN THIS BOOK WILL BE PRAYED FOR AT THE SHRINE.' She stood in the porch, turning the pages of the great book. Back, right back to – when? What date? When had Felix died? Her eyes ran over the columns. The pages were damp, they stuck together and revealed only a clump of months at a time, a huge aggregation of prayers. Patience was required; she started to scuff up the corners, looking for dates, for clues. But yes, here it is at last: her own handwriting.

RALPH ELDRED

ANNA ELDRED

KATHERINE ELDRED

Then the missing line; then

JULIAN ELDRED

ROBERT ELDRED

REBECCA ELDRED

Why did I think God would recognize our real names, our formal and never-used names, instead of the names we are called by? There: that's a puzzle. She reached into her bag for her pen. Her pen was a present from Felix. It was a serious and expensive object, made of gold.

Damn; not there. Her fingers probed, scraped the worn silk

lining. Perhaps a child had borrowed it. She plunged her hand into her coat pocket, and brought out a furred and leaking ballpoint, its plastic barrel cracked, its ink silted. She shook it, and tried a preliminary zigzag in a corner of the page. She shook the pen again, tapped it. If you could scribble the book over, make additions . . . But it did not seem decent to her to spoil the pages. Pray for Felix, she said to herself. Pray for Ginny. Pray for me.

She began to write. Her pen moved over the vacant line. The ballpoint marked the paper, but nothing appeared: only white marks. She shook it once, slammed it on the wooden desk. At last, like a slow cut, the ink began to bleed. Laboriously – the pen faltering, blotting – she filled in the missing line:

MATTHEW ELDRED

So that's done, she thought. She ran her finger down the page. Prayers answered; after a fashion. She hesitated, her hand in the air, then placed the defective pen beside the book. You could not know what desperate soul would come along, with no means of writing at all.

She stepped out of the porch. The air held snow. Often it promises, but doesn't perform; we're not very far from the sea. She put her hands into the pockets of her coat, and began to walk uphill to the car park. The cloud had thinned, and as she walked the sun showed itself, fuzzy and whitish-yellow, like a lamp behind a veil.